MU for

LOVE

or

WAR

MARTYN BURKE

TYRUS
BOOKS

Published by
TYRUS BOOKS
an imprint of F+W Media, Inc.
10151 Carver Road, Suite 200
Blue Ash, OH 45242. U.S.A.
www.tyrusbooks.com

Hardcover ISBN 10: 1-5072-0091-9
Hardcover ISBN 13: 978-1-5072-0091-9
Paperback ISBN 10: 1-5072-0090-0
Paperback ISBN 13: 978-1-5072-0090-2
eISBN 10: 1-5072-0092-7
eISBN 13: 978-1-5072-0092-6

Printed in the United States of America.

10   9   8   7   6   5   4   3   2   1

Library of Congress Cataloging-in-Publication Data
Burke, Martyn, author.
Music for love or war / Martyn Burke.
Blue Ash, OH: Tyrus Books, 2017.
LCCN 2016030930 | ISBN 9781507200919 (hc) | ISBN 1507200919 (hc) | ISBN 9781507200902
(pb) | ISBN 1507200900 (pb) | ISBN 9781507200926 (ebook) | ISBN 1507200927 (ebook)
BISAC: FICTION / War & Military. | FICTION / Literary. | GSAFD: Love stories. | War stories.
LCC PS3552.U7233 M87 2016 | DDC 813/.54--dc23
LC record available at https://lccn.loc.gov/2016030930

Martyn Burke gratefully acknowledges permission from Faber & Faber to use lines from "Journey of
the Magi" from *The Ariel Poems* by T.S. Eliot. Copyright © 1927 by T.S. Eliot and copyright © 1965
by the estate of T.S. Eliot.

Cover design by Sylvia McArdle.
Cover and interior images © Getty Images/Stocktrek Images; mishabokovan; sidmay; july7th;
aleksandarvelasevic.

This book is available at quantity discounts for bulk purchases.
For information, please call 1-800-289-0963.

DEDICATION

For Laura
Who has given me both the music and the lyrics

HOLLYWOOD IN TIMES OF WAR

1

According to what we've been told, the source of all knowledge is located somewhere just south of Sunset Boulevard. The problem is that Danny has lost the address.

This home of all knowledge is what's scrawled on some piece of paper Danny is frantically trying to find. It's where the psychic lives.

Danny doesn't want to get sidetracked by nuance and details. He just wants to get us to the ten P.M. appointment he's had ever since he got online in Afghanistan and e-mailed this woman, Constance, telling her that we'd be here on leave. She was supposed to have been booked up for months in advance with Hollywood types, trailing their mutually exclusive cynicism and neediness in one tight little bundle behind them. So Danny called in markers with her and got the appointment on three weeks' notice. Maybe this Constance is feeling guilty over the guys we lost after she'd e-mailed *I see a rough patch ahead . . . a rough patch.* In other words, death for Davis, Onuko, and Alvarez, who were caught out in the open in a Taliban ambush near Khost. The roughest patch.

Danny can't find the piece of paper and I'm getting edgy as the sheriff's deputies show up, parking their cruiser right in the middle of Sunset Boulevard between the two spastic ribbons of taillights. The deputies saunter through the traffic and the Mexican parking valets outside Screem, the latest hot club. They have that way of walking down to a fine art, the walk of the Men in Charge, stepping onto the sidewalk past all the airbursts of rope-line lust and anxiety wafting in on waves of studied indifference. They greet the bouncers like old friends. *A tradition of service* and all that *serve and protect* stuff cops always plaster on their cruisers to bring on the warm and fuzzies while they're busting you. The bouncers are standing there like cliffs to be scaled. As usual, there's one massive black bouncer just to make all the white people extra polite. A lot of the rope-line herd are decked out in their mandatory black, with a duster coat or two among them to accessorize that outlaw gunfighter attitude that usually backfires, making the rope line seem even more servile in their desperation to be chosen to get inside the club. The deputies are a study in form-fitting beige and starch that seeps all the way into their smiles as they stroll past the parking valets and go inside Screem so they can enforce the local by-laws and oh by the way, check out which movie stars are there so they can brag to their wives and families baking and garrisoned up in the boonies of Simi Valley or Santa Clarita, letting them know that they were in this cool Hollywood club hanging out with the A list.

Well, not really the A list. Tonight it's strictly C minus. Mostly television actors whose shows got canceled, actors who know you don't know their names and hate you for it. That kind of stuff. But still, most of the deputies live at least two area codes away, so even some guy on *Jeopardy!* can be a big deal.

Danny has taken all the pieces of paper from his pockets and he's laying them out on the sidewalk like he's going to do some incantation over them, hoping this psychic's address will miraculously rise from the lost and found of scrap paper. A lowrider Honda goes by with Mexicans pumping bass out of it like a rocket launcher. Danny doesn't even hear it.

"Damn," says Danny before he heads back inside Screem, sifting past the dead-eyed bouncers like they were invisible. It's one of the advantages to wearing a military uniform. Right now it's a free pass. In this war, at least. Choose any old vets and they'll tell you how soldiers got spit on coming back from Vietnam. Baby killers and all that. But in this war, we're strictly Teflon. Danny is still wearing the same camouflage tunic he wore back when I met him eight months ago, the one that a lot of people mistake for an American combat outfit until they see the little maple leaf flag on the left shoulder.

Me, I have no interest in wearing my uniform, but my jarhead haircut hasn't grown in enough yet so I might as well have a sign saying GRUNT hanging around my neck. The bouncers figured this out when we walked up to the rope line the first time, and after studying their clipboards like they were deciphering some code, they let us in ahead of the hordes of high-cool-factor types jostling behind the rope who erupted in silent confusion at the sight of us being waved through. Danny and I are so uncool we're cool. Totally. In fact, we are reverse cool here in Hollywood. Which is like four cherries on the karmic slot machine of cool here.

But, like everything else here, cool melts fast when it gets inside the heat of this celebrity beast whose entrails we're plummeting through. I'd give us another two, maybe three weeks till half of Hollywood starts showing up in combat gear. That'll be the end of our reverse cool, the moment when the sphincter comes into sight and we splat out into the rope-line sewer.

But for now we're a definite standout inside Screem, this big cavern of a club where everyone is pretending to talk while looking over each other's shoulders to see who they should really be talking to. Actually they're all yelling at each other from close range, trying to be heard over the amplified percussion. We had artillery barrages that were quieter. The thing about these places is that everyone seems like they're working hard to look like they're having fun. Seriously. It's hard to see if anyone is really having fun here. Everyone's looking for something or someone that will give them whatever it is they can't figure out that they're missing in their lives. And then the minute they find it, if they ever do, they never want to come back to all this enforced enjoyment. We even had a place like that in Kabul the ones the foreign-aid workers set up after the Taliban were driven out.

Although Screem won't really get going till about eleven o'clock, the whole place is the usual aerial assault of music from speakers pumping out a bass beat that's like a massive fist pounding on you.

You can almost feel your inner ear being liquefied. I'm lip-reading Danny while also looking over his shoulder—when in Rome, etc.—at a few amazing-looking women wearing skirts the size of ammo clips, clustered around the bar pretending to be interested in each other. This combat uniform of Danny's is definitely causing some quivering on the mating ritual compass needle. He doesn't even notice though. "Where did I write her address?" he keeps saying.

Then it's the light bulb going off. He pulls out his wallet, checks all his money, and suddenly bolts through the club. I follow him past all the female bartenders in their skimpy little T-shirts, past yet another roped-off sushi bar area reserved for the guys who want to let the rest of the world know they're being overcharged and don't have to care.

I'm groping past the dance floor, flailed by blasts of light whipping around like fire hoses that have seized control of themselves. I see Danny vanishing into the unisex bathroom, which is a cultural experience all its own. Even those earnestly liberated college dorms wouldn't prepare you for it. Sounds of male intestinal warfare thunder from beyond the cubicle doors, while attempts to casually apply lipstick are being valiantly waged in front of the mirrors. Instantly, I think of those bone-chilling old warlords we're supposedly civilizing over in Afghanistan. They'd take one look at all this equal opportunity unisex pissing, farting, shitting, and ogling going on in here and bayonet every damn one of us before we could explain the Western democratic values they're missing out on.

But Danny doesn't notice any of it. He's locked onto the little bathroom attendant, a wizened Mexican gnome who paws her tip jar with a desiccated claw of a hand as Danny gets her to pull out all the money in it. He's peering into the bills she takes from the jar until he stops, holding a ten-dollar bill aloft, and beaming.

"I wrote her address on a ten," he says.

At first I don't understand what he's saying. But then I remember he's used to all that weird Canadian colored money where all the denominations look different. "I thought it was a one." He holds it up, triumphantly showing me *Constance the psychic* and an address scrawled right under the *In God We Trust* part.

"Imagine. Coming all this way and then nada, zip. All because of a bathroom in a Hollywood club." I stare at him. "Hey," he says defensively, "is it my fault you guys have boring money that all looks the same?" I keep staring. "Besides, it's fate. It was meant to be. Constance will have all the answers." You can tell when Danny isn't convinced of what he's telling you. He always says, "Trust me" at some point.

"Trust me," he says.

Reading the address on the ten-dollar bill, we find the psychic's place. It's off Fairfax in an area of L.A. that used to be Jewish until everyone else took it over. It's one of those fake Spanish duplexes with a wall around it and a wrought iron gate illuminated by a streetlight, balancing on its cone of light over the stillness of the parked cars.

"Spooky," says Danny—this from the guy who crawls through the nighttime darkness of some Taliban-infested valley, waiting for when the makeshift door of some cave opens for jihad business at dawn.

There's two buttons next to the gate and beside the bottom one is written *Constance Amonte—by appointment only*. And next to that is one of those handwritten Post-its that says, *Please refrain from pressing the door buzzer until the exact time of your appointment. Thank You.* We sit on the fender of the Rent-A-Wreck Ford and wait.

"Watching silence is a real art form," says Danny, looking around like he was expecting some Pashtun fighter to leap out from behind the bushes. "Do you think she'll remember us?"

"Probably. Unless she has other guys visiting after they were fighting the Taliban."

"You think that's possible?"

With Danny, you never know what's serious. "Do you know what you want to ask her?"

"For weeks I've known. Do you?"

"I want to believe in all that stuff she was telling us . . ." I leave the rest unsaid.

The wrought iron gate suddenly swings open and a small man with gray hair hurries out. He's wearing one of those leather jackets that makes sure you know it's casual and expensive all at once. He's fixed on his cell phone until he sees us. "She's amazing," he says, as if we're all part of the same tribe, and then reacts to his cell phone, telling whoever he's talking to about something he's going to kill—*axe*—*axe* is the word he uses. And then we figure out it's a TV show he's talking about. Its ratings will go into the tank next season, he says.

"Whaddaya mean 'How do I know?' I just know, okay?" he repeats while getting into a big Mercedes. "I have this intuition."

We're both looking at our watches as Danny presses the button beside the gate and a slightly Brooklyn-type accent comes through the little speakers. "Are you the soldiers?" it wants to know.

We cross a tiny courtyard with a big stone fountain filled with dry leaves. At the big door, Constance is waiting. She doesn't look anything like our Afghan images of her. She's a lot younger than we thought—maybe thirty with a kind of Goldilocks tangle of blonde hair suspended over this high, round forehead like a frozen wave. Her face looks like it was pieced together from a bunch of different people. She's got big green eyes that, from the side, look like they bulge out a little too much, and her mouth is like something that's been cinched up too tight over this tiny little chin. She's wearing a big, bulky sweater that has a hole in one of the elbows and comes halfway down her legs. In an offbeat way, she's sort of attractive. Especially those green eyes. They have a way of looking at you and they almost draw you into someplace warm and mysterious.

"I'm tired," is all she says.

Inside, her place is all candles and heavy, dark velvets with a big oak table in the middle of the room with one chair on either side of it. Except for a leather couch, that's all the furniture she seems to have. Shiva-type Indian images are covering the walls and there's cats, just like we thought, but only one of them is black. The other's pure white. She introduces them as Alpha and Omega and right away Alpha is curling around my ankles. A good sign, apparently. "You can call him Alfie," she says, suddenly becoming more friendly. "And that's Meg." So we all talk about the cats for a while because everything's so awkward and both Danny and I have both lost our brains somewhere. Finally, she asks which of us wants the reading. When I tell her both of us, she makes a loud, exhaling noise and sits in one of the chairs. "Look, I don't usually do readings after nine o'clock. And I definitely don't do back-to-backs at this hour. It's too exhausting."

"Do you remember me?" Danny asks. "I phoned about a dozen times."

"I have so many clients," she says, looking as if she's heard the question before.

"We're from Afghanistan."

She goes blank for a moment. "Oh, that's nice," she says, as if it's somewhere around San Diego. "Now then, I'm not sure if I'll last much longer. I'm so tired."

Danny and I look at each other, wondering which of us will be the honorable gentleman and bow out. We're both looking for the women we lost. I want to find Annie Boo as much as he wants to find Ariana. But I'm on the verge of being sporting and all that because I can practically hear the jangling going on inside him. It turns out we don't have to make a decision, though. "Stop," she says sharply. "I'm picking up some kind of weird energy . . . very dark. Everything is going opaque." She looks from Danny to me and back again. "You go first," she says to him.

Danny beams and turns to me. "I was going to let you have it," he says.

• • •

It was one of those nights that keeps reinventing itself in your memory. What I remember the clearest is that thick orange candle Constance lit right after Danny sat in the chair facing her across that oak table. It flickered wildly even though there was no breeze in the room. But maybe it was me looking for signs. Then she looked confused, almost startled. She sprayed something from a little bottle and the whole room smelled like a breath mint gone bad. "Wintergreen, juniper, and tea tree. It clears the energy around me," she said, as if I should understand. "Witches hung juniper beside their doors to protect themselves. Centuries ago. Not like now."

Then she took out some cards from a little velvet bag and put them on the table and went through a series of questions about place and date of birth without ever looking at Danny. It was as if she were looking out the window to that streetlight. "I'm hearing so many voices," she said.

"What are they saying?"

"I can't understand them." There was a silence. "You are a hunter," she said. Part statement, part question.

"Sort of."

"There's something you're hunting now."

"Yes." Silence. "But why don't you ever look at me when you're talking?"

"I need to look through the window."

"What window?"

"It's a portal. A window, a mirror, a pond—where all the information comes through." More silence. "It's a man you're hunting?"

"Sort of . . . yes . . . no."

More silence. Danny was making me crazy. *Just say it, for christsakes!* "He's looking for the woman he practically died for," I blurted out.

"Shh," she said, shooting me a look that must have melted a portal or two in some other world.

"I have never loved anyone else. Not like Ariana," said Danny.

"Ariana?"

"The girl I went to school with. We were in love. Going to get married." He was almost having to force the words out. "But they kidnapped her. And sold her off to an old man. Back where she came from."

Constance stared. And then stared some more. "I see a white veil."

"A white veil?"

"Was there a wedding?" When she said it, all the color drained out of Danny's face. "I see whiteness. Something that looks like a veil. Yes . . . yes, a wedding maybe?"

"She had to marry some old guy. They would have killed her if she didn't do what they told her. But there wouldn't have been a veil."

"I see a veil. A white one," Constance said in that voice so flat her words sounded like they'd been ironed. "And you."

"Me?"

"When she wears the veil you are there."

"Are we getting married?" said Danny, suddenly exuberant, even hopeful.

"No." Then the silence of hope withering. "But she wants to talk to you."

"Oh God . . ."

"She is with you. Always."

"Ariana? Can you hear me?" Danny was almost yelling, clutching the table as if he saw her across from him.

"No. She can't. The energy flows are all wrong."

"I have to get through to her."

"Blood."

"Blood? What blood?" Danny's hand slapped the table. He was ratcheting up the intensity, his leg jackhammering under the table.

"A man's. She knows him, the one who is bleeding."

"She has a brother."

"You know this brother." Part question, part statement. "He was a friend of yours?"

"Once. Now we hate each other. I almost killed him."

"How?"

"In the war."

"Did you intend to?"

"It was war."

She heard this with her eyes closed, saying nothing. After a while she said, "There's more. Isn't there?"

Danny did not want to answer her. Finally he said, "He kidnapped her. His own sister. To marry her off to an old thug, a warlord, this guy Zadran, who has a tribe and . . ."

"Yes, yes, that one's alive, the one you think you almost killed."

Danny sat up like he'd been sprung on a stiff hinge at the waist. His eyes went wide as he tried to draw in her stare that was still fixed on the window behind him.

"He is laughing. He thinks he has won."

"Let him."

"I hear him." Another silence. "I have to stop for a moment," she said.

"Why?"

"Please. Give me a moment." She suddenly looked as if she hadn't slept in a year.

"Please," said Danny, sounding like he'd never sounded before. He looked like he was going to collapse. "Ariana. I need to know if she thinks about me."

"She is trying to reach out to you. But everything is blocked."

She took a deck of Tarot cards out of its velvet bag, told Danny to shuffle them and then pick four cards. She studied the cards he picked, asked him to repeat it, and then studied the results a second time. "I see death."

"What death?"

"Someone else's." She put the cards away and took something down from a shelf, something covered by a thick black-velvet cloth, which she removed. It was a mirror, not an ordinary one; it was almost black. She put it on the table and looked into it. "I had to stop because someone else has come in. He wants to talk to you."

"Someone else?"

"Another man. He was close to you. He died. And you blame yourself?"

"I don't know if I want to hear this."

"I see the color red."

"Oh God . . . no."

"What?"

"Red? Rubi? As in ruby red?"

"I need more information."

"Enrique Rubicalba. Rubi we called him. Born in Cuba. He was my scout for a while. Before Hank and I teamed up."

"What is a scout?"

"The guy who goes out with you. Who looks through the binoculars while you're firing at the enemy."

"Why do I hear music?"

"Liberace?"

"Who's Liberace?" she asked.

"Some flowery guy from years ago. He played the piano on TV and charmed old ladies who wanted him to marry their daughters when all he wanted was to marry their sons. Hank's mother downloaded all his records and sent them to me."

"All I know is that I hear music."

"It's Liberace. We played his music up in the mountains. Right in the middle of the war. We played it in the Afghan mountains because Ariana's brother absolutely hated Liberace. But the problem was Rubi hated Liberace too. Rubi was all salsa and congas and he almost went out of his mind when we were lying there, hour after hour, blasting out Liberace from speakers hidden all over that damn mountain.

"He got shot while it was playing. Rubi died listening to that stuff."

She stared at the mirror. "Do you have anything that belonged to him?"

Danny took out his wallet and removed a little photograph. "That's him."

She stared at it. And then at the mirror. "Rubi's ready to talk to you."

Danny was all wrapped around the big oak table, like his arms and legs were tentacles trying to subdue it. "Does he know I didn't mean to get him killed?"

A long pause. "He knows."

It was Danny's turn to sigh, which was actually more like a blast of throttled memories running for their lives. "Is he okay?"

"No."

"Why not?" Danny said with a kind of Marley's ghost look.

"Because he says he's going to have to listen to Liberace for all eternity."

THE MOUNTAINS

2

I believe in the dialectics of lousy first impressions. The contradiction of opposites and all that. So on the surface, Danny and I had no business becoming friends.

From the starting points of our lives, we had almost nothing in common. Neither of us could have remotely understood the other's life until we met over there on the side of that mountain where it felt like everyone was trying to either kill us or get us killed.

Or maybe it was simply the circumstances of that first meeting. Along with about a hundred other guys, I had crawled out of the Afghan mountains, all eleven thousand feet of them around the Shah-e-Kot Valley, with my ribs feeling like sandpaper just from breathing, and my head still ringing from the altitude and from our own 120mm mortars that had a way of sucking the clockworks out of an eardrum if you were too close. Two days earlier we'd dropped out of a frozen dawn into what turned out to be a hot LZ—which officially became hot the moment one of the big Chinooks, the helicopter we were in, got torn up by enemy fire as it was landing. In one fear-thrashed instant, we were hurling ourselves out onto the hard ground, a screaming kaleidoscope of rucksacks, weapons, men, ungodly sprays of blood, and the Copenhagen chewing tobacco that some hyperventilating grunt couldn't hold in.

Opening my eyes, I was staring into that loopy grin of his peering over the maple leaf patch the Canadians wore like a bullseye on their uniforms. I mean, for me, Canada might as well have been Mongolia. All I knew about those people was that they played hockey, fought a lot but acted polite. Danny was none of those things. Except for maybe the fighting part. That came to be true.

But that was only because of Ariana, after they kidnapped her.

• • •

Dialectics again.

That first time I saw Danny was moments after I was lying there exhausted and terrified, pinned to the mountain, watching the earth and the air regularly being ripped up as someone was screaming my name above the surround-sound effects courtesy of Central Command and its F-15s. It was Captain Ellers who was yelling at me. You could always tell when Ellers was upset because his face took on the symmetry of a pothole. Too small for his massive body, it looked like it was about to fly apart, as if the springs working just below the surface of his face were torqued way past the manufacturer's recommended tolerances. His mouth would be working in opposition to the rest of his face, like it was trying to quell an uprising somewhere between his eyebrows and his chin. It made his helmet bounce whenever the brigade commander's voice came on the radio. The brigade commander's main duty seemed to be assigning blame for all the fuckups to someone else in the lower ranks.

When I first got there he barely noticed me, the almost indecipherable crackle of PRC radios and squawk codes filling the air around him. "Zadran," was all he yelled.

"Sir?"

"Zadran," Captain Ellers rasped. "You the go-to guy for Zadran?"

If *go-to* was all about almost having been ambushed by that jovial throat-slitter, the Afghan version of the Frito Bandito complete with fat handlebar moustache, the guy who could shoot up your convoy in the morning, swear allegiance to you in the afternoon, and demand your wallet by sunset, then yeah, I was the man.

We were up at the Listening Post on the forward ridge looking over at the smoke and the immolated earth that heaved in peristaltic convulsions on the opposite hill. That was when Danny raced through enemy fire, making his cubist charge—everything about him looked like it was going in a different direction as he hurtled toward us.

"See that guy, the Canadian?" Ellers yelled, pointing to Danny careening through the smoke below us. "He needs to get to Zadran. You're it."

"It?"

"*It*," he yelled. "You and him. You're a team now."

"A team? What team?"

"How the hell would I know? Orders."

Watching Danny come swooping over a ridgeline, I began debating the merits of personal grooming. His enormous shirt was billowing around him like he had wings, and that thatch of reddish-blond hair looking as if it could get caught on the air alone. He was dishevelled in a totally different way than anyone else on that mountain. I mean, battle haute couture is not exactly Marine dress whites, but with him you just knew he'd never clean up properly. He was born disheveled, the kind of kid who wouldn't know what to do with a comb and probably hadn't ever bothered owning a suit.

"The psychic," he gasped.

"The psychic?"

"Are you the outfit with the psychic?" he wheezed into the thin air after he lunged over the ridgeline, sprawling beside me.

"How did you know?" It was something that our guys had tried to keep secret. Militarily speaking it was sort of embarrassing.

"Word travels. A psychic? Really?"

I nodded.

"Good deal," he said, reaching out to shake hands and introduce himself. "Danny," he added as the enormous sniper rifle swung around his shoulders, almost clocking him in the back of the head. "I need to get to your psychic."

• • •

Like most Americans, when I was growing up, all I knew about Canada was that it was some place north of Wyoming filled with people who were irritated because we didn't know anything about them. The Santa Monica school system wasn't too big on Canada. Mostly I grew up in the Ocean Park section near the beach with a mother who trailed husbands and lovers the way the surfers there discarded entangling seaweed, a mother who had led a life in Paris and London that humbled my schoolboy existence, a mother who, like a stopped clock, was unshakable in her belief that sometime soon she'd be right.

I think my mother's real name was Annabelle. But I'm not really sure. She was one of those creatures of the sixties and seventies who made themselves into what they had dreamed of becoming, and then couldn't sustain all the splendor they had willed into that image.

But even as a kid trudging off to school in Ocean Park, the low-rent section of Santa Monica, I knew my mother was unique. I figured out that she was like Mae West's old line about times being so tough she never knew where her next husband was coming from. I also figured out that my mother gave off lust like a crop duster. (An observation of uncomfortable Freudian implications but, as the Master said, sometimes a cigar is just a cigar.) The most fertile fields got sprayed the most. Many a night I was told to "do my homework," which meant to lock myself into my little shag rug bedroom while mother "entertained" the latest candidate chosen to propel her—actually us—back to the life she had known in Paris, where she was a house model for Chanel and Givenchy. Even in her more gravity-challenged years, she routinely chose suitors who dined in restaurants like Le Taillevent. (And would claim to have brought home a doggy bag for me, which I knew really came from the Tunisian falafel seller at the end of Rue Jacob.)

It wasn't that my mother was greedy. It was just that she changed somewhere around Number Three, the husband billed as a French aristocrat, whose proclamations of love were in direct proportion to the envy shown by other men when he was with her. The problem was that the aristocrat turned out to be a former waiter with a carefully invented past, impeccable manners—and women stashed all over the 8th Arrondissement. Something in her imploded around that time, and some illusion we all need in affairs of the heart clouded over, becoming so opaque that she could no longer see through to what had once sustained her. She simply stopped believing in what had been the goal of her entire life: love. Or at least the illusion of it. Even as an eight-year-old in that, my final year in Paris, I remember the change that came over her as she ditched the fake aristocrat, looked in the mirror a lot, stopped singing around the house, smiled less, and tried to feed us both on what were scraps the butcher gave her *pour le chat.*

Love became an abstraction for Mother in that headlong rush to reinvent herself. At least for a while. She dragged me from Paris back to Santa Monica, where she'd grown up. And began looking at men with an appraiser's eye.

Which is why, many husbands and lovers into the marital scorecard, she ended up with Albert, the biggest liar of them all. Albert drove a Rolls that was fourteen years old and was usually parked where the repo guys couldn't find it. Albert was short and shaped like a pear with a round, shiny face that looked like an egg with a jagged crack for lips, topped off by hair transplants that had gone seriously wrong and created a kind of unwanted Afro. As shrewd as they come, Albert had one goal in life: to be rich. Which is why he became Number Four.

Albert was one of those guys with the face of a weak king. Ten years earlier, he would not even have rated a second look. But the sight of that Rolls cruising up the hillside on Ashland Avenue toward our eviction-pending, run-down little stucco apartment clinched the deal. Within months after the wedding, the truth about Albert started to come out: The Rolls had five different sets of license plates to confuse the repo people, and that Afro was the result of Albert being too cheap to pay for a proper hair transplant job. He'd found an orthodontist who wanted to get into the transplant business and was looking for volunteers for an experimental procedure. The experimental part involved transplanting pubic hairs, which explained why Albert looked the way he did. Afterward, the orthodontist went back to teeth and Albert wouldn't talk about any of it.

Albert was shrewd, but he was also cheap, a truly dangerous combination. By the time the truth about Albert became evident, Mother had chosen to ignore it. Probably deciding that at this stage of her life she had no choice. I figured she was suffering from the Stockholm syndrome, because she started to become like Albert, who worked on the to-a-hammer-everything-looks-like-a-nail principle of instant wealth. Pretty soon she was examining everything we did as a way to make money. Just like Albert. She invented a dish detergent that doubled as a sexual lubricant and turned our kitchen into a bottling factory. After the lawsuits on that one, she and Albert went into ghetto foreclosures, but that ended when the Rolls was burned to the wheel rims by an angry homeowner in South Central L.A. When I got into scuba diving, there was the spear gun path to wealth. But that scheme pretty much took out the flimsy kitchen wall when Albert inadvertently fired the gas-powered prototype he was positive was going to revolutionize spear fishing and, incidentally, make us all rich.

At a certain age, I learned to tune out a lot of this. I'd spend hours down on Venice Beach either surfing or doing my homework. It was easier concentrating on things like memorizing the poems for English class or reading history. Trying to work at home was like painting in a blizzard. One day I memorized "Ozymandias"— "Look on my Works, ye Mighty, and despair!"—in between the best waves of the season. And when I quoted parts of it that night to Albert, he told me not to interrupt him, he was doing something important. He was watching a videotape about how to get rich in real estate.

The idea of being rich drove Albert with about as much subtlety as a dog looking for a crotch. Whenever he even looked around, you could almost feel dollar amounts being assigned to everything he saw.

But it was the franchise oil painting thing that really did them in. Albert looked at the millions some guy named Kinkade was making selling old-fashioned paintings and decided they could make those same millions by selling modern art. So Mother got a bunch of modern art books to study and then turned our kitchen into a culture factory where she was the artist. Her style was pretty much like throwing a bird into a jet engine while holding a canvas up on the other side. Everything she did was just one big splatter. The kitchen caught the worst of it. The walls became gelatinous with drying trickles of paint. I told them to forget about the canvases— just sell the kitchen.

But right when Mother's genius was about to be franchised to an unsuspecting art world, Albert's other big scheme—the self-heating coffee mug—somehow caught fire, which spread to mother's turpentine, and the only money they made was from the insurance claim.

After that, they spent a lot of time going to seminars held at hotel ballrooms where guys who used hair dryers and looked in the mirror a lot told hundreds of people how they could get rich quick just by signing up for expensive lessons in how to make fortunes that would pay for those expensive lessons. But after about a year of this, Mother and Albert had signed up for so many lessons they were going broke. They started making me answer the phone, because usually it was some collection agency threatening to sue them if they didn't pay what they owed on one of those sets of lessons. By the age of sixteen, I had already run out of ways to throw those bill collectors off their trail. Whenever I answered the phone: *Oh they died. Is there a message?*

Or: *They have early Alzheimer's.*

Or: *They were in a terrible car crash. They'll be late.*

Later Mother insisted that, being married to Albert, she should have applied for POW status. But I don't remember it that way. Sure, he was someone who had probably practiced road rage on his tricycle, but she could go toe-to-toe with him any time. I think that was part of the attraction.

For all those years, until Mother finally threw Albert out of the house, I pretty much existed on my own. It wasn't that she didn't care or was a bad mother. It was simply that she lived in a world where she was the only inhabitant. So I tried to do the same. And told myself that I was surviving just fine.

Until Annie Boo.

Legally known as Ann Boudreau.

She could have wrapped me up and taken me home. Maybe it was shell shock from being around Annabelle and Albert. But I loved her from the first moment I saw her. I didn't think that kind of thing ever happened in real life. It does. At least, it does if you believe you've been wandering through darkness your whole life, just waiting for a woman's crinkly little grin to light the way. A woman who looks at you for the first time like she's known you from before you even existed.

Annie had grown up in Venice—not the real Venice but the phony Los Angeles Venice, a couple of miles away from where I lived. Her family home was a crumbling old cottage on one of the manmade canals that became fetid in the decades they served as scenery for aging hippies. Annie never really had a bed or a room of her own because her flower-child parents formed serial karmic alliances with kindred souls they found on the Venice Boardwalk down at the beach. Those instantly kindred souls were often invited back to the little cottage where, in the dope-addled ebullience of a new and perfect spiritual connection, they were given Annie's room while she and her twin sister slept on the couch for as long as it took for that connection to fester into the inevitable recriminations of negativity, ripped-off stashes, or sexual imperialism. Which was when Annie and her sister would get the room back until the next round of karmic bliss blew through the cottage.

A week before I met her she had dropped out of Santa Monica College, deciding that hotel management was not for her; she was dressed in a long, flowing cotton skirt and blouse that would make a rainbow look drab.

With a bandana around her windblown blonde hair, she sat at a folding table on the Boardwalk and told fortunes. I didn't know when I first saw her that she wouldn't accept money for telling fortunes. And also that she didn't really believe she had any kind of fortune-telling abilities. "I do it to make people feel better," she said. "Isn't that enough?"

And it was. Her reward was watching people ingest all the hope and confidence that came from whatever she told them. They'd come in beaten down and leave high on the fumes of the future as they now believed it.

When I first noticed her—overheard her, actually—I was one of the production assistants in a film crew shooting a commercial for some new cell phone. I was sitting on a bench almost on the sand and heard a woman's voice. She was talking to a little old man who was dressed more like he'd just wandered off from a retirement home than someone hanging around the Venice Boardwalk. He was gaunt and wore glasses that slipped around his nose as if they had once been fitted to a larger face.

"She wants you to eat more," were the first words I ever heard from Annie as she peered from the crystal ball to the old man.

"I can't. Meals were always our time together. Without her, I can't."

"She wants you to. Your wife is worried about you."

"She is? You can see that?" He looked like he was going to cry. "But she died eight months ago."

Annie just nodded with that smile of hers that could have warmed an icecap.

Then he did start to cry. "Oh god. She's worried? About *me*?"

"Yes. She wants you to go out and buy—" Annie paused, staring more intently into that crystal ball. "—I see some kind of food she used to make. It's . . . it's—"

"Lasagna?" said the old man, looking amazed. "You see lasagna?"

"It's coming clearer now. Yes." Annie was fixed on that crystal ball. "That's what she wants you to go out and buy; take it home and eat it tonight."

"No one makes it like she did."

"She says you don't want to upset her, do you?"

"Oh god, no." The little old man was smiling and crying at the same time.

"And she says she loves you," said Annie Boo, staring into the crystal ball.

"Oh, thank you." The old man softly draped his dappled hand across Annie's arm. "Thank you."

Some people are just born with a smile and they can't suppress it no matter how life conspires against them. Annie was one of those people. From the moment she noticed me watching her from that bench, I was positive she knew what I knew—that we just got each other. Words were superfluous. Introductions unnecessary. We just *knew*. No attempt at impressing one another would withstand the zapping force of sly eye-rolls and slow headshakes, framed by that grin of hers that might as well have had a magnet built into it.

"I see a snoopy person listening to fortune-telling sessions that aren't meant for him," she said to no one in particular, staring into the crystal ball after the old man had left.

"What if that snoopy person was only sitting down to rest his tired feet and isn't really convinced that the crystal ball saw lasagna?"

"You know, that's the trouble with the world. No sense of magic."

"Oh, I'm not so sure of that. You probably got him to eat."

"He looked like he'd been starving himself since his wife died. So, where's the harm in a little magic?"

"Yeah," I said, thinking about it. "Magic is good."

"I'm Annie."

And she actually smiled the next day when she was presented with the latest get-rich-quick scheme that my mother had latched onto (battery-illuminated crystal balls), and, even better, when Annabelle tried to convince Annie of her theories on wealth and karma, she sat attentively listening, gently smiling.

And then Annie Boo went back to peering into a crystal ball—the one without the battery-operated illumination—and used her magic to tell people variations of what they wanted to hear, what would lessen whatever terrible battles they were fighting, and she did it with that crinkly little smile that became a beacon in some of my darkest nights.

Maybe it was because she touched me. It was her most natural response, her default gesture, reaching out and feathering her hand across my arm as that smile of hers encircled me. It was all that I had never known before. No one in my world ever touched. It was as if one of the senses had been stricken from the family repertoire, to be replaced with the heaviness of the arch question, the reproachful silence. The theatrical swoon.

With Annie it was all lightness, simply flitting across the surface on the wings of a smile. At the time, I needed that. And was grateful for it.

When Annie Boo and I kissed that first time, right after she met my mother, I told myself the planets had said to hell with karma and wealth and all the rest of it and had simply aligned the way they were meant to. Never before or since have I felt that strange simplicity of completeness that came from giving and receiving what was missing in each of us. We just filled in the spaces within each other in some quiet, warm way that makes me ache with longing when I remember those moments, the ones in the little guest house I was renting not far from the Santa Monica Pier. It was one of those 1920s cottage appendages with no insulation, and when the nights were chilled with the ocean dampness, all we had for warmth was each other. The nights drifted by in a kind of bliss that I told myself would go on forever.

She could be playful and loving and would sometimes gently sing an old hippie folksong, "The First Time Ever I Saw Your Face," and to this day its lyrics haunt me as I hear that sweetly laughing voice. Singing about the sun rising in my eyes. And the gifts she said I gave, gifts of the moon and the stars.

I believed her when she sang to me, maybe because I desperately wanted to believe.

But then one night she stopped singing and said, "Please don't love me." And a week later she made the same request.

Why? The word would come thundering through my head, sometimes spoken, other times strangled into silence.

"I want you to be safe," was all she would say. Again I would ask why, and she would look away and say something about not being able to explain it.

Which is when I would tell her, "I have no choice."

And I didn't.

• • •

And somewhere around here I think I stopped telling myself that no one ever really lets you down, you just misjudge them. I stopped because I had to. That was where I really had no choice. I loved Annie. And by loving her I began grasping at all that held her aloft, floating like a feather over whatever reality kept me bolted to the world I understood. And to ease the pain, I began floating too, suddenly untethered from all that had allowed my world to make sense. Drifting into the tabloid sugar-highs of disposable fame and sexual scandal. It is the air we all breathe now.

Like I said, Afghanistan made more sense.

3

In that infinite constellation of reasons as to why otherwise rational young guys would risk getting killed by vaporization, dismemberment, and whatever else could be dreamed up by the medieval minds we were facing, you have to start at the top and work your way to the bottom. Which, in the pecking order of noble intentions, would probably be where Danny and I resided.

At the top are those guys who are practically shrink-wrapped in the flag. They get it! And no matter how hard I try to be like them, I never get there. Cast from some alloy of history and patriotism, they know exactly why they're risking the package. They're the guys who look you right in the eye as they coat you with a thick layer of geopolitical goo beginning with September 11 and working back to some wormhole in your convictions as they remind you how you'd damn well better atone by charging into the great machine gun of history. These guys never blink. I envy them. I love having them in my platoon. But I sure as hell won't be hanging out with them, telling war stories years from now.

In the vast middle are the guys who are over here because they can't stand mortgage payments, PTA meetings, malls, marriage counseling, plumbing courses, and all the other avatars of two thousand years of testosterone distilled into a single drop of present-day ambivalence. Over here in the war, that one little drop gets redistilled into a hundred-proof buzz that comes out shooting flames. These guys cling to war because they've peered into the abyss and seen themselves punching a time clock for the rest of their lives.

And then there's me and Danny. I now know it was no accident we found each other in this maelstrom.

Right from the moment he asked about us being the unit with the psychic, I knew each of us was there because of a woman.

• • •

I am here because I fled. What I left behind was the reflected surfaces of more reflected surfaces. From Venice Beach to the clubs in L.A., everything had gotten so shiny that you'd go blind in the klieg lights of other people's hustles. Or maybe it was your own hustle coming back at you. That was the thing: You could never really tell.

Looking back on it all, I fled because I loved Annie Boudreau. I loved her in spite of those cortical neurons desperately firing reason into my thoughts in a futile attempt to fight off all the dopamine that got unleashed whenever I laid eyes on her.

In other words, Annie Boo had become kind of like a drug.

It was overwhelming me. With that same damn dream. But not exactly a dream, maybe more like a 3D nightmare on a loop, the one where I was on the shore running into the water with her, laughing and splashing until I realized she was somehow being pulled out to sea. I kept plunging in after her, reaching for her outstretched hand. But every time I lunged through the currents and almost grasped her, she was pulled farther away from me. I was in over my head, flailing at the water and reaching out, yelling at her to swim back toward me. But whatever it was that was pulling at her had her in its grasp and she receded farther out to sea.

The whole time, she was smiling, laughing even, and waving at me as she was swept out until she was nothing but a tiny speck of color in a vast gray sea of nothingness.

And then it would start all over again. Exactly the same, each time. Night after night.

After one of these nocturnal debacles, I went straight for Self-Help Shrink 101 and told myself, okay, you're freaked out over some force (read: Hollywood, money, drugs, rich guys—whatever) corrupting Annie Boo and taking her away from you. And meanwhile she's pleading and trying to figure it out herself as she tells you how much she loves you. So, big deal—other people have had to cope with worse. Get over it/deal with it/move on.

And all that.

But I couldn't deal with it. That sea I was lunging through on a nightly basis was filling up with acid. I had to get out of there before I dissolved in it. But I couldn't help it. I was in love—that awful, joyous kind of love that drains off all reason. To me, Annie Boo was like one of those perfect flowers that sometimes sprout in asphalt. You wonder how they could ever survive. And with her background, survival was a feat that made anything I'd endured seem puny.

I ripped away every self-protective instinct I possessed. At the same time as I stopped really knowing who—or what—Annie Boo was.

But all I did know was that I was trying to reach her, trying to help her come through those long metal nights of snorting press clippings, sleeping on mirrors, and Botoxing her innocence.

The changes in her terrified me. Once they started, she shed her layers of contentment until all that joy had been boiled down to a husk of sheer want. Angry want. Merely walking on the beach at sunset became a frivolous waste of time when there was preparing to be done: nails, hair, lingerie, makeup—everything that constituted a ticket into the back of one of the limos cruising Hollywood Boulevard. And also everything that led up to the three A.M. call, sitting on some filthy curb in her party dress, weeping into her cell phone, a bottle of Veuve Clicquot dangling from her hand like something from a charm bracelet as she slurred proclamations of her love for me.

All I could do was listen. I'd never felt more powerless in my life. I should have let the phone ring. But I always answered.

I couldn't help it. I loved her.

The thing about L.A., what it has honed, to an inquisitional knife's edge, is the ability to sense desperation. Show desperation, and the blades of a thousand smiles will leave you begging for a merciful end, confessing to the tabloids and the entertainment shows that carve off little pieces of you before you even feel the pain. That's what happens to you in that wilderness of shininess. There's no guidebook to help you cut a path through the endless thicket of smiles. And no retracing of steps. In the end, you're on hands and knees, groping for the map you lost on the trail. But it doesn't matter now. Because there's simply nothing left of the you you thought you were.

When I grew up there, L.A. seemed normal to me. But not now. Somewhere in all this mess it became the promiscuous virgin, flaying you in temptations while chanting rules you had to follow. In the nights after it ended between Annie Boo and me, I would spend hours up in the parking areas off Mulholland Drive, high above the endless city, sitting there drinking beer and watching the lights flicker into infinity. And wondering where in all that congealed tangle of asphalt and desire she was. It would have been easier to find her in a jungle.

And even now, I was wondering *what* she was.

So Afghanistan, for all its cold, exhausting terror, was a kind of relief. But still, the memories of Annie Boo weighed more than the weapons I carried. It was just all part of what I thought being in love was about.

Until I met Danny. He humbled me. It wasn't his intention but he did, just by listening to him talk about his days with Ariana as we drifted toward sleep in the cold fastness of those mountains. What he murmured wasn't what I understood went on between any two people who were attracted to each other. It went way beyond that. What I was listening to was practically a commingling of souls. And long after he fell asleep, I would lie there wondering why the weight of my memories of Annie seemed even heavier.

4

Sometime late in that first month, I saw Annie again down on the Boardwalk, telling fortunes. But this time something was wrong. It was Annie but it wasn't.

She stared right through me as I approached. Barely looking up, she negotiated a fee with the heavy woman seated in front of her. It was actually more like she was reeling in the woman, telling her tantalizing bits of some love-struck future and then demanding more money to keep going. I sat on that same bench trying to piece together what I was seeing.

Her voice was harder, almost metallic—like tinfoil being folded. And the faint, sun-burnished freckles on her face were now encased in heavy makeup, as if someone else had taken over Annie, replacing all that joy and gentleness with some creature crafted in one of Albert's get-rich seminars.

She saw me watching her. "Can I help you?" she said in that aluminum-foil voice.

"What's going on?"

"You got a problem?"

"Annie—"

"Wrong," she said. And then kept staring at me in silence.

And I was wrong. It was not Annie.

By some feat of perverse zygotic logic, she had a twin. An absolutely identical—I mean seriously eerie—twin sister who resembled her in every way but the ones I'd fallen in love with. Susan Boudreau—Susie Boo, they called her—was back in town, trailing Vegas behind her where she'd left federal prosecutors wondering if the short trail leading to some rich Lamborghini-owning lover turning up dead under the proverbial mysterious circumstances had anything to do with her.

Susie Boo was different from Annie. She spewed sexuality in carefully calibrated amounts, turned on and off at will and in ways designed to do the most damage to its target.

That night, the story of her sister, all of it, spilled out of Annie, framed by a jittery smile that had me peering into the black pit we all keep covered. Annie was endlessly protective of her sister, nervously pouring out stories intended to show me that whatever Susie might appear to be, there *was* a reason for it. *Really*—there were reasons for it all. Stories even.

There was the abandoned-by-her-father-who-couldn't-control-her story.

There was the never-being-loved-enough story.

But there was also the family tomb story—Susie Boo had discovered that the Boudreau family back in Louisiana had a much-sought-after above-ground tomb in a cemetery in New Orleans. She went back there, cleaned out the ancestral bones—including Grandma, who had only been in there for nine years—and then, at the age of eighteen, Susie Boo forged signatures and sold the tomb for enough to finance whatever she went on to do in Vegas for three years.

That night, after telling me all this, Annie and I slept in my little apartment. She shivered, called out strange names, and cried in her sleep. I lay beside her in the darkness, watching the Ferris wheel on Santa Monica Pier spin endlessly through the night in its neon journey to nowhere. She woke up as if she didn't know where she was, as if it were a trance she was in, undressing, pulling off the T-shirt she wore, and then whispering for me to hold her, to go inside her. This time it was all different. She made love as if she were single-handedly holding off the night, beating my shoulders with clenched fists as she thrust against me, crying and calling out words I could not understand until I withdrew from her, rolling over and listening to her cry until she fell asleep lying on her side, my hand stroking the contours of that magical valley where her hips descended to her waist.

I remember wanting to be religious, wanting to be able to pray for her.

And then one night soon after all that, I looked out to the ocean and saw Annie running in the surf. It was that same dream. She was dancing through the water, trailing colors as the waves crashed around her and then pulled her out to sea. I was desperately trying to hold on, to drag her back to the shore, to safety, but whatever tide that tugged at her had a force I did not possess, ripping her slowly away, swirling her far out into the ocean. And not for a moment did she stop smiling at me as she vanished into the blackness of the unknown. And then I awoke drenched in sweat with her looking down at me.

"I don't want to do this to you," she said. "Really."

"Do what?" I was still dragging myself back into the moment. She said nothing. "We can leave. Leave it all. Go somewhere else."

"I know. But my sister is here now." As if that explained it all.

"What has that got to do with anything?"

"We're twins."

"So?"

Again she was silent. And then she said what she'd always tell you whenever she didn't want to talk about something: "Well, that's another story."

It was always another story, at least whenever her sister was involved. And that other story was one that never really got told— just scattered and murmured in fragments of speech and averted eyes. It formed a kind of emotional moat I just couldn't cross. The castle was impregnable, behind some wall of her sister's suspicions. It was as if a part of Annie seized up whenever her sister was around. She would weave insistent proclamations of love for me into some fabric of self-recrimination, telling me how wrong she was for someone as good as me . . . and how much she loved me.

I used to wonder if it was all because Annie and her sister were raised by wolves, self-involved ones trailing platitudes in their wake.

And could it have been that her sister somehow protected her in those years? Was that the hold she had on Annie? Or was it that some hidden emotional scar tissue had stretched across Annie's image of herself, until all she could see was an ugliness and disfigurement that no one else saw? On all those nights, when that Ferris wheel went round and round in the darkness, the colored lights forging on in their endless journey to nowhere, I would listen to her tell me that I should find someone else, because she could never be what she wanted herself to be.

"What do you want to be?" I would ask.

"Good," she would answer. That was all. There was nothing more. *Good.*

The one time I got Annie away from Los Angeles, when we drove up into mountains between Palm Springs and Idyllwild, it was as if a spell had broken. That chrysalis of haunted looks fell away from those laughing eyes, replaced by a magical delight in gathering clouds roiling silently over the mountains, in the dustings of snow and the bolting of a deer that shot across the road. There were the nights, three of them, precious memories now, in the little rented cabin under a canopy of towering cedars. It had a fireplace whose flames somehow transfixed us until we found something else to laugh about, rolling on the bed and talking of the future, our clothes festooning the furniture.

"Further," she whispered to me in the flicking light. It took me a moment to hear what she'd said. I had drifted into some unworldly state, watching the light of the fire dance on her bare back as we lay across the bed. "I want to go further."

"Where?"

"Just somewhere further. Away."

"Why?"

"No one will know us."

"Why don't you want people to know us?"

"So I can be good." The light flickered off her back, rolling in across her legs and thighs in the silence.

I hadn't ever really thought of a future. I'd pretty much just existed by piling days on top of one another until they toppled over backwards and became the past. And then started all over with a new pile.

Our future ended when there was cell phone reception again. I hadn't realized how much I owed to the silence of the mountains, where our phones had stopped functioning, out of range of whatever towers that brought in the outside world. Only an hour into our drive home, near Banning at a gas station not far from the 10 Freeway, I went inside to buy water. When I returned to the car, she wasn't there. I got in, thinking she was in the washroom, until an image of her, small, distant, and frenetic, appeared in the rearview mirror. She was pacing back and forth beside the highway, staring at the ground as she talked on the cell phone.

I called out to her but the roar of the highway swallowed my words. Only when I got closer could I hear her pleading. "Susie, no, no, *no*! It's not like that . . . C'mon, please . . ."

She didn't notice me watching her. I went back to the car, got in, and waited. When she returned, the chrysalis had been reconstituted, her face blank until I spoke.

"You okay?"

She looked over, startled. "Fine."

It was the last word spoken until the tangle of interchanges outside L.A., when she reached over and rested her hand on my arm. "I'll always love you. I want you to remember that."

She was looking straight ahead.

• • •

It was the bony finger of Hugh Hefner that did it. That desiccated finger would have singled them out in some way that only Susie Boo could have organized, curling her way around the ankles of Hollywood like a cat.

Annabelle trumpeted the news, almost running up to me, holding the *National Enquirer* aloft, opened to the spread of the *Boo Two*, the two gorgeous blondes—identical twins no less—chosen by Hugh Hefner *to be part of his harem!*, the movable feast of blondes he claimed as his own in whatever way he wanted to consume them. The blondes of eternal youth who never aged because they were discarded regularly, replaced by their mirror images; the blondes who forever lived in the present because there was no tomorrow, only replacement, and *she'll be famous now—my son's girlfriend!* Ex-girlfriend.

Annabelle.

My mother was telling everyone who would listen that Hugh Hefner—*the inventor of Playboy!*—had confirmed her own son's good taste, *the man who discovered Marilyn Monroe!* the eight-million-year-old mummified hard-on *choosing Annie!* who would now be seen on television and, better yet, probably get rich. While regularly being impaled by a Viagra-mainlining *legend who will have her move into the Playboy Mansion with all his other blondes!*

I listened to Annabelle tell all the neighbors what a cool guy her son was for having spotted this Annie, such a famous person, way before she became famous.

In situations like this, you have no choice; you simply descend the usual rope ladder of despair. You know the drill: disbelief, rage, pleading, whatever. Until you're reduced to rubble. Even before you learn that whatever you say is *Wrong!* digging you deeper into whatever shit hole you happen to be in at the moment.

Racing over to her Venice cottage to confirm that all this craziness was not true, I almost ran headlong into a caricature. It was Annie, the new Annie, the ready-to-be-test-driven, sleek, late-model Annie, chopped, channeled, and polished to a high gloss of makeup, hair styling, and whatever else she had once scorned.

"Please." She said it like I was standing there holding a club or something.

"Please?"

"Don't make this any more difficult than it is."

"*Me* make it difficult?" *Wrong!*

"Don't upset my sister. Please."

"*Me?* Upset her?" *Wrong!*

"Just don't make her angry. I don't like it when she gets angry."

"*Her?* What about when *I* get—" *Wrong!*

"I have to go back inside."

I hadn't even noticed what she was wearing—a tightly cinched S&M outfit that no doubt would rock them at the Playboy Mansion. "Have you had something done to your breasts?" *Wrong!*

"No." Coming at me like a volley. ". . . *No!* No!" Fired from the moral high ground she suddenly found herself on. "Can't I wear a new bra without you telling me what to do? Hef likes it."

"Oh, I'm sure he does." *Wrong! For all eternity. And whatever follows after eternity.* "Aw Annie, come on . . . I'm sorry. For whatever I've done. Or haven't done to help you." The first non-wrong thing I'd said. For a moment she faltered.

"Hank . . . I can't explain."

"Annie . . ."

Behind her, from the party, the one being thrown in the little cottage on the canal by her dope-addled parents who had rationalized it all by deciding that Hefner—in anointing their recovering-virgin daughter in what would surely be a well-compensated defloration ceremony—did not in any way *contextualize the objectification of women as* . . . you know the rest.

Susie Boo was approaching, scorching all she came near. Brittle and spreading a shroud of control over her surroundings. She flailed me with her eyes, the way she did whenever she saw me with Annie.

"Annie, you're missing the party," Susan Boudreau said, now looking straight at me. As in: *Can I help you?*

"Coming," said Annie. She turned back to me. "All this—" she said, motioning around her, crinkling her nose in that little girl smile, "—it's another story."

And not for a moment did she stop smiling at me as she vanished out of my life.

• • •

For months afterward I held parties that were as wild as a cattle drive in a bungalow. Dissolute, frenzied, and stupid.

And the planes flew into the Twin Towers.

And I moved back into my mother's spare bedroom, caught glimpses of the Boo Two on *ET*. Fucked Muriel, the neighbor lady, when her husband was at work. Which was bad, *real* bad.

And regularly drank myself right into next week.

And enlisted, and then went off to fight for civilization as I understood it.

Yeah, that's exactly what I did.

More or less.

5

All this happened in those wild, early days of Afghanistan right after 9/11, back before the war mechanics tightened the bolts on the killing machine. Back then everything ended up being pretty much improvised, which is another way of saying that chaos ruled no matter how much the systems analysts tried to reason with all the usual madness.

Otherwise, Danny and I wouldn't have stood a chance of being paired up. And not just because of some regulation submerged in the depths of an Army Field Manual. Merely watching him come flapping over the opposite hillside had me figuring out ways to avoid going into battle with this overgrown kid who acted like nothing was important enough to be taken seriously. Under that thatch of unmilitary hair, some steering device straight out of a video game was seeing the world as a mad points system to be laughed at. At least, that's what came through in the confusion of that Listening Post with Ellers and the rest. Everyone was screaming into PRC radios, SATCOM phones, and anything else that could get across whatever degree of terror and desperation best described our situation as we were hurtling through a twisting black tunnel of fear with no visible guard rails. From the Somme to Hamburger Hill, unheard voices were calling out from military abattoirs. And now us? It was our turn now? With the added treat of knowing in real time that no amount of that shock-and-awe shit had stopped these Ninjas who were attacking us.

Each time air support vaporized a bunch of them, a new bunch would pop up from their caves and jeer. A goddamn horror movie on a loop was what it was. And we were a captive audience suddenly yanked onto the screen in supporting roles. While this guy Danny stood there in the midst of all that rasping madness, grinning like something about it all was absurd.

But nothing about it was funny, and I was *it*. No amount of trying to get Ellers to change my *it* status remotely registered with him as he screamed into various wired-up pieces of plastic and metal, trying to find out what happened to our Ninjas—the Afghan army unit, our so-called allies, our buddies who suddenly pulled a vanishing act whenever the first shots were fired.

I didn't remotely take Danny seriously. And that was my first mistake. That grin was just his default look, a kind of natural camouflage that hid something very different from what I saw that morning.

Once he got past the business with the psychic, he went on to what was more important. "So, you actually encountered Zadran?"

"About a month ago."

"Big guy? With a black turban and a moustache that looks like upside-down handlebars of a Harley? Leads a whole tribe? The Zadrans—the Black Zadranis."

"Yeah."

"Treacherous son of a bitch."

"You mean, like, smile and slit your throat?"

"Yeah. That."

"What do the Canadians want with him?"

"My battalion doesn't even know he exists."

"Then why are they after him?"

"They're not," he said. "I am."

I didn't know what to say.

"It's personal," he said.

"Nothing's personal. This is war."

"Zadran's got the girl I was going to marry."

"None of this makes sense. Aren't you from—"

"He kidnapped her."

Somewhere around then I realized that the grin had gone. It was as if he'd exchanged his face for someone else's. Someone else who definitely did not have a crinkly grin.

Even though he was a sniper with all the lone wolf qualities those guys have, there was also this Vesuvian side to Danny that pulled the doors of life off their hinges. It was that force-of-nature way he had. And maybe that grin of his that could warm an Afghan night at eight thousand feet.

I'd never seen anyone in a combat situation with as much freedom to do whatever he wanted. In those early days of the war you sometimes found guys like Danny who were practically freelancers. And since orders came down that I was to be OpConned, we became two freelancers. Danny was the sniper and I was the scout. Roaming the mountainsides of Shah-e-Kot as if we were the free spirits of the Apocalypse, somehow disconnected from the high-altitude warfare all around us. Even when the navy's F-18s ripped the sky in half, delivering thunder on demand, or the unseen B-52s left the mountains whimpering. That stuff was almost like it came from another war than the one we were fighting. Or maybe from the one Danny was fighting. Danny had this ability to make you want to help him, partly because help was the last thing he wanted.

Back then the Canadians were way looser than we were. And snipers in their army were given great freedom, often either ignoring or advising their own commanders all the way up to battalion level. It was as if their army had been peacekeepers for so long that they'd forgotten how to fight a war, and only raw Celtic hell raising kept them going. And yet, while our guys were gunning for targets at eight hundred meters out, the Canadian snipers were bringing them down at two thousand meters.

Being a sniper is one of the more bizarre professions. But definitely a growth industry in this, the crumbling of certainties on one side and the firestorm of certainty on the other. Where men of one side are required to lie in wait for hours so that they can put a bullet into a man from the other side who is too far away to be seen by the naked eye, usually hurling him backwards like he's been hit by a baseball bat. Or sometimes the target just slumps and vanishes below whatever cover he had thought was impregnable.

One sniper can spook no end of fighters on the other side. Think of it as the Great White of our fears: unknown, unseen, and striking when least expected. It makes you afraid of the whole damn ocean. Snipers tap into fears that can't be contained because there's nothing to contain, to see, to fight against, until that mind-altering moment when someone in a group simply explodes for no apparent reason. It sends fear rocketing through the bravest.

From what I saw there were two basic types of snipers. A lot of them I could imagine as farm boys who grew up popping gophers from two hundred feet and somehow evolved into staring through a 16x Leupold scope at bigger targets farther away. They usually were the strangely silent ones, weirdly mystical in their reverence for life even as they took it like so many gophers. The other type were the Finger-of-God guys, the ones juiced on adrenaline and channeling whatever furies had been bequeathed them as they feathered that trigger, just knowing it was their duty to implement a verdict from the Almighty.

Danny didn't fit into either category. He was all about finding the woman he loved.

For him, all of it—the sniping, the army, Afghanistan—was all just a means to an end that had nothing to do with any battlefield. Without even a helmet, with only his floppy hat, he would weave amid the fighting, hauling that drag bag of weapons, looking for a hide, sometimes for the hours and hours it would take for that one devastating shot that would wipe out some Ninjas who had been wreaking death from a machine gun nest or a mortar position. Hides could be rooftops, tall grass, dunes, whatever it took to conceal them as they waited.

Up in that clear, frozen altitude, Danny was like some disheveled kid who never learned to dress properly. His shirt, all the non-regulation yards of it, was billowing so much he sometimes looked like a displaced manta ray wafting its way across the mountain—the exact opposite of everything they taught in sniper school, where they learned to dress up like a Sasquatch in weird camouflage suits or use big rubber bands to tie twigs and long grass onto themselves so they could lie there for hours itching and sweltering, faces painted and bladders bursting while grim instructors watched approvingly.

Danny was none of that. He was Mr. Hide-in-Plain-Sight and the breaker of all the rules. Even his trigger finger was non-regulation. It looked broken, like part of a pretzel, zigzagging in ways no finger should ever be required to zig or zag.

Right when you thought Danny had all the invisibility of a circus elephant, he'd suddenly vanish. He'd go utterly invisible sometimes only from a few feet away, blending in with the terrain without even so much as a shadow to show that he was there. On that morning, I looked around and couldn't find him until I heard a whisper: "So, you actually met Zadran?"

I saw the dull glint of the big McMillan 50-caliber rifle barely visible through a goat-eaten tangle of juniper twigs on top of a little ridge. "Yeah. I just told you I did."

"Did Zadran ever mention me?"

"No. Why would he?"

"Just asking."

Then silence. "Glass that mountain," he whispered. "Near those trees. Tell me what you see." I trained my optics on the mountainside, scanning slowly until I stopped at the same thing Danny was watching through the 16x.

"See it?" Still whispering. It was an outcropping of granite under what looked like the mouth of a cave somewhere up around eleven thousand feet elevation. And in the linear compression of those scopes that flattened what was a mile away so it looked like it was a hundred yards from you, a looming, heavy machine gun appeared, one of the old Russian Dishkas, lethal enough to bring down a plane. It was manned by a Black Hat, which is what Danny called the Taliban, Zadran, and anyone else who wore black turbans. A black turban on a MAM—a military-aged male—and automatically the guy was a possible candidate for the crosshairs-on-the-chest award.

This particular Black Hat darted out to fire down at our guys and then ducked back behind the rocks. I didn't get a good look at him. But Danny did.

"Aw, shit," Danny whispered.

"What's wrong?"

"Too complicated to explain." Danny took out some green range cards and studied his scrawled writing. Then he put his right eye back to the scope and adjusted the focus ring. For several minutes he carried out a ritual of adjustments to his kneepads and then the scope, and then he muttered calculations of wind velocity, air density, and trajectory.

He painted the outcropping with a laser range finder. "One thousand five hundred and forty meters."

"A mile."

"No problem. I'm zeroed for one thousand five hundred." Then a silence that went on forever. And then: "Why are you in this?"

"In what?"

"The war. The army. All of it."

"What kind of question is that? We're at ten thousand feet waiting to blow away the local machine gunner and you—"

"Personal reason? I'll bet."

"It's all personal."

"A woman?"

"Why the hell would you ask that?"

"Just a feeling," he said. Silence. More scope dialing. "I apologize."

"Apologize for what?"

"For getting you into my own personal war. I need someone who's seen Zadran. And when I heard you guys had got shelled near Khost I knew it had to be Zadran who did it."

"Why don't we concentrate on taking out this machine gun?"

More silence. Neither of us had looked at the other for over an hour. We were both staring straight ahead, whispering, even though no one was near enough to hear us. Overhead, an Apache gunship flashed past, low and zigzagging like some cosmic elastic band of evasive action was at the controls.

"You got any more of those honey roasted peanuts?" Danny was whispering even though there was no one anywhere near us.

"Two bags. You want one?"

"Not while I'm working. Later."

From about a mile away there was a flurry of motion at the cave and the Black Hat reappeared behind the Dishka. He was young and behind him were older men in turbans pointing and giving him instructions.

"Oh, shit."

"What now?"

"He's probably only twenty. Twenty-three, tops."

"So?"

"I don't want to be Charles Whitman," whispered Danny.

"Just fire the fucking weapon. Before he wipes out our guys."

"But he's only a kid."

"What's with this Charles Whitman?"

"The coward in the Texas Tower. Back in the sixties. He started it all. The decline of our whole fucking civilization." Danny was whispering louder because that same Apache helicopter had circled back and came streaking in, heading toward a ridgeline. Suddenly a rocket-propelled grenade screamed into the air, blowing a hole in the Apache, leaving it rocking and spinning in the air like some giant insect doused with bug spray banned by the EPA.

"That RPG came from the cave!" I was yelling. No more whispering.

"Charles Whitman, nice blue-eyed boy, crewcut, early twenties, ex-Marine or something. Climbed all the way up to the top of a clock tower at the University of Texas with a bunch of sniper rifles and started blowing people away. Nineteen-sixty-six. He was the start of it all. The whole decline."

From the outcropping in front of the cave, the Black Hat had settled in behind the Dishka, his face emerging over the top of its distinctive round snout that spat flashes of fire. Urged on by the older men behind him, he was raining fire down onto the valley like an excited kid zapping a video screen. They all were laughing and pointing and jeering into the valley.

"Forget about it! We got a job to do."

"Laxatives have gotten slipped into the moral code," says Danny. The Black Hat guy was laughing now with a slight mirage effect through the scope, from left to right. "Technology has given cowards the edge. Cavemen just had their clubs. One on one. Now any whacked-out Charles Whitman can wipe out hundreds of people in an afternoon."

"Wind moving from left to right. Probably three to five miles an hour."

"Already compensated for it." Silence. "I worry about being Charles Whitman."

"Worry about getting us killed."

"Only reason I'm here is to find Ariana. Her brother had her kidnapped and given to Zadran."

The Black Hat fired off a sudden burst from the machine gun and way below, one of our M-Gators, those little all-terrain resupply vehicles that look like golf carts on speed, flipped over. Parts of it pinwheeled in different directions like it was cut into pieces. Along with the kid driving it, who was thrown out into a gully.

"I've never loved anyone like I loved her."

I didn't think I heard him right. "I'm on to other things right now, if that's okay with you."

"We were perfect together."

"You're in a fucking combat zone, for your information."

"Most people go through their whole lives looking for someone to love. They don't get to have what Ariana and I had."

"For christsakes you're a goddamn sniper in some sorry-ass army that hasn't been in a war since your grandma was knitting socks for the troops. Don't fuck this up."

"Have you ever known what it's like to meet someone whose soul shared yours as if they were one—and you were destined for each other?" It was as if he was stoned on his own memories. I was frantically looking from the scope to Danny and back again trying to figure out what the hell was going on. Down below us the M-Gator driver was rolling away from the jitterbug of 107mm Dishka rounds pulverizing the rock all around him.

This time Danny saw it. All of a sudden it seemed like the lights had come on again. He stunned me, firing once—crack!—then pulling the bolt back, ejecting the cartridge, chambering a new round all in a split second, breathing slow . . . slow . . . like he was in a trance, and then crack! Again crack! and again. One Black Hat after another exploded in a fine red mist, never knowing what or who had hit them from a mile away. It happened so fast that I actually looked up from the scope to see if perhaps what I had seen was a mirage of some kind.

Danny was waiting for any other signs of movement, feathering that trigger with that strangely crooked index finger. It looked as if it had been broken and then badly reset, curving slightly upward. He fired again and then, a mile away, all went quiet.

"Oh, God, I am so sorry," said Danny, looking at the dead guy so far away. Then he rolled onto his back and stared at the sky.

TORONTO AND THE MOUNTAINS

6

This is what I know about Danny:

He grew up roaming High Park, which stretched for miles across hills, wooded areas, and a tiny lake on the western end of the old part of Toronto. From its highest hills he could see the vastness of Lake Ontario a mile away and beyond that, America, which lay below the horizon about thirty miles away. In ninth grade, right before Easter, he found himself sitting beside a nervous, silent boy who was introduced to the class as Omar, who had just arrived from Pakistan. And, it was announced to the class by Mr. Holmes, the teacher who often wore a silver earring after school, Omar spoke not one word of English. But he was just like us, Mr. Holmes said so many times that the class began to watch Omar even more closely to see if it was true. For the three days until he vanished into the English as a Second Language class, Omar would show up in the morning and sit all day, his wide, brown eyes scanning the class, his face a mask that hid whatever was going on inside him. Danny felt it was as if Omar was being turned into a zoo creature, silent and stared at by the others. He tried not to stare himself but he was fascinated by the way this tall boy with the shiny black hair and tawny-colored skin could remain so isolated, so still and silent, yet give off a sense of utter vulnerability. His hands, Danny noticed, trembled whenever Mr. Holmes directed questions to the class. Sitting beside him at the back of the class, Danny motioned to Omar on the third day. "Me," he whispered, pointing to himself. "You," he said, pointing to Omar and then repeating it several times. Finally Omar pointed at Danny and whispered, "Me."

It was winter before they saw each other again. On the shores of the tiny frozen lake in High Park, known as Grenadier Pond, Danny saw two boys and a girl watching. Both boys were wearing flat, round wool caps that Danny had never seen before, and the girl was sheathed in silks that flowed from her head, tucked into a heavy lamb's-wool coat. Danny and several friends were on skates, engaged in the ritual of testing the ice to see if it was thick enough to support a hockey game, gliding slowly across the sheer surface, listening for telltale cracking noises. All of them had heard the legend of the pond since they were old enough to walk—about how, back when the country was a colony, British Grenadiers had fallen through the ice one winter in the early 1800s and their bodies were never found. Generations of schoolboys debated the depths of the pond, rumored to be deeper than any ocean.

Danny circled past the three onlookers and heard, "You!" The taller of the two boys was pointing at him. "You!" he called out again, his breath tumbling out in clouds of mist in the cold air. And then he pointed to himself and said, "Me." Danny circled back on his skates.

"Omar?"

Omar grinned. "Yes, me. Now, English okay. Soon, good."

Danny had never seen Omar smile before. "Good now," he said, looking from Omar to the other boy and the girl.

"My brother. Ahmed." Omar was motioning to the boy with a long, thin face that registered nothing. Ahmed did not smile and at first Danny thought he was not looking at him when he nodded a curt hello. Only later did Danny figure out that one of Ahmed's eyes looked off to the side while the other one stared straight ahead. Omar made no move to introduce the girl they were with and instead pointed to the hockey stick Danny was holding. "Me?"

"You," said Danny, giving him the stick.

By the time the other thirteen- and fourteen-year-old boys had decided the ice was safe, Omar was running and sliding across the ice, using the hockey stick as a kind of balance pole. And when the puck appeared, he charged after it, even though he was the only one not wearing skates. "Me! Maple Leaf!" he yelled, laughing, before his legs went out from under him.

"You. Boston Bruin," said Danny, flashing past him. As he was skating, Danny found his attention drawn to Ahmed and the girl on the shore, standing there like those statues he'd read about on that island in the Pacific. Neither of them seemed to be moving at all, but each gave off a different kind of silence. Danny circled away from the play, skating over toward them as Ahmed's wandering eye tried to focus on him. "Would you like to try?" he said, holding the stick out to Ahmed.

"No. Not try." Ahmed was looking even smaller and more frail than Danny's initial appraisal.

"Then how about you?" Danny said on impulse, holding the stick out to the silent girl.

Instantly Ahmed's hand shot up in front of the girl. "No. Not for her."

Danny wondered if he was imagining anger from the one eye that was able to focus on him. But suddenly the eye flashed to something past him, drawn there by frantic cries of panic. It came from the churning hole in the ice where Omar had fallen through, surrounded by yelling boys, scrambling back from the hole as the cracking noises beneath their skates sounded like gunfire. Danny raced toward the hole where Omar was churning the freezing water, crying out in sounds from some other language. "I'm coming! I'm coming!" Danny yelled, diving the last several yards, sliding on his stomach, and throwing his hockey stick to Omar. "Use the stick!" he screamed. "Use it against the ice! Hold yourself up with it."

"Cold!" screamed Omar.

Danny shouted at the others to organize a daisy chain of boys, all lying flat on the ice, holding the ankles of the one in front of them so if the one closest to the hole went through the weakened ice, the others would pull him back. Or so the theory went. No one had ever seen it put into practice. Danny was the one closest to the hole. On his stomach, with his neighbor, fat Freddie Trumbull, who was trying to get his chubby hands around the top of Danny's skates, Danny edged toward the terrified Omar. But the ice beneath him began to bow in a dangerous, groaning indentation.

"I'm coming back," Danny screamed, pushing himself backward to more solid ice, feeling the freezing water seeping through his clothing. He scrambled back on his skates, racing toward the shore, straight toward the trembling Ahmed, who felt like a bundle of twigs when Danny grabbed his arms, pulling him onto the ice. "You're the lightest. We need someone light at the end of the chain." But Ahmed somehow came unglued, shaking with panic, and before Danny could drag him even a few feet from the shoreline, he sunk to the ice, trembling and shouting in that same unintelligible language.

It was nothing conscious that made Danny reach out for the silent girl beside Ahmed, taking her by the arm, towing her onto the ice. She flashed an instant of confusion. Or was it anger? Or fear? From those wide, dark eyes Danny couldn't tell and, whatever it was, it didn't matter as his skates dug into the ice for traction. She felt lighter than Ahmed. Within a few strides, she was moving almost as fast as he was. "You. On ice. Flat!" he yelled in the stilted English he had used for Omar and Ahmed.

"I know," she replied in breathlessly perfect English that for some reason startled Danny. "I understand what you're doing."

They arrived at the churning hole as Omar was still yelling and grappling with the edges of the ice that kept breaking off in his hands. Without a word, the girl dropped to her knees and crawled closer to her flailing brother. The ice held beneath her.

Danny dropped to his knees behind her, waving at Freddie Trumbull and the others to reconnect the human chain, lying on the ice. He reached out and grabbed the girl's ankles as she sank forward onto the ice. Suddenly Omar's exhausted cries turned furious, with him and the girl yelling at each other in that different language, broken only by his cries. "No touch! My sister no touch!" The girl was yelling over him, turning to Danny, and shouting at him not to pay attention to Omar.

"Shut up or you're gonna drown," yelled Danny. "Do you wanna be saved or not?"

"Inshallah!" rasped Omar. "No touch her," as he tried to swat away the girl's hand, but the water-sodden weight of his coat, and his exhaustion, pulled his arm down.

"This guy's a wacko," yelled fat Freddie Turnbull.

"Another crack in the ice!" someone farther down the chain yelled.

"He won't," said the girl, turning to Danny. Much later, Danny came to believe that in that one moment when she turned back from where she lay on the ice to look at him, he knew they would be together. Danny played it out in his memory again and again over the next decade. And sometimes that look would go on forever.

"Your brother's going to drown."

The girl rose quickly, almost scampering on hands and knees, leaning into Danny, so close that he felt her warm breath on his face. "You cannot understand. Please."

It was all part of the same memory for Danny, that warm breath and her face so close to his own. And even though he was only fourteen and she was at least a year younger, he would, years later, insist that something irreversible had come from that moment.

Danny whipped around to the ice-prone human chain. "Tape!" he yelled. "Who's got the tape?" From somewhere in the chain an arm whipped up, flinging a roll of black tape toward him. It was the tape they used on the blades of their hockey sticks, and plucking it from midair, he unspooled a long strand. Grabbing two sticks, placing them blade to blade, and spinning the tape around them, he created one long pole that he thrust at Freddie Trumbull.

"Hold on to it, all of you, and pull us out."

Then, holding the other end of the makeshift pole, he shoved himself into the freezing water beside Omar, who was now lapsing into thick, unintelligible speech. Omar was weighed down by his waterlogged clothing and, for a moment, Danny almost lost him, until he could thrust the taped-together sticks at the boys on the ice, yelling for them to pull slowly.

Later, when they had gotten Omar onto the shore, lying bundled in their heavy coats, Danny knelt shivering beside him, wrapped in blankets that someone brought from a car. "You could have died."

Omar murmured something, his eyes closed. He sounded upset.

Ahmed interrupted, furiously pointing at their sister and firing harsh vowels in that language of theirs. "What is he saying?" Danny asked, looking across Ahmed to the girl with the large, dark eyes.

For a moment, Omar's sister didn't answer, averting her eyes. "He thanks you for saving his brother's life," Ariana finally said, still looking away.

7

We climbed through small arms fire toward the cave where those Black Hats had just gotten toasted by Danny. We climbed for a good part of the afternoon, all because of Danny's vibes. To Danny, vibes were a tactical element.

I was exhausted in all that altitude. At one point I was so fried I thought I was starting to imagine muzzle flashes, like little sparks behind my eyes. I had brain needles from all that thin air, my lips were getting eaten up by that cold, hard wind, I was dangerously low on water, and more than once aviation came in thinking we were Ninjas and tried to rocket us into Inshallah territory without the benefit of the seventy-two virgins.

But Danny was oblivious to anything but getting to that cave. "I think I saw something back before I dusted those guys."

"What?"

"A face."

"A face?"

"Behind the guy with the grenade launcher that hit the Apache."

It was all he would say until we had climbed up through the traces of snow to the granite outcropping where the machine gun stood silent on its tripod, surrounded by the bodies of the dead Taliban—who Danny couldn't even look at. The mouth of the cave had been hit with some kind of ordnance after we wiped out the machine gunners. The whole face of the cave was smoke-blasted, and not far from the entrance was a bizarre-looking little stick figure, frozen in some charred contortion with only the pinkness of its gums showing through the blackened sneer of death.

"I didn't do that." Danny stood in front of it, looking horrified. "Did I?"

"It's a goat."

"Oh. Yeah."

Whoever heard of a cave with a roof that leaked? This one did. Inside the cave, there was a dripping sound, like ball bearings being dropped into a metal pan. Everything echoed. An old, untended stove was wafting filaments of smoke that stung our eyes. Our flashlights grazed the vastness of the cave, actually more like a cavern cut out of the granite with angular wedge marks where it had been cut away with jackhammers. AK-47s were hung from spikes driven into the high walls. "Look." Danny sank to his knees in front of wooden boxes of ammunition and weapons. "Made in U.S.A." He was reading the stenciled words. "Canada. This is all American and Canadian stuff." In a corner was weightlifting equipment and skipping ropes next to the neat pile of Qurans. But Danny was barely aware of it all. He had moved deeper into the cave, his flashlight darting over a stack of grenade launchers and several pairs of Nike running shoes arranged near a radio that was connected to an antenna wire. Raw goat meat was hanging from hooks above a metal pan—the source of the dripping noise, as blood flowed down the freshly slaughtered shanks into the pan.

Suddenly he bent over, pawing through blankets, papers, and weapons until some gravitational force pulled him toward a pile of papers near the goat carcass.

"Do you know what you're looking for?"

"Not what," he said, "*who*. The face." He was on his hands and knees now, searching through a mass of papers, and then a duffel bag that he emptied out. Cell phones, dozens of them, clattered onto the granite floor. He crawled to a cardboard box covered with a cloth and turned it over. The box was practically a United Nations all its own, jammed with passports from places like Bulgaria, Britain, Kenya, Uruguay, and Trinidad. And those were only the first ones to tumble out. Many of them were blank with no names or photos. "Counterfeits," Danny said. We started organizing them by photos and found the dead Black Hat now splayed behind the Dishka, showing up in four passports from different countries. With a different name in each.

Danny stopped, staring into a passport from Belgium. Then another one from France. And finally one from Canada that got his thousand-yard stare from close range, like he was holding something that needed disinfecting. "This one is real." He started trembling and I couldn't tell if it was from rage or fear. "It's been two years since I saw him. I knew it. I knew it was him." He put the passports down on the floor of the cave, impaling each in turn with the beam of his flashlight.

"Omar," he said.

Staring out from the passports was someone who almost dared you. In everything. With dark hair and eyes that seemed to have glints where the pupils should have been. And set into a long face that looked pulled down into the weight of a full, black beard. *Omar Abdullah Shah*, it said in two of the three passports.

"The guy with the grenade launcher?"

"I saw him. I saw Omar. Right here. For one split second." Danny was whispering, like some mystical revelation had just occurred. "I almost got him. He knows it's me."

"Oh yeah, right. From over a mile away."

"Each of us can sense when the other is in a position to kill him. I'm going to track him until I kill him. Or he kills me. He knows it as much as I do."

"I don't recall this being part of any battle plan."

"This . . . *he* is why I'm here." Danny's words sounded tough, but his face didn't match. He looked like some kid about to get his marbles stolen.

He reached into one of his pouch pockets and took out two small photographs, each one laminated. The first photograph showed a grinning Danny standing with a dark-haired young woman with piercing green eyes and wonderfully geographic cheekbones framed by a headscarf. Her smile matched his. The whole image just radiated some kind of goofy joy.

"Me and Ariana," he said in a voice that might as well have had an orchestra playing behind it. "Omar's sister."

But something wasn't right. All the different parts of Danny were battling one another: his voice, his expression, his words, like they were about to be flung into some inner space reserved for lost thoughts. I looked more closely at the photo. Someone's arm and shoulder were next to Ariana.

"Show me the second photograph."

He put it in front of me as if I was being dealt a card. It was the identical photograph except it was wider and showed a third person, the one whose shoulder and arm were next to Ariana. It was the same guy in the passport photos. "Omar?"

He nodded.

In the photograph, Omar was a study in contrasts. Where Ariana and Danny were joyful, he was severe; where they were looking forward, he looked sideways.

"He had her kidnapped. Because she was in love with me," Danny said. "He was going to kill Ariana. All because of me. Because we loved each other. And because I wasn't one of them. But Zadran came up with a better idea. Zadran is from their tribe here. And he took care of their problem with Ariana."

Outside the cave, I checked the bodies of the Black Hats. "None of them is Omar," I called out to Danny, who would not look at them.

"Good," he shouted from a perch overlooking Shah-e-Kot. He sounded relieved. The noise of the battle came from about a thousand feet below us until a Black Hawk medevac helicopter flashed past, dodging an RPG that tore through the hues of the late afternoon sky like something slashing a canvas.

"What did Omar and Zadran do?"

At first I thought he hadn't heard me. He was watching the arc of the RPG. "Omar and I used to be closest friends. We grew up together."

I waited for what would follow.

"I can't talk about it," he said finally.

Omar was why Danny needed a psychic. He was obsessed with hunting down Omar. And the psychic could help. Surely. He kept saying how they'd been friends. Ever since they had gone to school together.

But it now was about far more than that. He thought the psychic could help him find Ariana. If she was alive.

8

Even as we're blazing up through map contours, a thousand feet at a time in an exhausting afternoon, I feel like there's three of us on this journey. Not only me and Danny, humping gear and setting up positions in these mountains. She's here too. Invisible. Unheard. But here. She's here because Danny has brought her along. I can almost hear him talking to her in something other than words. And I feel the aching. The fury. I wish I didn't. What we're doing is tough enough without all this shit.

A week after he pulled Omar from the hole in the ice at Grenadier Pond, Danny was crossing Bloor Street on his way home from school and he saw her. She seemed to be waiting for him. She was smiling, which he couldn't remember her doing often. At first he thought it was just a chance encounter, but halfway through the traffic he figured out that she was there because she knew this was the way he went home after football season.

"Be careful," she called out, the cars whizzing past him in both directions as he straddled the double yellow line in the center of the road. Without acknowledging the thought, he wanted to stay there in the middle of the traffic just to hear her say it again. That she was concerned about him made him feel better than anything he could remember. Better than getting his dog. Better than any football game he ever played in. Better even than when his father came home after having left the family for those five months—months that he remembered mostly because of his mother's anger about every little thing. It was an anger of hers that had started in those five months. And could never be extinguished.

"I'm okay." His words were drowned out by the traffic. He hoped he sounded nonchalant, the way movie stars like George Clooney or

Brad Pitt would be. Or maybe like one of the Toronto Maple Leafs. Hockey stars would definitely be cool, sauntering across the street to the beautiful girl on the other side. Even when they were only fourteen. So he sauntered the way he thought they would saunter for as long as it took for a truck to sound a horn that sounded like a freight train. He was pleased when he didn't flinch and she looked concerned.

By the time he reached the south side of the street, it vaguely registered that he could not remember the last time someone had been glad to see him. It was a simple, unadorned thought that over the years broke through the surface. It never left him.

"I have something to tell you." And when she finished telling him, he was embarrassed because he hadn't heard a word she'd said. He had been looking at the way her hair, jet black and shiny, parted slightly on the right side of her head, fell in waves that rolled occasionally across her left eye, only to be brushed back until the next cascade. Her normally serious expression was repeatedly wiped away by that blinding smile, erasing all that came before it. The funny thing was that her mouth barely parted, from the pouty fullness of her lower lip to the faint smile that lit up whatever his world was at any given moment. It was all in the eyebrows. They had a language all their own, arching to a crest above the outer edges of her eyes and then swooping down, like some tailing off of whatever emotion she was signaling.

She was almost a foot shorter than he was, and looking down into her face, Danny went totally blank. And congratulated himself on how successfully he covered up not hearing what she said. When she finished talking, all he could think of to say was, "Would you like to go for a walk?"

She would. And they walked through the huge park, around the ponds and over the hills until they came out the other side, not far from the edge of Queen Street, which was when she turned to him with a what-next? grin and said, "You didn't hear a thing I said back there on Bloor Street, did you?"

As he stumbled with fake indignation through parts of two different excuses woven into one impenetrable tangle of lost thoughts, she studied his face until she reached out, smiling, and put a finger to his lips. He stopped in mid-sentence, staring at her. Then they both laughed.

Danny couldn't remember feeling like he did at that moment. And long afterward, in the mountains of Afghanistan, when he was trying to describe it in words, he could not.

They walked up Roncesvalles Avenue because neither of them wanted to go home. Passing one of the last of the Polish restaurants on the street, she stopped in front of the big plate-glass window where the late afternoon sun was shining through to an old upright piano. "I play here. They let me."

Inside, Mrs. Cach, the old Polish woman with heavy legs encased in rolled-down sheer stockings, peered over thick glasses and polished knives and forks while Ariana played something Danny thought he'd heard before. "It's called 'Für Elise,'" she said.

"Slow," said Mrs. Cach. "Play slow. No hard. Soft. Play soft." With an accent that Danny couldn't always decipher, Mrs. Cach was Ariana's teacher. Every once in a while, she would glower over the top of her glasses, put down the knives and forks, come over to the piano, sit beside Ariana, and play what had just been played, but in a more fluid, graceful manner. Her fingers were short and stubby like fat little sausages, but somehow Mrs. Cach coaxed music from that piano that Ariana had not yet mastered.

"She's my secret teacher."

"Why secret?" Danny asked.

Ariana didn't answer.

By the time the chef and the waiters showed up, Mrs. Cach had gotten her request of "Beer Barrel Polka," which sent her stern face into an almost girlish fit of giggles over the way it was played. And then something called "I'll Be Seeing You." Ariana was pleased that Danny knew the name of the tune.

He didn't spoil it by saying he could barely stand to listen to it.

During the five months his father didn't come home, his mother played a version of "I'll Be Seeing You" sung by Frank Sinatra over and over again until Danny put the pillow over his ears and thrashed around on the bed, yelling to drown out anything that seeped through. His mother would sit alone in the living room of their little house near the pond, drinking Scotch until she started crying, and then yelling at the framed wedding pictures. One night she smashed the photos one by one as "I'll Be Seeing You" played in the background. "Lotta good that's going to do," Danny said later, surveying the rubble. Which only made things worse.

When Ariana finished playing "I'll Be Seeing You," she turned to Danny with a look that asked for approval without ever wanting to admit to it. For an awkward moment there was silence as they sat in the last warmth of the late-afternoon sun.

Finally, Danny spoke. "It was wonderful." She smiled.

Afterward, he walked with her as far as she would let him. She stopped on Queen Street a few blocks away from the grimy yellow brick apartments built forty years earlier for the lower rungs of the Anglo-Saxon ladder but were now teeming with a U.N. in miniature. "I can't let you come any closer."

"Why?"

"It would be bad for me."

"I don't understand."

"I know," she said soothingly. "It's okay. You can't."

"What do you mean I can't?"

"You have to promise me something—don't tell Omar."

"Tell Omar what?"

"About everything. About walking with me. About the old Polish lady. And especially about me playing the piano."

"Why?"

She didn't answer. But right after they parted she turned and called out, "Hey, dopey."

He did not have to turn around. He hadn't stopped watching her walk away. "*Me?* Dopey? Hah!"

"Hah," she said back at him. They looked for a moment, smiling. "What I said to you on Bloor Street—you haven't even asked me what it was."

Danny went blank. "I remember what you said."

"Oh yeah?" He knew that she knew she had him. "What?"

"Um . . . I forgot."

"You remember but you forgot?" She started laughing. "You weren't even listening to me. I knew you weren't."

"I was too listening."

"Oh right."

"You were telling me . . ."

"Telling you what?"

"Okay, okay."

She shook her head slowly with an eye-rolling motion he was to remember long after he last saw her. Her lips pursed in a little smile. "My mother wants to thank you for saving Omar. And so does my grandmother. She's here visiting. They both said you should come over for tea."

"Okay."

"No. It's not okay. They can't invite you. Only my father can do that. Even my grandmother would be afraid. She's a tough, funny old lady. But she knows she can only do what my father wants. And my father would never allow it."

"Where's your father?"

"Away," she said looking down.

"Away?"

She still wouldn't look at him. "Afghanistan. In some camp."

"A camp in Afghanistan?"

With a little nod of her head she turned and walked into the darkening eastern skies, passing through the lights of Queen Street. Danny watched her. When she was a block away she took a large scarf out of her pocket and quickly wrapped it around her head.

It was the same scarf she was wearing in the days that followed, whenever he saw her on the streets, slowly walking with her stooped and ancient grandmother. The scarf protruded so far in front of either side of her face that it seemed to Danny to be almost a shroud.

9

Maybe it was that both Danny and I were careening through battles looking for ways to find the women we'd lost. Maybe we understood that about each other before either of us had said a word. Maybe that was what did it.

In the mountains, we used to lie under the stars some nights wondering about this psychic. She *had* to be able to help. And then we got wondering what her place was like. We'd be out there breathing in that thin air that somehow seemed purer and colder than anything I'd ever inhaled, staring up at those stars that were so bright they shot spikey little shards of light into your eyeballs. I mean, you've never seen stars till you see them in those goat-stripped wilds of Afghanistan, those denuded, rocky hills without another light source around for about a caliphate or two away. There's zillions of them up there looking like they're about to fall on your head, twinkling away malevolently like some eerie celestial light show that can seriously creep you out if you can't hang onto the beauty of it all. And even creepier are those jagged towers of utter blackness, the mountains that loom over you in all that roiling night. They make you feel like a speck. Actually, a lot of things there make you feel that way.

Maybe that's why someone got online and found a psychic, some woman named Constance who lived in America and who tells your future. If you have one. A lot of our guys had their fortunes told online or by sat phone by this woman, and some of them aren't living anymore. The minute I heard about this woman, I wanted to know what she told them before that bloody operation in the mountains near Khost. *I see a rough patch coming up . . . IEDs. RPGs. Ambushes.* Oh never mind.

On those nights when we were out in the mountains we'd lie there wrapped up like mummies with weapons, debating what this psychic looked liked and what kind of place she lived in. The general consensus was that she was old, she probably cackled, and she lived in some Gothic place that looked Transylvanian, with vines and cobwebs all over. With black cats hissing everywhere.

No one knew exactly how we'd gotten involved with this psychic. The urban legend was that one of our guys, a gunnery sergeant, had somehow found her online and she did a cyber-reading for him. She told him that he would get back alive but she couldn't see anything about a home to return to. Two days later he was called out by the company commander and told that word from Pendleton was that his house had just burned to the ground. His wife got out alive, but his dog didn't.

Before the sun went down that night, half our base camp was trying to e-mail this psychic. Remember, this is in the early days, somewhere around a year or so after 9/11 when things hadn't been bolted down with a military pipe wrench the way they were later. Pretty soon guys were firing online questions like Katyushas, volleys of them, wanting to know if their wives were fucking the local football coach or if they were going to get home alive or if it was possible that God could intervene and give a certain major the clap.

The result was one big, fat cyber-silence. Nada until about a month later when one of the platoon sergeants suddenly got an e-mail message from her asking for his birth date and where he was born. A week after he replied, he got an e-mail telling him that she saw his left foot in a vision. The platoon sergeant laughed and went around doing some goofy *My Left Foot* routine like it was all a big joke until a week later, when he stepped on an old Soviet land mine and blew his foot off. His left foot.

After that, it was practically anarchy in the ranks. The whole company was coming unhinged. No one would ever admit to it, but whenever any of us got next to a laptop, we were all firing off birth dates, place of birth, height, weight, mother's maiden name, name, rank, serial number, shoe size, you name it. On the surface everything seemed cool. After all, we're Rakkasans—the legendary 3rd Brigade of the 101st Airborne. But if you looked closer you'd figure out that on one of the operations in the mountains where we were supposed to be like bloodhounds, chasing the Taliban across the border toward Miram Shah over in Pakistan, we were all thinking about what that psychic would say. It got so whacked that some of the drivers were even asking for readings from the psychic so they'd know where the IEDs were hidden, the ones that could blow up under their vehicles.

It became so obvious that Lieutenant Colonel Lukovich, our brigade commander, heard about it. We all thought Lukovich ate nails for breakfast so it didn't take a psychic to figure out what his reaction would be. Grunt-type laptops vanished like they were lepers at a fashion show.

But by this time I had discovered a secret weapon: the Canadians. A month or so earlier, one of the CENTCOM geniuses, the Gods of Tampa, sitting back there running the war from Florida, decided that we should be welded together with the Canadians like the Second Coming of D-day.

So that's how I got to Danny. And to his outfit, which was called—of all things—the Princess Patricia Regiment. So right off the bat you just knew you had an outfit primed for some American to make a smart-ass remark about Patsies or little princesses or whatever. Or at least, that's what we expected. But it was more in our minds than theirs.

They were the same but different from us. Tough, rugged soldiers who lacked our jagged edges and technology, but made up for it in a whole bunch of key ways. For instance, we'd shell something just a hair quicker than they would, but when they did it, all that was left was a sea of glass. Or when they dealt with the Afghan tribesmen they always started off way more polite than we did. But the end result was pretty much the same. A lot of them had been peacekeepers in countries where there was no peace—Bosnia,

Haiti, and other assorted hellholes—places they went to do all that moral-high-ground stuff that makes politicians all warm and fuzzy.

Finding Danny was like finding a direct line to the psychic. Unlike Lukovich, none of the Canadian commanders seemed to care, or even know, about psychics, so when I got OpConned to the Princess Pats, what we both really cared about was Danny's access to the Internet. Or better yet, one of their sat phones. Which all came down to one necessity: access to this Constance. By this time I was really buying into it all. I was definitely becoming a believer.

Because how else was I ever going to connect with Annie Boo?

Danny'd already heard about Constance so he didn't have to be convinced. But after I told him about the *My Left Foot* episode, he was . . . *determined's* not really the right word. *Obsessed* would be better. "She'll know where Ariana has been taken. Where Zadran's keeping her." He kept saying things like this over and over again.

Danny didn't merely *want* to talk to Constance. He *had* to talk to her. And not simply on whatever satellite phone he could borrow from one of the reporters. He was, he announced, going to find out where she lived and he was going there to meet her.

"Oh man. Can you believe this?" he whispered later that night. "She lives in Hollywood."

• • •

That night, Danny's major tactical concern was cell phone reception. I thought he was going to bust something inside him, stalking all over the side of that mountain, dialing the satellite phone, staring at it, and then muttering curses at the cellular gods before storming off to a different part of the mountain to repeat it all over again. I lay back on my rucksack and watched. He was the mountain's very own pinball.

But then suddenly he stopped. Even from about two hundred meters I could see his eyes. They were burning holes in the twilight. He beckoned to me, yelling from the plateau he was on, "It's working!"

When I got there he was dialing the number for Constance. You could see him preparing himself, taking the safety off his mouth and putting it on automatic, ready for the word burst that would get all he wanted to say onto her voice mail before it cut him off. His face was coiled to spring into action.

"Constance?" He looked around, whispering. "It's her! She actually answered the phone!"

He listened, like all those spring-loaded words had drained right out of him, down into the mountain. "Constance, Constance," I heard him almost pleading, "I can't make an appointment, okay? Not right now at least. But I will." A pause. "I only need a couple of minutes, okay? I'll pay for your time when I see you, I swear." Another pause. Then: "Constance, Constance. You're confusing me with someone else. I'm not the guy from Paramount. I'm in Afghanistan. Fighting." Another pause.

"Not that kind of fighting. It's a human rights thing. Fighting so that people can keep telling fortunes and . . ."

It went on like this for another few strangled exchanges, until finally I couldn't stand it any longer. So when he started into another *Constance, Constance* routine, I walked over and grabbed the phone out of his hand, holding him at arm's length.

"Hello, Constance? I'm a friend of Danny's, the guy you were just talking to, and let me put all this in context, okay? I'm part of the 101st Airborne and we're actually at war over here—"

"Tell him that she is alive," the silky voice on the cell phone interrupted.

"She?"

"Whoever he is seeking."

"Ariana?"

"Whoever he is seeking."

"She says she's alive," I yelled to Danny, not knowing that that was an issue.

"But she's being held by Luciferians."

"By who?"

"The Luciferians. Followers of Lucifer. She misses him. A lot. How old are you?" she asked, changing the topic before I could even grapple with the Luciferian thing. "You can only change at eighteen, thirty-five, or fifty. Those are the only three ages at which you can change, you know."

"I didn't know. I'm—"

"I'll be happy to see you."

"Thank you."

"I must go now." There was a pause. Then: "You are also coping with Luciferians. Aren't you?"

"Is Lucifer the devil?"

"When I see you, I'll do a reading." Then the line went dead. I wondered about Annie Boo being with a bunch of the devil's people. It was definitely a possibility.

And that was the moment when I first thought that maybe I needed to go and see this Constance too.

TORONTO

10

In the months after what Danny came to call their "piano day," he and Ariana were together only twice, each time for no more than an hour, walking along the streets near High Park. But they would talk often on the phone, the calls only happening when she phoned him from an old pay phone on Queen Street. She never specifically told him not to call her; it was one of those things that was just understood. He didn't push for an explanation the way he did with almost everything else in his life, knowing that she wouldn't talk about whatever it was that sometimes worried her. He understood that she would simply expect him to know, in the same way he knew so much about her—and she about him. All without really ever having put this knowing into words. It was some transmission of psyches to be completed wordlessly.

There was a week when Danny knew something had changed. Although the days were getting longer, Omar was never around in the evenings, not even on Fridays when they usually met and went to Sherway Gardens or one of the other malls. And Ariana looked startled whenever he saw her in the halls of Humberside Collegiate, quickly looking away and hurrying past. Once, she looked back at him, shrugged, and then vanished into her history class. And the calls from the phone booth on Queen Street suddenly ceased.

Only Ahmed seemed unchanged. The few times that Danny saw him on the streets, Ahmed refused to say hello, just walking past him with that same deliberate stride, his long, severe face framed by the beginning of the beard he was longing to grow.

After several weeks, he waited for Ariana on Bloor Street. She saw him as she crossed through the traffic. She stopped, with cars rushing past her in both directions, and looked around quickly as if she was trying to see if anyone was watching. Danny wondered why she had almost a pleading look. Later, he decided that this was the moment when he first refused to see things as they really were.

"Please."

"Hey. C'mon, what's wrong?"

She didn't answer. She just kept walking. And when he followed, she whispered, looking straight ahead, "Find some place my brother won't see us. Please."

They ended up in a nearby funeral parlor, sitting at the back in one of the pew-like seats, staring straight ahead into the open coffin of an old man with long strands of white hair combed over his baldness in a way that did not hold. The long white strands succumbed to gravity, falling in sheaves onto his yellow, silken pillow as if a mop was growing out of the side of his head. A few friends and relatives came and departed without disturbing the hushed atmosphere. Twice, old ladies stopped beside them, patting Danny's arm, and murmuring what a good man his grandfather was. And then they were alone, whispering to one another.

"Are you scared of me?"

"Danny, no." Said with troubled eyes.

"Then why all this?"

At first she couldn't answer. "My father came back."

"So?"

"He's been away for six months. Things are different now."

"Hey. My father was away too. He came back after five months. And everything was different. I barely knew who he was. My mother hated him more but couldn't live a day without him."

"My father is not like anyone you know."

He waited for her to say something else. She just stared ahead.

"When I get my licence I'm going to rent a car. I want us to go somewhere," he said, mainly because he couldn't think of anything to say. She hesitated, reached over, and then put her hand on his. It was the first time they had ever touched. And he hoped he didn't look stupid or anything because of the smile that he couldn't control.

Whoever heard of an out-of-control smile? And in a funeral home too. But with it came her quick, worried glances, looking around her.

"What? You afraid that old dead guy is going to wake up or something?"

"My father has just come from the mountains. Between Pakistan and Afghanistan. He lives there most of the time. He is very strong. Not like my mother. She is strong but in a different way. Even Omar is scared of my father."

Before Danny could respond, a man in a gray suit appeared beside him and said in a low voice, "Will there be anything else? Would you like the coffin to remain open, or would you like us to close it now?"

"Close the coffin. But do me a favor? Comb his hair properly."

"Of course, sir," said the man in the gray suit.

Outside, Ariana walked along the street several feet away from him as if there was an invisible person between them. "My father will invite you over to our place. He doesn't want to but he will. He will have Omar do it for him."

"Some invitation."

"He has to. My mother told him you saved Omar. So he has to."

"Why does he have to?"

"It's part of how we are. My parents are from a different way of life. In their heads, they still live in Miram Shah."

"Where's that?"

"North Waziristan. It's all tribes. Everyone, all the men, wear turbans and belts with bullets. I remember as a little girl wondering if the bullets were good luck charms. But then I found out how much killing those bullets did."

They walked in silence, stopping at a red light. "You saved their son. So they have to invite you. It is their duty."

"Do you want me there?"

"No."

Danny looked at her, expecting her to laugh as if all this was some kind of joke. "And please, please don't say anything about seeing me play the piano."

"Why? Won't they be proud that you're playing the piano?"

She tried to maintain a kind of smile as if it were part of a juggling act that suddenly crashed, brought down by the weight of a single tear. She turned and ran.

• • •

A week later, Omar silently pressed a piece of paper into Danny's hands. The address on it led him to the eighth floor in one of the teeming apartment buildings, warehouses of multiculturalism on Jameson Avenue. There was something about the starkness of their apartment that made Danny uncomfortable. The walls were painted light blue with no paintings or posters on them, only what looked like green signs with wiggly white writing. And the lights—there were no lamps like he was used to at home. Instead there was the bare ceiling bulb in the living room that made him squint as he sat on the rugs scattered across the floor where Ahmed and Omar sat next to their father, a short, powerfully built man with an unruly beard and a wide, stern face under a flat, sort of pancake hat.

Wearing what looked like a long gray shirt that went almost to his knees, their father leaned back on one of the heavy, dark-red pillows that were scattered around the room and watched Danny as he and Omar talked. Omar was reduced to nervous attempts to fill the silences that hung in the room, unlike Ahmed, who seemed content to act bored, waiting for it all to be over.

Danny felt their father's stare as if it were a beam of heat, the kind they had gotten as kids by holding a magnifying glass at a precise angle that caused a point of light to burn a hole in a piece of paper. Once he attempted to return the look but quickly turned back to Omar. There was something about the man that made both him and Omar feel the need to talk even when they didn't want to.

But what most got Danny's attention were the doors in the apartment. They were all closed as if compartments of life differed from room to room and had to be kept apart at peril of contamination. From beyond the door behind Omar's father, he could hear female voices, one of them being Ariana's. While he was listening to Omar nervously telling his father how he and Danny went to the same school, he strained to hear what Ariana was saying. All he could make out were muffled words in a language he could not understand—words that ceased instantly when their father leaned back and rapped his knuckles on the door.

Ariana appeared almost immediately. Danny started to make some kind of greeting, but it evaporated within him. She was instantly different, remote, and unapproachable, dressed in a long black robe, her head tightly encased in a silk shawl as she stooped before her father with a tray filled with glasses of Pepsi and 7UP. Danny was aware of that one wandering eye of Ahmed's. It kept drifting back to focus on him, as if he was checking for reactions. Danny sat back on the big cushion and tried not to pay too much attention to Ariana. Her father reached for a glass without looking at her. She then turned to Danny, staring down at the floor while she held out the tray. He took a glass from it, murmured a thank you, and no longer cared if Ahmed was watching him. A woman, Ariana's mother, Danny assumed, came from behind the same closed door with a tray of almonds and candy. She had a face that was unlined yet tired, with no makeup. She wore the same encasing clothing and never looked at him. She put the tray in the center of the room and hurried back into the void beyond the door. Neither Ariana nor her mother had spoken a word. To Danny, as he watched the back of Ariana's shroud erased by the swinging door, they were like ghosts.

"So. You save my son," said Omar's father in a heavily accented, raspy voice. "This is good." It was the first full sentence he had directed at Danny. Everything else had been nods, word fragments, and those impaling stares. Danny wasn't sure how to respond.

"Omar is my friend," he said, settling on something that sounded safe. But Omar's father seemed first puzzled, then vaguely irritated. He looked over to Omar, who acted as if he hadn't heard anything.

"Friend." His father said it as if he was weighing the options. Omar looked straight ahead. "Where do you pray?" his father asked, his face pointing to the floor, but his eyes blazing upward so he was almost looking through his eyebrows.

It was the first time anyone had ever asked Danny such a question. He had no idea how to answer.

"I sort of say thank you a lot."

"Thank you?"

"Yeah. Like things are going good so I really should look on the bright side."

"Bright side? Bright side is a God?"

Danny was completely confused. No one else he knew talked of God except at weddings or funerals. "I'm sorry sir, I don't understand." He saw Omar looking hard at the wall.

"Omar pray five times a day."

Danny was even more uncertain. This talk of praying was not anything anyone he knew ever did—other than *Say your prayers*, the standard catch phrase they all used when something bad was about to happen, like when exam question papers were being handed out. No one Danny knew ever prayed. "Five times?" was all he could think of.

"Every day." Omar's father turned to his son, who nodded quickly without looking at Danny.

"Wow."

"Why this 'wow'?"

Danny felt sweat trickling down his back. All he wanted to do was get away from this stare that he was hoisted on—this strangely grinning but irritated look. Danny thought of the time his cat playfully pawed a trapped mouse back and forth before annihilating it. The stare was drilling holes in him. "I guess that's a lot. Five times a day."

"How much do you pray?"

"Um . . ." Danny shrugged. He didn't know what else to do.

"You do not. I know." Omar's father was almost smiling. "We know no one of you pray. Only us. Good for us. Bad for you."

That smile didn't change—but suddenly it became different in Danny's mind. And at the time he wasn't sure what made it different. It was only later that he realized that it was the combative version of Ariana's smile, showering you with mixed messages and irony beneath those arched and formidable eyebrows.

"Have more candy," said Omar's father.

• • •

There's a night that Danny remembers from that time, one of those nights he talks about up in the mountains when he's trying to work through why it all happened the way it did. It's the night Omar was blowing smoke on Bloor Street, practically pawing the ground like rutting season had begun and announcing he was going to get laid that night—"Just you watch." All of which is probably why Danny keeps talking about some of those nights so much. Because there just ain't any sane way to really think your way through them and come to an explanation that makes sense. At least not the way we normally think things make sense.

They were standing there on the edge of High Park waiting for fat Freddie, who had a car. Freddie was the only one whose parents let him use their car on Friday nights, so automatically he became cool. In a kind of honorary way.

"But your father said you—"

"Fuck him," said Omar.

"Your old man's a pretty tough guy. I thought you were worried about him finding out."

"He doesn't know a goddamn thing about what I do," said Omar, hoping his father wasn't around to hear him. "He spends all his time away, back in Miram Shah and places like that. And Afghanistan. Shit holes. Mud. Everything's mud. The streets, the walls, everything. Made of dried mud, camel shit, and god knows what else. And then he comes back and it's nothing but pray-till-you're-a-fucking-zombie, man. We're like fucking prisoners. You can't listen to music. And TV? Forget that. He saw me watching *Friends*, where Ross gets it on with Rachel, and he ripped the cord right out of the wall, yelling about living among prostitutes. It's like a fucking monastery in there, I'm tellin' you."

"Yeah. The other night?" said Danny. "When I was there? I thought he was going to make *me* pray before he let me out of there." Omar nodded and said nothing.

Later that night, Omar turned to Danny. "Do you like my sister?" The sucker punch of questions, coming from the blind side. Not asked with any ill will or menace. But somehow feeling like being asked to hold a grenade. Nothing scary about it unless you handled it wrong.

"Your sister?" Said with the requisite yuck factor and a shrug. "She's nice."

"Aw, c'mon, man. Nice? That's it? *Nice?*"

Stay away do not touch move on. Danny was seeing this—the two of them just talking—like it was an old video game with instructions flashing. Everything was lit up. "Yeah. She is." Omar looked at him sideways and shook his head.

"Hey. Back when you went through the ice, why didn't you want me to hold your sister's ankles so she could save you?"

"I was different then."

"C'mon. You were drowning."

"Are you deaf? I'd just come over here then, okay? That was back when I was like my fucking brother, Ahmed."

"*You're* deaf, you moron. You almost drowned because of that."

"You like her, don't you?"

Topic change! Danny scrambled through his thoughts, wanting to get away from anything remotely connected to Ariana. "Fuck you, Omar. You always do this." He knuckle-punched Omar on the back of the arm, and they jostled each other and laughed as horns honked on the street, and they ran for fat Freddie's car, which for some reason had stopped in the passing lane.

They jumped into the big SUV, yelling at Freddie that he was dumb for holding up two lanes of traffic.

"Oh yeah?" said Freddie. "If I'm so dumb then how come I got us a Bonus Night?" Then he made the tires screech until the end of the block as Danny and Omar laughed and yelled at him to slow down.

Bonus Nights were the main reason fat Freddie was so popular. It meant not only having one of his parents' cars—it meant they got the whole house as well. Freddie lived in one of the big houses in the little hills on the other side of Grenadier Pond. At least once every month or two, Freddie's parents flew to New York for the weekend, leaving him food in the refrigerator and a warning not to throw any parties while they were gone. Freddie had his bored *Oh yeah right. Like I'm going to have a party or anything* routine down to an art form.

Omar lived for Bonus Nights. Four days after the first one, he announced that the mere fact Freddie hadn't been slapped stupid meant that his father didn't keep track of the condom stash in the sock drawer. Or the porn collection. In English class, Omar held up *Saturday Night Beaver* when Ms. Kershaw's back was turned, grinning and dangling the DVD just beyond Freddie's lunging grasps from the next row of desks.

At Freddie's place, Omar went right through the living room and into a little den as if he lived there, opening up a wood-paneled compartment that held two long rows of DVDs and videotapes. "Classics," Omar announced, pulling out a handful. "Vintage porn. *Behind the Green Door, Deep Throat—*"

"Jesus," said Freddie. "I didn't even know it was there . . ." His voice trailed off as he pulled out DVDs and stared at their covers. "Wow. Lookit those."

"How do you know so much about this stuff?" Danny asked.

"Like you don't? Time for your education, my man." Omar slapped him on the back.

And even now, Danny talks of how the Omar he pulled out of the ice was not the same Omar who gave him that slap on the back, the kind of hearty slap that frat boys strive to master, the kind men of power use to establish superiority, the kind Danny used to think only Americans could really pull off. The old Omar, the Omar who was his father's son, would never have attempted it. But except inside their apartment when his father was home, there was no old Omar. There was only the new Omar, who had his hair cut to look like George Clooney's, the Omar who had the gorgeous Bonnie Frangilatta threatening any other girl who stopped at his locker, the Omar who led paintball raids across the woods in High Park.

The Omar who told Danny he could talk to him more like a brother than to Ahmed. Geeky, scary Ahmed, who prayed to Allah enough to deserve a new eye.

On the next Bonus Night, Omar talked Freddie into inviting two of Bonnie's girlfriends over to his house. Freddie was becoming obsessed with being found out by his parents, but he gave in when Omar told him that he'd gotten Bonnie to invite Sue Chapman, whose name Freddie called out whenever he watched porn. Freddie had always felt like a worm in Sue Chapman's presence. In three school years, she'd never even looked at him before—and now she was actually coming over to his house! He watched *Porn-ifornia*, his favorite DVD, and imagined himself and Sue Chapman out there under the palm trees, fucking their brains out. He cleaned up his bedroom for the first time since summer, hid the *Penthouses*, and spent hours in the sauna for his sure-fire way to lose twenty-five pounds in three days. He just knew he'd be buff at the end of those three days.

Danny had fantasized even more than Freddie—ever since the Monday before the first Bonus Night, when Omar had come to school with a grin. He hardly ever smiled unless someone made him laugh, but now it was as if he had a joyous secret he couldn't wait to share. "He's gone. My old man. Gone," he said finally. "For maybe six m-m-months. First he goes to Tucson. Then Pakistan."

Danny decided that if Omar was free, then Ariana would be free too. Or freer.

"No way," she said when Danny told her of his plan. "Are you crazy?" She spun around, walking away into the pedestrians on Bloor Street. She turned back, irritated that he hadn't moved, and came hurrying back, in flight.

At least that's the way Danny remembers it: with her hair being almost like shiny, black wings, falling and rising around her head, in a way that he keeps thinking of and tells me about sometimes, looking through the scope, when he doesn't want to pull the trigger, when he only wants to go back and live in that moment.

She said it all with those eyebrows arching to that crest above the outer edges of her eyes, the way they did whenever something about him either irritated or pleased her. "Are you crazy?"

"You already asked me that."

"Well, you must be. How am I ever going to get out of our place on a Friday night, even if my father's gone away?"

"You already told me your friends got out."

"Yeah. They lied. About studying the Quran together."

"So?"

She looked at him until her gaze faltered and she had to turn away.

• • •

About an hour or so into the next Bonus Night, every room in Freddie Trumbull's house was being used. Downstairs, Freddie was being ordered around by Sue Chapman and her best girlfriend, Dorothy, who were drinking margaritas, listening to music, and phoning boys. Each time they dialed another number, they would yell for more pizza and Freddie would race in with slices of the extra-pepperoni he'd ordered using his father's credit card and hoping that maybe this was when he could really talk to Sue. But after Sue announced that Jerry, the second-string running back on last year's football team, was coming over, she quickly went into the guest bathroom, put two fingers down her throat, and threw up, missing the toilet by a considerable distance. Someone later told Freddie the bathroom mirror could probably have sold in some modern art auction.

The upstairs rooms were technically not in use, at least not yet, but Omar had earlier announced while watching porn films that he was claiming them as the spoils of sexual war. But at nine o'clock he was still watching television with Bonnie Frangilatta, who was getting totally confused. She began worrying that maybe Omar didn't find her attractive, even though she had worn the blouse that opened down to her bra and was rubbing her hands all over him and saying maybe it would be better if they went upstairs.

From out past the door of the TV room came Sue Chapman's moaning and cries of "*Oh! Jerry! Yesss!*"

"Can you keep it down?" Omar yelled, and Bonnie Frangilatta told him he was so funny.

Only Danny was not really a part of Bonus Night. He had showed up with the others, contributing to the tangle of bodies packed into Freddie's parents' SUV, had joined in the laughter and raw jokes once they got to the house, but then after a few minutes had quietly sifted out to the patio, where he checked his watch and then ran as fast as he could over to the far eastern edge of Grenadier Pond, and the little road on the side of the hill in High Park.

Ariana was waiting for him, whispering from the shadows, barely visible as he ran up the hill. When Danny came close, he saw her trembling ever so slightly and in one simple, unplanned moment he put his arm around her. He had never reached out to touch her before, not even holding her hand, somehow deciphering and abiding by the rules that came with being who she was. But now those rules fell away for the instant it took her to reach out, and for him to put his other arm around her, pressing her against him, feeling the shivers that flowed down through her body in waves. "What's wrong?"

"Nothing," she said, not looking up at him. "Nothing. I . . ." Her voice trailed off and then: "I don't know how to . . ."

"Shh." Uttered so softly she barely heard it.

"Okay." For a while they stood wrapped around one another, listening to faraway noises of the city and the waterfall sound of rushing traffic coming from the Gardiner Expressway beyond the edge of the urban forest, near Lake Ontario.

Danny felt her breasts pressed against him and the sensation surprised him. He had thought of her as being beautiful but in a different way from anyone else he had ever known, and unlike all the other girls he had been with, her body had somehow not really been part of what he felt. It was shrouded by the rules—always *the rules*—that swaddled her in layers of clothing, even on warm days, and kept out thoughts of anything but how much he lived to see her.

"I have to go soon."

"We just got here."

"I know, I know."

"Your father's away."

"He's never away."

"I don't understand, of course he's—"

She put a finger to his lips. And then slowly removed it.

• • •

It was only later, when she sat up from his coat that he had laid across the ground behind the rows of spruce and cedar trees that he understood the fear she felt. It was a voice, calling from far away.

"Ar-iana!" It came curling around the hills like some auditory tendril.

"Ahmed," she whispered, and he felt her go rigid. As they scrambled to their feet, he tried to calm her.

"He's not close."

"You don't understand. He is. He always is."

They scrambled out from the protection of the treed area they were in and climbed to the top of another hill, looking down on a ravine with a road that ran through it. "Please," she said several times. But it was not a plea; it was more of a statement.

Below them, a flashlight beam scanned the underbrush and then the parked cars. A man got out of one of the cars, angrily charging the beam, yelling at Ahmed to mind his fucking business and sending the light careening all over the place accompanied by fearful apologies.

"How does he know?" Danny said.

"He knows. He starts by thinking the worst about me and then working backwards. Somewhere along the line he gets it right." The flashlight beam retreated farther down the ravine, flailing across bushes and trees. Ahmed passed under a faint street lamp, a stalking, distant figure in a long white robe and green cap.

"Arian-a!"

"He heard that some of the girls come here at night. Ever since he transferred to that school, the one out in Pickering where they pray all the time and study the Hadith, he thinks I'm going to become a whore."

"That's stupid. I'm going to—"

She reached down, holding his hand, squeezing it, and then brushing his cheek with her lips. "Good bye," she whispered, and then took off down the hill, leaving him still feeling her warm breath on the side of his face.

"Wait!"

"Please don't come with me." She turned, and from where he was, Danny could no longer make out her face in the darkness. "It will make it harder on me."

"I don't understand this."

"You can't."

"Why can't I?"

"*Pashtunwali*," she whispered from the near-darkness.

"*Pash*—" She had vanished. Danny listened as her footsteps crackled through the underbrush on the side of the hill.

Far below, an old car approached the ravine from the south, its muffler blasting away and one of its headlights shining up into the air, a quivering wand of light. The car came to a stop, an emphysemic jumble of rusted metal that sputtered and called attention to itself. Its one errant headlight shot high onto the hillside, framing Ariana in its gray glow, Ariana, frozen in a clearing and not sure which way to turn.

To the north, Ahmed's flashlight beam was still slashing at the darkness when suddenly it stopped for a moment and swung around the ravine toward the noise of the car. Then it flashed upward, joining the headlight, and an alloy of lights shimmered on the faint outline of a woman on the hillside.

"*Ariana!*" Danny had never before heard her name sound ugly. Screamed in an angry slash of sounds.

Ariana ran until she was beyond the palsied headlight and the fainter beam of the flashlight that swung wildly as Ahmed raced toward the hillside, his white robes flailing around him. Which was when Danny went crashing through the underbrush, tumbling down the hill in the darkness, and making enough of a commotion that Ahmed stopped in confusion. Danny veered off, heading in a decoy maneuver, hurrying among the trees. He was heading almost in Ariana's direction, trying to confuse Ahmed and to lure him into following the noises in the dark while giving her enough time to reach Queen Street.

But then everything got instantly darker after an explosion of light in his head.

He awoke partly wound around the tree he had crashed into. He was aware that footsteps were coming toward him. And that damn beam of light. That shone on him.

"Turn the goddamn thing off."

"*La ilaha illa Allah*," said the voice from behind the beam, sounding to Danny like something that was shattering.

He rolled around on the ground, holding his head. "Fuck, fuck, fuck."

Ahmed leaned over, above the flashlight beam. "That was her?" he screeched, part question, part accusation. "She was here. *Here!*"—all of it sounding to Danny like some rising note of hysteria that scraped against the pain he felt in his head. "Ariana? *Where?*" Like a needle being shoved in his ear. "You know! My sister. She is prostitute and you—" With one wild swing, Danny reached up and connected, his fist landing sideways on Ahmed's head, spinning him around so he fell backward down the hillside. He was surprised at how light Ahmed felt, like hitting a pile of twigs.

"You are with prostitutes. All of you. She is with you," Ahmed yelled.

"You fucking wacko," Danny was yelling back at him and then suddenly was laughing, without knowing why. All he knew was that it felt better. Maybe because it made Ahmed angrier.

"It is not for laughing."

"Yeah? Take a look at yourself."

Some calculation of risk for Ariana raced through his mind. To defend her too much would send Ahmed screeching into a fit of certainty, confirming what he already believed.

"My sister. She was here!" Ahmed said struggling to his feet.

"*Your sister?*" Pumping the words so full of absurdity and ridicule that they had a force all their own, shaking Ahmed loose from his certainty. "Are you crazy? What the hell would your sister be doing here?"

Ahmed wavered. The zeal broke, leaving only indignation, which was not enough.

"Why would a nice girl like your sister be here in the park when dipshits like you are all over the place? Hey Ahmed, you know you got a problem? So tell me something: You ever been with a woman? I'll bet that's the problem, huh? See now—"

"No!" yelled Ahmed. "No! It is *haram*! And I—"

"Then don't talk to me about whores," Danny yelled. "I've seen you checking out the cheerleaders when they do cartwheels and their underwear is sticking up in the air. C'mon, you can tell me. You're a crotch hound, I can tell."

"Filthy! All you—you are the same as a dog! The Prophet, peace be upon him, has shown us. Infidels, you will see jihad—"

"Hey, bro," said Danny, remembering how Omar had once called out to another kid from Pakistan.

"I am not your bro! Don't you ever call me bro!" Ahmed was spitting all over as the words flew out of him.

"Sorry bro," said Danny sweetly and then felt something shattering part of the hand he instinctively raised when he saw something flash toward him.

• • •

Danny lay beside the swimming pool, rolling around on the chaise lounge, groaning in pain and holding his index finger, which had been shattered by whatever Ahmed had swung at him. The pain came at him in waves, lessening slightly when he held his hand in the cold water of the pool. Inside Freddie's place the voices were louder than when he'd left almost two hours ago. There was yelling from the ground floor. The French doors opened as Freddie yelled at someone inside that he was not the goddamn maid and that he could even buy a Porsche if he wanted to. Freddie came outside, pacing back and forth before he noticed Danny. "Don't puke in the pool," he said.

"Fuckin' animals, man. I'm telling you. That Jerry, what a dick. She's crawling all over him. After I got her exactly what she wanted! Who else knows how to get a pineapple and olive pizza, man? I got it for her. She's gonna lose out, man. I'm gonna lay down the law."

"Freddie, what are you doing?"

"Pissing in the bushes. What does it look like?"

"Just checking."

"You wanna go in there and piss in a bathroom that looks like the pizza from hell? After she pukes all over the goddamn place. It's a fucking petri dish in there."

From beyond the open French doors, Sue Chapman's voice sounded in a symphony of vowels played on an instrument whose notes had been calibrated for effect. *"Ferrr—ehh—deeee!"*

"What?"

"You are so *meeeeeean!*"

"What—*what?*" A look of panic came over Freddie's face. He zipped himself up and raced toward the house, vanishing into a volley of vowels about how *meeeaan* he was for hiding the *keeeeys* to his parents' car when all she wanted was to drive Jerry home and—

Danny stuck his mangled finger into the pool, waiting long enough for the throbbing pain to subside as he heard Sue Chapman promise to be back in ten minutes—fifteen max. On one of the glass-topped patio tables there was a bottle of some kind of liquor, over half full and burning as it went down his throat. But the burn felt good because it made him forget about the pain in his hand. And the more he drank, the more both the burning and the pain went away. He looked at the label that said *Napoleon* in big gold letters, thought maybe History wasn't so bad after all, and then laughed at his own little joke before drifting into a fuzzy haze that ended when he sensed someone else was standing over him.

"Omar?"

"Fuck, man."

"What's wrong?" Danny said, wondering if it came out as *Wasswrong?*

"I kept seeing my old man."

"Where's Bonnie?"

"She's a b-b-bitch, man."

Danny wondered why Omar was suddenly tripping over words, sometimes verbally jackhammering consonants. "I thought you liked her," he said.

"Yeah. Well. Whatever."

"Seriously."

"She . . . she didn't c-cut it."

"What are you talking about?"

"I thought she c-could handle it." Omar grabbed the bottle of brandy and drank one long gulp from it. "She's supposed to be so fucking hot, man. But you think she could handle it? No f-f-fucking way, I'm tellin' you."

"Handle what?"

"Making my old man go away!" Omar almost exploded as if it was all so obvious that any moron should get it.

Danny sat up, wrestling with the dampness of the cushions on the chaise lounge that clung to him. "Your old man's in Arizona. Or Timbuktu, or wherever."

"You know you really don't have a clue, do you?" said Omar indignantly. "He's in here, man," he said, pointing to his head. "That's where that motherfucker is. I'm up there in Freddie's bedroom with her and you'd think that she would at least have enough hots to make me stop hearing *haram*," he said, throwing himself back on a chaise lounge and finishing the brandy in one gulp. "She was supposed to be so fucking hot, man. Biggest fuck in the whole school. And could she handle it? No way. All I could think of was my old man yelling all that shit at me."

The French doors swung open and Freddie trundled out like he was powered by steam. "Shit, shit, shit."

"Go away," said Omar.

"I live here."

"What's that got to do with anything?"

"She said ten minutes. Fifteen max." Freddie was yelling now. "That was an hour ago. And she's still not back. If my parents knew someone was driving their car—"

"Freddie go away, willya. We all got our own problems."

"Jeeze," said Freddie and then trundled back inside.

Danny felt the pain in his mangled finger coming back and suddenly wanted to be anywhere but where he was.

"Hey, Danny, do you know what you want to do when you grow up?"

"I dunno. Why are you asking me that?"

"I want to know what it feels like."

"What are you talking about?"

Omar didn't respond, and for a moment Danny thought maybe he'd left. He was standing in the shadows. "My old man's a fucking t-terrorist."

"So's mine. They all are."

"I'm serious. You know why he's going back to Peshawar?"

"If I don't even know where it is. Why would I know why he's going there?"

"He organizes money for bin Laden."

"What's bin Laden?"

"Not what—who. You'll figure it out."

"How am I going to figure it out?

"You will."

Later, when the planes flew into the Twin Towers, Danny wondered if he had been involved in a kind of historic moment, there at Freddie's place. But then up there in the mountains on one of those quiet, cold nights, after telling me about that night at Freddie's, he decided that it was just another one of the warning signs that everyone saw but no one understood. "People aren't built for warning signs," he said. "Just being born is a warning sign."

I told him I'd get back to him on that one.

THE MOUNTAINS

11

That night, most of us were extracted. (Who thinks up these words? When I hear we're being *extracted* I think of a rotten tooth being yanked out. The military loves words like that.) We watched from inside the Chinook as it rose into the thin mountain air, a fat bird struggling for flight. The traces of unmelted snow gleamed in the moonlight like gashes on the faces of the now-silent mountains around Shah-e-Kot. Back at Bagram, the mandatory proclamations of tactical brilliance from the geniuses were celebrated in spite of evidence to the contrary.

I lasted a day there and then managed to get re-OpConned, sent back to the Canadians at Kandahar, which meant jumping another Chinook, this one suddenly developing rotor problems, making the TuffBins I was sitting on feel like the innards of a cement mixer. I stepped off the helo barely able to walk, staggering over to our Rakkasan billets at Kandahar airport, a truly bizarre modern structure like inverted concrete beehives dropped down on the medieval landscape.

Danny was waiting for me.

Hovering was more like it. And when he saw me staggering toward the billet with a rucksack that suddenly weighed a thousand pounds, he swooped down on me like a hawk with a secret. Still wearing British desert fatigues, with a billowing shirt that never seemed to touch his pants, he flapped his way toward me, propelled by the force of the loopy grin that belonged on someone half his age. Or maybe I was just imagining it was a grin.

"Constance."

"What about her?"

"Awesome," was all he said until we were in his tent and he was hunched over his laptop. There were messages from Constance, most them sounding like fortune cookie stuff, the kind dreamed up by the Mexican busboys at our Chinese takeout joint back home in Santa Monica and believed fervently by dentists and lawyers going through bad divorces—*Love will be yours if you are daring*—while eating chow mein alone in their new single-bedroom rentals, leaving them pumping fists in the air and resolving to hit some bastards with that class action suit that would definitely get the attention of the blonde paralegal in litigation who—

And yet, once you read through Constance's fortune cookie stuff, there was one of her messages that really got your attention: *You have missed something of importance. Something in a dark place. Something that was used to steal from you.*

Danny was excited as he read it for what must have been the hundredth time.

"That cave—'*a dark place.*' And those boxes, the ones we saw in the cave. Filled with fake passports and the weapons our guys gave Zadran. That's how Zadran would have paid Omar. In guns. To buy Ariana. That was the dowry. Instead of camels or mules, Zadran bought Ariana from her own family with guns. That's how the weapons got there. Ariana was sold—*stolen.*" The words came tumbling out like some speeded-up revelation brought down from the mount around Shah-e-Kot. "Omar wanted weapons; Zadran wanted her. So they sold Ariana to him." He looked like he was talking to me, but really he wasn't—*you have missed something.*

By this time, even our guys had gotten back into the Constance business. Lieutenant Colonel Lukovich was now in the States, and the new guy hadn't yet figured out why so many of these laptops were appearing all over the place. Forget Clausewitz. Sun Tzu. Patton. Now it was Constance, master military strategist. Three centuries of incrementally rational military thought went right into the voodoo dumpster. You might as well have had a witch doctor running the OpsCen tent—*Sir, considering the psychic intel we've received from Hollywood, don't you think we should avoid Objective Blue and go for Objective Orange instead—*

Like I said, this was in the days before Big Army moved in and made the whole Afghan thing a subsidiary of War Inc. These were the days when our guys rode horseback into battle whenever it made tactical sense, and no one filled out forms or consulted with military lawyers. These were the days when rules were being made up to fit whatever we needed them to fit. It was war fought from the bottom up, with all the attendant loopiness that drove most of the generals crazy.

Dear Soldier, I wish you all the best and all good fortune and I know that my previous readings will bring you—which was pretty much a form letter from the Other Side, but Danny didn't see it as that. For him, Constance's e-mail was The Sign that was coming from Ariana. She was out there waiting for him, in the murderous fastness of those mountains a few kilometers and a dozen centuries away. She was out there, loving him as she had loved him for all those years when they were growing up. She—

I watched Danny convincing me, convincing himself. And I cringed on his behalf.

• • •

Here's what you need to know about my guys, the Rakkasans: One day in World War II, the Japanese woke up and saw the sky fill with American parachutes. They started yelling, "Rakkasan," which means something like umbrellas that come down from the sky. The name stuck. Back then our guys just loved saying the word—go ahead, try it. *Rak-ka-san!* It had no end of ethnic superiority possibilities. Then those same guys added some Hoo-Ah! cluster of Latin words no one understands but feels jazzed about—in this case it's *Ne Desit Virtus* (Let Valor Not Fail)—words more or less designed to provoke sneers among a segment of the Chardonnay crowd on both coasts. Which does not stop newly minted batches of Rakkasans from getting sent off to war with all this *Ne Desit Virtus* business ringing in their collective ears. And the truth of it is that, when the incoming rounds start obliterating your immediate surroundings, all that Hoo-Ah! stuff surely does give aid and comfort to those whose woebegotten hides are on the line for whatever doctrine the Free World has sent us to drum into the heads of murderous tribals living a century or two behind the civilization curve.

The Canadians were cursed with being pretty much the same as us and yet not at all like us. It was the paradox that they lived with, and usually railed against. They didn't have all the Hoo-Ah! stuff. At least, not like ours. Once in a while they'd do a crazy move, strutting around like roosters and raising that goofy flag of theirs, the one with the red target-practice maple leaf for a bull's eye, planting it on some godforsaken piece of ground that wasn't going to see a subdivision anytime soon. Like they'd studied the Iwo Jima photograph and thought they could improve on it. But for the most part they were just people trying to remember a skill they had collectively once possessed and forgotten—in this case, warfare.

The Canadians seemed to have no institutional memory of war; the last one they'd been in was fought by their grandfathers, so they mostly made it up as they went along. This Princess Patricia outfit that Danny was a part of was given to fits of egalitarian goofiness and Celtic mayhem that our Big Army would generally have regarded as mutiny. One of their quainter rituals was the so-called field days, which would have had our generals calling for the military police. In these things the lower ranks would challenge their officers to wrestling matches, which, once you got past the thin veneer of civilization, occasionally turned into caste system vendettas.

On that day when Danny was telling me about Constance, someone came in the tent and tugged at him, trying to draw him into what was billed as a tag team wrestling match. Danny shrugged him off; all he wanted to do was talk about Constance. "She knows. I can feel it." *You have missed something of importance.* "That psychic knows how to get to Ariana."

I hadn't told Danny about the message I'd gotten from Constance. The one that might as well have been branded onto some part of my mind: *She hurts. She needs you. Be kind.*

"What the hell are we doing here?" Danny was stuck somewhere between confusion and irritation.

Someone else grabbed his arm again. This time he didn't resist and he was pushed out of the tent into the center of the massive cluster of soldiers, which had all the military discipline of a mosh pit.

In the center was the alpha male, the battalion commander who didn't need the insignias to prove it. Actually, there'd be no place for any insignia since he wore only cutoff jeans, the muscles of his shoulders and arms rippling, not in that body builder condom-stuffed-with-walnuts way but more like one of those construction guys whose hand swallows yours when you shake it. Like I said, our Big Army would be reaching for the rulebook on this kind of thing—a colonel putting himself up as a possible punching bag for some grunt.

But this Canadian colonel had already wrestled a couple of guys into roadkill. And you just knew that somewhere behind that buccaneer's grin, the battalion commander was listening to some malt whiskey chorus of ghostly highlanders demanding genetic continuity. When Danny was pushed in there like Big Bird, it definitely looked like a continuation of some clan battle. The colonel, with sweat pouring down from that mowed wheat sheaf of red hair going gray, just grinned. "Okay, last one. Two minutes, max."

But Danny had a different chorus in his head. "Sir, I must warn you," he said to the battalion commander. Remember, this is Big Bird talking here, so the words got pretty much drained of any menace.

"Duly noted, son." There was almost an imaginary knife between the teeth in that buccaneer's grin. The battalion commander moved his arms in flowing motions, like waves of muscle, beckoning.

"Sir, I must inform you: I really don't want to fight. I am thinking about the woman I love," Danny announced.

The battalion commander was covered in that moon dust, the powdery coating that covered us all in Afghanistan like we were in some talcum powder factory. Danny looked like he was his own ghost. His sweat was running into the moon dust, giving him a kind of war paint in reverse.

"Excuse me?"

"I am in love, Sir. You really don't want to fight me. Not while I am thinking of the woman I love."

The battalion commander did a kind of double-take. He looked from his men to Danny and back again. Then he started laughing, a full-diaphragm, bellowing laugh that as much as commanded laughter from those around him.

Which he got. The whole circle bellowed back in laughter as the battalion commander whipped his hands around the back of Danny's neck in a full wrestler's maneuver. They were bent at the waist and joined at the head in a tangle of arms. In all that dust and commotion, they looked like Siamese twins feverishly arguing over which way to go. Danny was whipped and pulled all over the circle, even though he was a lot taller than the battalion commander. He was like prey in the jaws of one of those predators you see on the Nature Channel in some show that Darwin might have produced. The circle fell almost silent out of respect for the about-to-be-dead.

But then something happened, something pure Danny. He slithered away from the battalion commander's grip and flung himself off to one side, spinning through the dust, staggering to his feet and lurching through the cloud of moon dust as if different parts of him were going off in their own directions. "Sir," he announced, wafting away the dust, "I am being forced to fight in the name of the woman I love."

"Huh?" said the battalion commander. He was at the intersection of irritation and control, that moment for someone of power who suddenly has to cope with someone who does not care about power.

"Sure. Whatever." With that same knife-between-the-teeth grin. He lunged toward Danny, who sidestepped him like a bullfighter swirling a cape of pure naiveté.

"Sir, she is out there in those mountains. We were supposed to be married."

The battalion commander was now beyond theatrics; the narrowing of his eyes could be read as either anger or panic. In a crouching stance, he circled Danny, who was still staggering until that one instant it took for him to make a lunging strike, catapulting the battalion commander back into the dust. Danny was on him like he'd been spring-loaded. The prey became the predator in a blur of arms, legs, and frenzied eyes.

Danny wasn't only fighting the battalion commander; he was battling everything that stood between him and Ariana. And no one else knew it, especially not the battalion commander, who was pinned into the dust, flashing desperate, angry glances as he tried to find a major, a captain, anyone who could do what he could not do, which was pull rank and end this debacle. There was no way he could assert the full withering power of his position in the hierarchy, not now when he had so grandly cast it aside to show that he did not need it. Not now when he was being wrestled into flattened crab-walk submission by this puny beanpole.

The air around that human circle suddenly screeched, like something was being shredded inside your eardrum, a shock-wave effect that jarred the whole writhing, bellowing, moon-dusted collection of unleashed testosterone. The screeching ripped away the moment; it came from the bagpipes played by a knobby-faced regimental sergeant major, whose years in the army officially rendered him wiser than anyone else.

That wisdom included the knowledge that none of the two hundred men forming this circle could ever fight to the death for a man humiliated as badly as their battalion commander was now about to be.

I couldn't tell what this bagpiper was playing, but it was something that obviously stirred the circle into mumbling things that made no sense *true patriot love in all thy sons command* and except for the crab in the center that was still flipping onto its back and then slapping itself into the dust *with glowing hearts we see thee rise* the whole throng was singing along.

The bagpiper was playing their national anthem.

Pretty soon they were all standing at attention, eyes straight ahead, bellowing out *we stand on guard for thee* until even the crab disengaged, becoming once again Danny and the battalion commander, both staggering into an exhausted facsimile of protocol, each of them realizing that national honor was now at stake. Side by side, they stood trying not to fall over as they joined the circle belting out *O Can-a-da, we stand on guard for thee.*

And when it was over and the circle was desperately looking for ways to pretend none of it had happened, Danny walked past the colonel and said, "Good job, Sir."

"See," Danny said, lurching over to me, "he doesn't have any hard feelings."

"Oh yeah? His face was like a cat's when you catch it taking a dump."

But Danny didn't get it. He simply couldn't absorb the reality around him. Which was that a battalion commander, with his depleted reserves of hierarchical power, was staggering away, trying to make jokes about it all with desperate-eyed captains who laughed too easily.

That was the moment when I knew that, in some karmic workshop where spirits write destiny, I was being assigned the role of Danny's protector.

• • •

Danny was one of those among us who have not been given the codes. Or maybe it's just some inner fount of optimism which erases judgment that does not fit what they have decided to believe. Danny was one of them. Some kind of guile had been bred out of him. For someone roaming the seething Afghan mountains with an awesome instrument of destruction in his hands, he was an innocent when it came to anything that did not conform to his belief that nothing could prevent him from finding Ariana. Who was out there. Waiting for him.

And I confess to a moment of envy. I wanted that kind of belief too. So I could find Annie Boo.

12

Those stars again. I just couldn't stop looking at them. Or thinking about them and what they said about us.

Almost everywhere in Afghanistan the stars are terrifyingly bright. Whatever your preferences for all the light-polluted places we live in, you just understand things way better by going back into places still waiting to update the oxen. The Afghan nights are blacker than any shade we've dreamed up on our civilized color chart. They yield more rawness and awful truth about the human condition in one bandit-ridden, Taliban-filled night than a decade of nights in places where the darkness is blown out by the local mall lights. You stand there in that Afghan blackness where the closest light bulb is at least two tribes away; you stare up at those stars blasting out photons with an intensity you've never known, and you just have trouble getting seriously ecumenical. No matter what the body count is that day in the eternal Bad Guys versus Us struggle, you just have to wonder how all those stars out there can be created by more than one God.

But if God is on our side, and the Ninjas are claiming the same thing, where exactly are we? I always wondered about that.

• • •

When your mother tries to tell you how to fight the war you're in, the generals are in trouble. My mother's theory of war was simple: *Be nice to them. And then when they see you're being nice they won't want to fight.* Of course! That's it! God, if only! *If only* we'd seen it before—*The Strategic Thoughts of Annabelle*—niceness as a geopolitical strategy. Hitler, so utterly undone by a box of chocolates from the nice Jewish people that he races to have the gas in Auschwitz shut off. The Taliban, weed whackers in the human petunia bed, blubbering with gratitude over the free tickets to Disneyland. Osama bin Laden sighing with remorse because he got comped in that nice Las Vegas . . . *See?*

Annabelle's Theory of War caught up to me in the mountains when one of the support soldiers reached into the big yellow mail sack and pulled out a bulky padded envelope with Annabelle's grand handwriting that had grown more florid as she got older. In it were the obligatory updates on the Boo Two as told by the tabloids—*Twins in the Playboy Mansion!*—that pretty much drove needles into my eyes reading them. *Boo and Hugh—an item?* with photos of Hugh Hefner looking about as leathery as the average eighty-something, draped around four gorgeous blondes who were probably still in diapers when he started collecting his pension. The photographs in those magazine articles were like cluster bombs, detonating multiple images of Annie lying under the sagging folds of that leather as he—

Oh, the carnage of it all.

My mother knew exactly what she was doing. She had never forgiven me for "letting that girl get away." *That girl* had represented Annabelle's chance to recreate herself; her one last shot at redemption and social rebirth, sweeping herself back onto the A list by trailing the beauty that was Annie behind her. The beauty of *that girl* would absolutely, certainly, be a reflection of Annabelle herself—*every*one who was *any*one would see the similarity in an instant, a few years removed perhaps, but who was counting?

I crumpled the articles into a ball and fired them into a pile of trash. But the padded envelope was the oracle that wouldn't stop. All sorts of stuff kept tumbling out of it. There were two versions of my horoscope with Leo outlined in yellow highlighter: *Risk should be avoided this month*; an article on the importance of taking herbal remedies for the prostate; another article about syphilis; in other words, the usual Annabelle package.

But this one had something different. Besides the usual letter, it had two homemade CDs on which she'd written *Music to Make Love or and War*. The *and* had been rubbed out, written in again, and then finally crossed out.

The letter was pure Annabelle. Each of her letters had a theme that was practically megaphoned off the pages. The last one was about how fashion models today don't have the class that they did in her day. Reading it in the midst of a rocket attack on a dust-blown plain in Zabul Province somehow didn't do the subject justice. Scrambling for cover from what turned out to be Chinese-made 107mm rockets fired by the Taliban into our forlorn Forward Operating Base tends to interrupt one's train of thought.

This latest letter was about Albert. It was even more unreal. Suddenly, Albert was a good guy again. No more *shithead, ruined-my-life* stuff. Suddenly he was one seriously *outstanding* man. *Up*standing, if you can believe it.

"You okay?" Danny asked. We were sitting on packing crates outside the big tent where he was trying to figure out a satellite phone he'd borrowed for ten minutes talk-time from a reporter. Danny was a master at finagling sat phone time from reporters.

"No." I was still reading. *Misunderstood?* Albert? And *so discerning*! I read that word at least ten times, wondering if I was missing something—I mean, Albert was about as discerning as a buzzard in a dumpster. If there was a buck to be made, he was Mr. Nice Guy. Other than that, he was just another hustler in the ring, punching his shadow. . . . *but you've always been too hasty to condemn poor Albert*. Poor Albert? What happened to the never-darken-my-door-thief-swindler-con-artist Albert? Where did that Albert get to? *And just to show that he has no hard feelings* . . . Albert, of all people, having hard feelings? . . . *he has downloaded—is that what they call it?—some wonderful music for you. Which I chose, of course. I let Albert use your computer here so he can start this wonderful new business of his, making CDs for shut-ins and widows—*

I dropped the letter.

"You okay?"

"You already asked me that." I was staring at the homemade CDs Annabelle had sent me, wondering if something about them was contagious.

"Things change."

"This doesn't."

"What's that?"

"Music for love and war."

"*Or* war," Danny said, squinting at Annabelle's scrawl.

One of the other Rakkasans, a kid whose real name was something like Bakassaro but who was known as Battle Zero, looked over from where he was cleaning his rifle. "It's the same thing where I come from."

Battle Zero had a tight little face that looked like it never saw the sun, and big ears that moved when he got excited. "Cool. CDs. Ludacris? Mötley Crüe? Snoop Dog?" Battle Zero's ears started jumping. He grabbed the CDs and studied the handwritten notes on the cover.

"Liber Ace," he said. "Never heard of him." He jammed one of Annabelle's CDs onto his player and hit Play. And then his face practically melted with confusion. He strained, listening into his headset, like something was pulling that already small face down into his shoulders. Battle Zero looked as if he was listening to someone being tortured. "What the fuck is this?"

He whipped the earphones out of the CD player, hooking it up to little speakers on the edge of his cot. They poured out some other universe of bouncy piano music, sounding like something stuck between classical and white guys' reggae. "Does the person who sent you this like you?" he asked.

"I'm not sure."

On both CDs was one word written in Annabelle's loopy scrawl: *LIBERACE*.

"Libb-er-ach-che," I said, enunciating carefully.

"Libber—?" said Battle Zero. "Who would do a thing like this?" he said, staring into the music like it was something he should spray with Raid.

That tinkly music started driving them all crazy. A kid named Rubi started yelling, "Turn it off!" and "Enough already!" from inside the tent. Rubi had been born in Cuba and everyone liked him. He and Danny had been together on a couple of short missions. After a few more bars, Rubi stuck his head out of the tent. "What the fuck is this?" he yelled. "A new interrogation technique? Audio waterboarding?" Pretty soon the whole mountain was yelling insults at Liberace's music.

"'Kitten on the Keys'?" said Battle Zero, reading from the handwritten list on the back of the CD cover. He hit the Forward button. "*Warsaw Concerto?* Who listens to this crap?"

It was the laughter that surprised me: gleeful, exuberant, almost giggling. It came from Danny. "I love it!" he said, leaping to his feet to stop Battle Zero from turning off the music. "It's perfect."

"You're kidding."

"Trust me," said Danny. "I'm not."

"'Indian Love Call'?" said Battle Zero, reading the notes again.

"It's the most beautiful music I've ever heard."

It dawned on me that Danny might be serious. He was staring into something only he could see, something let loose by that tinkly, weird music.

"Man," said Battle Zero, looking to me for help, "is this what posttraumatic stress is like?"

But Annabelle the oracle was not finished. Out fell one more of my mother's gifts to modern warfare: a thick, shrink-wrapped, cardboard lump that landed at my feet. It was something that had to be unfolded before its full splendor was revealed—a life-sized poster of a prancing, middle-aged white guy with pompadour hair and wearing tighty-whitey little short pants, diamond-patterned knee socks with diamond-patterned shoes to match, and a spectacularly fringed Star-and-Stripes shirt.

"Wow. Faggy," said Battle Zero.

"It's Liberace."

"He's dead," said Danny.

"No wonder," said Battle Zero.

"Your mother's a genius," Danny said. But I was too busy reading the rest of her letter:

> " . . . *and if we, the rich, white world, stopped being so selfish and donated more of our culture to those unfortunates who don't have it (instead of trying to make a profit off it), this world would all be one big happy family . . .*"

"This is brilliant," Danny said. And for some reason, he really meant it.

> "*. . . And so if you let them hear the musical genius of Liberace, which Albert has so generously downloaded for you, those Talibans will almost certainly want to be your friends, and . . .*"

. . . And what, Annabelle?

Yes, what? All the gentle lacerations that never heal with Annie Boo? The ones frozen in the aspic of the *People* magazines that you send? Her and Hef? Her and (fill in celebrity blank here)? Her from a million paparazzi angles destined to flash through the zipline of our collectively deteriorating attention span? Is that why you're sending me *People, Us, National Enquirer*, and all the rest of the air candy we dine on in our endless banquet? Or maybe—just maybe—is it because Annie is the You that never happened?

And if so, what the hell does that say about me?

Signed: yr lving son.

• • •

That night, the Apache gunships roaring into the air to take out whoever was mortaring our south perimeter kicked up enough of a downdraft to knock poor Liberace over. That life-sized, prancing poster of him dressed in those tighty-whiteys and all that fringe was spun against the tent, but he suffered no grievous injuries and, once righted, was still frozen in his leg-kicking pose with that megawatt smile.

But the attack had a soundtrack, just like in Hollywood. Liberace's "Moonlight Sonata" was ending when we heard the distinctive *crummp!* mortar sound that preceded the explosions. They were perfectly timed to synch up with "Beer Barrel Polka," which cut loose as something blew out beyond the wire.

For Danny, this mortar business was just some annoying irritation. He was fixated on Liberace—his showing up was a sign, he just knew it. Liberace was some sort of cosmic messenger and Danny wanted Constance to tell him what it all meant. *Crummmp!* He redialed her number on the sat phone. "Answering machine," he said. "Five times."

Crummmp! And then a distant *thump! thump! thump!* as the Apaches let loose with their 30mm guns. Like in horror films, the night tends to expand your imagination when scary stuff is involved.

"Leave a message."

"It's too complicated." A mortar hit somewhere closer in. Whoever was shelling us was bracketing. "Watch out for Liberace."

For most of his allotted ten minutes on the reporter's sat phone, Danny just dialed, listened to the message, hung up, waited a few minutes, dialed again, and repeated the whole exercise. "These Hollywood people," he said. Somewhere, in his mind, ten thousand miles away in California, a woman was watching the phone ring and not answering it. Because maybe it was not cool to answer your own phone in Hollywood.

Finally, when he was about eight minutes into his sat phone allotment, he left another breathless message. "Hello? Constance? It's me again. Danny. In Afghanistan. Listen I'm sorry to bother you. I don't know what time it is over there in California, but it's eight o'clock at night here in Afghanistan and I really need to talk to you. See, I know this sounds weird, but Liberace has sort of shown up here. And I know it's a sign because I'm trying to find my girlfriend, Ariana, who was kidnapped and taken over here by her family, especially Omar, her brother, who used to be my best friend but now is trying to kill me before I kill him and if there's one thing that would send him around the bend, make him absolutely bat-shit crazy, it would be Liberace, because—"

Crummp! He abruptly stopped talking and stared into the phone. "It cut me off," he said at almost the same instant that something exploded on the packing crates—you could almost hear the fins on the mortar round rotating, it was so close, sending Liberace pinwheeling into the next tent. After we lurched to our feet again, Danny ran to pick up Liberace. Dusting him off, he said, "We need him."

"For what?"

"To get Omar."

"Liberace is going to bring down Omar?"

"Of course," he said. He was looking at me as if the answer was utterly obvious.

• • •

From the LZ, we left the platoon we'd flown in with and walked through a small valley, through fields and villages with no one visible, usually a sign that the Taliban were nearby. The silence of those mud-brick structures came from some different age, from some other place than the one we knew. The stillness alone made your skin crawl. The slightest sound was amplified in your mind. A cloth banner, flying raggedly over a grave, made a snapping sound that sounded like gunfire by the time it got through to my brain.

Farther up toward the mountains we saw a woman collecting scraps of firewood from the goat-ravaged trees. Dressed from head to foot in a light-blue burqa, she turned, probably startled as we approached—I say probably because there was no way of telling—she was encased in that burqa like it was a shroud. She stared for an instant through that heavy mesh opening across her eyes. Then she fled across the mountain like a sky-colored ghost.

Danny stopped, swaying under the eighty pounds in his rucksack until I thought he was going to fall over. "Aw man."

"What's wrong?"

"That woman. She could have been twenty—she could have been sixty. Who knows what was underneath that thing. She was erased, man. *Erased!* That's what they do. That's what they're trying to do to Ariana. But she won't let them."

"Are you trying to convince me? Or are you—"

"Don't even go there."

"Break! Break! Break! Gabriel Three—" The radio crackled with our call sign. Coordinates were relayed quickly back and forth. Two of our guys were dead and another wounded after a Ninja RPK light machine gun opened up on them, daisy cutting the terrain on the other side of the mountain. They couldn't get to the wounded guy because of the fire from that machine gun with its two-hundred-round drum.

Danny and I pushed ourselves up through more map contour lines than I wanted to know about, climbing maybe fifteen hundred meters straight up. And then we had a view of the problem. One of the Americans was lying on a plateau way below us, slowly bleeding to death from a major leg wound. Every time one of the Rakkasans tried to go to his aid over the ridge line, the RPK would blister the ground in front of him.

I glassed the other side of the plateau and found the RPK on an overhang on the other side. Two Taliban fighters manned the machine gun, one firing, the other preparing to load. The one firing had a black turban and a full beard. The other one wore a flat, round, *pakol* cap and played cheerleader, yelling whenever the machine gunner fired.

Instantly, we were all business: doing a laser check on the guy with the turban who was firing the machine gun; it came up with 1,920 meters. Then calibrating the remnants of a cooking fire behind them, which yielded a calculation of about four minutes left for the drifting smoke; then dialing that windage into the scope; checking and rechecking the notations in the logbook that Danny carried: altitude, elevation, temperature, trajectory, and velocity. And finally crawling, ever so slowly, to get to the place where that single round of 173-grain ammunition would not be deflected by the barrel of the machine gun.

That was what we did. Those were the fierce, intense moments we needed to get the mil dots in the scope lined up right below that black turban and beard.

But really?—that was not what we were doing.

Not even close. Only later did I realize it.

What we doing was avenging Ariana. And whatever she was going through.

As we crawled through the scrub brush, Danny whispered the whole time about Ariana. About how Omar and he were both here in these mountains. About their brother. Their father. Whispering, inching ahead. About Zadran, who would be protecting Omar. And still whispering as he lined up to fire. And again as I murmured recalculations: *One thousand eight hundred and ninety-two meters . . .*

The whispers were about how Ariana's family hated music. Music was the work of Satan. The Prophet had said so. And how Omar had talked to his father, who was fleeing after 9/11 and had issued his own decree: No music. Especially no piano music. Piano music was evil.

And so, Liberace was now our fiercest warrior. The piano player. Liberace would wreak havoc on Omar.

Exhale, Danny. You are in another world now. A world where time slows down. Ex-hale. Softly. And feather that trigger with that crooked finger, eye to the scope, pulling back oh-so-gently, and—

A mile and more away, the black turban flew into the air as a fine red mist exploded from the machine gunner's chest.

And a second or two later, the cheerleader also lay dead, and the Rakkasans scrambled onto the plateau toward their wounded comrade.

"Ariana," was all Danny would say.

• • •

Later, toward nightfall, Danny again unfolded the life-sized poster of Liberace. He took it out to where the groove in the mountain pass ascended for perhaps three thousand feet like a vast scar in the looming granite.

In the face of the gathering clouds, he strode to the highest point of ground, a tall, shaggy-haired kid with Oakley wraparound sunglasses, baseball cap, the beginning of a blond beard, headphones with a radio mike, desert camos, T-shirt, and a Glock or two, all of it accessorized by the *deshmal*, the warriors' fashion statement, the brown-and-white checked Afghan kerchief that draped over his shoulders. A rifle hung at his side in one hand as he planted the poster with the other hand so that Liberace faced the mountain, beaming and prancing into the darkness as if that smile alone could light up the night.

Then he implemented *Annabelle's Theory of War*. He took Albert's downloaded disk and inserted it into the CD player. From two portable speakers, Liberace, prancing in that frozen pose, belted out "Polonaise in A-flat Major," and the Afghan mountains ricocheted with his music. Such *nice* music! Liberace's tinkling, bouncy notes filled the passes, blasting through caves, bouncing off the rock faces, and soaring into the cold mountain heights.

"*ARIANA!*" Danny yelled into the mountains. His voice came back to him in waves of echoes.

"Omar," he said quietly. "We'll know Omar's out there when someone attacks Liberace."

Whatever concerts Liberace gave or pranced through while he was alive, the response was nothing compared with this, his most fervently attended performance. Because, from somewhere in the gathering clouds jostling against the highest reaches of the mountain, the glint of tracer bullets flew out, arcing toward us. They lacked the trajectory, and sank into the void below Liberace, who was now arm in arm with Danny, waving into the distant gunfire.

"*Omar!*" Danny yelled. "What's the matter, Omar?" *Omar Omar Omar* the echoes responded. "Let me see Ariana!"

Another burst of tracers raced through the gloom as Liberace pounded out something called "Mexican Hat Dance." Danny stood beside the cardboard standup poster, bracing it against the wind that had whipped up. The bullets came closer but could not reach what must have looked like two friends enjoying the view.

TORONTO

13

Omar had become so tall and physically strong that the phys ed teacher approached him, looking for a linebacker for the football team. Omar had to ask Danny what a linebacker was and when he found out how long the daily practices were, he decided on a carefully laid-out plan. "I'll do it just long enough to destroy that prick Jerry."

Jerry was the enemy. Ever since he'd wrapped Freddie's parents' car around the telephone pole on the Lakeshore, thereby ending Bonus Night forever, Jerry had been dickhead, fart face, and ass wipe. It didn't matter that he was supposed to be the football star of the upcoming season. Or that he was poised for whatever greatness such things bring to someone who vacationed in California every March break. Even Sue Chapman's three weeks in traction after the accident did not diminish the luster of what lay ahead for Jerry.

"I'm g-g-gonna crush him" was Omar's pronouncement.

"Forget it," said Danny, staring into the furrow that Omar got between his eyes whenever he was seized by some anger over something that made no sense to anyone listening. Danny had started to decode Omar's fits of fury. They were always about something else than what he was talking about. Danny saw it mostly when Omar was talking about having to go to the mosque out in Scarborough, the one his father took them to. They were increasingly accompanied by a slight stammer as he exploded his way through whatever sentence he grappled with. And usually the fits ended up with some comment about his father. "Fucking di-dictator."

"Jerry's not such a bad guy," Danny said as Omar's brow furrowed into that knife-edge of emotion he sometimes showed. "He's just a lucky guy who's got it all."

"Guys like that? They're a fucking fraud, man." Omar's pronouncements about Jerry were often made in front of Dorothy, his new girlfriend after Bonnie Frangilatta, who was practically slandering him to anyone who would listen. Now, whenever he encountered Bonnie in the halls, Omar wouldn't look at her, and twice he shoved guys around him, especially after she asked, "Fucking the mirror are we, Omar?"

"Dorothy's better, man," he would say. "Way b-better." Which didn't really make any sense to most of them because Bonnie practically dripped lust and Dorothy wasn't exactly loaded with the same juices.

Dorothy had been Sue Chapman's closest friend, the one who would usually get drunk whenever they went out. But that didn't bother Omar. "You just like undressing me when I'm passed out," she giggled once when Danny was driving and she was between them.

The following Friday night in Kenny Brunton's house, Danny descended from upstairs, where the singles were acting like it didn't matter what was going on in the basement, where the near darkness was filled with writhing, groping, and breathless whispers from a dozen couples. He could barely see across a candle's flame as Omar stripped most of the clothes off Dorothy, who mumbled and giggled in a vaguely vomitous way. Omar stared down at her, running his hands across her breasts. "Yes," she mumbled. "Yes."

The stairs creaked under Danny. Omar looked up across Dorothy's nakedness to where Danny stood. For a moment, neither of them said a word.

"Jerry doesn't know what he's in f-for."

"You okay?"

Omar only spent four days on the football team. None of the coaches had ever seen anything like it. This Paki kid, they called him. Even in the practice sessions he was blasting through the offensive line and cutting down blockers like they were so much

Styrofoam. And crushing the running backs with scythe-like tackles aimed below the knees. There was no half speed, no let's-just-walk-through-it for Omar. It was annihilation or nothing. No matter how much the coaches tried to explain, no matter how much he nodded as if he understood it was just a practice session, he still came crashing in like some heat-seeking missile programmed for one thing only.

"It's a game, asshole," screamed Jerry after he stopped throwing up, crawling on hands and knees across the field after Omar had driven his helmet into his ribs, a kind of human pile driver. Omar went back to his position, with those eyes peering over the facemask. The kid who played defensive tackle swore he looked like Hannibal Lecter. Which he didn't. It was just all that concentrated energy, perfectly focused in a way that no one else on the team could even approach.

Two days before the game against Runnymede, when Bonnie Frangilatta was on the sidelines leading the cheerleading practice, Omar disregarded the playbook that called for a no-contact-zone defense and crashed in past the offensive tackle, a blur of vengeance for some wrong that no one could identify, cutting down Jerry on a draw play, flying at his knees with such force that the snapping sound caused the cheerleaders to stop in mid routine and turn toward the agonized screaming on the field.

Two days later, Runnymede won by five touchdowns.

Jerry was in hospital and Omar never showed up for the game. The following day, frustrated confrontations by the coaches were met with a stare that made them step back. "Why would I care about a game?" Omar said, almost whispering in a way that made them turn around and walk away, shaking their heads. None of them could figure out what had happened.

But Danny knew.

• • •

Not long after the Runnymede game, Omar phoned Danny. Little Big Horn was on, he told him. That was what they called the paintball fights they had, where one side was Custer and the army and the other side was the Indians. Omar had announced he was an Indian. Not the kind from India, he made clear. The other kind. And he was Crazy Horse. Enlisting Freddie and Brunton and a couple of dozen others, they had staged what Omar called warm-up fights, blasting away in the more secluded hills of High Park until the police chased them out.

But now Little Big Horn was on. Tonight! It *had* to be tonight. "I don't know if we can get all the guys on such short notice," Danny said.

"You have to."

"*I* have to?"

"You know what I mean. C'mon, man."

"I'm busy, Omar." Danny was looking across to Ariana, who sat on the couch, rocking ever so slightly back and forth. She would look up at him for a moment, brushing the cascade of shiny black hair away from her eyes. And then look away whenever he replied.

"I'm coming over, man. I need to get it going."

"Don't come over. I got homework." Ariana flashed a look, her dark eyes widening. Danny reached out, putting his hand on hers. All she could hear was her brother's voice crackling distantly in the phone Danny was holding. It was an urgent, loud voice. "Omar, what the hell is that all about?"

"My father's c-coming back tomorrow, g-goddammit."

That night the paintball war was fought along some tribal passion that most of the players could not begin to understand. High school in the west end of Toronto prepared them for none of the fierceness Omar infused in it all. In their confusion, it began simply as the same goofing-around game they always played.

But blind fire soon raged. Snap battles broke out everywhere across the hills, the rules were disregarded, half the players were zombies, and trees ended up as abstract art.

Danny was one of the Indians; it was part of the unspoken order of battle that he and Omar were usually on the same side. Danny and Omar. Sitting Bull and Crazy Horse. In most of the Little Big Horn battles they overwhelmed the cavalry. But on this night, nothing worked. It was all chaos. And all Danny wanted was for it to be over so he could get back to Ariana before she had to go home.

Freddie pretty much ended it all when he ate the paint, taking a direct hit from Chapchuk right in his mouth. And while he was being hosed down, he threw up all over Adamson, Watson, and Gilmore, who were part of Custer's cavalry, and everyone started accusing everyone else of dirty tactics. The hillsides echoed with wimpy war cries and confusion until the police cars showed up and they all scattered.

Danny took off, glad to have it ended, just wanting to get out of the park and get to where Ariana would be waiting for him. He kept running until he reached one of the picnic tables, telling himself he was free of it all.

And then he heard footsteps coming up behind him. Omar. Not even out of breath. "Yo."

"Yo, yourself."

"Want a Coke?"

"I gotta go."

"Sorry, okay? I get wired. So I overdo things. What of it? Don't you ever feel like you're under a goddamn avalanche?"

"What are you talking about?"

"Everything." Omar was walking around the table. "It's too much."

"What is?"

"All of it." Omar waved a hand around in the air.

"I gotta go," said Danny.

"Hey wait."

"Why?"

Omar walked around in a tight little circle. "I don't have anyone else to talk to."

Danny made an instant calculation. Ariana was waiting for him and there was only an hour before she would have to go home. So: how to say just enough to Omar without being trapped? It was a variation on the calculations he had made again and again in the previous month. Like how many hours it would take to get to a distant multiplex where no one would see them at a movie and get her back in time. Or the hours that one of her Muslim girlfriends felt comfortable covering for her. Or the hours, sometimes days, that Ahmed would be at the Islamic school outside the city. "So what's going on?"

Omar kept making his circles in silence. Then: "Don't you feel it?"

"Feel what?"

"The tension, man. The goddamn tension."

"Maybe not like you do. What are you tense about?"

"Stuff doesn't fit together."

"Stuff?"

"I'm a talker, man."

"So? You're talking to me."

"Yeah. You're the only one. Everything is compartments. I spend my life making sure I'm not talking to someone from one compartment about stuff in another compartment. Nothing fits together. Ahmed— he'd have a shitfit if I talked to him about what we do at Freddie's, the women, the drinking. And the porn. He'll bring the Prophet down on me for that. I'm going to go to our own kind of hell for drinking and porn and all of it, man. You know that?"

"You'll have tons of company."

"You know the problem with p-porn?"

"No, what?"

"It makes you crazy. You always want more." He wasn't sure Danny even heard him, staring off into some proprietary distance. "Hey, you listening to me?"

"Course I am."

"Who the hell can I talk to about that stuff? You're it, man. The only one who's not in a compartment. And Bonnie—forget Dorothy, she's never sober enough to figure anything out—but B-Bonnie? Can you imagine dragging her to the mosque, bouncing out of her blouse?"

"Now, why would you want to take Bonnie to a mosque?"

"She needs to go, I'm telling you. She's way too mouthy for her own good."

Omar was talking so loudly that a family two tables away stopped what they were doing and looked at him until ice cream from their cones ran all over the children's hands. "And you know what I dreamed about last night? Putting Dorothy in a hijab and a niqab—the whole package from head to foot—with only her eyes showing and then pulling it up and boning her from behind. Fucking her until she practically converted or something. Except she'd probably puke before she came."

The family quickly gathered up to leave, wiping ice cream away, the mother tugging her oldest daughter toward the car.

"It's like being in solitary even when you're surrounded by people. I used to talk to Ahmed all the time. When we were little. Before we came over here. And before he started memorizing all the suras in the Quran. All hundred and fourteen of the damn things—do you know what kind of guy does that? A guy who never even thinks about boning Dorothy. Or anyone else."

"Maybe that's all they think about."

"Now what the hell do I have to talk to him about? Or Freddie? Or Kenny? Or anyone? Do you know what it's like being in a bottle? Living in compartments?"

"What about your sister?" Tempting fate. Danny wanted to take the words back as he spoke.

"My sister?" Omar looked appalled. "What about her?"

Let it go. Don't push it. "Can't you talk to her?"

"Would you talk to her?"

Run. Escape. Send up decoy flares. "Is that what the Crazy Horse thing was all about tonight?"

"My old man's c-coming back. I told you, right? He's right out of some other cen-century." Omar was pacing around, staring into the ground. "The tension, it makes it g-go away."

"That's it? *That* was why it had to be tonight? All that panic to have the battle tonight?"

"Battles can be good, you know."

"For what?"

"It's like wildfires in the forests. They look like disasters. But really they're clearing away all the crap that chokes off everything."

"I didn't know we had crap that was choking off everything."

"Don't you feel the high?"

"I'm late."

"For what?"

For your sister. "My parents." Danny got up to leave.

"There's only you, man. You're the only one."

• • •

The old house on Algonquin Avenue, a block away from High Park, was scheduled for renovations once the trustees had resolved the land title problems for the estate of the elderly Ukrainian widow who had died three months ago. Danny's father had twice been scheduled to begin work on it, but each time legal problems delayed settlement of the estate. Danny's offer to "look in on it once in a while" was received with no afterthought by his father, whose home renovation business was already overwhelming him.

After leaving Omar, Danny circled back through the park, sprinting across Parkside Drive. And then after walking up and down the block to make sure that no one was watching, he hurried up to the door on the shadow-darkened porch and tapped quickly, three times, on one of the beveled glass panes, waited for a moment, and then tapped twice. The door opened and fetid air from within the house rushed out at him, like the breath of something that had died.

She was waiting for him. She had backed away and stood in the only illumination there, the silver cast from the street light outside. It was a pale light that concealed more than it revealed, and he could not tell if she had been crying. "Sorry," he whispered. "Omar. He wanted to talk." There was no reply at first, until she reached out and took his hand.

He knew exactly what was to come.

She would wait until he made the next move, putting one arm around her, perhaps brushing back the waves of dark hair from around her eyes, holding her, dancing to music that only they heard, trying to keep it light, swaying until they were pressed against one another. Lost utterly within whatever voids they filled for one another, and in the moment before he kissed her he would tell himself that this time it was different, it was as he had imagined it to be.

Not once had they ever undressed. The closest they had come was on a Saturday afternoon when Ariana had begun removing the outer layers of cotton that she had to wear. They were the folds of cloth carefully arranged to cover this new body of hers with its suddenly full breasts that still felt like they were not really a part of her. On the streets she had begun covering herself more completely. The mere thought of her father or of Ahmed watching men look at her was enough to make her wrap herself in layers of cloth.

In the entire three-story house on Algonquin Avenue, there were now only two pieces of furniture to show that lives had been led there. There was a battered old C.M. Schroder grand piano with a missing middle C key, standing in the oblique silver light, a bulwark against the tide of oblivion engulfing those departed lives. In the same room was a brocade-covered couch, a faded voluptuary to which he would lead her, where she would smilingly recline, pulling him onto her. For a single moment they would be embracing, wrapped around one another with an urgency, a simple desperation that would always veer into the complicated physicality of clothing being rearranged. And it would end as it was destined to end, in confusion and awkwardness with one barely audible word: *Please*. It was a clean, sharp ending as irrevocable as anything he knew of. *Please*. She always said it. And he always stopped.

"I'm sorry," she would say.

"It's okay," he would rasp breathlessly, lying but not wanting to hurt her.

"I'm not good for you. Someone else would be better."

"I don't want someone else."

There always were minor variations on what followed. On the previous Friday night, there had been explanatory fragments about her family and the tribal way things were done. And the codes. Endlessly there were the codes, the *Pashtunwali*, the way their lives *had* to be led. Always, the codes of *Pashtunwali* had to be obeyed. Or so she said. She had reached down, putting her hand over his as it rested on the curve of her hip. She had moved his hand across her stomach, releasing it to explore on its own. He had reached under her blouse, caressing the outline of her breasts, but when he reached around to unhook her bra he felt her entire body stiffen.

"Whatever happens . . ." she had said.

Now he waited. She did not finish the sentence. "What about whatever happens?"

The silence of the old house was so complete he thought the dead were listening. "Please." And then only silence that he did not intrude upon.

Nothing in his life had prepared him for the confusion of lying there in the darkness with a girl who was suddenly sobbing uncontrollably. He did the only thing he could think of. He put his arms around her and wondered what to say. He told himself he had to say something. So he said, "I love you."

And then a few minutes later in the silent stillness he said, "Would you play something for me?" He had no idea why he said it. Maybe to make her laugh at how awkward he felt. Or perhaps to change the topic. Or maybe just to make those *Pashtunwali* codes go away.

Codes. He forgot the word until later, much later, in the mountains.

She had looked at him laughing and maybe crying at the same time. And then he had stretched across the old brocade couch, listening to her play the battered piano and wondering if there really were marmalade skies the way the Beatles said there were.

She played with no middle C key and he never noticed. It was as if something in her took flight when she played. It came from some new confidence acquired in all the hours of practice, a kind of joy that flew from the music. And from her. She suddenly stopped playing and said, "You have to take me away. You know that, don't you? It's the only way." It was all so simple. So straightforward. What was there that was so difficult to understand? . . . *take me away!* It was that simple.

And yet, he missed it.

For all the years afterward he asked himself what was there that he couldn't see?

I know. I could see it, those invisible welts lying across some part of a soul. The scars he kept hidden behind that crinkly grin. Or tried to. But it became as if old wounds were suddenly ripped open up there in the Afghan mountains, when he would stride into the twilight loudly and blasphemously invoking whatever gods could hear him in the gathering gloom, asking that he be made to suffer, not her. Yelling to Jehovah Shiva Buddha God Allah Jesus and all those in between. Raging at them. And then talking to her, telling her he was sorry, as if she was out there listening to him, just beyond the next mountain, telling her that he would find her, he would, he swore he would.

That he loved her. And that he would take her away.
Finally.

But tonight? None of it was as it had been in their past. "Please," she said. "For many reasons. Some of them I can't ask you to understand. But I want . . . I want . . ."

"What?"

In the glint of the pale, hard light he saw her eyes in some strange alloy of shame and longing. She buried her face in the brocade. "I want to feel you inside me."

It did not happen. At the moment he leaned over her in the darkness, he felt a shudder, almost a convulsion, sweep through her as she began to cry. "I'm sorry," she whispered over and again, tears flowing onto his hands as they lay there in numb exhaustion, naked in so many ways. Then she was silent, still, and finally said one word: "Zadran."

"What's Zadran?"

"Not what—who. He is a chief. From Miram Shah. In the tribal area. He is very powerful. My father comes back here tomorrow. Zadran will be coming soon after. To see my father."

"Is that a problem?"

"Yes. I think so. A very big problem."

"Why?"

She didn't answer.

14

That year it all changed.

Sayyid Shah had returned from the mountains of Pakistan and Afghanistan and marveled over the difference in his sons. Ahmed had almost grown a full beard. And Omar was as tall as he was. And strong, which pleased Sayyid Shah more than anything else about his son.

Almost immediately, Omar changed. He began avoiding everyone he once talked to, showing up at his locker in the morning, going through classes in silence, and then leaving after school before Danny could find him. In the middle of the week, he simply stopped going to school. Ahmed was seen hurrying along Queen Street, a hunted quality to him, his errant eye flailing like a searchlight separated from the darkness. But it was Ariana who seemed most affected. For several days she did not come to school. When she did, she brushed past Danny, vanishing into the crowded hallway without a word.

In the afternoon, he saw her seated on a chair in the hall not far from the entrance to the auditorium. She was staring straight ahead.

"What's wrong?"

"I can't talk about it." He could barely hear her. "Please."

Danny walked down to another part of the hall, put his back against a locker, and slid down to the floor, never taking his eyes off her. *Keep it light—somehow.*

"What are you doing?" It was the first hint of urgency in her voice.

Make her smile. "You obviously don't want me around, so I'll just hang out down here." He grinned and felt awkward for doing it. *Try!* "And if you won't even look at me I guess I'll have to sit here till you—"

A door to the auditorium opened and the halls echoed with student musicians rehearsing some Tchaikovsky piano concerto minus the piano. A man Danny recognized as one of the music teachers stepped out into the marbled stillness as Tchaikovsky was pushed back inside by the force of the heavy door closing.

"Ariana? Are you sure about this?" he asked. Said gently, almost kindly, Danny thought, watching from the length of a hallway. To Danny, the teacher was definitely older, which was anyone about forty or more, with thinning gray-blond hair and little wire glasses on a round, ruddy face.

"Yes. I'm sure." Her whisper echoed faintly and died, scattered in pieces across the marbled floor.

"I don't understand." The teacher spoke as quietly as she did. "You have a gift. And you want to stop playing?"

Ariana stared into the floor and slowly nodded.

"I've taught here for sixteen years. I've waited for your kind of talent to show up. For selfish reasons perhaps. It's the kind of talent that makes someone like me know he made the right decision when he chose to teach music."

"I'm sorry."

"It's not your fault." The teacher let out a breath that was a statement all its own. "We all have strange elements in our lives that make the rational somewhat irrational." Danny liked the teacher immediately. He cared. A lot. You could tell. Danny sat on the floor motionless, wondering if the teacher would look down the hall and see him watching it all.

But the teacher was staring off into a place only he could see. "When I heard you play that Gershwin concerto I almost wept. Most people mangle the opening."

"Thank you." She shook her head slowly.

"I'm very confused. So I have to ask you something," he said. "Why? Why are you giving all this up?"

"I have no choice."

"We all have a choice."

"Not all of us."

"I don't understand."

She looked up at him for the first time. "Where I am from it is different."

"How?"

"Music is evil."

"Evil?" A flicker of a confused smile flashed across his face. "You're joking. You don't believe that."

"What I believe is not important."

"Then what is important?"

"The only thing that is important is what I *have* to believe."

"Now I understand even less."

"I'm sorry."

The music teacher seemed lost in thought. "I am not religious. Not at all. Friends of mine would laugh at me for what I am about to say: I pray for you." He opened the door again. Tchaikovsky rushed out.

"Thank you. For everything."

The music teacher started to say something, stopped, and then returned to the auditorium, the music blasting out until the heavy door closed behind him. Danny sat on the cold marble floor waiting, somehow sensing that doing nothing was better than doing anything. She got up and quietly walked out of the school.

He did not follow.

For hours afterward he tore through all the possible places Omar could be: the hills in the park, the Starbucks on Bloor Street, Freddie's, even the train tracks they often walked along. Finally, he found Omar in the dankness of a video arcade on Queen Street near Dufferin. The clanging, shrieking, and roaring video screens blazed against black walls, like a tunnel with fluorescent lights hanging unevenly from chains, accessorized with cigarette butts and ripped AC/DC and Metallica posters pinned onto all that blackness. Omar was strangling the steering wheel in front of a big screen, his digital race car careening into other vehicles.

"What's going on?"

"I'm three laps from the finish line." Omar's eyes stayed fixed on the screen. "*That's* what's going on."

"Hey, c'mon. I'm just asking a question."

"I'm busy."

"What's happened? With all you guys?"

"*All* us guys? You talking about Ariana?" said Omar.

Stay away. "That wasn't my question."

"Sure it was. Hey, bro. Ain't nothin' you can do." Omar cheered as his race car crashed into a wall in a hail of sound effects and kept going.

Don't. "Why is she quitting the school orchestra?"

"Hah! That's what it's all about, ain't it?" The video game wheezed to a sudden halt. "Shit." For the first time, he looked over at Danny. "She's grounded, man. No more music."

"What's wrong with her music?"

"*Haram*," said Omar, waiting for Danny to show some degree of comprehension. "N-n-not allowed," he said finally.

• • •

Twice he waited for Ariana on Bloor Street. He stayed until it was obvious she would not show up that day. Somehow she found other ways to go home, or perhaps she left early. Finally at the end of the week, Danny talked Freddie Trumbull into cutting classes. Freddie's new car, the Toyota he got from his father when his parents separated in late August, served as the surveillance vehicle parked on Jameson Avenue.

"We gotta watch out," said Freddie, opening his second SlimFast. "They got laws against stalking you know."

"I'm not stalking her, okay?"

"What are we doing, then?"

"Surveillance."

"Cops do surveillance."

"I'm worried, okay?"

"About what?"

"I don't know."

"Did I tell you that Sue Chapman wanted to know if I could drive over to Oakville and pick up this special new crutch she's been fitted with?"

"Did she ask you to do her laundry too?"

"Fuck off Danny. I'm getting close, I can sense it. Pass me another SlimFast." Danny drummed his fingers lightly on the dashboard and handed him a can. "How'd you get that weird crooked finger?"

Danny didn't hear him. "Take a look." On the opposite side of the street, about half a block away, an old white Buick with rust marks all over the fenders had stopped. Four men got out, leaving the driver to find a place to park. One of the four men was Ariana's father, Sayyid Shah. With him was another man with a big turban that had to be tucked back into shape after he got out of the car. The man had angry eyes and a moustache so big and black that it made Danny think of a broom. The other two men were a kind of security detail, bodyguards dressed in tight-fitting, round, white caps and Afghan kameez—knee-length shirts with a slit up the side—over billowing pants. They were waving cars to a stop so the man in the turban and Sayyid Shah could cross the street. And then the two men hurried ahead to open the door to the apartment building.

"Look at that willya," said Freddie indignantly. "Guys dressed like it was fucking Halloween or something. They act like they own the joint. I mean for christsakes, would we just blow into their fucking countries and stop traffic? What a bunch of dickheads."

"That's Ariana's old man. And some guy named Zadran. A big warlord. From over there."

"The guy's a Paki too, huh? Jeez. So, what now?"

"I go up there."

"And do what?"

"Get them to feel they have to invite me in for dinner."

"Oh, right."

"Her father won't have a choice. It's part of their code. This *Pashtunwali* stuff. It's a kind of code for how they have to live. If you're in their home, you're their guest and they have to treat you like some long-lost friend. No matter how you got there. You're smiled at. Given food. Hospitality. The works."

"And then what?"

"Once you leave their place, all that changes. They can fillet you like a fish if they want to."

"You are out of your mind. Why would you want to go there?"

"Because I got a bad feeling. I need to see some things for myself."

"What? Like you want to watch your own nuts roasted over an open fire? After they've cut them off with their daggers? These people aren't like us, man."

"Yeah."

"Danny, listen, man, you gotta stick to your own tribe."

"She is my tribe," said Danny, getting out of the car. "My whole tribe."

"You know what my old man would do if you banged on the door when he was throwing a dinner party for the honchos he works with? He'd file a class action lawsuit or something."

• • •

The elevator rattled to a stop on the eighth floor, its doors opening into a cacophony of hardened apartment odors. The stained vinyl wallpaper changed hue in the twitching overhead light. He walked toward the loud voices coming from behind the most pungent of the doorways, the one with some kinds of spices he hadn't smelled before. He hesitated, knocked, and then listened as the voices fell silent and then rustled in urgent whispers. The door opened as far as the safety chain would stretch and a bodyguard's eye fixed upon him from slightly lower than his own eye level. A word was spat out, one he did not recognize.

"Hi," Danny said, plastering a smile across his face. There were more words spat out from behind the door. "Oh, I'm a friend of the family." More confusion. He heard Omar's loud whisper: "You idiot!" And then in broken English: "It is this Danny." The door was unchained and opened. The bodyguard glared at Danny, who looked past the man, into the room where Sayyid Shah and Zadran sat together on the heavy rugs on the floor. Omar and Ahmed sat beside their father, and one of the two bodyguards sat beside Zadran.

Sayyid Shah never took his eyes off Danny. "He saved Omar. Omar would die. Back. Years now."

"Ah," murmured Zadran, "*Assalamu alaikum.*"

Ahmed said something sharply to Zadran and his father in Pashtun, and then an angry fragment of English: "He is not with us."

His father waved him off with a motion of his hand. "He is here now." He turned to Danny. "Welcome." With his face arranging itself as a mask of stone. "Omar, prepare this person to be our guest."

Omar got up, motioning sharply to Danny, and led the way down the small hallway toward the bathroom. Danny could not hear what he was muttering. All the doors in the darkened hallway were closed until one of them shot light through a crack. Ariana flailed him with panicked eyes that Omar did not see.

"In here," Omar called from the bathroom. "You have to wash."

"Coming." Danny made a calming motion with his hands. Her eyes lashed. The door closed.

In the cluttered bathroom, a cave of wall-hung toothbrushes, shampoo bottles, soap-on-a-string, various articles of indescribable clothing, and towels piled behind the door, Omar was waiting. "F-fuck you!"

"What are you, the official greeter?"

"You re-really fucked it up this time, man."

"C'mon, man. I just came by to see if you wanted to—"

"There's some heavy shit going down, man. You d-don't belong here." Omar grabbed Danny's arm, his words pouring out in an urgent jumble. "Okay, here's the drill. You wash your hands. Sit with your legs crossed when we start eating. Only use your right hand. Take the food with three fingers. Don't stick your hand into the food up to your fu-fucking elbows. Understand?"

Danny waited until Omar stopped breathing like he'd just run a race. "What's up, bro?"

"I'm fucked, *bro*. That's what's up. Me and my sis-sister."

"Jesus, Omar, what's happening?"

"This is bad, man. Bad! Z-Zadran's an eight-hundred-pound gorilla. He could wipe any of us out. Even my old man wants to please him. And that's the problem. So I don't n-need you sticking your fucking nose in here t-tonight." He threw a towel at Danny and started to walk out.

Danny grabbed his arm. "What about Ariana?"

Omar looked at him for a moment. "Well how about that." He shook free and walked out.

Minutes later they all sat together on the heavy rugs, reaching for food from the various platters that had been silently set in front of them by Ariana and her mother. And sometimes by her hunched old grandmother, who came and left like a ghost who flicked glances toward Danny. He ate only enough to act polite, and he tried not to be obvious, watching Zadran, who had fixed Ariana with an appraiser's stare. From the instant she entered the room, Zadran's eyes flashed to her and never left until she departed. Once he caught Danny watching him; for an instant, Danny knew they understood each other perfectly. He knew it even more when Zadran said something in Pashtun and ordered Omar to translate: "He says that our sister is well trained." Zadran looked right through Danny as Omar said what he had to.

"Tell him your sister is a very versatile and independent young woman."

"Ain't going to translate that, man."

"Translate!" said his father.

Volleys of Pashtun followed, with Zadran motioning toward Danny. Ahmed turned to Danny, his wild eye coming unhinged so that it flickered back and forth. "He says that the Quran provides for cases of independence, also called disobedience. By either denying the woman your bed or . . ."

"Or what?"

". . . by beating them." Ahmed allowed himself a small slit of a smile as his good eye held perfectly still.

"What is that supposed to mean?"

"Drop it," whispered Omar. Ahmed leaned over and talked in Pashtun, and then after several exchanges he turned to Danny. "You will want to know that we all agree our sister is not obedient."

"And how is that?"

"She was secretly disobeying Allah."

Danny sat for a moment in silence. Utterly unsure of which way to answer. And of where the traps were. "Really?"

"Yes. With music. The Hadith from the *Bukhari Shareef* condemns those from the Umma for *ma'aazif*—music," said Ahmed. "It says it is the same as fornication and the drinking of wine."

"I don't have a clue what you've just said."

"My sister was practicing evil things and now she is not. My father and I have stopped it." Ahmed and Zadran began talking among themselves in a language Danny could not understand.

"Every one of us hates the fucking piano," Omar whispered. "*Hates* it. So drop it."

Danny waited for the other language to cease. "Your sister has a talent, a gift that you can't begin to understand," Danny said to Ahmed. He wondered if it was crying he heard from the kitchen. Or if maybe it was the old-fashioned steam kettle shrieking on the stove as it came to a boil.

. . . and now when he wakes up in the mountains, flung from his sleeping bag in the middle of the night, stumbling into the tripwire that detonates our personally embossed form of hell, he thinks of that moment. And if it was really her or if it was the kettle shrieking as they made tea for the men.

He wonders. Still.

• • •

Omar left the next day.

It was almost a kidnapping. And when he started crying out on the street, he had to be forced into the rusting Buick on Jameson Avenue by his father and one of Zadran's bodyguards. He was to be taken back to Miram Shah with Zadran and sent to a religious school, a madrasa, that his father had chosen where his progress would be carefully watched by Zadran. As a favor to Omar's father. And a sign that the two families were now joining together.

• • •

"I think maybe it was planned a long time ago." Ariana was standing in the silvery light flooding into the emptiness of the old house on Algonquin Avenue. "When my father decided Omar was being pulled away from the Umma. By the kind of life he was getting into. That he would not be able to cope with what is ahead."

"What *is* ahead?"

She didn't answer. It was now a week since Omar and Zadran left and two days after her father took off, going first to Hamburg and then some place in Afghanistan. She had sought out Danny, forcing a note into his hand as they passed in the hall at school. *7 P.M.?* was all it said.

It was different this time, right from the moment he tried the door of the old, empty house and found it unlocked. She was waiting for him when he arrived, breathless. There was none of the past awkwardness when they touched, the throttled forays into some steaming tangle of lust and regret. She simply stepped forward and kissed him.

"Why—?"

She put a finger to his lips. She reached around behind her and unraveled the scarf that hung around her head. It fell to the floor. Then she removed the clips that held the shawl encasing the upper half of her body. It too sifted onto the floor. She stood in a white blouse and a cotton skirt of many colors. She began unbuttoning the blouse. When she got to the lowest button, Danny reached out and took her hand. "What changed?"

"I may have only one chance."

"For what?"

She said nothing, removing her blouse, not even looking away as she had in the past whenever he touched her. Running his hand gently across her bare shoulders and then down her back, waiting for her to stop him when he reached the clasp, he spun into torrents of confusion. Falling with her onto the old brocade couch, tearing at clothing and whispering fragments of feelings, he pressed his lips against hers, overwhelmed by his own clumsiness and desire, both carrying him mercifully forward past all the awkwardness engulfing him.

But later, in the months and the years that passed, up in the mountains, Danny swore it was the music he remembered the most, the music he somehow heard even before it was filling the room. No one was playing that battered old C.M. Schroder grand piano with a missing middle C key, standing in the oblique, silver light like a bulwark against the tide of oblivion engulfing—no one!—there was no one playing it! But he swore the music was there. As he rose above her and she spread herself out below him. It was there!

• • •

He fumbled and apologized to her but then felt her hands around his face focusing him on her faint smile, pulling him down toward her—and then into her. The music was *there*—he knew it was—when she cried for an instant as he went deeper into her, hearing her cry out again from somewhere that seemed so far away, with tears streaming down her face and pulling him into her, whispering words he could not translate, as he found some rhythm given him by raw instinct, thrusting into her in the undulating motion that suddenly bound them together.

And it was there, this music, when it was over.

He lay beside her on the couch and passed his hand across her blood, which was soaking into the brocade. "This was your first time?" he asked. Her eyes remained closed, her arms around him. For some small eternity they lay there in silence with only the sound of their breathing.

But then the music was there before him as she rose and walked through that silvery light to sit naked at the piano playing "Für Elise."

He lay watching her in the faint filigrees of light and shadow as the onrush of moments passed into memory. It was an image of their nakedness together that he would recall. For as long as he lived the image would be relived somewhere in the farthest reaches of himself as she would return to life, his life, again and again playing the piano, her eyes closed and the light shimmering off the contours of her uncovered body.

She finished playing "Für Elise." There was silence until, with one hand, she played a low, slow chord and looked out into the light from the street. "I am afraid."

"Of what?"

"That there will be no more music.

"My father's brother killed the brother of Zadran twenty-one years ago. It was part of a feud that no one really knows how it started. It was in the blood by the time I was born. Our family originally was from Bannu and theirs was from Miram Shah. They slit each other's throats for years. Bodies were found by the side of roads, some without heads. It has gone on for all my lifetime. And long before."

She played the same chord again and again.

Waiting for Danny to say something.

"I can understand the words. But not what they mean. No one on my block came close to slitting anyone else's throat. The most intense part of my life has been fighting with Freddie or making the football team or getting a date on Saturday night."

"Danny."

"What?"

She was crying. "It has to be over with us now."

"Ariana—"

"It ended the other night. When you should not have been there. It ended before your eyes."

"What are you talking about?"

"*Vani,*" she said shaking her head.

"What's that?"

She rose from the piano bench and walked back to the couch. She took his hand in hers and passed it across the warm moist place on the brocade.

THE MOUNTAINS

15

That evening Liberace was unfolded and set up prancing into the night. That big poster of him waved at a herd of goats on the hills below us. The herd was almost entirely black except for a few white ones wandering among the others like threads being pulled. The entire herd was in a jostling quest for the leaves on the few remaining trees that had not already been nibbled bare. A few camels showed up on another hill, peering at the goats with a ruminant's disdain for all the hyperactivity below.

Danny was using his rucksack as a pillow, doing the usual, staring up at the stars that were beginning to poke holes in the sky. He had set up the speakers about eighty yards away, facing the mountain. Just far enough away so that if anyone attacked, we'd be off to the side.

"I'll Be Seeing You" was wafting out into the void. With the bleating of the goats providing the vocals.

"There's three goat herders down there. They're staring up toward our position. You think maybe they're music critics?"

"The purists always hated Liberace," he said.

"Yeah, but the Taliban are purists."

"Yeah. That's the point."

Later, after the CD player had gone through all the music, I was deep into my watch-for-shooting-stars game that was better in Afghanistan than anywhere else because when those stars took off in that perfect blackness, they really ripped through the night. It looked like slashing a canvas with a blowtorch. Way better than my earlier, sinsemilla-fueled days on the beach in Santa Monica. Danny was completely still and silent. I thought he was sleeping until: "It was her father." Silence.

"And?"

"Her father came back. It was all over then. But I didn't know it. I didn't want to know it." More silence. "I still don't."

• • •

No one ever talks about *Pashtunwali* up here in the mountains. They don't have to. You feel it. Crawling all around you like a thousand-year fog. No one escapes it. The old-time Special Forces guys, the ones who go native in grand style, put it in ways you can really understand: *Who the fuck has ever heard of a code of honor that exalts treachery and throat slitting as the best way to achieve that honor? And all these dumb motherfuckers live by that code.* There's lots of little footnotes up here, all of them drenched in blood, and the feuds go on for so many generations no one can remember which of the addled ancestors started it all. But honor—or *nang*, as they call it here—is automatically the motive for most of the party-trick decapitations that go on in the night. Murder mysteries would definitely not sell well over here—there's simply no mystery in it at all.

And then there's *miratha*, which, as an added bonus in the whole *Pashtunwali* thing, means that if your *nang* is seriously bent out of shape, then go for it, march right into your enemy's village and annihilate every living male. A no-penis-left-alive policy. And just to put it all in perspective, this is the twenty-first century, not the twelfth.

(Well maybe for Muslims it's only the sixteenth because that's how long it is since Muhammad first got his own revelations. But that's another story; don't even go there. You end up in no end of soggy comparisons to the Reformation and all that, not to mention accusations and footnotes from righteously tenured professors you've never heard of.)

The real root of this *Pashtunwali* thing is *zan, zar,* and *zamin,* which, not so loosely translated, means women, gold, and land. In that order. If you mess with a Pashtun's *zan* or his *zar* or his *zamin* then you're into throat-slitting territory. His *nang* will get seriously bent out of shape. Which is pretty much why we're here—me and Danny, at least—freezing our asses off in these Afghan mountains. Because Ariana is Pashtun and *Pashtunwali* is what this is all about. And Danny is going toe-to-toe with it all: *nang, zan, zar,* and *zamin*—something that legions of dead Victorian Brits and dead Soviets whose bones litter the countryside here would no doubt advise against.

Danny is seriously messing with the *zan* end of things— women—endlessly telling himself that he'll find Ariana and they'll live in a cabin in the woods or whatever and raise a herd of kids. And you have to ask yourself: is he just totally oblivious or is this really some grand obsession, some love affair that makes the rest of us look like mud wrestlers at the ballet?

• • •

Two days later our radio came alive. *Reaper One? . . . Come in, Reaper One.* Which was us. (Whoever gave us that designation did not include irony as a factor—Reaper as in Grim with a One tacked on.) The radio was our master with us, its servants, bowing to the voice from the Gods of Tampa, the CENTCOM brass sitting back there on an air base in Florida watching the whole thing play out on video screens with images from their cameras in the drone way above our heads. They, and the Lesser Gods of Bagram outside Kabul, collectively hurled thunderbolts commanding Danny and me, mere grunt-type mortals, to slog up to a mountain LZ on a tiny windswept plateau barely big enough for a sparrow to land on, and then get choppered into another mountain area somewhere between Khost and Gardez.

We flew over sheer mountain walls, as straight as the side of a New York skyscraper, only taller. The mountains flashing past the open back of the helicopter with the machine gunner balancing on the ramp made your mind play games right up until it roared out into clear skies and landed somewhere east of the phony border between Pakistan and Afghanistan. Our orders were to support a Special Forces team that had a little problem. No one spelled out exactly what this little problem was. Right off the top, something didn't compute.

Why were the Gods of Tampa sending us, a puny, two-man sniper team, all this way? "We're way off the reservation," said Danny, moving faster down into the treeline once we left the chopper, stopping only to punch eight-digit grid coordinates into the store-bought GPS.

"Zadran's territory," he said, and then kept going, strangely excited. For a moment I thought that maybe Zadran was the reason we were here, the image of him with his Frito Bandito moustache and black turban appearing out of the mist a couple of months ago at the roadblock outside of Gardez. Everywhere you looked, his men were appearing out of that same mist, all around us.

"Zadran!" Danny yelled into the mountain air, as if someone would be out there listening.

It was when the shadows were shortest that we first saw the horses, the ones that Special Forces Team 590 was riding in on. There was something about seeing them that fried the wiring between eye and brain. These guys, about a dozen of them, farm boys and surfers, riding these small, fierce Afghan horses, were a collision of centuries, like seeing Henry the Eighth stepping out of a Ferrari, these guys with satellite radios riding in on saddles that looked like they were designed by Genghis Khan. You told yourself it was real, you were seeing it, but some rebellious neurocircuitry behind your eyes just didn't want to close the deal.

Danny unfolded Liberace again and set him up on the side of the mountain while the Special Forces Team 590 watched as if someone was burning the flag. Liberace's prancing in fringe and those tight little white shorts was just not what they were all about. They didn't say anything. They didn't have to. Those guys could use silence better than a fist. For a bunch of Kansas farm boys or Laguna surfers or wherever they were from, these guys were world-class fighters who had gone seriously native, making a fashion statement all their own. They were dressed in varying combinations of American military and Pashtun warrior, complete with checkered neck shawls and the occasional Afghan kameez. All of them had mastered the art of the dead-eyed stare, which was what we were getting.

Actually, it was Liberace getting those stares as he waved and pranced into the wind. Liberace gave these Team 590 Green Beret guys a slow-motion fit. But it was nothing compared to the reaction of the Afghan soldiers they were with—about a hundred of them. The Afghans had their own circuitry blowout, bunched up behind a hill on the other side of a little gully, a milling collage of turbans, *pakols*, and AK-47s, all of which seemed to be pointing at Liberace. Or was I only imagining it?

One of the Special Forces guys rode up to meet us, like he was stepping out of a spaghetti Western, only wearing a baseball cap. He had what Annie Boo would call a high-cool-factor, complete with the Oakley wraparounds, a headset connecting him to the Lesser Gods of Bagram, an M4 dangling at his side at the end of a bronzed and muscular arm, a ton of pouches and bullet belts looking like a carapace that a turtle would be proud of, and all of it deliciously accessorized by that over-the-shoulder Afghan throat slitter's checkered-pattern shawl that Liberace would simply die for.

"Call me Tom," was the first thing he said. Which probably meant his name was anything but Tom. Most of these Special Forces guys, once they got up in the mountains, had names like Wolfman or Dice or Spinner. Tom, or whoever he was, had not stopped staring. "What the fuck is that?"

"Liberace," said Danny. Acting just as cool as Tom, who dismounted.

"Get rid of it."

"Uh-uh." Danny looked surprised that Tom wasn't kidding. And when Tom made a move, Danny did too, standing in front of Liberace. "He stays."

"Not even close, pal," said Tom in a real quiet voice, his eyes narrowing. On the plateau behind us, the other Special Forces guys had dismounted, looking pretty much as slit-eyed as Tom. Several of them had lit up those little truck-stop cigars, Swishers, which definitely added to the spaghetti-Western feel of it all.

"You fight the war your way, I'll fight it my way."

"Jesus Christ," said Tom, looking around and making a whistling sound through his teeth. "Hey, pal, we'll talk about court-martials later but—"

"I'm not in your army," said Danny, pointing to the maple leaf flag insignia on his shoulder.

"—in case you hadn't figured it out, we're both fighting the same war."

"Not quite."

Right then, at the very moment they were teetering on one of those *Oh yeah? Says who?* numbers, one of the Afghans defused it with a different threat. He was climbing toward us, jabbering and pointing at Liberace. Tom called out something to him in Pashtun, which was obviously a kind of "Cool it," because the guy muttered something and then settled into his own version of the thousand-yard stare. Which he did really well.

"Atif there is freaked out."

"I can see that," said Danny.

"Is this really necessary?" Tom was looking at Liberace.

"I'll explain later."

"Yeah?" said Tom. "Well, Atif is their head guy and he wants to know why a woman is dressed like that and why a big picture of her is here in the mountains."

"Tell Atif that Liberace is a man."

"I already did. He said no man dresses like that."

"Damn," said Danny. "What we got going on here is a cultural divide."

"Like hell we do," said Tom, taking off the big Afghan shawl on his shoulders and draping it around the lower half of the cardboard cut-out. Liberace looked like he was wearing a skirt, and Atif seemed to think that was just fine. He and the other Afghans stopped jabbering among themselves and went back to pointing their rifles somewhere else.

Which was when that noise sounded, that terrifying *snap!* you hear differently in the thin air of mountains than anywhere else—the sound of a bullet breaking the sound barrier.

The bullet that ripped through Liberace.

We all hit the ground and when we looked up, Liberace had been spun completely around but amazingly, he was still standing, a small-caliber bullet wound right through his reinforced cardboard heart. But still he was prancing into the wind.

"Damn!" said Danny, looking over at me. *Omar* was the other word hanging out there just waiting to be said. But it wasn't. And I was too busy finding cover to pay much attention to him anyway.

Tom lifted his face from the dirt and looked up at Liberace, still beaming and prancing with that ragged hole in his chest. "Helluva fighter," Tom said.

• • •

The simple question was why the Gods of Tampa went to all the trouble of ferrying us—me and Danny of all people—up to that particular mountain. The simple answer was pretty much what it is for most things that get overcomplicated:

In other words, the lawyers got involved.

It started off pretty simple three days earlier when the drones had relayed images of Tampa's least favorite warlord, Zadran. With a column of his men, he was moving from a compound near Gardez up into the mountain we were now on. A mountain that was pretty much infested with Taliban. Zadran and his men had obviously arranged a friendly meeting with these Taliban. Which, on the surface, was strange because after all the bales of cash the CIA had dumped on Zadran, he and his tribe were officially supposed to be our allies.

Which logically meant Zadran should be waging war on the Taliban instead of drinking tea with them. But the problem was that Zadran had the loyalties of a bond trader on a bad day. He spewed love onto whoever happened to be the highest bidder. And right now no one was sure whose side he was on.

He remained the same smiling bundle of treachery and violence he had ever been, jovially untroubled by loyalty as it was understood by the Gods of Tampa. Not to mention his troubling tendency to rain mortar fire down on our guys from Sarabagh to Orgun whenever those bales of CIA cash didn't show up on time.

The surveillance images on those wide screens back at Bagram and Tampa were now showing some kind of overly long meeting going on between Zadran and the Taliban. And whatever they were meeting about, the Gods of Tampa were displeased and wanted to send a message. Somebody's first suggestion for a means of communication had been to drop a two-thousand-pound JDAM—which would pretty much have ended the meeting. Vaporized it, actually.

Which was when the military lawyers got involved at the Judge Advocate General's office, seven thousand miles west of here. Those military lawyers back in the States only had to dangle the thought— War Crime—and the entire JDAM bombing plan crumbled while all that due diligence stuff ensued. Conventions of international law were weighed and mulled while forlorn grunts like us froze on mountaintops, waiting to find out if we could just get on with fighting the war.

We were guessing that the problem here was probably that it could turn into one of those General Accounting Office scandals in Washington. Because, after all, handing all those bales of CIA cash to Zadran and then incinerating him with a JDAM could lead to a lot of messy Senate subcommittee questions about all that taxpayers' money going up in smoke. Literally.

But right now all we really knew was that it was getting damn cold on this Afghan mountain and some guys in warm offices in Washington were probably looking up *Allies—vaporizing of:* while making dinner plans at some French restaurant.

If Zadran had not been an ally, this whole legal mess would not have happened. Which is where we came in.

Or at least where Danny came in.

One of the Lesser Gods had apparently decided that what our lawyers said didn't apply to someone from another army. Someone like Danny. So being a Canadian was one thing, but being a sniper was another. Especially a Canadian sniper with a McMillan Brothers .50-cal bolt-action long-range sniper rifle fitted with a Lilja barrel and modified with shortened bipods, Leupold optical . . . and all those other specs that don't register with people outside the circle but translate into one simple fact that everyone understands: it was way better than anything we had in the American army. Which was the other reason Danny and I were here: that overgrown gun of his could hit targets our own snipers couldn't even get close to.

It was the stiletto instead of the hammer. The Gods of Tampa wanted us to send a precise and specific message to Zadran. Instead of vaporizing the whole tribe, they were letting him know that he was lucky. This time. Only a few of his people were being annihilated. Next time . . .

"Three kills needed down there." Tom was pointing to figures way off in the distance. "Like having a field-goal kicker who can get the job done from sixty yards out." Tom had already forgotten about Liberace. "Except we're seventy yards out."

I was probably the only one there who noticed the little shock wave go through Danny. The same one that went through him when anyone casually mentioned that he was needed to end a life.

Like swatting a fly.

• • •

We glassed the mountainside in the direction Tom was pointing; a group of six men could be seen moving slowly up a steep trail. Three of them were prisoners and looked like they were having trouble walking, stumbling, their hands tied in front of them. One of them was being jabbed by a rifle butt to the back of the head. "Two 'terps'—Mo and Ali is what we call them," said Tom. "The guy behind them is a teacher. The previous teacher at the school near Sarabagh was beheaded by the Taliban last August, his head stuck on a pole driven into the ground in front of the entrance with the Arabic sign warning that teaching females violates Allah's will.

"Mo and Ali are names we gave the interpreters. They're our guys. They worked for us and somehow Zadran's people caught them at the bottom of the mountain. About two hours later our intercept guys started picking up radio traffic between the kidnappers and Zadran, who's up here somewhere on the plateau. Right after that, the captives were being marched up the mountain as Zadran's offering to the Taliban, a sign that he can deliver whatever he wants to deliver. Mo, Ali, and the teacher are lambs being led to slaughter. Right before our eyes."

Zadran's three prisoners were now about an hour's trek from the plateau. We found the ragged little column by scanning until we first located a man cradling an RPG-7 rocket launcher, and then farther east and slightly below him were two lighter Russian machine guns. Glassing straight down about fifty meters below the machine guns, we saw the ledge that led around the mountain to where the meeting was supposed to be happening. "Black Hats," Danny said, looking through the binoculars at the three men behind the machine gun.

"Chechens. Uzbeks. Pashtuns. All mixed in. As much al-Qaeda as Taliban."

"This is why we're here?" Danny sounded as if he would rather be doing something else.

"Unless you know of a good bar nearby," said Tom.

"We just ran a laser check," said Striker, another Special Forces guy with a Southern accent, a big full beard, and a doo-rag tied around his shaved head. "Twenty-four hundred meters."

"What's twenty-four hundred meters?"

"From here to those poor bastards, Mo, Ali, and the teacher being dragged up the mountain," said the Southern accent, sounding surprised and vaguely irritated that Danny would even have to ask.

"Can't do it," said Danny, sounding relieved. I knew where this was going. "Even Hathcock couldn't do twenty-four hundred meters." Hathcock was some old Marine in Vietnam who used to crawl through jungle gunk and take out Viet Cong at ungodly distances—or so the legend was, the one that every sniper practically had to memorize before they let him touch a weapon.

"You can do it."

"How do you know I can do it?"

"We checked. Let's go."

"Are you sure these really are bad guys?"

"Am I sure?" Tom was getting a bad case of slit-eye all over again. "What the fuck do you want me to do? Run down there and ask them why they're dragging those poor motherfuckers up the mountain?"

"Okay, okay." A long, fretful pause, looking around, shaking his head.

"We don't have a lot of time."

"You're sure?"

"Hey—pal, we can't call in air support and drop a bomb because we'd kill the terps and the teacher too. So take out those assholes willya?"

"Life isn't something to be taken just like that."

Tom, Striker, and all the other Special Forces guys exchanged looks. "Jesus Christ. A fucking Guinness Book of Records here—a sniper with an identity crisis," said Tom.

"Just shoot the motherfuckers," said Striker.

"Why are you even over here?" said another Special Forces guy.

"To find the woman I love." Danny said it like it was the most normal thing in the world. He was calm, almost serene.

There was a complete, pure moment of infinite silence. And stillness—stillness as absolute as can exist in this cosmos. As three Special Forces guys stood there like those pillars of salt in the Bible. And then:

"Fucking Canadians." Tom shook his head almost sadly.

"They'll do it to you every time. I had a brother-in-law once. From Winnipeg. I know," said Striker.

"You know what?" I asked.

"Whatever Americans want to do, Canadians want to do the opposite. Just to prove they're not us." Someone else agreed and started talking about a hockey player he once knew.

Danny wasn't paying attention. He was looking through the binoculars. "I just want to be sure, that's all."

"Sure? You want us to have Wild Eye come round from the plateau and tell us his plans for those poor bastards being dragged up the mountain? Barbecued or roasted on a spit?"

"*Wild Eye?* What's Wild Eye?" Danny swiveled, remnants of his serenity falling away like something that had shattered.

"Not what. Who. The skinny fanatic with the goofy eye. The one who's leading that sorry-ass bunch. One of the sons."

"Wild Eye?"

"That's what I said."

"Sons of who?"

"Some fucking al-Qaeda big shot. He's got two sons over here."

• • •

The range was quickly dialed in at 2,438 meters *alpha two-four-three-eight . . .* farther than anyone had ever attempted in any war *zeroed to two-zero-zero-zero* as the elevation fine-tune ring was adjusted and movement compensation factored in *muzzle velocity 2,590 feet per second* and wind calculations *four minutes hard right.* Through the scope *fine-tuning to match numbers,* the three captives were being lashed up the mountain, clubbed by rifle butts whenever they fell.

"Crosshairs center mass."

"Roger center mass," as the countdown went on like the last moments before a space launch.

That crooked finger feathered the trigger and all breathing stopped.

It was so numbingly different from mere everyday war with its usual maelstrom of death and destruction in all the screaming chaos and random madness as the beast devoured thought and made any act almost accidental.

Time ceased to have any delineation and instead flowed seamlessly, drowning out the unheard ticking. Through those scopes, in some way creation and destruction come together as Zen in whatever universe the mind finds itself at that moment. Alpha and Omega. Life, and now death, in that moment of knowingly turning away from reason and humanity.

In other words, it came down to God the Creator, the Destroyer, in one man's finger.

The lead captor went down first, sort of slumping over when the bullet hit, as if he'd suddenly gone to sleep. The second guy, the one with the rifle butt that had battered the teacher, was more horrendous, kind of a watermelon-hit-by-a-baseball-bat explosion, which, apart from the sheer spewing spectacle of his head exploding, defied the bloody physics of war. If a human head is about sixteen inches in diameter, even the best match grain ammunition can only hold to an accuracy of about nine inches per thousand meters. And this mountain trail was way over twice that far.

The third captor—the skinny fanatic with the goofy eye— instantly became a cat looking for a tree as dogs closed in. Covered in another man's blood, Ahmed went into a screeching fit of terror. In the silence of the scopes, you had to imagine the bellowing shriek that came out of him from twenty-four hundred meters away, spinning around, looking for this source of unimaginable terror from above. In a move of sheer instinctive survival, he grabbed the battered teacher and held him in front of himself like a rag doll shield, not sure from where this vengeance was coming.

"What now?" said Danny, taking his eye from the scope for a moment.

"Wait," said Tom. "He'll screw it up somehow. He always does."

Through our scopes, Ahmed's roiling panic was telescopically compressed as he clung to the teacher for the moment before the two terps began swinging their bound fists at him, raining down wildly uneven blows until the man fled, bellowing silence across all that distance.

"You got a clear shot," said Striker, looking through his binoculars.

Danny remained motionless, his crooked finger on the trigger.

"You got a clear shot," Striker said again, his voice rising in volume with each word. Still, Danny remained eye to the scope, motionless.

"Something wrong?" Tom said, not in a pleasant way.

Danny leaned back like he was thinking of something. "He's done. I don't need to take him out."

"Jesus Christ," said Tom.

Through the various binoculars and scopes we all saw the two terps and the teacher tumble down the mountain, running in a different direction from Ahmed, out of range of any possible aerial bombardment. At which point Tom nodded to his radio operator.

"*Break, break, break!*" screamed the radio operator into his mouthpiece.

• • •

It was as if the mountain blew up. A single B-52, an F-16, and two Apaches provided destruction in varying degrees of precision. The shock waves pounded you like a huge fist and then a plume of smoke billowed volcanically from the other side of the mountain as the Special Forces guys rode in to make sure that there were still men left to interrogate once Atif and the Afghans overran it.

Danny's call rang down around them as they mounted the horses. "Don't kill him!"

"Anything else?" someone called out.

By the time we packed up Liberace and got to the other side of the mountain, the plateau was charred for as far as we could see. It was like the world suddenly turned black with flecks of color moving through it: a ragged red neck scarf on a staggering, insensate Taliban whose eyes were rolling, a woven green-and-orange saddle being dragged by one of Atif's men, and a lone surviving green banner flying above a recent grave. The earth was steaming. Moving across the plateau toward a cave in the side of a small rise, I stopped twice, lost in the acrid fumes of explosives and blood, baked together in a fine mist that made it like some version of Hades with the damned stumbling all around. Occasionally you'd stumble over one of the Taliban, fallen, limp and intact, his innards obviously rearranged by the massive blasts, mouth open and moving, eyes staring at the ground like a fish would stare at a dock it was on. Danny was ahead of me, plunging through the fumes toward the shattered opening of the cave where the Special Forces troops were quieting their roiling horses.

Even through the fumes you could see the pale guy in the filthy white robes and black turban. "Ahmed," yelled Danny as he charged forward toward the man who looked completely terrified.

• • •

It was not the way failed martyrs were rumored to be—blazing defiance at infidels, invoking fate and Allah all as one. Instead, stripped of his robes and turban, shivering in the moist heat of the huge carved-out cave and sobbing uncontrollably, Ahmed lay tied to the planks of wood that hours earlier had been the door to the cave. The whole cave was lit by ChemLights—the kind ravers waved overhead at rock concerts back home. They were now nestled in water bottles that became makeshift lanterns, giving the blasted-out rock-face walls of the cave a weird yellow and blue glow as faces loomed out of the darkness. There were new men who had suddenly descended from the fabled black helicopters, in this case ordinary Apaches. They were CIA operators, men who had fought their way across eastern Afghanistan in the months after 9/11 and were impatient to get on with it. Dressed in a collage of improvised combat gear, they were barely welcoming and cared nothing for credentials, certainly not of the snipers who made this moment possible. "I know him. I need to talk to him," Danny had said, forcing his way into a circle of hard stares. Only the grudging intervention of the Special Forces guys like Tom kept us anywhere around the terrified, convulsing figure of Ahmed, tied to that door and being moved slowly up and down like he was on a seesaw.

One of the new men pulled up a packing crate and sat very close to Ahmed, whose wandering eye seemed to have come unhinged, flailing in its socket. "You have the choice. You can either answer our questions. Or we will make you answer them." The man was older than the others, perhaps close to fifty, wiry with arms that showed a lifetime of physical activity, and a taut, almost sad face slightly hollowed at the cheeks. He was smaller, and had an unruly thatch of tightly cut steel-gray hair that had thinned slightly at the center. "Do you understand?" Said quietly, almost politely.

Ahmed shook so hard his nod was barely distinguishable.

"Good. You obviously understand English."

Again the same shaking, as if Ahmed was freezing in that humid, steaming cave.

"What's your full name?" As the digital record light shone solid red.

"Ahmed Shah," was the burbled reply, through lips bubbling with flecks of blood and saliva.

"Where is your brother, Omar?"

Ahmed's lips were clenched and quivering. Sweat poured off him as he shook his head fiercely and gave a strangled little squeal.

"We'll try this once again, Ahmed." Said so soothingly you'd almost think it was a shrink talking to a patient. "Your brother, Omar, sent you to do this, didn't he?" More clenched mouth and closed eyes. "He is really the one, isn't he? He calls the shots. C'mon, Ahmed, we know. He's tougher than you are. Tougher than your father even. You're not really cut out for this. There's no shame in that." It was almost a practised pause that followed. Calculated for maximum effect of what followed: "Your father's dead. You know that, don't you?"

Ahmed went wide-eyed, straining against the ropes that held him. His good eye blazed and the other one darted from side to side. He shrieked something none of us understood and then spit in the face of the man talking to him. The whole cave went silent; all murmurs ceased and the man stared off into space, Ahmed's spit trickling from his forehead. Slowly, the man untied a small neck scarf he was wearing, wiped the spit from his forehead, and spoke to no one in particular. In the green-and-blue ChemLight illumination, all tension seemed to have drained away from the man. His voice was somehow distant, almost serene. "My cousin John was my hero. You know what it's like to have a hero when you're nine years old? And he's fifteen? You know why he was my hero?"

The man waited patiently for some response from Ahmed, who shook and shivered, looking straight ahead.

"Do you know why he was my hero?" the man repeated quietly. Still not looking at Ahmed.

Ahmed managed to force his head into a back-and-forth, spastic shaking motion.

"Because he showed me how to throw a spiral. Do you know what a spiral is?"

More spastic head shaking.

"It's the way you throw a football. Most nine-year-olds can't throw real spirals. But I could because of him. Trivial, huh? Making such a big deal out of it. But what was really the big deal was that he loved helping us. At the time he showed me how to do it he was the biggest football star in any Boston high school. And then at Michigan. He could have turned pro. He could have done almost anything."

The man stopped talking, staring off somewhere. The others in that cave, all of us, wondered in silence.

"But the truly amazing thing was that he stayed my hero way after we were both grown up. Do you know how rare that is? John became a doctor. Most of his time he spent working overseas. In war zones. Hellholes like this. Not many people help in this world. But John did."

For the first time, the man looked at Ahmed. With a cold, hard look, one drained of everything. Ahmed shook violently, strapped onto that door.

"And then one day not long ago, he got up before dawn at his home in Boston, caught a plane for Los Angeles, and was blown to bits about an hour later when it hit the building in New York. And when I think of what he was and then look at you and your brother or your father, wiping your spit off my face is a small price to pay for why I am here today. I asked to come here. You know that? I went to my bosses and begged, pleaded to be sent here just so I could do things like this. They told me I was too old for this stuff. But I told them, "No, I'd just be there to do what any nine-year-old would do." They didn't understand that. But you do, don't you?"

Ahmed looked up, writhing and sobbing, trying to form another bubble of spit in his mouth, nodding his head as he did.

The man uncoiled, pounding that rolled-up, spit-covered neckerchief straight into Ahmed's face, slamming him against that wooden door with two ferocious blows. Then he grabbed Ahmed's hair, yanking his face forward toward the laptop that was thrust in front of him. "Okay, asshole, spit at this." The screen on the battered laptop filled with an image. It was the blasted body of Sayyid Shah, Ahmed's father, frozen in a rigor-mortis contortion with an arm halfway across his chest as if shielding those dead, open eyes from the stares of those looking down on him. "Two days ago. On the other side of Khost."

Ahmed stared into the laptop and shrieked incoherently, straining at the ropes that pinned him to the door. The man kicked a support out from under the wooden plank and it swung down with a jolt, a seesaw with all the weight on one end. Ahmed's head was lower than his feet. "Where is your brother?"

The shrieking continued.

The man nodded and another of the new men poured water on Ahmed's face so it went into his mouth and nose, causing him to choke and flail his head around. "This is for John," said the man. "Even though he wouldn't want me to continue." Pieces of cotton were forced up into Ahmed's nose and more water poured into his mouth, which created an explosion of spray when he gagged.

"I have another way," said Danny, stepping forward. "Stop." At that moment the little maple leaf flag on Danny's shoulder might as well have been etched in flashing neon. They all looked around, irritated that an outsider was there in the cave.

"Get that guy out of here," someone said. Danny had planted himself not far from the sputtering, gagging Ahmed. For a moment, the chain of command within the cave seized solid. No one quite was sure who should make the next move.

The move was made outside the cave, by others. An Em-Biter radio crackled with urgency. And some kind of commotion sounded, coming from beyond the shaft of blinding sunlight where the door had once been. Voices rose and fell, with names called out. The CIA man rose from beside Ahmed and hurried into the shaft of light. Others followed. Only Danny, Tom, and I were left in the cave with Ahmed. With his head pinned to that door, he looked around with that one eye flickering until it settled on Danny. For a moment he froze, straining against the ropes, and then everything within him let go. All the tightness, the shrieking ceased and in their place came a look of mute confusion.

"Hey, I got a treat for you," Danny said, loosening the ropes around Ahmed's torso. "Not a fair fight, this one, huh? You being cinched up and all."

He unpacked a small knapsack as he talked, almost uninterested in Ahmed. He took out the little speakers and his Walkman, hooking them up, and then, when he hit Play, the cave reverberated with tinkly piano music. "'Stardust,'" said Danny helpfully. Ahmed closed his eyes like his face was being cinched backwards. "*Ma'aazif.* That's what you called it, didn't you? Music."

Tom looked confused. "What is this? A fucking dance club?"

"Liberace."

"Am I missing something?"

"Ahmed? Is he missing something?" said Danny. "Hey, let me turn the volume up a little more." The whole cave felt like a wind tunnel experiment on chimes. The tinkling was deafening. "You like Liberace, Ahmed?"

"In the name of God, the compassionate, the merciful," Ahmed yelled, his feet still tied to the planks of the door.

"It's the same music your sister played. More or less. Piano music," Danny said.

"I knew, I knew."

"Ariana. Where is she?"

"I knew."

"You knew what?"

"You. All of you."

"All of you what?"

"She is impure because of you. All of you."

"Naw," said Danny, leaning back, looking like he was dealing with someone who just doesn't get it. "Don't start with that impure crap again." Ahmed exploded in a burst of rage and spittle.

Danny held up his hand with the crooked finger. "Remember that night in High Park? When you were looking for her? Remember that night, huh? Sure you do. You remember. All that 'prostitute' stuff you were yelling? Well, you know what? Your sister is the purest person I have ever known. Was it tough to live with that? Knowing what you are? And what she is?"

A kind of rage-filled laugh came from Ahmed. "She is married now."

Silence from Danny. Then: "Kidnapped. Not married."

"Her husband is here." Rasped, defiantly. The tinkling had stopped.

"Where?"

It was the first time Ahmed seemed pleased about anything. "Here!" he rasped, motioning with his head toward the loud voices beyond the blinding light.

• • •

When Zadran was brought into the cave, the first thing you noticed about him was the dried blood from his left ear, leaving a trail down the side of his neck, partly framing that bulbous face. Blood was on the necks of several of his bodyguards, who had not held their mouths open when the bomb detonated a couple of thousand feet above their heads. The blast hit with a thousand or so pounds pressure per square inch and blew out eardrums all over the mountain. With his huge black moustache and knifing eyes shrouded by a hedge of black eyebrows that flashed a sign language all their own, Zadran held his hand to his ear, snarling fury at the Americans around him and yet groveling in his own way. It was an art form—attitude and fawning all at once. Uriah Heep, Fagin, Shylock, and all those others I couldn't keep straight back in high school. He switched back and forth between the two so quickly that he had us all, strangers in that cave, exchanging glances. He was surrounded by a small, jostling, yelling group of his men, all disarmed. They cleared a path for him even though the Americans had backed off so much there was nothing to clear. It looked good, though, and gave Zadran the stamp of importance it was presumably intended to. The huffing and puffing went on until Tom stepped in front of them, drilling Zadran with that spooky gimlet stare of his and casually holding an M4 about chest high.

"Enough," said Tom quietly.

The jostling and yelling continued at some decibel-overload level. Tom fired a burst into the ceiling of the cave that sent Zadran clutching his ear and those around him scattering in a shower of falling rock. Stillness.

"Much better."

Zadran was stooped over, his eyes sweeping the room like a scythe. His two-colored turban had been loosened by the earlier blast, and in its unraveling, dignity was becoming an issue.

"Okay, let's get a few questions answered," said the wiry man from the CIA, the one who had been interrogating Ahmed. "Why were you meeting with this guy?" he asked, pointing to Ahmed, still strapped to the seesaw door.

The thought jumped through my head: *What is wrong here?* They never interrogate two guys in the same room! They always split them up and get them to rat on each other. I mean, even the Taliban probably watch *Law and Order*.

The question was translated for Zadran, who erupted with indignation. "He has never seen this man before," said the translator in a pale imitation of Zadran and pointing grandly to Ahmed.

"Then what was he doing coming up the mountain with hostages?"

Another blast of indignation, with secondary flare-ups among his entourage. The whole cave reverberated with alpha-male huffing, like Elvis impersonators, only Zadran got to be Elvis here. Which is when I started wondering if the fix was in, if the CIA guys knew something we didn't and were just playing for theater here.

Danny leaned over to me and said something I couldn't hear. I didn't have to. All I made out was ". . . Ariana."

"What about her?"

"The women they think are—"

"He says to inform you we are on our way to Bannu," shouted Zadran's translator, his finger rising through the air like it was cutting a hole. "Crossing the mountain is the shortest way to Bannu."

Danny stepped forward, saying nothing. Zadran didn't see him at first and when he did, it was as if he was trying to remember something.

"You and Ahmed know each other," said Danny.

When the translator used Ahmed's name, the puzzled look intensified. Zadran shrugged and grew more irritable.

"You know who I am," said Danny.

"He says he has never seen you."

"Sayyid Shah's apartment. In Canada. With Omar. And Ahmed." Danny motioned to Ahmed strapped to the door. "And their sister. You were there. You know them all."

Still clutching his ear, Zadran looked from Danny to Ahmed and then to the cluster of Agency men and back again. Something in him faltered. Only a few people there noticed it. Ahmed saw it.

"Canada?" Zadran rasped out the word in an accent so thick it came out *Keh-NAH-de*.

Danny nodded.

Zadran suddenly smiled, as if *now* he had someone to go up against, one single opponent. An opponent he knew could do nothing to him. He broke out laughing. He stepped toward Danny and snapped his fingers in the air. One of his men instantly produced a big leather pouch from which Zadran removed a plastic cover, aware that a dozen weapons were trained on him. Which made him smile even more. His eyebrows arched so that his face seemed cinched around that enormous nose. "Yes! Yes!" he said, taking out a photograph of himself in front of a traffic-clogged street with dusty brick apartment buildings. "Me. Jam-sen!"

"Jameson Avenue," Danny said.

"Yes, Jam-sen. Me-you!" He held aloft another photo. Danny, Omar, and Zadran were side by side in a room.

"Let me see that," said the Agency man, scrutinizing the photo for a moment before turning to Danny. "We need to talk." The photo was whisked away by Zadran, playing the role of magician building up to a sleight-of-hand finale. He held up a photo of a barely recognizable scowling man with a multicolored turban and a moustache the size of a squirrel, sitting cross-legged on carpets and cushions. Beside him was a young woman in a green dress and a big pink headscarf. She had an expression frozen somewhere between terror and confusion.

"Me! And wife."

There was a silence that was somehow deafening. Or maybe I was just imagining the inside of Danny's mind.

"Ariana. My wife! Me!"

Danny started breathing in short, jagged bursts as if he was having trouble breathing. "Fuck you! She's not your wife. You kidnapped her."

Zadran didn't need to have it translated. He laughed until he almost shook. He was winning. "Me? No! Omar give me!" he said, pointing to Ariana. "Omar! He give!" Then he turned and said something to his men that yielded laughter and chattering.

The Agency man turned to the translator. "What does he say?"

"He says, 'This poor boy.'"

• • •

There was no way to hold Zadran there. The Gods of Tampa had suddenly awoken and decreed that, treacherous as he was, he was still *Our Ally*. And had to be allowed to leave. Someone in the pantheon had inhaled the fumes from Washington. A little double cross here and there shouldn't stand in the way of the Greater Good. A few embezzled millions shouldn't cloud the Big Picture. And throw in some rumored cache of Stinger shoulder-fired missiles that he was supposedly hiding, and the *Be Nice* factor trumps all. The decision had been relayed before he even entered the cave. From then on, it was all just theater and we were the spear-carriers, the Rosencrantz and whatshisname of the piece.

Zadran swept out of that cave, knowing he had just served up a full-course banquet of marinated shit and we were his official tasters. He knew—that malevolent old prick—what none of us yet knew. He had figured out that even the most corrupt link of the geopolitical chain needed to be protected by those tugging on it. Otherwise you're only left with a bunch of round metal links attached to nothing.

America loathed him/America loved him. It was all the same. There was nothing we could do about it. And he knew it.

The final cut-bait order from the pantheon came in on one of the Em-Biters, those little radios that Tom and some of Team 590 carried like they were there to balance the weight of the chewing tobacco pouches. So Zadran just sifted out of there, that fuck-you, yellowed-piano-key grin growing by octaves. Danny yelled at everyone standing still in that cave, telling them that Zadran could not be allowed to leave. And then found himself crosschecked by a rifle when he got too close to Zadran.

When we went outside into the blindingly blue light of three thousand meters elevation on a clear, sunlit late afternoon, we all blinked in the glare, stumbling into all that death and perfection. Zadran was already a hundred or so meters down the eastern side of the mountain, on his way to Bannu in the wildest part of Pakistan, when he sent his translator back with a message. It was for Danny. "Tell the boy," Zadran's message said, "that I beat her when I found she was a whore."

Danny stood there like he had grown into the granite. Absolutely still and blank. "And something else," said the translator.

I said it for Danny, who was suddenly mute: "What?"

"You will never find her. He has her in a hidden place."

On the side of the mountain, Zadran could be seen waving to us, and laughing.

The sun set like it fell out of the sky.

16

The artichoke. In other words, one of my mother's letters—you'd have to peel away the outer layers endlessly until you got to the core of what Annabelle was saying. You'd read the artichoke for about the tenth time but by then you were more uncertain about what the hell she was saying than when you started. It was just layers of maternal encryption. I mean what mother ever writes: *Just remember that dignity and sex always collide.* Or how about: *Let no one slip a laxative into the Moral Code I have instilled in you.* Sitting there on that frozen mountain, with dead guys dug into it in their new little graves, the ones with the long poles sticking straight up and the skinny, ragged Islamic banners flying from them like some used-car lot of the dead—it gets you thinking. Especially when their replacements are already out there, waiting to kill you, and your mother is talking about laxatives in the Moral Code. *Just remember—moral diarrhea is just as smelly as the real thing.*

But that was not the part of the letter that required the real code-breaking skills. That part was always about Annie. It was like that in every goddamned letter. Annabelle had a genius for maternal payback, leaving rapier slashes across your soul as she showered you with a hard rain of love and concern. A month ago her letter had a newspaper photo of the *Boo-Two!* Annie and Susie, with Hugh Hefner at some nightclub. Both of them looking lacquered, with rictus smiles that simply were not Annie. It just wasn't. But this latest letter was the complete negative image—jammed with whole pages of the *National Enquirer* with big parts torn out and a Post-it stuck beside each jagged void saying, "I didn't want this to upset you, so I tore it out."

Me upset? God forbid. Reading about the tedious love lives of Hollywood stars and—*this part (fill in your own blanks about the*

Boo Two) censored. I sat staring at it and then held the jagged void in the middle of the *National Enquirer* up into the Afghan air, framing those graves with Brad, Jen, Angelina, and Britney.

"What are you doing?" That wasn't the real question Danny wanted to ask.

"Gimme your sat phone."

"I need it."

"What if I need it more?"

"Constance. I need to call her."

"So do I." He didn't respond. "Annie," I explained.

He looked at me for a moment. And then passed me the phone. "Batteries are low."

I dialed the number on the other side of the world. The number on another of my mother's Post-its, the one under the notation *Highly recommend you do* not *call this number!*

From across the world, the female voice that answered the nonrecommended number exploded into the sat phone with a laughing, shrieking, giggling "HELLO?" My silence produced another "Hello?" this one irritated and surrounded by loud male voices.

"Is Annie there?"

"Who is this?" Silence. "Oh fuck," said Susie Boo.

"I want to talk to her."

"Don't you ever leave the fuck alone?"

"No. I don't."

"Aren't you in bumfuckistan or somewhere?"

"Something like that."

"Well, we're in a limo, dude. And your vibes don't fit." Spat out in a voice strained through steel wool dripping in daiquiris.

"Put Annie on the phone please."

"We're on our way to Vegas and—" The earpiece suddenly filled with voices, and out of the audio maelstrom I was sure I heard Annie cut through it all, and I wanted to imagine her grappling for the phone.

"Hank?"

"Hi."

"Oh . . . oh god . . . I thought . . ."

"Hey. I miss you."

"Oh Jesus I—" Her sister was yelling something in the background. "I'm with some people."

"What people?"

"Please . . ." She was crying. "Some new . . . new friends."

Suddenly there was a jostling sound and a man's voice came on the phone. "Hey pal, get your own fucking party."

"I have."

"Well, quit horning in on ours when these broads are on the meter."

"What meter?"

"Go fuck yourself." The line went dead.

Highly recommend you do not . . . !

Who else could get me to make a call like that? Annabelle is such a genius.

• • •

Sometime later that night Danny left, sifting into the darkness unseen.

In the commotion on the mountain with so many different units, all reporting to their own command centers and their own nationalities, his absence went unnoticed. A note on the drag bag we used said simply *Back soon. Don't wait up.* Inside the drag bag everything seemed to be there—at first. The big McMillan rifle, the suppressive fire weapon, the tripod, the scopes, all of it was there. But I kept pawing through, thinking something was missing, some weapon I could not remember was not in that tangle of metal, plastic, and composites.

Two nights later, from inside the folds of Gore-Tex, came a crackling, muffled "Reaper One, this is Dark Side. Do you copy?

Over." In the infinite darkness I was flung, spring-loaded, out of my nocturnal fog and I grappled through the sleeping bag for the radio but suddenly heard someone quietly responding, "Reaper One. Over." It was Danny.

"Dammit, where you been?"

"Out there," he said, his voice coming through on the radio sounding as bored as a guy ordering a cheeseburger in the drive-thru line. *Out there*, as in: out there in that infinite blackness of varying degrees of savagery stitched together with isolated acts of countervailing nobility. Wandering alone among the turbans, a pasty gringo out for a stroll *out there*. Like a walk in the—

"Where, out there?"

He came back into our camp hours later. "Man, I'm tired," was all he said. And within seconds he was gently snoring under those jagged beams of starlight.

Before dawn I was awoken by a muffled voice coming from the depths of the sleeping bag next to me. "I need to know. Is she okay?" It was Danny talking into the sat phone. Silence. "You're sure?" More silence. "I just did something bad. But good too. For her I mean. I hope it helps. I need to know. Is it going to help?" More silence. "Awesome. Thank god. So, tell me, am I going to be with her? I mean, some day?"

I whipped the sleeping bag off. "You're talking to Constance?" He waved me away, his arm flailing like a bird trying to take off with one wing tied down. "No! Please you gotta—" He looked at the phone. "How can she tell me that and then just hang up?"

"Tell you what?"

"To make an appointment."

"She always tells you that."

"She thinks Afghanistan is somewhere near Palm Springs."

"Get real."

"We got to get over there."

"We are over there."

"I'm talking about Hollywood."

"Where were you for the past two days?"

It was as if he hadn't heard me. "Don't you want to know your future?"

I thought about it for a while. "No." I went back to sleep.

Minutes before dawn, the sky filled with Chinooks extracting Team 590. The guys with John's cousin, the Agent, had already vanished. The whole plateau was silent, empty. Inside the cave were the burned-through ChemLight bottles littering the place. The seesaw door that Ahmed had been tied to was still there. But Ahmed was not. The litter and crap all over was positively eerie.

Sometime after the sun had warmed us out of our insulated jackets, I checked that drag bag again. Everything was still there. But something had been added, returned, really, to the bag. It was a small-caliber Russian SV-99 weapon, good up to a thousand meters. The kind of weapon that might damage but not necessarily obliterate. Depending on the skill of the shooter, of course.

Exactly!—the skill of the shooter! Skill, as in being able to hit a small target—moving from somewhere within the far end of that "about a thousand meters." And if he was anything, Danny was skilled. Rumors flew in several different languages. Rumors about a ghost that had recently roamed the mountains. An avenging spirit with wings that flapped as it leaped across the ground.

After he was hit, Zadran was said to have been carried the last part of the journey on a stretcher, borne aloft by frantic men stumbling toward the medics in Bannu. He was said to have sustained a catastrophic wound below the waist. A bullet fired from some hidden place, from somewhere no one saw, had struck him on a part of his body he refused to let others see. It was known that the loss of blood spewing from his groin area nearly killed him.

He survived.

• • •

Liberace was becoming a real warrior. I mean, have you ever heard "Warsaw Concerto" being blasted through Afghan mountain passes? Echoing and re-echoing off all that zillion tons of vertical rock, zigzagging up and down, backwards and forwards until it comes back at you like needles being jammed into your brain from every angle imaginable? But that's nothing compared to "Kitten on the Keys." You just knew that thing could penetrate rock. It had *cruel and unusual* written all over it. There was no cave deep enough up there in those Taliban-riddled mountains that could ever withstand that tinkly weapon that ended up sounding like pipes falling on each other. It was the original bunker buster. Or daisy cutter. Or whatever those weapons are.

The problem was that Liberace had what they call blowback. At least for Danny. Whenever we let loose a barrage of piano music, he'd start thinking of Ariana and then get to seriously weirding out. Like that night as we lay there in the crystalline cold of three thousand meters altitude, staring up at those zillion stars firing fusillades of photons at us. Swaddled in some high-tech sleeping bags but really relying on wool military blankets—*green* wool, the only kind that kept out the cold—we shared a merciful silence.

"She was a virgin."

"They all start out that way you know."

"You're not helping," he said.

"Well, what do you want me to say?"

"I figured it out. It was Ariana's way of turning herself into damaged goods. After we made love. Those tribal chest thumpers like Zadran need to deflower the bride themselves. They want virgins. It's part of the whole *Vani* deal."

"You ever thought that maybe she was just in love with you?"

He didn't answer for a while. "You know the really terrifying thing? What cuts a hole in my nights?" Mortars sounded from far away with a distant *thummmp* and then it was the stillness of all those photons. "That he didn't send her back. When he found out she wasn't a virgin. She must have been counting on that."

"Maybe he didn't have an alternative."

"He had an alternative, all right. And that's what scares the hell out of me."

"What?"

"He could always beat the shit out of her. For as long as he wanted. And no one would stop him."

"What about her family?"

"Are you kidding me? She's someone else's property now. That's how they all look at it. Besides . . ."

"Besides what?" Nothing. I thought he was asleep.

"Swear to God . . . I'm going to get Omar."

Once in a while history has a nasty way of running through your head when you're here. It unspools in some old analog loop that has played soundlessly in the widescreen crania of generations of sane people who found themselves wondering what they're fighting for. Don't get me wrong—we believed in all the drum-and-bugle pep rally stuff about fighting Terrorism and all that. That's not the point. The point is that Afghanistan is littered with the bones of a dozen drum and bugle corps. One or two per century on average. The Brits, those poor Victorian bastards, left their wounded behind as the Afghan women would stalk through the battlefield when the fighting was over, deadly ghosts clutching the long scimitar knives they used to fillet nice boys from London and Bristol, handing them their entrails, their private parts, smilingly watching them die in horror. And the Russians, stoned on brake fluid, drugs, and rock 'n' roll, dying in the mountain passes like insects as their own empire collapsed.

They don't talk about this at the pep rallies.

But if they did, Danny would be one of those lucky ones who wouldn't even care. Danny is not here for history. It makes it so much easier. Being here for Ariana makes it all so simple. I envy him. There is a kind of purity I long for in the dark fastness of those Afghan nights when the air almost crackles around you.

I think of Annie Boo and wonder what steps are still out there for me to retrace. And if I even could.

• • •

All through the shifting darkness of that night, he whispered out his own little hymn of pain, a torrent of memories: of how her black hair swirled in shimmering waves when she turned her head, about how he almost buckled the first time she smiled at him, about how he ached every time he heard her music in his thoughts, and about the way they completed each other, and . . . It went on and on, all through another perimeter mortar barrage that was pretty much ignored, and then sometime after quiet had descended again he remembered God's Valley, the slope from her hips down to her waist as she lay on her side. He relived running his hand gently back and forth into this Valley, the place where all life begins, the place of creation, where God resides. And from there, lapsing into the stillness that nurtured all this quiet frenzy that had turned in on him.

It was grief, plain and simple. I saw something like this only once before. Danny would try to talk you out of calling what he felt as being grief. But it was. Ripping through him, a blade with sawtooth thoughts, shredding memory and leaving shards of pain all around. Just like what I saw when I was seventeen with the father of a friend of mine. After his wife washed out to sea. They saw her go under far out there, the rip tides doing their work. And the father went more or less mad. Mostly because her body was never found. He kept expecting her to walk in the door. It got so that he'd almost fight anyone who suggested she wasn't going to show up.

Danny would never think of it this way, but Ariana had sort of washed out to sea. And he was sure she'd be walking in the door any day now. I sat up and realized that this was a replay of the nightmare about Annie I used to have.

That night I lay there in my sleeping bag, in all that frozen stillness, and figured out something when I stared up into all those stars. Some of them had died eons ago. But their light from when they were alive was only now reaching Earth after zipping along for a billion or so years—so what I was looking at was no longer there. My memories of the great days with Annie Boo might be exactly the same.

I had stashed the *National Enquirer* photographs of the Boo Two next to the two grenades I carried. Thinking that maybe taping them to the grenades might be therapeutic. It didn't really help. I was as bad as Danny.

I'd been using the latest bulky envelope from my mother as a headrest until I succumbed to the temptation to open it again, turning on a flashlight in the depths of the sleeping bag. In the midst of her letters was a phone message with the logo of a printing company in Santa Monica. On it was my mother's loopy handwriting: *Tues—2 P.M. Mr. Jones called for you. Very important you return his call.* As if I was going to take time out from a firefight or something and return a phone call in America.

There were two other phone messages with orders to call this Jones. I didn't know anyone named Jones.

Then there were my mother's latest letters to cope with. Annabelle had outdone herself. In the first letter you could almost hear the flutey mixture of indignation and insecurity as she wrote of the *unbelievable!!! deal* that she and Albert had gotten on a *spectacular* foreclosure deal on a house on the rim of Santa Monica Canyon. She and Albert were *friends again—well, actually, more than friends because he is such a genius, a true!! genius when it comes to business and money.* The letter was filled with this genius of Albert's, spotting this unbelievable deal that they went to see in the driving rain, beating out dozens of other bidders because Albert planted false information about the place being rotten with termites. Even now they were planning to fluff the house, flip it for a much higher price, and make money, more money than . . .

Then there was the second letter. Ten days later. When it had all changed.

Albert: dickweed; asshole; small man syndrome. Etc. . . . *conning me into putting my retirement fund into a house on the edge of a cliff—a whole cliff!!! that gives way in the driving rain, taking the house with it sliding down that cliff into the houses below . . . I am almost destitute . . . Etc. . . . and now Albert, that little shit, is now driving around in a brand new . . .*

Etc.

• • •

That night in the depths of the Afghan darkness, we almost killed a little girl.

At 0-something, half the plateau bolted out of sleep with the clacking of rounds being chambered in some locked-and-loaded wet dream. All over the night, voices and lights snapped out of whatever fog they were in.

But it was Danny who was first in on what was happening. Way before even the perimeter guards sent up the flares, he knew something was there. He sat up like he was hinged, breathlessly fired out of whatever dream was torturing him. I was still thinking about *I am almost destitute and that little shit is*—when he rasped, "You awake?"

"No."

"It's here."

"You're creeping me out." Which was true. It was almost eerie, the way he looked around.

"Constance said I would see a sign. From Ariana. That sign— it's here. Somewhere. I know it."

"Hey. I don't mean to burst your balloon, but that sign stuff is bullshit. My mother used to read tea leaves. Every time some guy showed up she'd say he should watch out for a sign. They'd leave thinking a traffic light turning green was a sign."

He wasn't paying attention. "The sign—it's here. I know it." He started groping around in his sleeping bag, coming up with the night-vision goggles and then vanishing into the darkness. Only moments later, the whole plateau awoke with that paranoia that rockets through the dark when noises happen where they shouldn't. All that chambering was clattering away when *Hold fire!* sounded. It was Danny—*Hold your fire it's a girl!*—yelling over the din, cutting through a jumble of *what the fucks?* as a bizarre sight appeared before our eyes. A little Afghan girl in a turquoise headscarf was standing in the center of a suddenly floodlit plain. She had wide, dark eyes that calmly looked at the rifle barrels flashing toward her like compass needles.

They were all fixed on this little girl, maybe eight, nine years old, maybe less, holding a flashlight and covered from head to foot in a dark blue robe and that headscarf around her shining black hair. She was serene, as if it was the most natural thing in the world for her to be out on a mountain in the middle of the night. And the way the Afghans think, maybe it was. Cause and effect just aren't linked the same way here. We'd had panic-in-the-night moments before, ones where you couldn't begin to understand the thinking that went on. Once, a herd of goats barreled in, driven right through a battalion-strength outpost. The herd ended up as stew for a week, accompanied by payoffs to the indignant goat herders. Another time, a camel train walked through an encampment before dawn, almost scaring a squad witless and provoking curses in several different languages.

But this little girl merely acted perplexed, looking at the weapons all around her without a flicker of fear, her large, dark eyes almost demanding that we explain our presence there.

"She's carrying something!" a voice in the darkness snapped.

Another voice—"Yeah, she's hiding it"—unleashing a platoon's worth of suicide bomber thoughts.

"Whoa! Back off," yelled Danny, stepping into the light. "I can handle it. I speak some Pashto." He walked slowly toward her.

"Don't get too close," one of the company commanders yelled. But he didn't see what Danny saw: the eyes and the hair. A few feet from her, he bent down and said something in that language of theirs. She looked at him with one of those Mona Lisa smiles that aren't really smiles. He said something else and she shook her head, this time showing the first flicker of emotion. She shook her head again, clutching whatever it was she was holding even tighter.

Danny kept talking to her, and slowly she parted one of the upper folds of her blue robe. She held her two hands toward him. In them was something, gray and rustling.

"What is it?" someone called out.

Danny looked from what was in her hands to her face. And then he smiled. The girl returned his smile as if relieved that he approved. "It's her bird. It got free. She went looking for it."

The girl suddenly burst into a chattering volley that Danny translated. "It's a songbird. Her family kept it alive all during when the Taliban were running the country. They banned music. So her family raised songbirds."

The girl said something else, and Danny was suddenly almost laughing. "It was the only way they could hear any kind of music."

Danny's joy shook free of its reins and took off. "You see?" he yelled.

After that, there was no way you could have pried Danny loose from that sign stuff. He practically went into free-association freefall, thinking everything was a sign: that little girl was the young Ariana coming back to him; it was Ariana's spirit seeking him out; it was Ariana calling out to him about her music; the bird *definitely the bird!* was a sign *for godsakes I mean a songbird?* A bird that made music when it was forbidden? *What more of a sign could you ask for than . . .*

And the dead satellite phone got prayed over all night as if incantations could somehow bring a now-worthless piece of plastic and metal back to life. He became obsessed with it, driving the radio operators crazy, bugging them to help, to MacGyver the thing back into life so he could talk to Constance again and find out what all the signs really meant. But that particular sat phone remained worthless. Mute, gleaming, and unable to communicate with the satellites overhead. Sometime before dawn, when I was back bundled into my sleeping bag, I heard the usual rustling that always preceded the crazy-making *Are you awake?* whisper. I was tripwire ready for indignation but he crossed me up. "I figured it out."

"Figured what out?'

"Our lives. Maybe just my life."

I thought about this for about as long as it was worth. "Yeah? And?"

"We gotta get out of here. Fast."

"Why?"

"We need help." Silence. "I'm scared."

"You're scared?"

"That I'm never going to find her." More silence. "Unless I get help. This country's huge. I need to go and get help. Fast."

"Go where?"

"Constance," he said.

I sat up and looked at him.

"Hollywood," he said.

HOLLYWOOD

17

Getting out was the easy part.

Danny convincingly pulled in the Canadian military's *disease or trauma that has detrimental and significant effect on the member's ability to perform assigned duties* clause that sprung him for fifteen days' compassionate leave.

I started by going to the XO and babbling something like, "Sir, my mother was in a house in California that slid down a cliff and I think she's okay but I can't be sure and I'm pretty damn worried about her." All true of course—except for the Timing Is Everything element—because I didn't mention that she was in the house, or what was left of it, two days *after* it slid down the cliff, inspecting the rubble.

Permission granted.

From Bagram to Dallas I left a vapor trail of the Annie Boo blues. All the way into California, courtesy of nice people who donated frequent-flyer miles to the USO so distraught defenders of the Free World like me could end up lurching off a red-eye into one of those remote airports east of L.A., the ones ringed by concentric circles of tract homes, strip malls, and ragged Chamber of Commerce billboards welcoming new investors.

Already there are two voice and three text messages on my phone from Danny, who got here two days earlier. They pretty much boiled down to *found us gr8 place in H'wood.*

The *gr8 place* turned out to be the Star-Brite motel *in the heart of glamorous Hollywood!* whose online home page somehow forgot to include among its *spectacular views!* the scenic shots of ravaged tweakers on the street below us, the ones who'd been up for two meth-fueled days straight, the transvestite hookers teetering on platform heels, and a healthy sampling from the left side of the bell curve, all working the same taco stand outside our window, a block or so north of Santa Monica Boulevard. And for our added enjoyment, there's the usual serenade at three-digit-decibel levels of hip-hop from some basehead sitting in his chopped and lowered Civic, waiting for Mr. Crystal to show up. Meth and tacos are what passed for health food on this block.

• • •

For the first two sessions with Constance, we kept being drawn back to the same thing: "Why do I hear so much music?" she asked.

"Liberace," Danny said. "I told you about him and—"

"No." She shook her head and looked up at him. Even from where I was sitting, I felt almost drawn into wherever those big green eyes of hers were leading. "Not this Liberace. Someone else is playing."

"A woman?"

"Yes. I think so."

"Ariana?"

"A woman who is where something is missing."

"What's missing?" Danny asked as Constance picked up the black mirror.

"The portal is bringing in broken music." Quickly, she picked up that little bottle and sprayed the ripe mint potion all over.

"Why are you doing that?"

"I feel danger," she said without any further explanation.

"How can music be broken?"

"It is. She is trying to fix it."

Right at that moment, while we were hurtling through this musky velvet tunnel of memory and image, one of those things happened. The kind of thing that causes most people to put you in the wacko category if you talk about it. But there's not a damn thing you can do because you've seen *it* and they haven't. And now you're a believer. *It*, in our case, was the white cat, Alpha, or Alfie, as she had instructed us to call him, which leapt up onto the big oak table. Constance shot off her chair like something had detonated underneath her. She was giving off a weird little barrage of breaths. "This has never happened before." She looked terrified.

"Cats jump up on tables all the time."

"No. Not during a reading. *Never!*"

It was as if she was expecting the cat to do a head-spinning thing like that kid in *The Exorcist*. Or some slime tentacle like in *Alien* was going to shoot out of Little Fluffy.

But it didn't stop there. Alfie, that white fur ball of entitlement, sauntered across the table and sat on the black mirror, the one that was the portal and all that business. I was about to make some joke—*If a white cat sits on a black portal*—when the damn thing starts meowing like crazy.

But it turns out that it's not the one doing the meowing. All it's doing is moving its lips. We've got Alfie the lip-synching cat on our hands. The real meowing is coming from below the table. It's the black one, Omega, sitting directly below Alfie and bellowing out some cat aria like a diva.

Constance backed away from the table like Alfie was about to explode. "It's a sign."

"You think?" Danny said. He and Constance were in lockstep on this one, doing some kind of psychic three-legged race. They'd lapped me and were going for the gold.

"The white cat mouthing the words of the black cat that come to it through the black mirror," she said. Awestruck would not come close to summing up Constance at that moment in time.

"You're missing something," Danny said. "Listen."

We all listened. All I heard was a black cat meowing under a white cat.

"Don't you get it? It's music. A kind of music."

Constance agreed. "*Yesss*," she said slowly three times. I was beginning to wonder if maybe the Afghan mountains weren't a better place to solve what was ailing us. Or at least a simpler place. "This woman? Ariana? There are Luciferians using her voice."

"What does that mean?"

"She wants to talk to you. But there are others, devil-people, who are preventing her. Their voices are blocking out hers."

It was right then that the two cats had their otherworldly accreditation revoked by a pounding on the door that sent them diving for sanctuary beneath a couch. When Constance opened the door, some other guy was there, jonesing for his future-fix, looking like he'd stepped out of a Calvin Klein ad. We heard him talking through the partly opened door. We only heard fragments: "*jesuschrist!* . . . I need to have you on standby in real time, okay? . . . I made an offer . . . a hundred K square feet in North Hollywood tonight . . . zoned mixed usage . . . I need to know if I should pull the trigger . . . *I need . . . I need . . . I need . . .*"

Maybe it was the whininess. Or maybe it was our general pissed-off truculence over having to sit in the fading aura of two transcendental cats and listen to this little shit. Stepping out of that Afghan night does give you a certain attitude injection that lasts longer than the guy's Botox. We walked up behind Constance, opened the door and stared at him. His reflex defense was to get puffed up like someone had stuck an air hose in his ass for about as long as it took for Danny to fix him with that look of his, the one that could get stray dogs barking. The guy deflated like a party balloon, sputtering all over the cheap stucco, leaving trails of indignation like so much snail slime.

They all drive Porsches here.

• • •

We'd returned from her place, neither of us saying a word about it, all the way back to the Star-Brite.

We lay there in geometric patches of streetlight and darkness, on two big beds separated by a collage of dubious stains and cigarette burns on a rug that was marginally worthy of being framed. Neither of us spoke for a long time. We were both replaying our time with Constance, trying to figure what it all meant. If it meant anything.

"What did you think of Constance?" he asked.

"When she's doing her act, you look into her eyes and you just know someone else is doing the driving."

"Chinese food—the minute you get out of her place you want more. Only your brain's stopped working in all that fog." Which was true. Maybe it was having your senses strained through all that darkness and incense and then draped around Shiva and God knows how many other deities peering down from framed posters all over the place. I definitely started seeing things in my mind.

It was my turn to sit on the tiny space that passed for a balcony at the Star-Brite, so I got to watch the tweakers at the taco stand scratching and jitterbugging their way across the sidewalk in spastic circles, waiting for their meth to show up, checking the newspaper coin slot for the hundredth time, and parading through my fears like some ragged advance guard of an omen. Watching them, and thinking of Annie somehow made them linked and I didn't know why.

Back in the room, lying there again in that geometric light and darkness, I thought Danny was asleep. "Jesus!" His head arched back, looking at the wall behind his bed. "Oh, man. I don't even wanna know."

"What now?"

"Look." He was pointing at the wall.

About a foot or so above the laminated headboard were two faint and greasy outlines of male handprints, spaced just far enough apart to let the imagination soar.

"Why would a guy be that far up on *this* bed leaning forward, supporting himself by putting his two greaseball hands on the wall, in front of where *I* am supposedly sleeping tonight?"

I was trying to think of the word we learned in Ms. Lechowski's English class for when nature adds to drama with things like thunder or lightning. Because right then, as Danny was having a fit about the greasy handprints over the bed, one transvestite hooker at the taco stand outside started screeching at another tranny, reaching high C in some demented aria that threatened him/her with what would happen if he/she didn't get the ice out of his/her ass. And the second one was yelling that whoever hid it from the cops up his ass got to keep it—"*So unless you intend to kiss my neon ass motherfucker you can go back to getting something else rammed up your own sorry butt and leave me the fuck alone, you get what I'm tellin' you?*"

"You listening to this?" I asked.

Danny stopped his own rant for a moment, listened, and then said, "I'm not meant to sleep indoors anymore."

He started to get up, slumped down again, and said, "You know the scariest thing of all? Ariana's mother. She's a ghost. Invisible. I can't remember one damn thing about her. I must have seen her five different times. And I can't even remember what she looked like. She would come in, this little ghost, bundled up in all that cloth, serve the tea, and then shuffle out. That's what they want to do to Ariana. She won't let that happen. She won't," he said for added emphasis.

After a long silence I asked, "What are you going to do if you find her?"

"Not if. *When*," he said.

"When."

He lay there staring at the handprints for a while. "I don't know." More staring. "I'm going to ask her to forgive me for not protecting her."

"Hey. Women rule. It's the zeros, the new millennium."

"The zeros of which century? Ours or theirs? I'm going to ask her to marry me."

"I thought you already tried that."

"Things were different then."

"Yeah, she wasn't married then."

"She's not married. She's kidnapped."

That night, Danny and I had the biggest fight we'd ever had. The problem was that I was starting to think Constance was possibly a Grade A wack job. I mean, even with all that spooky cat wailing, portals, and witches' juniper, I wasn't sure I really believed the whole fortune-telling business. I started wondering if maybe I'd always wanted to believe in Constance more than I actually did believe. Maybe I was too afraid of risking whatever chance I had to find Annie Boo on some woman who burned incense and peered into crystal balls. Or it could have been having Annabelle as my mother. And watching all her tea-leaf readings.

Whatever the reason, Danny just couldn't handle any doubts about Constance. Not after all that cat-on-the-portal business. He was a believer now. Totally. Which is where the argument started.

Sometime in the middle of that night, I woke up when I thought I heard him talking to someone. He was lying on his bed, sort of mumbling under his breath. I couldn't make out what he was saying, but I felt like I was intruding on something private.

"Hey."

"What?"

"Who you talking to?"

"Oh . . . sorry 'bout that."

"What's going on?"

"I don't want to talk about it."

"Wait a minute—you wake me up talking and then you say you don't want to talk?"

"You'd think I was insane."

"I already do."

He lay there on the bed. This time it was the ceiling he was fixed on, where the occasional passing headlights would rearrange the shadow patterns. "I talk to Ariana sometimes. I swear to God it's like she can hear me."

"I think we need to go slow."

"What are you talking about?"

"I'm not sure I believe in all this voodoo we heard tonight."

"It's not voodoo," he said indignantly.

"Hey. My mother told fortunes."

"Meaning what?"

"Meaning I'm not sure about it all."

This was obviously a direct hit on the emotional ammunition dump. "Constance is not telling *fortunes*!"

"I've already been through this with my mother."

"What's your mother got to do with anything?"

"She's just kicked her husband out. For the third time. Every time she does that, she starts reading tea leaves. Which she says give her messages from the other side—whatever that is. And then she says, 'He's dead to me! I might as well be in mourning.'"

Which was true. Whenever Annabelle pitched Albert out she made sure I knew all the stages of mourning so I'd be sure to be sympathetic when she smashed the china or keyed Albert's car. There was Isolation. Anger. Denial. And some other things, and maybe not exactly in that order. That stuff always confused me.

"I know all the stages," I lied. "There's Anger, Denial, and Isolation. You're in denial."

"What the hell are you talking about?"

"Like my mother. With her tea leaves. They're a kind of denial."

"Constance is not tea leaves." He sat up in that same spring-loaded way he did in the Afghan mountains whenever his sleep got mortared.

"Look, let's run through it, okay? Ariana's locked into South Waziristan or some fucking camel town, married to that fat dickhead with a Groucho Marx moustache whose balls you shot off way too late to stop him from probably filling her up with baby dickheads who will grow up to come hunting for you. Maybe she's gone out of your life, okay? *Gone.* No matter what some wacko fortuneteller says."

"*Fuck you!*" he yelled and then leapt up with a whole lot more *fuck*s, flipped the bed over, kicked the dresser, whipped open the door, yelled at the transvestites down at the taco stand not to answer the questions of the cops who'd just showed up, slammed the door, locked it, and then with his back against that door, slid down to the stained carpet and was quiet.

"Feel better?" I asked after a while.

"If the cops storm this room, filling the place full of bullets, do me a favor."

"What?"

"Tell her I love her."

"No problem." I waited for a while. "Acceptance. Stage Four."

"I repeat . . ." He didn't finish the sentence.

"What if the bullets go right through the door and hit me instead of you?"

"Then I'll be sure to tell Annie Boo that you died in a hail of bullets in a bed in Hollywood. It'll make a great legend that she'll tearfully tell her other lovers. All dozens of them."

That was the last name I wanted to hear—the one I craved, longed for. "You know, sometimes you are truly a goddamn idiot. You just pushed the wrong fucking button." Hot bubbles of indignation burst all around me. And he knew he had me. Which made me even angrier.

"Oh, so *my* buttons are okay, but poor sensitive you—"

"Reasoning with you is like putting contacts on a blind guy."

"Wow. Just because I talked about Annie Boo's other—"

"Yes!"

"You know what you need? You need a session with Constance."

"Tea leaves."

"How'd she know about Ricky Rubi then?"

"Luck."

"You sure about that?"

I wasn't. And staring off that Star-Brite balcony at what passed for my own personal Hollywood, I decided that the whole Annie

Boo journey was weird enough to begin with. And somehow Constance was only going to compound all that weirdness. If I was looking for that to happen, I could always let my mother handle it.

"Constance is a genius," he said.

"Then she's your genius."

He thought about that for a while. "You're gonna miss out. Already she broke the code, you know. She figured it out—the broken music thing she was talking about. 'The portal is bringing in broken music'? With that cat? It was that old beaten-up piano, the Schroder. The one in the empty house on Algonquin Avenue that Ariana and I went to. She played it even though it was missing a key."

"Wow."

"Okay. Be a moron. 'Now Ariana's trying to fix the music'—you heard Constance say that."

"Yeah? And? What exactly is that supposed to mean?"

"She's trying to reach me. Like I'm trying to reach her." Sitting on the floor, his back against the door, Danny's face was completely in the shadows. "She *is* trying to reach me. I know it." Only when a car passed by on the street outside and the shadows were fought back by the charge of reflected light that passed across the room could you make out the expression on his face. It was like someone who'd taken a direct hit.

"Hey, let's talk about sports. Or beer or something," I said.

"Oh, great idea." His voice was so low I could barely hear him.

But neither of us could think of anything to say. We just sat there in silence as the light and the shadows fought for supremacy on the ceiling.

"That first time? When she and I were naked together," he said. "When I almost made love to her? I didn't. Because she was crying so hard when I was . . ."

"Was what?"

Danny sat there staring at the floor. I thought he hadn't heard. He had. He just didn't want to answer. "You're right," he said after a while.

"About what?"

"We should be talking about sports or something."

• • •

Back on the Star-Brite balcony watching the tweakers:

I folded and unfolded one of the scraps of paper with two phone numbers on it. They were the phone numbers I used to dial to talk to Annie. I'd carried and cared for them all through the Afghan mountains, inscribed on a growing number of pieces of paper in various stages of decay. You could never be too safe with something so precious.

On that other piece of paper was Annabelle's *Highly recommend you do* not *call this number*. Coming off the page like a dare.

I had spent all those months over there looking at those three numbers, waiting for this moment, rehearsing it, refining it, that pause after she answered, which was when I would say quietly, "I'm here," and then listen to her telling me . . .

. . . I never really settled on what she would tell me.

But now these numbers immobilized me, blotched markers eating into tattered shards of paper that I had carried like talismans. It wasn't until the first wedge of light over Hollywood sent the tweakers stumbling home on silent streets that I got the courage to dial the numbers. One of them had been her cell phone; another was the house on the Venice canals; and the third one had simply shown up a year or so ago on Annabelle's caller ID. I was no longer sure which was which.

The first number yielded a Spanish-speaking female voice on the answering machine. The second one told me I had come to the right place for health care products. And the third one, the *Highly recommend you do* not *call this number*, lay across the screen on my cell phone in my own version of perpetuity as I tried to imagine her voice. I phoned.

But what came through that cell phone was an angry, sleepy male voice gaining consciousness with each new curse. *Didn't I know what the fucking time was? Didn't I know that he hadn't seen that fucking bitch in a year? Didn't I know . . . ?*

I knew none of it.

18

The sound was like having a kazoo playing Beethoven in your brain.

I grappled my way out of a dream-riddled sleep, blinking into the sunlight as the musical clatter went full *fortissimo*. On the next bed, Danny might as well have been in another county, snoring like a rusted muffler, not even stirring as his cell phone blasted out its strangled symphony. I found the phone under the nachos bag and flipped it open.

It was Constance. "Is this one of the soldiers?"

"Yes."

"I haven't ever called someone who I've done a reading for. Never. *They* call me."

"Thank you."

"I've been working the caller ID list on my phone, trying to find out which one was your number."

"We were going to call you."

"My cat just died."

I waited for some punch line.

"*Hello?*" Exasperation blasted through the phone. "*I said, 'My cat died.' Didn't you hear me?*" She was talking very fast. And emotionally. Not at all like last night when she had this low, slow way of talking.

"I'm sorry. I didn't know what to say."

"Alfie, the white one. When I woke up he was dead."

"That's horrible."

"I'm devastated."

"I can understand that." But I was lying. I had come from seeing men destroyed, obliterated, vaporized. So I could not really understand. I apologize to all cat lovers. But I was no longer capable of that kind of understanding. At least, not yet.

"It's a sign."

"It is?"

"Alpha—Alfie—was only the mouthpiece last night when Omega was channeling all that evil. He paid the ultimate price."

"He did."

"I need to see you. Immediately. I'm canceling all my appointments today."

"Danny's asleep."

"Immediately."

• • •

Danny and I hurried through a Burger King, a second-hand clothing store on La Brea, and a florist on Sunset Boulevard where the lady didn't know what kind of flowers to buy for a dead cat. So we bought roses. We walked up to Hollywood Boulevard feeling that we were not mere tourists, the kind of people surprised by seediness where there was supposed to be movie-star glamour. But still, walking past the place where they hold the Academy Awards, we looked around to see if anyone famous was hanging out. We went further along the street, holding the roses and reading the names of the famous people in bronze stars on the sidewalk in front of cheap souvenir stores, Scientology centers, and wig stores. A lot of those names we'd never heard of. Paul Muni? Jesse Lasky? It got better when we turned down Vine Street and walked across James Dean.

But by this time Danny was starting to believe everything we saw was a sign. That business of the cat dying had really unleashed a torrent of symbols. When he saw a woman with beautiful, dark hair walking in front of us, it was Ariana's hair, a sign that she was trying to be with him. And when another dark-haired woman was standing outside the Egyptian Theatre on the other side of the street it was Ariana waiting for him. And when a white Mercedes pulling out from a curb parking space was hit by a black Chevrolet it was like Alfie and—"Don't even go there," I said to him as we walked over the Beatles and then Marlon Brando.

By then I realized that every tourist in the whole place was walking along, reading the names just like we were.

We headed south, and then east into another world past Larchmont Boulevard. A world of small houses bristling with claims of bigness. *Old* small houses, built in the silent film era, daring you to ignore the ghosts of Hollywood, of lives led and dreams born dead for years afterwards. For me those were the real signs. The whole place gave me a chill. But maybe that's what happens when you've been raised at the beach where the closest you get to mysticism is someone talking about UV protection or a great wave.

Constance's place looked so different in the light of day. There was none of that unleash-the-werewolves spookiness. Daylight had burned off all the Gothic battlements we'd imagined the previous night. Now it was just one of those crummy two-story, stucco apartment buildings, the ones with a forlorn interior courtyard that had been dropped across Southern California in the 1960s like warts on the landscape. But it was a crummy stucco building with a new Cadillac Escalade parked outside in a red no-parking zone. Of course, the black Escalade was on its way to becoming another sign, but before Danny could even say anything, I rolled my eyes and he shut up.

We stood with our roses in front of the wire mesh security gate and the push button intercom that stood sentry for Constance. The buzzing noise ushered us inside, up to an exterior walkway that seemed to bounce when we walked on it. Dressed in a T-shirt and silk cargo pants, she was waiting for us, looking haggard, that tangle of Goldilocks hair flying off in all directions as if she'd just gotten up. Right away we knew the roses were somehow a problem. She didn't even want to touch them when we offered them to her. "Oh . . ." she said, not taking her eyes off them. "Thank you. But all flowers are wrong at this moment. Unless they are black."

We ditched the roses and tried to think of one black flower either of us had ever seen as we waited for Constance to finish with the Escalade guy who'd refused to cancel his appointment. Sitting there on that exterior walkway that went past the individual apartments, we could hear the guy going crazy—*"You never said anything about this. It could be a tumor for christsakes. I been coming here for two years and all you ever said was something about a cloud being over some part of me? That's it? . . . I take vitamin E, omega-3, selenium. All that shit, so tell me how the fuck it's possible . . . Just tell me how to fix it, okay? Please? I don't have time for this."*—each time followed by some low murmur from Constance until she said gently that his time was up until next week. *"Next week? I think I might have a tumor and you want me to wait until next week?"* The Escalade guy left, barreling out, stepping over Danny and me like we were speed bumps. He looked younger than he was, wearing an expensive leather jacket and jeans with a crease in them. "Kind of guy who shines his feet and then puts his shoes on," Danny muttered.

We waited for a while, heard nothing but silence and then decided to go inside. For some reason we felt almost obliged to tiptoe in. She was seated at the wooden table against the wall in the small living room. Sunlight streamed through the pale orange curtains. Heavier black velvet curtains had been pulled back to the edges of the living room. A single candle was lit and flickered for no reason I could see.

And on the floor in a corner near the kitchen was a white towel draped over something that bulged.

"Hello?" I said.

She didn't acknowledge me. She didn't even look at us. She was staring into a small bowl of water. As if she was in a trance, she reached for a mirror and put it into the bowl, staring into it again.

"What are you doing?" Danny asked.

"Scrying," she said with her eyes closed. As if we were supposed to know what she was talking about. "When I scry I get information from anything that has a reflection," she said, staring into the mirror in the water. Her voice sounded like it came in from Burbank. "Yes . . ." she said. "Oh." A silence. Her eyes were closed. "I'm going in," she said, rocking slightly back and forth.

We stood there waiting for whatever was next.

"Sit," she said, waving her hand, her eyes still closed. Danny looked over at me. I nodded and he sat in the single chair in front of her. Her eyes remained closed. "Last night when I saw you I sprayed wintergreen here in the room. I need to protect myself. But I didn't do enough. I told you—witches will put juniper branches beside their front door. To keep out evil spirits. I should have put juniper up by the doorway, a lot of it. But I didn't. So evil spirits got in past the door. And Alfie paid the price."

I quickly checked out the entrance to the apartment. What looked like Christmas tree branches were now hanging from a nail beside the door.

Her eyes opened. It was almost a shock when they did. Danny looked uncertain. "I'm really sorry about your cat. I was just trying to find Ariana. Maybe we shouldn't be here right now."

She didn't take her eyes off him. She got up slowly from behind the table, walked over to the white towel, and removed it from the floor. Like it was all some kind of drama. With her pulling aside the curtain in a theater. Under the towel was Alfie, starring as the dead cat.

"Evil came in here last night. Alfie paid the price. But we are not finished."

I'd wanted to ask *the* question, easing into it in *did-he-have-a-good-life?* terms, but instead I went straight for it. "Let me ask you something. How old was Alfie?"

"Thirteen," she said, as if that had nothing to do with Alfie's demise. A thirteen-year-old cat suddenly croaks and it's a mystical event? I tried to flash Danny a look, but the ghost of Alfie was obviously pawing with his mind. "*We* are not finished," she said again, looking right at Danny.

"Okay," he said uncertainly.

"You're going to bury Alfie."

A cat? We're burying the cat? My mind went tumbling through a kaleidoscope of flashbacks to other dead, human dead, strewn across the mountains. And now we're burying a cat? "Hey Danny, maybe we should—"

"Of course," he said.

"Afterwards," she said. What *afterwards*?

"After what?"

"After we get to the trauma that made Alfie die," she said, switching on a lamp beside the window and then turning out all the others in the room. She sat down and took the Tarot cards from the velvet bag, looked at them, shook her head, and uncovered that black mirror and looked into it. It was like she was inspecting it for flaws.

"You have kept something from me," she said. Almost like an accusation.

"What are you talking about?" Danny wouldn't look directly at her when he answered on behalf of both of us.

"Maybe it wasn't lying," she said. "But something like lying. Concealing?"

"No." Danny almost leaned into the word.

"Yes. That's why Alfie died. He was using up all of his energy. He was a channel for something bad. Even healthy psychics get sick a lot because some channels aren't clear. We have to clear the channels. But a cat? Poor Alfie didn't stand a chance."

"Yeah," he said quietly.

"Death. One you haven't talked about."

With almost a jolt, Danny's eyes suddenly focused on her.

"A man?"

"Oh jesus," Danny said, looking like I'd never seen him before. And that was the instant I figured out that we were in an elevator after the cables had snapped. With me pushing buttons for every floor all the way down.

"And this woman you seek . . ."

Danny suddenly started to shiver as if he was freezing. "I don't really want to go into this."

"Someone died."

"Yes." Danny's whisper came from some part of him that was far away.

"When you were with the woman. The one in the white veil."

"Yes . . . sort of." Silence.

"You still don't want to talk about it?"

"No."

"Fine."

"Wait . . ." Danny was twisting in the chair, going through some personal portal all his own. "My father . . ."

"Your father?"

"He shot himself."

"He . . . ?"

Nothing. Silence.

"It took me a long time to figure out that maybe it was his way of warning me."

"About what?"

"About not taking chances."

She got up and pulled the towel back over Alfie as if he had done his job and it was time to bring the curtain down. Then she sat across from Danny and waited.

"After Omar left, Ariana and I were supposed to meet again at the house on Algonquin Avenue, the empty house, the one I was supposed to be looking after for my father until the estate was settled and he could do the renovations." He stopped and was staring blankly at something only he could see as his hands silently strangled the edge of the table.

As close as I was to Danny, I wasn't sure I should be there. I looked toward the door. I just wanted to leave. I felt something was about to be said that was just too personal.

"I got there early, before Ariana. I knew something was wrong the moment I went inside. Like some cold, invisible wind was blowing, the kind that freezes in your spine. I called out, 'Hello?' and there was only silence. I was almost creeping through the darkened rooms where the streetlights lit the crevasses. In the shadows, way over in the corner of the back room, past the big sliding doors that were pushed back, my father was there. He was sitting on the floor, his eyes wide open. Like he was watching me. He seemed so peaceful. Looking right at me. It took me a while to really see the big pool of his blood that had run from his chest down across the floor until it congealed in a dark sticky circle. The gun was lying beside him.

"I stood there like I was nailed to the floor, trying to say something to him. But no words would come out. I couldn't move. It was only the sound of Ariana's footsteps outside that shook me loose. I got to the door before she could open it, making some excuse about my father coming to the house unexpectedly.

"She never knew. That entire evening I was an actor. I wanted desperately to break down and cry. But I didn't. And to this day, I'm sure she had no idea."

In all those months of wandering the Afghan mountains with Danny, of talking about the most personal parts of our lives, not even a hint of this had ever come up. "You never mentioned anything about this," I said.

Constance answered, not Danny. "He couldn't."

"I should have known. It was there all along and I never saw it. I could have stopped it."

"How?"

"After my father moved back with my mother, with us, he just wasn't the same person he used to be. I remembered when I was little he used to laugh a lot. He was great fun to be with. He was my hero then. But when he moved back into our house there was no laughter, nothing. Just him and Mother, two people who went right back to being welded together by whatever they loathed in each other. I thought maybe he came back because he felt guilty about leaving me behind. He always wanted me to take over his business. The more misery there was in the house, the harder he worked at that business.

"But when I look back on it all, I think I always knew he was going to kill himself. I just *knew* goddammit."

Constance was still looking into the black mirror. "But I see someone else."

"My father came to me one day out of the blue, about a year after he'd moved back in, and said something about how we all have only one soulmate in our lives. And whatever you have to do, you *never* let her go. Never walk away. I thought that was pretty strange, coming from him. He never usually talked like that.

"But back then I didn't pay much attention. Whoever does at that age? But I didn't understand anything about either of them back then. My mother'd gone back to smashing their old photographs, thinking it would make him mad. But instead of losing it he'd just watch her and say nothing.

"I didn't even pay attention when he came back late one night and just sat in the car until dawn. I went outside because I could hear the car start about four times. He'd start it, put it in gear, sit for a while, and then shut it off and sit there some more. I saw something I never wanted to see. He was crying. I couldn't believe it. My old man—crying! He was the toughest guy I ever knew. Nothing got to him. But here he was. Sitting there alone. Without a sound. I could see his face in the light. It was like, tears were pouring out of him. I backed away. It totally freaked me out. I couldn't handle that. And now? All I can think about is why? Why didn't I just go up to him? Why didn't I say something? Because I knew. I just *knew.*

"So, in that instant, in that old house on Algonquin Avenue, something in me was not surprised. And there he was, sitting on that floor. Staring right at me after he shot himself. I had *known.* And I hadn't tried to help him. And to this day I don't know why.

"At his funeral there was one car that hung back from the others in the cemetery. I had seen it parked outside the funeral parlor. It was a gray Mercedes, pretty new, and driven by a woman who had sat at the back in the chapel. She was attractive, with shiny black hair, and looked sort of darker than most of the other people there. She never made eye contact the whole time. She was crying, though. Very quietly.

"At the cemetery she didn't get out of her vehicle. She was there watching as the rest of us were heading up to the gravesite on that little ridge. I was at the end of the group of people going up there. I turned around for some reason and went back to the little road where she was parked. 'I'm his son,' I said.

"'I know,' she said. She was still sitting in the car. 'I've seen photographs of you. A lot of them.'

"I asked her if I should know who she was, and she said, 'Just someone who loved him.' She looked straight ahead when she said it. She wouldn't look at me. I started to walk back toward the gravesite and then something made me turn again. 'Why didn't you and my father stay together?'

"At first I thought she hadn't heard. Then she said, 'I still don't know.' She was still looking straight over the steering wheel. 'Maybe he let his fears become a wall he couldn't climb,' she said, and for the first time she looked at me. I thought she was asking me for some kind of understanding. 'After he went back to your mother, I married someone else.'

"Then she drove away. Really slowly. I never even knew her name. I think about that woman. A lot."

Constance could have been in a trance, for all I knew. She sat there listening, staring straight into the lamp. She finally said something: "I am hearing music again."

"Is it 'I'll Be Seeing You'? That Frank Sinatra song? The one that my mother started playing again? About a million times after the funeral? When she decided she loved my father again?"

"No."

"Is it Liberace?"

"Maybe."

"And?"

"He will help you. And . . ." Her eyes closed. Her lips began moving in some silent conversation that only she could hear.

"And what?"

"Alfie."

"What about Alfie?"

"He was speaking for your father. No wonder Alfie died. He was overtaken by the voice of a dead man."

"Alfie was my father?" Invisible parts of Danny started flying off in all directions.

"Be still," she snapped without opening her eyes.

"A dead cat was my father?"

"You're blocking the energy." Constance raised her voice for the first time. "Be still." She opened her eyes and looked into the light behind Danny. We were back to that same jangled silence, the one that seemed louder than any mortar attack. "Alfie paid the price."

"I'm sorry."

"Put your hands on the table. And turn them over." Constance held her hands over Danny's. Then she slowly lowered them until they rested on his. Her eyes were closed. "Yes." Quickly, she took the Tarot cards from the small velvet bag and laid them out in front of her. She looked from the cards to somewhere past Danny's head and then back again. "She is alive."

"Of course she's alive."

"There is no 'of course,'" she said. "But this woman you are looking for has survived."

"Survived what?"

"She waits for you. It will not be the same, though."

"What won't be the same?" Danny was in static motion, the way he got when he was tense, his leg jackhammering under the table.

"All of it. It will all be different when you meet her."

"Will she recognize me?"

"That is not the question." Constance was looking off into that light. Her voice again came from somewhere far away.

"What *is* the question, then?" Danny looked at her as if a stare could pull an answer out of her. She seemed not to hear him. *"What?"* Then suddenly he sat back. You could almost hear the tumblers falling into place, unlocking some vault within him. "Oh god. Are you asking . . . Is that the question? . . . Is that what you want me to understand? If *I* will recognize *her?"*

Constance did not answer.

19

It went on. In circles that kept coming back to that same silence. I was gagging on all this karma and anxiety.

I began looking for a way out, some graceful exit from the bombardment of whatever it was that Constance was dropping on us. I started to move toward the door, muttering a kind of preliminary goodbye.

Constance seemed to snap back into whatever world we were in. "Wait a minute. Are you leaving?" When I nodded, she looked indignant.

"Well, what about my cat?"

Somehow I got put in charge of Alfie.

We wrapped him in a towel that was taped together so that the only part of him you could see were his legs. The problem now was rigor mortis, so Alfie's legs stuck stiffly straight out through the openings in the towel.

My initial impulse, which was simply to run like hell, got overruled by Danny, who wanted all the time with Constance he could get. There was almost an anxious quality to him now, exasperated maybe because he wanted to hear things that she wasn't telling him.

The idea of this outing, we were informed, was to give Alfie a clairsentient sendoff. Or something like that. It had to be done by everyone involved in his demise. Which is why Danny and I were there. We'd started by standing in the Sunset Plaza parking lot overlooking a good chunk of L.A. I suggested we send him to the spirit world like the old-time Comanches or Sioux or whatever tribe it was who stuck their dead up on wooden platforms and let the birds peck them clean. I figured that should pretty much do it for Alfie, who was dangling from my side by a carrying harness

I'd made out of 7-Eleven plastic bags. Perfect to hook over a tree branch and the birds do their work.

But apparently this was not clairsentient enough. Constance seemed to be drifting into a daze. I started to feel almost sorry for her. There was a kind of frail quality, as if something about being out in the light of day diminished her. "The ocean," she said, like it had been revealed to her in a vision. "The ocean is calling Alfie."

So with me sitting in the back of Constance's old brown Ford Taurus with a green driver's side door and a shattered rear window that was held together with gaffer tape, we started west toward the ocean. I told myself I was doing it for Alfie. On several counts this was difficult to sustain. The first was because Alfie was lying wrapped up on the seat beside me, with his legs sticking more or less straight up. The second problem was that Constance drove like a bank shot to the side pocket. She was all over the road. She drove as if she was still doing a reading. Her attention was in some other world, everywhere but on what was in front of her or on either side. Sitting in that back seat, bracing myself in whatever way was possible for the crash I knew was coming, I yelled over the intermittent symphony of horns for her to drive in a straight line.

It was like reasoning with a grenade.

At one point, after she had nearly sideswiped an eighteen-wheeler on the Hollywood Freeway, I yelled something about her getting us all killed. She turned around, that mass of Goldilocks curls spinning like blonde wind chimes, her little chin holding aloft a look of impatience. "Why are you so jumpy? There's no need, you know. I had a reading done a month ago. I'm going to die in an earthquake in Mexico when I'm eighty-six years old." As she said it, she was heading straight for a concrete bridge abutment that we would have hit if Danny had not grabbed the wheel and steered us back onto the inside lane.

"See?" she said as we lurched back into the lane.

I took over the driving, which seemed to be well received all around. That left Alfie buckled into the front passenger seat, legs in the air, while Danny and Constance were in the back seat. It almost turned into another session because Constance was staring out the side windows—*transing*, or whatever she called it—while Danny was going crazy wanting to ask her questions about Ariana.

He asked it outright. "Please, I just want to know where she is."

But Constance acted like she hadn't heard him, talking endlessly about clients—"Without naming names. I'm not a 'read-and-tell' kind of psychic, you understand." All the way along Sunset Boulevard it went on, past Beverly Hills and out into Brentwood. I heard things like, "I had a client up there on Rockingham, divorced now, and I told her that was . . ." And then every mile or so it was leaning over, looking down at Alfie who was lying there trussed and stiff on the front passenger seat.

When we got to the end of Sunset Boulevard where it meets the ocean, she leaned forward and said, "Alfie wants you to go north." I thought of asking her how she knew. I mean, Alfie was still lying flat on his back with his legs sticking straight in the air saying absolutely nothing. But after thinking it over, I decided the answer would probably just lead to more questions.

In the back seat, next to Constance, Danny was strangely silent.

We drove up the Pacific Coast Highway to where it becomes two lanes in each direction, past the Topanga Canyon road and the Malibu Colony. Constance was fixated on the hills on our right. "What are those hills?"

"The Santa Monica Mountains," I said.

"I never get out this far." She looked out the window as if she was in a foreign country.

"They have some nerve to call those things mountains." Danny said, looking up at about three thousand feet of big hills.

But Constance suddenly came alive. "Stop the car please," she said. "Here! Here!" I pulled over to the dirt shoulder of the road and she jumped out. She stood staring at the mountains. "Where are we?"

"That's Malibu Canyon over there."

She sank to her knees, closed her eyes, and ran her hand back and forth a few inches from the ground. "We are close."

Back in the car, we kept going north through Malibu, stopping once more, turning in at Paradise Cove, which she dismissed with a wave of her hand, and then going a couple of miles north to where Zuma Beach blossoms through the windshield as the roadside hills are peeled away.

"Ah," she said. She was smiling and staring up at the mountains. In the rearview mirror she looked serene once again. "I feel Alfie's energy." Danny was sitting beside her, staring out at the ocean in some world of his own.

Not far past Zuma Beach a road turned inland, first passing a patch of scrawny tract homes and then rising up into the mountains past flimsy mansions built in defiance of nature. Further past these was the remoteness of asphalt intrusions into places no road should sensibly go. It was on one of these that we stopped at a turnoff overlooking the Pacific Ocean below us.

"Alfie is home," she announced.

Fine by me. Truth was, Alfie was starting to get a tad whiffy. After all, the poor thing had been dead now for at least sixteen hours and not even the car's wheezy air conditioner was wafting Alfie out through the open windows. Constance seemed not to notice. She had already grabbed him by the 7-Eleven bags and had laid him gently on the ground. "Help me," she said. Which in this case meant gathering twigs, bark, and branches that I first thought were meant to be a good way to cover up Alfie in his final resting place. But it turned out it was Alfie covering the bark, in a lovingly constructed funeral pyre she was making for him.

Constance took out a plastic lighter and set fire to the twigs. "Cremation," she said. "The surest path into the next life."

And basically, that was the moment that I became an accessory to a crime.

Because, at that instant, I was silent in the face of whatever clairsentience trumped common sense. Or, put another way, I just stood there—even as I remembered what I'd read years ago about why Los Angeles was not fit for habitation: the earthquakes, the lack of fresh water, the mudslides, and all the rest. But the big one that stuck in my mind was, believe it or not, *resins*! The gooey stuff that is loaded into all those twiglike bushes and bark covering the hillsides of L.A. The resins that explode like a bomb when they ignite. No mere charring and crackling for these L.A. bushes—uh-uh, we're talking flamethrower stuff here. These little bushes can literally blow up and hurl flame at you from all directions. All because of the resins.

I knew that. And yet, still I blankly watched Constance light the twigs and bark under Alfie, for some reason frozen into inaction. I probably even knew that bark was from one of the big eucalyptus trees, the rocket-propelled grenades of the local flora. To this day I can't explain it. That was my part of it, my little chunk of guilt. But that alone didn't open the gates of hell. It took nature to do that. A sudden wind whipped down the side of the huge hill, so hot and arid that you felt invisible sparks flickering across your body. It eddied and whipped around like a decoy before the blast out of the east that slammed in with a force that almost knocked us over.

"Santa Anas," said Constance. "Winds of evil." She yelled something else that we couldn't hear because that eucalyptus bark, loaded with enough resin to humble napalm, suddenly exploded all around Alfie.

Alfie practically levitated above the inferno. "Oh dear," said Constance as a satchel charge of manzanilla twigs blew up.

For me, *Oh dear* was not what first came to mind as I grabbed Constance, dragging her out of the way of the horizontal geyser of fire that shot out, peeling the paint off the trunk of her Taurus. Wind-whipped and leaping like a deranged dancer, the fire shot across the thin strip of asphalt to the underbrush on the other side of the road. Which was where the eucalyptus trees themselves were standing, with their sleek, scaly trunks suddenly reminding me of artillery shells.

We barely made it into the car as that patch of mountain blew up around us, the eucalyptus tree canopies erupting in sequence like Katyusha rockets.

"It's like calling in air support right on your own position," said Danny, looking amazed that I could get the Taurus out of there before the tires melted. We hurtled down the zigzag road with the rearview mirrors billowing with fire and the horror of what we had just unleashed.

Constance was practically swooning. Staring out the back window, she kept calling out, "Darling Alfie!"

"We're practically ecological war criminals, do you know that?" I yelled. The car skidded around a curve, heading into the Doppler effect of the distant, onrushing sirens.

But she was operating on a more transcendental level. "Alfie was special," she said proudly. "But who would have thought he had it in him?" In the rearview mirror I caught Danny's wild eyes signaling me to let it drop. "Alfie is showing his anger," she said. "Over what happened to him." Police cars flashed past, a zipline of lights and sirens. Constance was exulting in it all. "The ocean," she said grandly, stating the obvious. "We must reach the ocean."

That was the easy part. Just straight down the mountain with a few minor course adjustments and we were at Zuma Beach watching Malibu burn on one side and the endlessness of the ocean on the other. Danny could only look at the ocean. In the warmth of the late afternoon sun he suddenly looked older than I remembered him. Or maybe just tired, more tired than I'd seen him after any of the battles we'd been in. The kind of exhaustion that comes when something inside slips and the floodgates can no longer hold.

"You okay?" I asked.

"What the hell are we doing?" he said so softly I could barely hear him. "We wipe out mountains over there all the time. So we come all this way here to America and do the same thing?" Over at the water's edge on that huge beach, Constance was standing knee-deep in the surf, eyes closed, her blonde curls piled like a parka hood around her small face. Danny watched her circling in the water. "What the hell are we doing? We should have saved ourselves the trip."

Constance slowly turned around, her eyes opening. "Earth, water, wind, and fire," she said.

"Been there, done that," said Danny loud enough for her to hear. You could have cut paper on the edge in his voice.

"Excuse me?" she said. You could tell she'd grown accustomed to reverence from her clients.

"Coming down that mountain? After we've just fucked it up more than a B-52 attack? I started to wonder why we'd come halfway around the planet just for this."

"Oh, *really?*" she said, eyebrows arching in tiny, sharp parabolas. I've always thought that *really* and *fine* are two words that women say way better than men. For starters, they come gender-equipped with their own personalized exclamation marks that no guy can duplicate. And, they come with about a million different meanings per word so that a *really* one day can mean the exact opposite of a *really* the next day. And no mere male is strong enough to cart around a dictionary big enough to translate every curled vowel, every different estrogen-soaked inflection that make Chinese intonations seem almost monotone.

"Yeah, really," Danny said. Not in an angry way. It was just a tired, depressed, guy-type *really*. Flat. Unnuanced. But you could tell that, to Constance, it pretty much had the sound of a gauntlet being slapped down.

"Meaning what?" she said, wading out of the water, the forces of the Hollywood belief system rising invisibly behind her.

"*Meaning* that I came all the way from Afghanistan, crazed over the woman I love, praying, pleading for answers about how I find her. And what I end up with is a dead cat that sets Malibu on fire."

She circled him, saying nothing. You could almost hear terrible things in all that silence. Even the waves made no noise.

"I vote we get out of here," he said.

"Why?" she said. "What's the rush?"

"Oh, I don't know. Maybe before we poison the water. Or cause an earthquake."

"What are you afraid of?"

"It doesn't matter."

"I'm serious."

"So am I."

She drilled Danny with a silent *really?*—another gender-specific tactical advantage—and then marched up the beach, the sun at her back. "Stand over there," she ordered. At first Danny did nothing. I thought of two gunfighters waiting to see who would draw first.

"Why?"

"So you can go back to Afghanistan with more than a dead cat." She adjusted her sunglasses, lowering them, looking over them to the ocean. Then she raised them again.

She stared past him. And then she took off her sunglasses, holding them up to the sky. "Polarizing," she said. "Takes away the reflections. Bad for scrying," she said. "Give me a minute." She squinted into the sunlight and the ocean in silence.

"She sends you music. This Ar—Art—"

"Ariana?"

"Yes. Ariana."

Merely her name stopped Danny in his tracks. "She does? The broken music you were talking about?" All that edge crumbled. Suddenly he was back to being the mendicant waiting for crumbs of information.

She stared into the ocean. "No. It is not broken. I hear a name. Another woman's name. Elizabeth? Liza?"

"Elise?"

"Yes. Maybe. This woman you want to know about, this Ariana, she plays this Elizabeth or Elise music. Again and again. But only in her mind."

Danny said, "Then it *is* broken. She played it on that old piano with the key missing."

"No," Constance said. "No, wait." Behind her, all of Malibu looked like it was in flames. The news helicopters circled like mechanical vultures, waiting to feast on their own kind of carrion. Others in the same flock came clattering up along the coast and then cut inland.

Constance looked over to me. In a way I didn't like. A seriously impaling way. She looked back at the ocean. Then at me. Back and forth until I asked if something was wrong. She didn't answer. At least not immediately. She went back to looking straight at Danny for a moment. "It's not you," she told him. "The broken music is his."

She was pointing straight at me.

I snapped out of whatever mind space I was in. "I don't have anything to do with this."

"You do. Someone you love is trying to make music. But something stops her before she can finish it. *That* is the broken music," she said.

"What about Ariana then?" Danny said, irritation, or maybe disappointment, stringing his words together.

"Her music never leaves her head. She is blocked somehow." Constance turned back to me. "But this broken music you will hear comes from another woman."

"Is her name Annie?" Suddenly all this psychic stuff didn't seem so insane. "Annie Boo? As in Boudreau?" As I heard—

The first time ever I saw your face
I thought the sun rose in your eyes

It was in the rest of the lyrics where I almost lost it—the part where the moon and the stars were the gifts she was giving me. The moon and the stars back in all those frozen nights, staring up to the skies and listening to distant battles in the mountains—and why hadn't I known it? It was Annie! Then and now. The broken music had to be Annie! She was singing to me?

"I'm tired," Constance said. "Very tired. The light is growing dim. I'm having trouble feeling energy."

"You have to tell me." Instantly I was a believer, a zealot practically. All my *what a crock*s vanished.

"I feel noise," said Constance. "She is somewhere where the music is too loud. She is looking for you there."

"Where is music too loud?"

"There are too many people."

"A club," said Danny. "Like the ones we saw."

She stared at the sky like some revelation was about to come from it. "You are both looking for the same woman," she said.

Danny and I looked at each other. "*What?*" he said impatiently. "You haven't understood what we've been saying, so—"

"*Enough!* I only tell you what comes through to me. *You* are missing something. Both of you."

"What are we missing?"

"I told you. You are both looking for the same woman."

"No, look, there's *two* women." Danny said, irritated by what she saying. "There's Ariana and then there's—"

"There's one," she said, interrupting. I could see panic in Danny's eyes. Panic in a place where no danger ever seemed to intrude. "Physically there are two. But really there is only one woman, one single source of energy. She is following a life imposed by others. Terrible things are all around. And she loves you." She was looking right between the two of us.

"And that is why the two of you found each other," she said.

"We didn't just find each other," Danny said. "It was a fluke. He got OpConned to our unit and—"

"It was no fluke. Each of you was out there in the universe, waiting to be found by the other.

"It was the women who guided you," she said.

20

When we were in the Afghan mountains we would sometimes watch the F-15s come swooping in. Twice, when we were fighting Taliban who had vanished deep into their caves tunneled miles into all that granite, the planes had dropped something we later learned was a BLU-118B bomb. More specifically, a *thermobaric* bomb, a word none of us had ever heard before. All you needed to know about those bombs was that you did not want to be anywhere in those caves—even miles down in the most remote manmade recesses of that hollowed-out mountain—because those thermobarics were going to blaze through all the miles-deep twists and turns and blow all your deep-fried innards out through your nearest available orifice.

"Thermobaric" was the first thing Danny whispered to me as Constance was walking back to the singed Taurus. He was totally unnerved by what she'd told us and was trying to come up with something catchy to make like he didn't take her all that seriously.

"Totally," I whispered back. We were both still absorbing what she'd said, pretending to cope with it. She had reached into some of the sanctuaries we'd preserved in the deepest part of our defense mechanisms, vaporizing illusions we'd held dear.

At first I thought what she said was a bad joke of some kind. But then the idea of Danny and me having somehow been looking for one another across an invisible universe, joined by a quest for a single soul in the body of two women, sank in. And for a while we both quietly disintegrated after pretending to be too cool to take her seriously. I asked Danny, "Do you believe her?"

"Sort of. I guess."

"Yeah me too. Because, I mean, who can believe in that psychic stuff?"

"Yeah."

"But we should humor her."

"We should."

"It would be rude to act like we didn't believe her. Like it was all bullshit."

"Absolutely. We don't want to hurt her feelings."

• • •

We sat there on the beach for hours. Constance phoned for pizza and as Malibu burned in the background, the deliveryman came trudging across the beach with dinner. I lay on the sand watching Constance check for double pepperoni.

"You thinking what I'm thinking?" Danny asked.

"I don't have a clue what you're thinking."

Constance made another phone call, talked in low tones, and then announced that it was time to go. We endured a wordless drive back down the Pacific Coast Highway, with news choppers blasting back and forth overhead in their quest to fill their assigned wavelengths with images bearing the precious word *LIVE*.

We wove the winding thread of Sunset Boulevard for about ten miles, driving inland to the overpass across the 405 and looking down on endless beads of white and red lights inching in opposite directions. The sun had set and darkness rose out of the east above Beverly Hills. "I'm still hungry," she said.

We got through Beverly Hills and into West Hollywood, to the diner in the middle of The Strip on Sunset Boulevard, the one where the younger movie stars hang out between clubs, order cheeseburgers, and show that they haven't moved off normal no matter what kind of car they gave the valet to park. The whole place was artfully over-lit, loud, and packed. Kind of a cafeteria with money, where some invisible scorecard of life hung over everyone.

A couple of the girls walking in behind us had legs taller than some people I know, and the movie stars sitting at the counter pretended not to notice them. Cool ruled.

But when Constance walked in, half the heads at the counter swiveled. It was our first real insight into the power she wielded here. The young woman taking names for the waiting list looked up, saw her, and with arched eyebrows immediately escorted us past the waiting hordes to a booth beside the huge window overlooking Sunset Boulevard. Constance was the queen of cool, making eye contact with no one, ignoring stares, and pretty much exuding the kind of perfected disdain that makes people in this town desperate to be seen with you.

"It's only an act," she said before either of us could say anything. "I usually don't come to these places. I'm only here because of you."

"What has this place got to do with us?" Danny asked.

"I phoned someone. I'm waiting for them to show up," was all she said staring into the menu.

An actor who I recognized from some magazine cover tried to get her attention and finally came over. He was about our age, intense, and wiry. Everything about him was screaming money and cool; he was expensively scruffy; his jeans and leather jacket were skillfully distressed; and his hair shot out in all directions like spiky razor wire, something that would have taken hours to get that casual. He leaned into our table and, without even looking at us, said, "I need to see you. It's urgent. I've got two feature offers. Both shooting in October. I've got a decision to make."

She looked up for the first time, her little china-doll face framed by all that hair. "Phone me," she said sweetly.

"Maybe we could do it now?" But it really wasn't a question. Not even close.

She hesitated. The actor was aware that, in the midst of all that noise and rushing waiters, a lot of eyes were on him. He remembered to grin. "I'm with these two gentlemen," she said.

The actor stood up, looking at us for the first time. "Who are you?" It was as if he smelled something bad.

"Friends," I said. He was waiting for me to say something else. I didn't. He thought for a moment. You could see he was weighing the options. Or maybe thinking about all the cell phone cameras just waiting to be whipped out of purses and pockets.

"My apologies for interrupting," he said, widening that grin into something that did not match the look in his eyes. He gave the table a quick, sharp tap—which reminded me of an animal pissing on something to mark claims of territory. For public consumption he winked at Constance and then went back to the group he was with.

"He'll call," she said. "They always do."

Sometime around when the milkshakes showed up, I had stopped hearing whatever it was that Constance and Danny were talking about. All around us were young women, sculpted and polished into confections to be dispensed by the machinery in this town. I found myself thinking of Annie and not wanting to connect her to what I was watching. But it was impossible not to. Danny barely noticed me leaving the table.

From the other side of that window, out in the parking lot, you could see him hunching over the table like he was being drawn into whatever she was saying. I stood out there feeling a million years old even though we were the same age as most of the people going in and out. When Annabelle answered the phone and I said, "Hi, Mom," there was a long pause and then: "I just saw Annie and her sister on *Entertainment Tonight*."

"I'm fine too, Mom."

"Now, don't you go guilting me. I've moved past guilt. Living with Albert did that to me. The only blessing from such a nightmare. Cynthia has helped me see that."

"Cynthia? The real estate lady?"

"That was last year. This year she's a therapist."

"Are you okay?"

"You mean, except for nearly dying when the house slid down the hill? I'm fine. Thank you for asking."

"We already talked about that, Mom. When I landed in New York. Remember? A few days ago."

"Are you still in New York?"

"Not exactly. I'm on my way to see you. Tomorrow."

"Someone's been looking for you."

"Who?"

"That Mr. Jones. I told you about him. A nice man. Very clean-cut. The kind Annie probably would have liked. You just never dressed rich enough. That poor girl needs a man who—"

"Mom."

"I'm only trying to help."

"Who's this Jones guy?"

"He didn't say. He wants to talk to you, though. Such a nice man. I saw him sitting in a car outside here last week."

Something about this spooked me. I didn't know anyone named Jones. Or why anyone would be staking out my mother's place, waiting for me. "Mom, I don't know who the guy is and I'm not interested in—"

"I invited him to come back. And told him all about you. A real gentleman. And he agrees with me and Cynthia that Albert is a devious gigolo."

"Don't tell this Jones guy I'm even in town."

"He thinks you're a hero for fighting for your country."

"I gotta go."

"You have no idea how difficult it's been for me."

"I do, Mom. I do."

• • •

Back inside the churning diner, Constance followed me with those green eyes of hers, all the way to the booth. I wasn't so much walking toward her as being reeled in.

"She was watching you," Danny said.

"The window," she said. "It enabled me to go in."

"In?"

"Where I saw her. This woman you want to find. She is surrounded by people, all of them touching her. There is the color red. Lots of red. But then something strange happens. Someone near her dies under strange circumstances—"

"Who?"

"I don't know. But this woman, the one you are looking for, she has a mask. And it looks exactly like her. But it's not."

It must have looked like I hadn't heard Constance. All sound vanished—the voices, the laughter, the yelling and the fires of unmet ambition roaring, stacked high with the kindling of sculpted smiles all around us.

Or maybe it was because of the dancing eyes that hung just over my own portal in the darkness of all those mountain nights, a portal into a warmth I had never known before.

Or since. Annie.

And why was this guy smiling and shaking my hand after he gave Constance an air kiss and slid into the booth beside her?

"Eugene is the man I was waiting for."

"Constance rules," Eugene said, grinning. He was short, about our age, almost handsome in some vaguely Latino way, his dark hair as carefully in place as everything else about him. "Half this town relies on her to tell them what to do."

"Oh, stop," said Constance, pretending to sound irritated but looking pleased.

Eugene had no rough edges, at least outwardly. Unlike the others there, he scored low on the grunge factor. In fact, he was almost well dressed, wearing a blue blazer over a turtleneck shirt. He switched effortlessly into Spanish when the waiter came over, and then wove both languages together as he acknowledged endless drive-by greetings, knuckle taps, grasped hands, and other hormone-based codes of Sunset Strip as they flashed around the booth we were in.

"Constance tells me I'm your guide."

"Didn't know we needed one," Danny said.

"You do. Trust me, you do."

Eugene took about a dozen glossy cards out of his coat and laid them across the table. Names like Viper Room, Ivar, White Lotus, Bliss, Pearl, Geisha House, and Eden were among those that leapt from all that gloss and graphics. Across some of the cards was the inscription: *A Eugene Fulton Presentation*. "Clubs," he said. "I'm a promoter. I live in this jungle. And so far it hasn't eaten me alive." He was still grinning. "But give it time."

"Eugene knows this world," said Constance.

"Look, the first thing you need to know anytime you go into a club: Everyone in the place is miserable. They're all looking for love. And the minute they find it—or think they've found it—you never see them in there again. Until it doesn't work out. Then they're back, plowing the same rocky ground all over again. As miserable as ever and smiling like they love it. Problem is, all they know about love is that it was what made their momma cry while she was in the lawyer's waiting room."

I thought of Annabelle.

"I told Eugene I definitely didn't want you two going back into war without him helping you," said Constance.

Eugene gave a mock salute. "My marching orders." The grin hardened. "But tell me that this horrendous rumor isn't true," he said, "about one of you looking for the Boo Two. Anything but that."

· · ·

Out in the parking lot Danny stopped walking. "I have to go back," he said.

"Back where?"

"Afghanistan. Where else?"

"Go," I said. "I mean it. You have to find Ariana."

"I don't want to leave you here. Not in this zoo."

"Hey. If I can survive Shah-e-Kot, I can survive Hollywood."

"You're delusional."

"I'll be fine."

"They're way more vicious here."

"And what are you going to do about it?"

"Two days."

"Two days what?"

"I'll stay for two days."

•••

Eugene was a different kind of scout. Constance said that if anyone could get to Annie Boo, he could. He was as wired into that scene as anyone could be, and within a couple of hours after we'd left Constance and the diner, we'd followed him past rope-line throngs and been waved through guarded doors by human-wall bouncers who gave him the obligatory hand-clench and hug. Names like Deep, Nacional, Bar Fly, and Spider Lounge blended in with all the others, some of the clubs being packed and writhing amid shades of darkness with women in G-strings dancing on pedestals, while clusters of guys stood under them staring up and shifting around like chimps on Viagra. And still more places a block or so north of Hollywood Boulevard, ones that had potted palms, Moroccan-tiled floors, latticework, and rumors of George Clooney or Brad Pitt having just left.

Always, they had *just left*.

It was all sort of like being in the middle of a movable opera performed by a garage band. Stage props like Ferraris or sculpted women back from a weekend in Dubai were waved onstage as needed. Eugene was everywhere, serene and magnetic and cool. In fact he was the arbiter of cool, and when he met someone who did not possess the mandatory high-cool-factor, he passed judgment on the offender:

"When that guy eats he needs mud flaps."

Or: "She has all the grace of a cow on skates."

Or: "That guy's so boring. His idea of daring is to leave his umbrella at home."

He led us through VIP rooms, which were really just more roped-off real estate containing more guys with a need to show off in front of women who needed to be with guys who needed to show off. Actually they weren't really rooms, they were just open spaces with a rope around them because the aim was to be seen. Spending all that money to get in there wasn't really worth it if you weren't envied by the peons on the other side of the rope.

The VIP Bottle Guys, the ones who sold five-hundred-dollar or even thousand-dollar bottles of mediocre champagne to the men in those areas, were usually the best source of information, according to Eugene. They saw it all. Every club we went to, he checked with the bouncers and the Bottle Guys.

But Annie was nowhere. Again and again Eugene wove enquiries about sightings of the Boo Two into the rounds of hugging, clenching, air kissing, and all the rest of the rituals. No one had seen them for at least a week. Merely the mention of their name raised eyebrows on the men who were asked. But Eugene was as skilled and smooth as the army recruiter who had signed me up. Everyone wanted to talk to him.

It was only later that Danny and I figured out what made us so uneasy about him. "The Edge," Eugene said as we were driving along La Cienega in the quest to find Annie Boo. "You have to have The Edge in this town. Without it, you're just another fire hydrant for all the two-legged dogs of this town."

"What Edge do you have?" Danny asked a few minutes later as we left the sonic assault of Zama where it felt like the bass from the speakers was rearranging your vital organs.

Eugene didn't answer. He'd already gone on to rolling calls, as he called it, hitting the speed dial on his cell phone—*Ashley? Hi!*—and talking to women—*Tara? Remember me?*—he had met on the street or in other clubs.

He was constantly in motion any time we got out of his car, with some inner compass needle leading him straight to beautiful women, moving toward them in a long duster coat he sometimes wore for effect, occasionally finessing a huge roll of cash under it just for luck. "Rule number two: Cash, cash, and more cash," he said, looking us up and down like an appraiser. "You guys need some fluffing." That grin was back.

Fluffing, in our case, was some theme, some narrative as Eugene called it, that we needed to be more accepted in the clubs. Eugene was relentless. "What other clothes you got? You need to change."

"We're fine."

"You're not, trust me. You look like you've been up in the mountains burying a cat."

"Did Constance tell you about the cat?"

"More than one way to be a psychic in this town. Gossip is power. Get changed."

There was one reason that any further resistance to his demand pretty much crumbled. Speaking for myself, I was worried that all those months in the mountains had sort of desensitized any smell receptors. Not taking a shower from one astrological sign to another does that to you. You could smell like a dog in August and not even know it.

While he waited outside the Star-Brite motel, we changed into the only other clothes we had, which were the same fatigues we wore in the mountains but freshly laundered and without the jackets. We decided that our ratty, khaki-colored T-shirts would have to do.

"Think we should we stick a pencil through this thing and tell him it's a bullet hole?" said Danny, holding up his T-shirt.

"Sorta hate to disappoint him, don't you?"

But we did anyway. "No medals?" said Eugene, looking disappointed when we got into his SUV.

He kept pumping us for details about being combat soldiers. Both of us turned into verbal anorexics on the topic. Neither of us felt like telling war stories, especially here. Or anywhere. But he kept probing with all the *You-ever-kill-anyone?* type of questions. You could almost see his mind working with every question he asked, always angling for something.

"Hey Eugene, you looking for The Edge here?" Danny's voice was as flat as I've ever heard it.

"Found it, guys," he said. "Found it."

"Care to share?"

"You wanna know about The Edge? Simple. The Edge is publicity. Any kind of publicity. Good, bad, it doesn't matter. We live in a world of no repercussions. Outrage lasts as long as a cigarette. Shame is oh-so-yesterday. Lemme tell you a story. True. Swear to god. It happened two weeks ago. A dwarf, a real honest-to-god dwarf, about three-foot-something, showed up at Strut, a nothing place on Hollywood Boulevard. Over near the Roosevelt. Feisty little prick. With a woman about twice his height. An Amazon— he'd be going down on her just by giving her a hug. Gorgeous chick. Everyone thought it was a stunt of some kind. But the promoter, a guy I know, was smart enough to have them whisked through the door. He was also smart enough to know that some kind of freak show was going to break out. Turns out this woman was actually into dwarfs. Go figure. They really turned her on. And this little bastard knew that every guy in the place wanted to drop-kick him into the balcony and grab his gorgeous woman. So when enough eyes were on him, he gets her to hoist him up on a stool at the bar. He pulls down the top of her dress. Right in front of the whole place while the music is blasting and everything's going crazy. And he starts sucking on these enormous tits of hers. While she's standing there like nothing's happening, reaching for her martini and taking a drink while this little prick is doing his lactation act in front of the whole place. *Well!* Let a million cell phones ring! Is there a god of clubs? By midnight the place was packed. The guy I know, the promoter, went over to that dwarf and told him he and the Amazon had a free pass to anything in the club—the door, drinks, food, anything. He even offered to send a limo for them.

"But you know what? The dwarf and this girlfriend of his simply drove off into the night and never came back. The promoter almost tore the town apart trying to find out who they were. He must have called every casting agent in town, every porn producer, even endocrinologists for christsakes—can you imagine calling up doctors and asking for a list of patients who were dwarf tit-suckers? But nada. Zip. They'd just vanished. And after days of driving himself crazy, he looked out on the multitudes who'd packed the clubs he promoted for three days running, and realized he didn't need them anymore. Merely the rumors flying around that the dwarf and his woman might show up were enough to fill the place three times over. Now *that's* an Edge."

"Hey Hank," said Danny. "This is what we're fighting for."

I thought about it for a moment. "Sounds okay to me."

"Yeah. Probably."

And in a weird way it was. After what we'd seen of women over there?—those fearful slaves scurrying around like shrouded Afghan ghosts, dressed from head to toe in burqas, the steaming cloth prisons they're forced to wear, with only a mesh grating across the eyes?—even the Amazon-dwarf show was more civilized than that.

And in the end, maybe that's what it's come down to: We're fighting for the dwarf and his girlfriend.

• • •

"We're here," said Eugene, stepping out of his car parked halfway into the street as the parking valets swarmed it. We were standing on a street off Hollywood Boulevard, staring up at some old hotel that looked like Humphrey Bogart or Cary Grant should come walking out of it. It was one of those Hollywood Spanish places that should only have Packards or Duesenbergs parked around it. But instead there were Hummers and Ferraris fighting for supremacy in the valet pit and a rope line that looked like it probably went to some casting office.

Eugene never broke stride all the way past the bouncers and up into an outdoor pool area, where a skinny, tough-looking woman in her thirties was waiting. Dressed in jeans with a crease, a silk blouse, and expensive leather boots, she looked us up and down. "These them?" she asked.

"Certified war heroes," Eugene said, motioning to us. "Would I lie?"

21

We were told their names were Sari and Raquel. It was obvious we were expected to know who they were. One of them was famous for being famous and had a reality television show about dating. The other one was an actress whose career was in trouble, having rolled her car off Mulholland Drive into a ravine in full view of the pursuing paparazzi, and even worse, gotten bad ratings for her TV sitcom.

All we knew was that Sari was the taller one, blonde and attractive in an odd way where nothing about her face quite fit together, but it worked for the cameras. And Raquel was the shorter one, breathtakingly pretty in some scalding concoction of childlike innocence and jailbait wantonness. She looked out on the world through confused, haunted eyes above pouty lips and a rare smile that could change her whole face.

They were sitting at a corner table at the open-air club around the hotel pool, shielded from the gawkers in front of them by radiating layers of security and people who looked like they were paid to be friends. The whole place was a kind of fish bowl without the glass, with exotic creatures flitting all around while trying to act casual. The music was the usual ear-cleaving assault from the air that the partygoers called down on themselves. With woofers that almost had you checking your pants.

It took us both about five seconds to register the same unspoken thought: The Edge. "Hey Eugene," said Danny, "this certified war hero wants to know the fastest way out of here."

"Guys, guys," Eugene said with a voice that had lost all its humor. "This is all business, okay? You give me what I want; I give you what you want. *Capiche?*"

"And what do we want from you?" said Danny.

"His girlfriend. Annie," Eugene said, motioning to me. "You do for me—and I do for you. Okay?" It was meant as a question, but it wasn't.

Over at the table, the skinny woman standing behind her shot a look at Eugene, who gave her a thumbs-up gesture. The woman looked at us as if she was evaluating a purchase. Then she nodded to Eugene. "They're perfect for Sari and Raquel," she said.

"Who's that?" Danny asked.

"Carla. She's a god in this town. A fucking god."

"What do Sari and Raquel have to do with anything?"

"Hey pal, it's simple. You fall in love with them." We both just looked at him with a syncopated *Say what?*

"You gone deaf?" His grin was back.

"God, I hope so. Did you say . . . ?"

"That is precisely what I said."

"Fall in *love*? With them?"

"Oh, like this is hardship duty? Two women so gorgeous they cause chromosome damage just by being near them? And you're bitching at me? Every other guy in this place is trying to get into their thongs for christsakes."

"Hey, Eugene—*pal*," I said, "let me explain something. We came here trying to find the women we lost. Start. Finish. How's that for simple?"

"You're both idiots," said Eugene. "You don't really fall in love with them. Just make it look like you are. I told you—this is a trade, okay?"

Our blank stares sent him onto a new level of irritation.

"Look, lemme *'splain* something to you: This town is all about trade-offs, okay? All you have to do is agree to a little harmless PR. *'War heroes fall for stars.'* Easy! *Simple!* And then I get you to where Annie Boo is. Simple."

I could hardly hear him because of all the yelling that suddenly came from the end of the pool. One of the women had been pushed or jumped in. She was quickly followed by another woman, a tall redhead. They bobbed up and down as if they were arguing in the pool while flashguns from a dozen cameras blasted away. But something didn't make sense. Neither of them had gotten their hair wet and their makeup was dry. The dark-haired one had breasts that looked like flotation devices. Not to be outdone, the redhead made sure her skirt floated on the surface of the water.

"See? Now *that's* PR!" Eugene was almost hyperventilating with glee.

In the midst of all the chaos there was a guy standing off to the side of all the braying. He looked even less like he belonged than we did, but for different reasons: He looked like he'd just stepped out of an old fifties movie where he played the accountant. He had short hair, almost a military cut, and wore a suit, white shirt, and tie. And spookier, he was looking from something in his hand— something like a photograph—and then up at me. And then back to the photograph.

I grabbed Eugene's arm. "Who's the guy in the suit over there who keeps looking our way?"

"Are you serious?"

"Of course I'm serious."

"He's your friend. Why else would we let a dork like that in here?"

"My friend?"

"Jones. Said your mother told him you'd be here."

Suddenly Jones lunged through the tangled, laughing crowd, charging toward me. All I knew was that whoever this Jones was, I didn't want to deal with him. It all smelled like something Annabelle had cooked up in another of her New Age schemes to plunder with the blessings of the Buddha or whatever deity-of-the-month happened to be smoothing over the nasty bits around the edges of all the lacerating self-interest that made going to Afghanistan seem sane.

I was seized with some physical reaction, a fear of going back to where I had escaped years ago, as this Jones fought his way through the tangle of enforced spontaneity and missed Danny's pincer movement, a leg trip that sent him hurtling into the pool.

• • •

Eugene made sure we knew how he'd saved us—that he'd made those human-wall bouncers push the dripping-wet Jones back into the pool as we raced toward black SUVs that appeared out of nowhere. They came equipped with wannabe Secret Service–types wearing suits and talking into their wrists. As Eugene yelled like a cattle herder, we piled into an SUV and the whole motorcade took off. Driving west and then north into the hills like we were about to come under attack, everything flashed past in a deeply tinted blur. The streetlights barely registered through all that side window tinting, and when one actually did I saw something mounted on the dashboard.

"Tell me that's not a camera I'm seeing. Pointing right at us."

Eugene stared straight ahead, acting like he was deaf.

"A *video* camera? Eugene?"

"What?—you think I own all these vehicles? And hire these security guys? And drivers? Get real. We needed someone's help to pay for it all."

"What's that got to do with a camera being there?"

"It's from *FYI*—you know, the show about Hollywood celebrities. They own all the vehicles."

"What's that got to do with us?"

"I'll explain when we get there."

"The camera's moving back and forth. With no one holding it."

"Oh. Yeah. It's a remote camera—controlled from some studio."

"What studio?"

"Where *FYI* does its shows."

"*What?* And it's recording us right now?"

"We're almost there."

The motorcade screeched to a halt in front of a Spanish-style house on the hillside. When we got out of the SUV there were black curtains all the way up to the front door. "Why the curtains?" I yelled over the uproar of walkie-talkies and two-way radios.

"All the paparazzi are on their way up here. *FYI* wants an exclusive."

"An exclusive what?" Danny said and then, before either of us could say anything else, we found ourselves standing inside a round stucco vestibule, a kind of hacienda-type of place with a huge living room, brightly colored manzanilla red couches, and doors that opened onto a balcony that overlooked the city. The living room was filled with camera equipment and technicians racing around as several men in suits sat poring over legal documents spread out on a coffee table.

And lying on the lounge chairs out on a big balcony, smoking cigarettes and looking bored, were Sari and Raquel.

• • •

From close to the top of the Hollywood Hills, the city looked almost pretty at night. All the lights of L.A. lay below, twinkling into a haze-induced infinity. We were standing at the back of a big old house built on the hillside almost straight up above the Sunset Strip and oozing that fake Spanish-style charm like so many of the places here. From the winding hillside street, it looked deceptively small, a one-level, red-tiled house behind a white stucco wall. But from the back lawn it rose, floor after floor, up the side of the steep hill, each level presenting a tiled veranda or balcony to the vastness below.

Carla, the skinny woman from the club, the one with the boots and pressed jeans, came up to us. "Ah, good. Now we can start," she said in a voice that reminded me of a dull razor doing its work. When I shook her hand, it was like holding loose twigs. "We have a few legal documents for you to sign. Releases."

"Ma'am, I'm not sure you understand—"

"Look, we don't have time to fuck around," that razor doing its work. She had this weirdly carnivorous look in her eyes. If it came from a guy, you'd think you could be in a fistfight before the next sentence came out. It was pure, innate aggression wrapped in a carefully calibrated smile. Quite a skill. "Look, let me tell you where *I'm* coming from, okay? I got one girl whose series is on life support and she just got caught in a cell phone video fucking the props guy. And the other one whose next film will tank and who can't stay sober or straight for two weeks. So we need an image makeover. Clean. Wholesome—like war-hero wholesome. So you're it."

"We're not—"

"*Please!* We don't have a lot of time. I need you to listen to me." With that same look, the impaling one. You could tell that Danny had gotten to her with that expression of his, the one that said nothing was worth being taken seriously. It drove intense people like this skinny woman completely insane. But you could tell she was like that most of the time anyway. She was from the class of the professionally offended. "So listen, *FYI* will need an interview with you guys, war stuff and all that, understood? They're paying for all this *meshugas*," she said, motioning to the commotion around her. "All you have to do is drive the girls around for a day or two. We'll provide the cars, you go to a few clubs with them. And then after that we let *Extra*, *ET*, and *E!* to do a piece about them finding Mr. Right, and then tearfully waving goodbye while you guys go off to war—that is what you do isn't it? War?" She practically slashed us with that look of hers and then scanned the room. "Where'd Business Affairs get to for christsakes? I need those releases signed."

She vanished into the swirl of technicians and men in suits, leaving us with Eugene. For the first time, he looked uneasy. "Just go with it," he said.

Danny looked from him to me and shook his head with a weird little smile. "Wow," was all he said.

"Carla's a genius at damage control," Eugene said, anxiously looking toward Danny. "Oh, and I got a call from Constance. She says she's got something for you. She said she went in."

"Went in?"

"That's what she said."

"I want to see her," Danny said.

"You can't leave now."

"Hey, Eugene, I came here for one reason. And this ain't it."

Danny took a step toward the front door. "You don't get it: *They're* here," Eugene said, almost panicking as Danny opened the big front door.

The night exploded.

It was like the door was booby-trapped, detonating a blaze of light upon light, a searing white phosphorescent flashbulb assault on the eyeballs. In the millisecond after it subsided, a forest of faces shuddered out of the darkness, all of them bellowing and distorted like melted plastic suddenly frozen. Those paparazzi voices had a blast pressure all their own—menacing, pleading, ordering. *"Hey GI Joe, look over here!" "Hey Daniel didja fuck her yet?" "Hey, I did your mother last night. That's it, look over here."*

For an instant we were immobilized in that avalanche of flashbulb antagonism and noise. With all our combat training, with all our experience in high-stress, quick-reaction, life-and-death situations—and here we seize up? In Hollywood? It was Eugene who lunged from behind the door, slamming it. The sudden silence was startling in its own way. "Paparazzi," Eugene gasped.

Danny was furious. "Did you hear what they were yelling at me?"

"They do that to everyone. They want you to lose it. They get way more money for a photograph where the guy goes berserk."

"Yeah? We're out of here."

The skinny woman, Carla, had returned. "*We* use the paparazzi—*they* don't use us, okay? Control. That's what this is all about. Think of it as being in your very own shark cage. Fuck it up and you're just so much bait. When you walk out of here, you're gonna do it with Raquel and Sari. Now talk to the Business Affairs guy over there," she said, motioning to a guy in a suit with no tie. "He's got a release we need you to sign."

I went out to the empty balcony and looked at the lights while Danny found a leather couch, sat down, and stared off into space. No one bothered to follow either of us. There was still too much chaos mixed in with a kind of general free-floating attention deficit disorder, so no one stayed focused on anyone else for very long.

The prettier of the two movie stars, Raquel—was sitting alone in the shadows. I was aware of the smoke from her cigarette before I realized she was there, staring straight ahead. "Hi," I said. She didn't reply, sitting there manically smoking that cigarette, her arm snapping it back and forth toward her mouth in a kind of periodic salute.

"I'm not going to let you fuck me, if that's what you're thinking," she said finally, still looking straight ahead.

I didn't even bother replying. I just shook my head.

"You think that's funny?"

"No. I don't."

"Just because you're a goddamn war hero?"

"I'm not a war hero."

"Then what are you?"

"We're soldiers."

She said, looking amazed, "Then what the fuck am I doing here then? You're supposed to be a goddamn hero. I don't want to have my name out there with just some ordinary generic-brand soldier."

"I don't either."

"Well you're going to be a hero when Carla gets through shaping your life." She thought for a moment. "Just like I'm a fucking movie star."

For some bizarre reason I almost felt sorry for her. "Hey, if someone like me has seen pictures of you, then you're a movie star."

248

"Oh yeah, sure." It was the first time she'd looked over at me. She was one of those women who could project vulnerability and ferocity at the same instant. But the effortless beauty she had been gifted with pretty much neutralized whatever she was saying. For a moment, I forgot to listen. "What photos did you see? The ones when I rolled that fucking car off Mulholland? Rehab number one? Or maybe number two? Or maybe the barfing into a storm drain on Sunset?"

"None of the above."

Silence. "Yeah right." More silence. "I'm still not fucking you." There was a perverse charm to her wizened cynicism. It was like an old person's anger bubbling up fecklessly from a child inhabiting the body of a beautiful woman.

"I wouldn't worry about it I were you."

"Even if Carla wants it for the through-line," Raquel said defiantly.

"What's a through-line?"

"The story. They've got a whole story for us. Didn't you know? Scripted hour by hour. You and I sleep together for like three nights before you go off to war. I tell *ET* and *People* and *TMZ* how proud I am of you. I give some dipshit reporter an exclusive on how I realized because of you that I, like, needed to turn my life around and shit like that. Then in front of about a zillion paparassholes I, like, wave goodbye with tears in my eyes or shit like that as you get on the plane and go off to fight for your country. Wholesome shit like that." The cigarette went up to her cherubic lips in another of her salutes. "You mean you didn't see the through-line they came up with?"

"They actually have a script for all this?"

"Two. A second one if you get killed over there in . . ."

"Afghanistan."

"Whatever. And, like, if you go lights out, I'm supposed to go and meet the plane with your coffin. Dressed in black. Bawling. The whole fucking bit."

"I'm touched."

"But don't worry—if I have to go do the widow bit, I'll tell them how great you were in bed. How we'd just fuck ourselves blind trying to make a baby war hero." She giggled for a second and then went back that brooding silence.

"I thought only your movies were fiction."

"What fucking planet are you on? Everything is fiction now. On the set or off the set. It doesn't make any difference now. My whole goddamn life is fiction." She threw herself back in the big overstuffed chair. "Honestly," Raquel said to no one in particular, "this sucks." She lit another cigarette. "I'm supposed to drive a fucking Prius. It's part of the package. Carla wants everybody to know that I'm helping save the world by cutting down on greenhouse gas. She thinks it'll cut my probation time. What kind of car do you have?"

"I don't have one."

"What? You take the bus?"

"I don't need a car."

"Seriously?" She looked almost appalled.

"In a war zone?"

She looked confused. And then, for some reason, defensive. "Well, how the fuck am I supposed to know?" She sat back in the big chair. In profile she was even prettier, but it wasn't her appearance that in some strange way made her interesting. It was that vacant vulnerability, once the fierceness subsided. It was replaced by a kind of confusion that made you think she could almost detonate. "I don't like your attitude," she said.

"I didn't know I had one."

She acted as if she hadn't heard me. She sat staring straight ahead. And then suddenly, she smiled. It came out of nowhere. "Got any beans?" she said brightly.

"Beans?"

"Happy pills." When I shook my head, she giggled. "When I was in high school, I sold my cheerleader's uniform for a two-week supply. And some benzos."

"I didn't know there was a market for used cheerleader's uniforms."

"Old pervs love them. The smellier the better." A transient observation drifted through her thoughts like prey to be caught. "You know, Sari likes your friend."

"Yeah?"

"Yeah. She'll fuck him. She told me she would, back at the club. But she wants to hammerhead." She giggled again when she saw I didn't know what she was talking about. "Mixing Viagra and happy pills—Ecstasy. She tries to get all her guys to do that. I hated it, though. It was like fucking a jackhammer."

I just laughed at her. I didn't really mean to, but it was a spontaneous response. And amazingly, she laughed back. "I'm gonna get us a treat. There's got to be one here somewhere." She bounced to her feet, and suddenly she did a strange little shimmy, her arms vanishing inside her blouse and reappearing, holding her pink, lacy bra, which she waved in front of me. "Da-*da*!" she laughed, spinning around and throwing it over her shoulder before walking into the chaos of the living room, where lights and cameras were being set up. "Gotta go to the bathroom," she yelled to Carla before she vanished down a hallway.

I was left on my own on the big balcony. The lacy pink bra hung from a tall, red bougainvillea, regimental colors of whatever forces were doing battle in the interiors of her mind.

On the terraced hillside at the back of the house, Sari was hurrying toward the house, racing grimly through the pools of landscape light. For an instant she saw me, said nothing, and kept walking through the French doors on the lowest level of the house.

From somewhere below there was a soft clicking noise, the kind Danny and I made over in the Afghan mountains when talking was too dangerous. An almost unnoticeable glint flashed from the darkness near the end of the property. I made a single clicking noise in return.

At the end of the property, Danny was lying on his back, staring up at the sky. "Weird not being able to see even one star," he said.

"What was with that Sari? I just saw her barreling back to the house."

"Strange, that," he said. "She was saying we should mix cough syrup with cocaine and then get laid up in that tree there, but all I did was talk about Ariana. And how much I miss her." He squinted into the smog trying to see a star. "These Hollywood types retract their wheels before they get liftoff."

For a moment, the distant noises of L.A. at night had a strange music all their own. From up at the house someone called our names. Lying on our backs under the gray shroud of the night sky, we ignored the voice. "I was just counting up the number of people I ever really loved. I only got to two—my old man and Ariana."

"Hey!" The bellowing came from the top balcony, way behind us. *"Where the hell are you guys?"* It was Carla. For a really thin woman, she had amazing lungpower. *"We need you up here."*

I lay back again, staring at the gray shroud of the sky. I started counting up the number of people who'd heard me say I loved them. I stopped after my mother, my grandmother when she was alive, and Annie. "I only got to three people. You think maybe we're weird that way? I mean, shouldn't we have about a dozen or more?"

From back on the top balcony, all that lungpower was still shredding the relative silence of the night. Carla was getting a little screechy and yelling for Eugene to *do something*! "The photographers are getting impatient." We could see several security guys approaching, obviously sent to bring us back inside the wire.

And then everything changed. To pure panic. *"Call an ambulance!"* It was a scream that cut through the night. The security men above us instantly lost all interest in what they'd been doing as *"Help!"* came through the walkie-talkies and *"Hurry, hurry, tell 'em it's a goddamn emergency,"* was screamed from the balcony.

"Eugene? Anybody?" yelled one of the security men into his walkie-talkie. "What the hell's going on?"

The reply crackled with a lot of static for such a short transmission. "She pried open Carla's medicine cabinet. It was locked. She pried it open."

"Meaning what?"

"Meaning she got the fucking Demerol and injected it into herself. Along with some other shit she took."

"What other shit?"

"We think blow. Maybe sherm. Just get up here."

"I ain't doing the mouth-to-mouth again, pal. She puked in my mouth last time," said a security guy.

"Just get the fuck up here!"

We weren't even trying to avoid them anymore. We just pulled ourselves up the steep part of the property and stood on the grass, listening to Carla's frenzy and a barrage of sirens getting closer. You could hear her yelling that everything was okay like a kind of ringmaster of denial. *She's fine, do you understand? Fine.* We got back to the house about the same time as the paramedics crashed through the door, accompanied by sheets of white lightning from those flashbulbs. Raquel was lying unconscious on a couch, the silent center of a constellation of self-perpetuating panic. Carla was yelling orders and camera technicians and security people came racing back and forth with water, ice cubes, blankets, electric fans, hot towels, cold towels, and whatever else she demanded and then discarded in quick sequence. Several paramedics came barging in through Carla's screeching—"*There's really no need to*"—and went straight into their drill of pulse, blood pressure, heartbeat, and pupil dilation as their team loaded Raquel onto a gurney without paying any attention to Carla, who was still yelling for hot towels just to show that she was in charge. The paramedic pushed past her, wheeling the gurney toward the entrance. "Not that door! There's too many—"

"Out of the way, lady," one of the paramedics shouted as the door was opened and the night exploded all over again. The paparazzi were one seething organism, a roiling, contorted ball of elbows, screams, and faces that had become masks, festering around that gurney like a swarm of jungle insects suddenly discovering carrion. Police and fire department vehicles came screaming up as the ambulance doors were slammed shut and it lurched into the hillside darkness, trailing a multicolored tail of paparazzi motorcycles, blasting out flashes and screams, illuminated as it careened all the way down the winding hillside roads toward Sunset Boulevard, by the lights from the news helicopters that had taken up the scent.

The noise and the flashes receded, and within a few minutes the house was empty except for a couple of technicians putting the video equipment into shiny metal cases and two police officers putting pill bottles into plastic bags.

We went past the yellow *Do Not Cross* police tape into what must have been Carla's bedroom, which was a static avalanche of pink frilliness. Teddy bears and dolls like silent sentries guarding the framed photos of her and every movie star we'd ever heard of. We *liberated*—to use one of Annie's parents' favorite words whenever they stole anything—two fluffy down comforters.

All those months in the mountains somehow had changed us. Sleeping indoors seemed so unnatural, so we went back out to that grassy overhang, rolled ourselves in the comforters, and watched Los Angeles twitch beneath us.

The mere thought of Annie sent the jackals in my head scattering thought and devouring composure. She was down there somewhere among all those lights. I was fine, or sort of, until the memories came flooding back—the wind-whipped, sandy-blonde hair under the bandana being brushed away from in front of a smile that drew me in across the days and months and years since I had last seen it. And I remembered as if it was now the velvet warmth that came when her hand rested on my arm and gave me a sense of completeness. And then there were the times when all I wanted was to shut it all out.

"Hey," said Danny. "What was that business about us both being after the same woman?"

"Probably nothing."

"Yeah." We both stared at the lights some more. "I mean, that psychic stuff only goes so far," he said.

"Absolutely."

"Pretty ridiculous when you think about it. I mean, Annie lives here and Ariana's over there. How can they be the same woman?"

I'm not exactly sure why I had a need just to lie back, stare at where the stars should be, and then drift into sleep as fast as possible. We both knew that what Constance had said was somewhere between my mother's tea-leaf readings and some higher plane of understanding. Or a curtain neither of us really wanted to look behind.

"It makes no sense," was the last thing I remember him saying.

"Yeah, what does she know?"

22

Going to see Annabelle the next morning, I had to stop twice on the way to steel myself. Or maybe just to practise deep breathing.

I stopped on the bluffs of Palisades Park, that thin sliver of grass guarded by sentinel rows of skinny palm trees swaying like giant green sunflowers high above the nearby Santa Monica beaches, enormous fields of sand sprouting tourists and beach towels. It was almost the same place where Albert had told me that the reason people were crazier here was because ever since the Tigris-Euphrates, thousands of years ago, they had been moving west, looking for something better. And if the place they found wasn't good enough, they could always go further west. But when they got here to the edge of California, there was no *further*. This was it. And when things didn't turn out the way they wanted, the only journey left was in their heads. Which is why this is where all the nuttiness starts.

I remember as a kid listening to Albert tell me this and deciding that he was some kind of warped genius.

"Oh, you mean Mr. Pubic Head," said my mother when I mentioned that memory. This was not long after she'd yelled to the neighbor that her son, the warrior, was home. I'd just walked from Palisades Park to an old stucco bungalow near the rim of Santa Monica Canyon where Annabelle was housesitting for two months while the owners were in Europe. It took less than an hour for me to start thinking of reasons why I didn't want to spend a lot of time here.

"Look!" she proclaimed angrily, standing on the rim of the canyon overlooking the houses and trees down below. "A felony! Perpetrated by that waddling charlatan."

I looked over to the opposite side of the canyon and wasn't sure what she was pointing to. "I don't see anything."

"Precisely," she said, pointing again.

I looked more closely. "You mean that empty patch of ground on the other side?"

"That 'empty patch of ground' just happens to represent my entire life."

I thought about asking her if she wanted to rephrase that. But decided that it would be too much trouble to explain why.

She insisted we inspect that empty patch of ground. Which meant going into the garage of the house she was looking after and using the owners' new BMW. By checking all the possible hiding places in the house, Annabelle had finally found the keys to it a week ago, and now had the problem of the newly wrecked front right fender. "It's not my fault," she said, more or less aiming the car down West Channel Road. "If they had just let me have the car to drive, I wouldn't have been so nervous."

On the other side of the canyon, she parked on that empty patch of ground. At its highest point there was a view of the ocean stretching from Catalina Island in the south all the way up to Point Dume, the big cat's leg of land stretching out from the Malibu coastline. "You are missing it entirely," she announced in that voice intended to let me know she simply could not *for the life of her!* understand how I could survive even one day without her.

Below her in splintered contortions was a tangle of wreckage, a kind of massive doll's house tossed down a steep little hill. Broken walls, or what was left of them, gouged at one another. Splintered rooflines took off at random angles, and curtains, clothes, and a twisted refrigerator lay scattered around and partly submerged in the mud from the hillside that had collapsed. It was all stillness except for a woman's stocking, the old-fashioned, long, silk kind, that wafted from a tree, a pallid banner of a life once led.

"My *savings!* which that colossal runt fleeced me out of in order to invest in this catastrophe."

"Mom, c'mon, you said the two of you went into this foreclosure business as a way to—"

"Perfect!—the house slides down the hill and you're taking *his* side?"

"No, I am not taking his side. Forget Albert, will you?"

"*Forget Albert?*" she almost yelled. "He got the insurance money. Which he used to buy a drunk tank up in Malibu. It's making a fortune. Everyone wants in on the rehab business now. It's the wave of the future."

"Let it go, Ma. Move on."

"You realize this wouldn't ever have happened if you hadn't broken up with Annie." Guilt 101. Prof. Annabelle at work.

"Exactly how did you come up with that gem of logic?"

"It's obvious." She pulled a tissue from her pocket and dabbed her eyes. "I wouldn't have gotten tricked into this because we would have been all one big happy family."

I thought about that for as long as I dared. One big happy family. It sounded so strange. I couldn't remotely figure out how that would work. Annabelle, Albert, Annie, and me. "There you go again," she said. "Withdrawing. You do that all the time."

"It's called thinking, Mom."

She wasn't listening. "Oh good," she said, pointing to the other side of the canyon and the house she was staying in. "There's that nice Mr. Jones."

"Good?"

"You need to meet him. At least *someone* thinks your mother is charming and intelligent."

I could barely make out the man in a suit standing beside a large gray car, the same middle-aged guy with the jarhead haircut who was stalking us at the club. It looked like he was talking on a cell phone. "You keep trying to sic this guy on me. Who the hell is he?"

"*He*, at least, is gracious and polite. And he agrees with me about Albert being a worm." She waved a pink scarf up and down, looking over to where Mr. Jones was now walking back and forth in the distance. "*Yoo-hoo.*"

I got up and gave her a hug. "I'm outta here, Mom."

She looked at me, appalled. "Why on earth are you leaving?"

• • •

By the time I got back to the Star-Brite, Danny was sitting outside on top of his duffel bag. "We got a choice. I'm gonna let you decide," he said. "Choice number one." He held up his airline ticket printout. "We blow this town before it takes another shot at us. I'm locked, loaded, and ready to sprint. Or choice number two is sitting right over there." He pointed toward the taco stand across the road, which was now a hive of tweakers buzzing around, looking to score some ice, and one dazed transvestite hooker almost falling off his platform heels while lurching toward a pickup truck that had pulled over.

"Become meth heads and forget about everything? Starting to sound like a better idea than anything else."

"Not there. *There*," he said, pointing more precisely. A brand-new black Dodge was parked farther up from the taco stand. In the light of the setting sun, I could barely make out someone sitting behind the wheel, talking on a cell phone. "Eugene."

"You're kidding."

"I told him we have one more day here. He says he wants to make it up to us. He has something he wants to talk to us about."

"What?"

"No idea. He said he wanted you to hear it. I told him we'd phone him but he wanted to wait."

"Annie?"

"Probably."

My expression must have changed ten times before he turned and whistled loudly.

In the distance, Eugene jumped out of the car, still talking on the cell phone and waving as if we were old friends.

• • •

That night, I found Annie. Exactly as Eugene had promised.

All his spies, his sources, were telling him that tonight was going to be huge. And the Boo Two kept coming up on radar screens all over the buzz world.

"Yeah?" I asked as we were standing on the Sunset Plaza median, watching the usual nighttime caravan of expensive cars slowly cruising The Strip, all of them dripping testosterone out the tailpipe. "So what's the catch?"

It was the first time I'd seen Eugene look insulted by anything. "Man, and I thought I was cynical. Here am I, just some hustler who shills flash and trash, thinking wow—I have a chance to do good for someone, to help a guy fighting for his country. And what happens? I get it thrown back in my face. Okay, sorry I mentioned it. Let's just go home."

"Wait!"

About an hour later, when the night was getting started, we moved out. It was another Hollywood recon patrol, for me more hair-raising in its own way than anything we did in Afghanistan. I was so tense that once, when a car backfired, I almost dived for cover.

"That posttraumatic stress is a bitch," said Eugene. "I had it once in high school."

Eugene had worked his entire network: the bouncers, doormen, women who ran rope lines, paparazzi, and news crews. The word was that at one of the clubs tonight there was going to be a shootout between rich geezers who came armed with blondes. But no one knew which club was going to be the O.K. Corral.

"You sure you want to do this?"

"You know any other way?"

Danny thought for a while as we were driving. "I'm wondering if Constance isn't right about some things."

"Yeah?"

"What are you going to do if she doesn't want to see you?"

"What's that got to do with anything?"

For a while he was just watching the neon floating past the passenger-side window. "Nothing."

But we both knew it did.

Eugene was driving with one hand, dialing with the other, yelling instructions into two different cell phones, and writing notes while changing lanes and making illegal U-turns into valet lines. There was White Lotus, and after that, Dublin, where some star named Justin had a huge birthday party thrown for him. And Deep, a place in the old Brown Derby at the corner of Hollywood and Vine where the coolest rooms were converted meat lockers.

And somewhere else on Melrose where strippers danced across the bar in a tiny, packed club reeking of temporary exclusivity. Eugene worked the room like he did all of them, introducing us—*"just back from the war, both of 'em"*—in ways intended to score points with people like the gaunt, intense director of the biggest hit movie of last summer. Or the innocent-looking young girl from Kentucky who sweetly bragged about having worn out a platoon's worth of lovers three nights earlier.

In the midst of it all, I went back to remembering those old photographs I'd seen years ago, the ones of Bogart and Bacall and Clark Gable and Cary Grant and all the other old-time movie stars, elegantly decked out, dining in the Hollywood nightclubs of their own era. And wondered what they would make of it all.

Eugene wheeled around in mid-cell-phone conversation and made a trigger-pulling motion with his free hand. *"Combo!"*

Combo was on La Cienega about a mile south of Sunset. It was apparently the petri-dish club for whatever was going to break out between rich, powerful old men and their young trophy women— and when it happened, Friday was *the* night to be there. The limos were lined up outside like press releases. "Awesome!" was Eugene's seal of approval bestowed upon the scene as we cruised past. "No way we're driving up in a Dodge, guys." After parking the Dodge four blocks away, we walked past the longest rope line we'd seen, into a corona of news camera lights and paparazzi, restless for action, and then into a wall of security who looked like guys who'd been court-martialed at least once.

"Hefner's here. See that limo?" yelled Eugene. The long white limo with the Playboy bunny logo was parked in front of the main entrance, blocking just about everything else. It squeezed the overflow rope-line crowd onto the narrow sidewalk so that everything became crazier than it really needed to be as people pushed their way into view of the door crew. It was one of those go-figure moments—all these twentysomethings crazed to get into a place just because some old guy, an eightysomething, was inside with four blondes.

Eugene and the black-suited guy at the door did the knuckle-punch hug and the *these-guys-are-just-back-from-the-war* number that had become standard foreplay. For a moment they were deep into conversation, each nodding, then more grinning and knuckle-punching as the guarded door swung wide open for us, delivering body blows of bass rhythm pounding our innards from the huge speakers.

The noise in Combo was of the usual battlefield caliber, sometimes sucking the speech right out of your throat. Fake breasts and movie directors were duly pointed out by Eugene as they poked into one another, and the host of a cable network show trolled for the youngest women in front of us.

On a mezzanine balcony we followed Eugene to a place that looked down on the dining room, an island of status surrounded by the sea of foaming ambition in the outer areas of the club. The island even had its own perimeter, with plainclothes guards stationed at the wide entrances to the dining room, keeping out the peering hordes who surrounded it on two sides.

Below us, over in the far corner, in a huge maroon-velvet booth was Hugh Hefner, looking old and almost dazed as the blondes on either side of him laughed, leaned around, and shouted to one another over the din. "You're looking at history, guys," yelled Eugene. "He's slept with at least six generations of women. Now *that's* a man! And imagine what the first woman he ever fucked looks like now."

Eugene was already moving down that railing overlooking the other tables. Most of them had an older man in the center— sometimes just flat-out *old*, shriveled guys, warmed by the rapt adulation ladled out by granddaughter-age women whose bubbly proclamations were met with knowing smiles as an alternative to adjusting their hearing aids.

It all had the undercurrents of a desiccated frat house, where overpriced bottles of Mumm's were the entry key, summoned to the tables in price-is-no-object waves from withered hands.

The team of security guys in front of Hefner's booth used their iron fist-velvet glove finesse. They all stood looking outward at whatever was coming at them. One of them, a guy about forty, wearing the only plaid blazer in the place and looking like he would mug a Muppet, was particularly skillful at handling anyone who got too close to the big booth—*Hef! Love ya, man. You rock, man. Hey I got an idea for you*—The plaid blazer had a standard routine for handling intruders: a chiseled smile, a few cautionary words, and then, if that did not work, a fierce grasping of an elbow in some judo grip, causing the intruder's face to erupt as if he'd been shot through with a live wire that sent him scurrying back into the vast pool of unrequited ambition.

The security guys had their own choreography, sensing when Hefner made a move behind them. Almost in unison, they took a few steps out toward the center of the dining room, creating more space as Hefner was being eased out of the booth by the giggling blondes. It looked part of an obligatory ritual—*Hef's still got it!*— dance number with one or all of the blondes, like his energy level was Botoxed by those thousand eyes on him. And then summoning up a world-weariness appropriate to someone who has done it all—a legend deigning to mix it up with all of *you*!

But something was wrong, like a soloist playing from a different score. Every dance step he took with those blondes was completely off tempo, a sclerotic, jerky series of arm jabs and shuffling connected to absolutely nothing. It was as if the founder of the Playboy empire, the man who could not remotely remember the number of naked women he'd had standing in front of him, had suddenly come down with a touch of palsy. Looking out on the world with a rictus smile, as fixed and as rigid as a stone carving, he showed a kind of confusion. Suddenly, almost imperceptibly, he faltered as the blondes swept out like lifeguards all around him, throwing out safety nets of manufactured joy and *oh-isn't-this-so-silly* giggles as they steered him back to the booth.

"Bingo!" yelled Eugene, cradling his cell phone. They say *Bingo*? Even in the most grimly cool place in town?

"What's up?"

"That was my buddy at the door. The show's about to start. Milo is showing up in a few minutes. Let's go." He was gone before we could ask any questions, pushing through the crowds and yelling over his shoulder as we followed. Whoever Milo was, he was here to do battle! The challenger.

"The battle of the blondes. History in the making, man!"

Everything here was history, according to Eugene. But this was *primo*! Milo was apparently some old guy who owned a record company and started thinking he never got enough credit for all the hit records made on his label a decade or so ago. At the height of his success he'd thrown the obligatory political fundraisers at his Beverly Hills mansion, making lofty speeches, extolling virtues he himself had never lived by. But then the music, his music, faded, moved on, and what was left was a man who drew blank stares from maitre d's at the newest, hottest places all over town.

If fame had eluded him once, he was now back for Round Two, determined to out-blonde Hefner at his own game.

"What's this got to do with us?" And then silently answering my own question almost before I'd finished asking it. Following Eugene all the way down to the big entrance doors of that club, through the sweating, yelling jostle of hormonal imperatives, I felt a growing dread. I wasn't sure I wanted those doors to open.

Eugene could have been a mind reader. "The Boo Two are part of it," he yelled back to us. "Milo's latched onto Hefner's rejects." The big doors swung open and the light from a hundred tiny suns blinded us as we stepped into the maelstrom.

"Showtime!" yelled Eugene.

The challenger's stretch Mercedes drove up and the place went even crazier. Out of the back of the Mercedes stepped the first of five blondes, representing a kind of glamour that could have been dated decades ago if it wasn't for the validation of the frenzied yelling and the news cameras they provoked. For one desperate instant I clung to hope. Maybe Annie wasn't—

It all shattered, something sheer and fragile, falling away in panes in front of me as Susie Boo stepped out of that limo, as brittle, as perfect, as manufactured, as anything human that had been endlessly worked on could be. With practised breathlessness, she beamed to the crowds.

And then my dread knew no bounds. The dogs within my mind devoured the shreds of hope as Annie—or a sleek, vacant facsimile of the Annie I had once known—stepped out of the limo. I barely recognized her. The flashbulbs seemed to reflect off her like she was chrome. For an instant she looked dazed, forgetting to smile until her sister said something and her lips parted mechanically.

I didn't have the slightest idea what I should do.

Last out of the Mercedes was Milo, a little ferret of a man with dark, impaling eyes, a despot's smile, and a prosthetic hand encased in what looked like a sequined glove. The blondes, all of them, formed around him urgently like they were part of a marching band. As the bouncers cleared a path, they became a moving chevron with the little old ferret at the front where cameras from either side could catch him in profile, leading the charge of perfect breasts.

The chevron flared out, filling the space created by the bouncers who pushed the civilians back. The kaleidoscope elements of blonde hair, white smiles, and identical, red, form-fitting gowns blossomed on cue. Annie had her back to me only an arm's length away.

"Annie!"

And she turned around.

Was it joy? Or fear? Or maybe both on her face when she saw me?

The glittering procession toward the big doors of Combo suddenly faltered as Annie stood there frozen, mouthing my name into the uproar. The line she was attached to came to a confused, shuddering halt. Susie Boo, who was on Milo the ferret's other arm, saw me and fired off a furious look like something out of a nail gun. Without missing a beat, she tugged at Annie, jump-starting her back into the procession as the ferret looked around through hooded eyes for the source of this outrage, this scene-stealer of his grand and expensive entrance.

He saw me, and for an instant I could have sworn he recognized me.

"Good evening, Mr. Milo," Eugene yelled in a voice that was loud enough to be picked up by the syndicated TV cameras.

Only later did I wonder about this.

But at that one moment, inwardly crumbling at the sight of Annie, I could absorb none of it. I was taking hits from all the incoming images that made no sense in any way that I could cope with. Seeing this overcompensating little ferret strutting through the chaos with Annie—*Annie!*—on his arm, commanding the flashbulbs like forked lightning, I stood there with all the noise drifting away from me in a kind of silence of my own making, with music drifting into my head, only the melody, no lyrics.

But I supplied the words that no one else heard—*And the moon and stars were the gifts*—Except maybe Annie as she turned toward me again in that scintilla of time before the momentum of the ferret's daisy chain of blondes tugged her into the darkness of the club.

Of course! That was the music! *That* was what Constance was talking about. *Yes! But why are people looking in my direction? All of them?* It was only later that I could replay it all with any kind of coherence. I became aware of a finger pointing straight at me. Eugene's finger. "Here's our guy," he yelled to the bouncers. And everything suddenly seemed to be happening in slow motion.

The real tip-off should have been all the Combo signs that were strategically placed for good camera as I was centrifugally pulled forward into the gravitational maw of the publicity monster that devours what it has just destroyed.

And why was the ferret suddenly back outside? Nodding to someone? He was nodding first to Eugene and then to someone I had to crane my neck to see:

Jones.

Into that melee, guided by Eugene's ringmaster's finger, jabbing through the blinding white fog of the news lights, stepped Jones. I couldn't put one single piece of this damned puzzle together. *Jones?* Up close he looked like one of those old guys who use shoe-black on their hair. With a flourish that he must have practised a thousand times in front of a mirror, he slapped some papers with the words *Superior Court* into my hands. Like arrows rushing to a single target, all the news microphones shot toward Jones, his cue to intone morality like a Pentecostal smelling a conversion. I heard his words like they were being bounced through some vinyl sewer: " . . . he knowingly, illegally, and repeatedly downloaded music by Liberace, a blatantly illegal action and theft of music by downloading . . ."

And: "The Recording Industry of America cannot and will not tolerate the illegal downloading of music that is robbing the record companies of . . ."

And: " . . . this man is being served with notice of our intention to seek damages . . ."

And: ". . . asking for damages of ten million dollars for said illegal piracy of the music of Liberace and . . ."

And on and on until I started to laugh. Eugene. What a genius. An amazing puppet master.

And he was right. In its own minor-key way, this *was* history. Because here, in these first few years of the twenty-first century, an entire industry was crumbling—the music business—melting in the heat of a zillion illegal downloads by kids more nimble than the analog dinosaurs running the record companies. *Fuck 'em! Enough is enough! Sue 'em!* was the only threat these dinosaurs could think of, yelling from their cash fortresses built by the Beatles, Elvis, and all the others, at these cybertermites busily eating away at the foundations. It was a threat intended to spread terror in the dorm rooms of the nation, freezing fingers on the keyboards of a larcenous, ungrateful demographic. Find a few of these hooligans and make a full-blown-media-circus example of them.

Apparently, I was one of the designated hooligans.

Laughing probably made my situation worse. "It wasn't me," I yelled. "I didn't download a damn thing! It was Mr. Pubic Head." And it was. Albert. Using my computer while I was off at war. Downloading music for another of his get-rich-quick schemes. But no one paid any attention to me.

And: ". . . I want to bring in Mr. Milo . . . who graciously agreed to be here tonight as one of the most respected music pioneers of our time, in order to . . ."

And from somewhere in that thicket of microphones, I saw Eugene grinning a kind of leering what-the-hell'd-you-expect? grin.

What's the big deal?

Milo, the wizened ferret, stepped into the hungry glare of those syndicated television cameras, pointing that artificial, sequin-covered hand at me like a prosecutor skewering the defendant. "With this one subpoena, we in the recording industry want to call attention to the outright theft, to the illegal downloading of music, stealing revenues from the poor artists, the record companies, the . . ."

"Get real. It's Liberace," I yelled. "This is the best thing that happened to him since he died. And probably even before!"

Milo's sequined hand shot toward me again. And it all became *blah, blah, blah, blah* . . . in the midst of the roiling media where microphones flailed like cudgels of the information age and sun guns blocked out all the light.

The story had already been written, filmed, edited. Nothing mattered. We were all just shooting a script. The machine had to be fed.

So Danny decided to feed it. Really feed it.

He had been watching from the throng, yelling into that vinyl sewer words that no one heard. He shot a glance to me, and then when he couldn't stand it anymore he simply snapped, going full Canadian, wading through the bouncers, who stumbled backward, caught off-guard. And with one, almost rocket-propelled fist, he caught the wizened ferret somewhere in his middle, lifting him clean off his feet.

Milo looked like his shoes had exploded.

It was a raw, unadorned explosion of primordial justice. It was one of those moments you know are just *wrong*! You're raised to believe civilization depends on it being *wrong*! Vigilante justice is *wrong*! But I do confess to a terrible sense of satisfaction on seeing that multicolored projectile explosion of bodily fluids from the ferret's various orifices. *Mea culpa.* After all, the spectacle was essentially devoid of any higher purpose except to provide highlight-reel immortality for the screaming-segment producers who were already gleefully editing the sequence in their heads.

• • •

It took until almost dawn before the ferret could sweep aside the tatters of his rage and figure out—aided by his PR consultants— that by pressing charges against a war hero, the ferret would simply call attention to his own five marriages, bitter former employees, and nonpayment of royalties to old singers he no longer cared about. The real capper came when one of those consultants googled Danny and learned that he had been recommended for a Bronze Star, a U.S. Bronze Star. But by then I could see that Danny no longer cared what was going to happen.

23

Hours earlier, in the midst of that chaos outside the club, with Milo the ferret being carried to his limousine, oozing, gagging, and screaming *No pictures!* as the media monster devoured him, Danny, from a tangle of restraining arms and voices, nodded to me. It was a quick motion of his head, directed toward the door. It was the kind of gesture we'd sometimes tossed silently to one another in Afghanistan when words were a problem. In all that diversion he loudly provided for me, I stepped behind a jostling tangle of testosterone and slipped unnoticed into the club.

It was like stepping into my own private inferno, complete with a pulsing, heavy-metal soundtrack blasting through the red-tinted light and darkness that strobed through the throngs.

It was easy to find Annie. She was standing off to one side, away from the ferret's other blondes, who were laughing hysterically at something that held them together in a tight little coalescence. It was obvious none of them knew what had just happened to Milo outside.

I walked toward Annie from the side. She was in a world of her own, singing. Actually it wasn't really singing—it was more like a kind of belting out of words. With her eyes closed, clenched, she yelled out some strange words. It took me a moment to understand what I was hearing:

Dirty deeds done dirt cheap

It was lyrics that were blasting through the enormous speakers. They were from an AC/DC song I used to hear as a kid.

Dirty deeds done dirt cheap

I touched her arm. "Annie."

Her eyes clenched shut even tighter. Again and again she yelled the same lyrics, even when the music changed—*dirt cheap*. I stood in front of her, gently placing my hands on her arms. I could feel something seismic within her when I did. She was rocking back and forth in a tiny, pendulous motion, a magnified trembling. "Annie. It's me."

But her eyes clenched still more tightly shut. I waited. The lyrics came in drum rolls, identical and repetitive. *Dirty deeds* . . . Finally I leaned over, very close to her face, and said again, "*Annie!*"

She opened her eyes as if she was startled, breathing in bursts. Then tears rolled down her cheeks and everything seemed to let go at once. I almost had to hold her up, moving her back into a corner in the shadows. "I'm sorry," she said over and over again, until it too became a loop. Her eyes were glazed and the tears were almost bubbling from them.

"Annie? What are you on?"

"Please . . . don't."

"What drugs, Annie?"

Over her shoulder I could see the ferret's security team hurrying and herding the other blondes toward the door. Susie Boo was yelling and pointing toward the back of the club, but the ferret's men were in too much of a hurry. Stragglers in that herd would be left to fend for themselves. Susie was almost carried out by a guy who looked like a sidewalk slab dressed in a suit.

"Oh god, I'm so sorry," said Annie, her head sinking into my shoulder and her makeup running all over my shirt.

• • •

Danny had "liberated" Eugene's Dodge and tossed me the keys. Annie slept all the way to the ocean. The last store open at the end of Washington Boulevard, down near the pier, sold beach towels so I bought five of them and two big T-shirts, went back to the Dodge, picked her up, and carried her out onto the sand, to where it crests and then gently runs down to the surf.

She didn't awaken, not even as I was putting the big T-shirt over her—and over that red dress. In the near darkness of the beach, the dress still caught glints of light. As I pulled the T-shirt down, there was something that seemed right about making that dress vanish under it. The girl I remembered from somewhere near here, telling fortunes and smiling as she brushed away her sandy hair blowing from under a colored bandana—*that* girl would never have worn a dress that made light glint. I kept telling myself that. It was my way of looking for certainties where there were none. And at that moment, I desperately wanted certainties. However I could get them.

I wrapped the beach towels around us, a terrycloth cocoon that kept out the chill air that came off the ocean. I leaned back on my elbows, looking out into the obsidian void that lay before us. We were at the end of Earth, Annie and I.

She made little noises, fragments of words as she lay nuzzled into my arm. Then she was still again.

Not far to the south of us were the simple lights of the Venice Beach pier, the unadorned concrete structure that stood like the chrysalis of its gaudy cousin, the Santa Monica Pier, a mile or two to the north. That one was a whirl of light and color, bouncing through the night, the Ferris wheels and roller coasters circling to nowhere, a rouged calliope blasting its recorded mirth out across the waters. Annie and I were between the two. I lay looking from one to the other and then settled back, listening to the waves and remembering all the nights in Afghanistan when I'd prayed for this night to happen. And now that it had, with Annie lying pressed against me, in some state beyond mere sleep, I had no idea what was really happening.

I fell asleep like I usually did now, searching the sky for stars.

• • •

She was sitting with her back to me, looking out at the ocean as the dawn wedged away the night. The red dress lay on the sand beside her, like something discarded from another presence. She only half turned when I sat up. "I need to ask you something."

"Okay."

At first I thought she hadn't heard me. Then she said, "Don't try to save me."

I lay there listening to the waves rolling in for a long time. "I didn't know I was."

She reached out and put her hand on mine. It was the first real act of touching I had felt in years, and it caught me completely by surprise. This simple little gesture shook loose any defense I'd encrusted around some fragile, secret place where only I existed. A flicker of panic, of vulnerability lit up this refuge. Then the warmth of her hand brought a stillness I had almost forgotten.

She continued looking away. "I am not who you want me to be."

"I never wanted you to *be* anything. You just were. Are."

"I'm not strong enough, even for that." Her voice was so quiet the waves almost muffled it.

I reached around and gently tried to move us both so she would look at me. "Hey. It's me." I wanted her to see me, to know that I was smiling, and trying to keep it all from getting difficult. To let it be like it once was. She kept her eyes lowered and slowly shook her head.

"Bad things happened."

"I don't care."

"You can't say that. You don't know what happened."

"Is all this because of Susie?"

"Don't blame her."

"I'm just asking."

"I owe her."

"What do you owe her?"

"You wouldn't understand. We're twins."

"You're not her."

"Maybe I am."

"Is she the one who organized this Milo and his five blondes circus?" It was a word I instantly wanted to take back. But it had an unplanned effect. For the first time, she looked at me.

"Circus?" she said, her eyes trying to hold back indignation and failing. "Milo's saved us."

"From what?"

"I told you—bad things happened." I waited out her silence. "Susie's boyfriend went to prison. And all the things he gave her, the car and the condo, got seized by the court. And . . ." She was shaking her head. I waited. ". . . I was with someone."

With. The all-purpose word in conversations like this. Draining away all meaning.

"With?"

"He was the brother of Susie's boyfriend. He took care of me."

I didn't want to hear any of this. But choice was not an option now. She was turning away again. "What happened?"

"He was murdered," she said in a voice so faint the waves smothered it.

It was as if sheet lightning had gone off in my mind. I couldn't move. The words bubbled out. "He wasn't really a drug dealer. They said he was, but he wasn't." She was crying. "He was only helping his brother, the guy Susie was getting all the gifts from, and I wanted to help her. But it wasn't his fault that the guy in Vegas got stiffed. It wasn't him, it was his brother who did it."

I lay back with it all drifting away from me as the words kept pouring out of her. ". . . He wasn't a dealer, he wasn't . . . and after Milo paid off the people in Vegas, he took care of Susie and then me . . ." and in some bizarre moment all I could think of was that poem "Journey of the Magi," which I had memorized on this same beach over a decade ago. I'd crammed, in between waves, fearful of getting kicked out of the English class the next day, and resenting having to learn such gibberish.

And then, amazingly, discovering that I loved it, that I somehow thrilled to the images that the poem unleashed in my mind. The same images that overwhelmed me now, of the Magi discovering what they came to wish they had never learned. And how they could no longer be the same after Bethlehem and this *hard and bitter agony* of theirs, living with what tore down old certainties.

I remember sitting on the beach, seeing the Magi making their journey home to emptiness once they had learned what they did not want to know.

I should be glad of another death.

As should I now. Not literally, but something that would take me away from the devastation.

"I told you. I told you, bad things happened," she said.

Yes, you did, Annie. You did.

With the voices singing in our ears, saying
That this was all folly.

She had turned to face me, looking right at me now and wanting me to hear her while some drumroll in my head was playing out that this was all folly. But if it was, why couldn't I stop that sheet lightning behind my eyes?

"I wish you hadn't come here," she said. "It was easier remembering you and knowing that when I could get myself clean again, you would be there. I didn't stop loving you, you know."

"Maybe I'm not smart enough to follow all this," I said. It was my turn to look away. It felt safer that way. "I keep coming back to one word: Why?"

"I don't know."

"You're a free person. You make your own choices."

"Junkies don't think that way." She had gathered up the red dress and raised herself to her feet.

"Where are you going?"

"My mother still lives in the same place on the canal." A memory flooded back, the frivolous couple who had been her parents, seeking out self-involvement however they could find it. "My father died last year."

"I'm sorry."

"I didn't cry," she said. "You know, for a long time my mother used to ask me if I'd seen you. She said I should have stayed with you."

"We should have let the mothers handle it all."

"You think?"

"Annabelle never missed a beat. She kept a pipeline of *National Enquirer*s coming all the way to the mountains in Afghanistan. She made sure I read this stuff about you. And your sister. And sometimes afterward I didn't much care what happened to me over there."

"It went both ways."

"What does that mean?"

"Your mother would photocopy your letters and get them to me. No matter where I was, she could find me. I would end up reading them. I didn't cry when my father died, but I would cry when I read your letters."

Annabelle?

"Why would you care? When you were *with* someone?" I'd fallen into Annabelle's job—loading on guilt. And I instantly wanted to pull it all back.

"Because of a nightmare that always came back to me. The nightmare started right after I reread one of your letters. One day I would leave all this, I'd get clean. And go looking for you all over, and finally find you and be telling you how glad I was that I'd found you. And while I was telling you, a woman appears in the background with children and I just knew who they were before you said anything. And in my dream you were looking at me strangely and I couldn't figure out why until you held up a mirror. And when I looked in the mirror I was old, really old, and chewed-up and horrible-looking. And I looked at the woman in the background and it was me, but me when I was young, like when you first met me."

"And that's it?"

"Almost. I remember looking at myself in the mirror and thinking, 'This old hag doesn't deserve him.' And then looking at the other woman—in my dream it was me when I was young—and thinking, 'She could make him happy.'"

"There's only one of you."

"There's been two of me." She smiled the saddest smile I'd ever seen. "Gotta go," she said, slinging the red dress over her shoulder. I started to get up. "No," she said. "Don't."

I watched her recede across the huge beach, walking into the dawn. When she got to the asphalt bicycle path that lay like a scar across the beach, she turned around. "I'll come to you," she yelled. "I'll clean up."

"Come back now," I yelled.

"No. It can't work now."

She was right. I watched her walk away and imagined that I saw blood all over the sand.

24

I have found grace where I least expected it. Sort of like a flower growing in concrete, these things simply should not *be*. Because by all the laws of cosmic probability, expectations have a gravity all their own, some inevitability that allows us to believe we understand our tiny worlds. Sheltering us from the endless surges of uncertainty and surprise that could otherwise burn through our puny circuitries of comfort.

And so it was with Annabelle.

My mother, the sharpshooter of the emotional drive-by, leaving you lovingly mowed down, riddled with passing words. "Oh, I see in the *National Enquirer* that Annie is wearing diamonds now. Did you buy them for her?"

That Annabelle.

After watching Annie vanish into infinity across that endless beach, I went there, to that little stucco bungalow on the rim of Santa Monica Canyon. I still don't know why. Maybe it was all because Annabelle was my mother. Maybe that's the only gravity that matters, the genetic pull of one body, one mind, one history, acting on another. Einstein never came close to figuring that out. $E=mc^2$ is nothing compared to the planetary pull of a mother.

She was sitting there staring out across the canyon at the wreckage of her fortune, the shards of what she and Albert had bought lying there in temblor-loosened mockery. I expected another tirade about Albert. But there was only an unusual and serene silence as she sat drinking her tea and searching my face for clues that were obviously not hard to find. Neither of us said anything for a moment.

"So," she said with finality.

"Yeah," I answered, nodding. And that was all.

The silence went on. I sank into the leather couch, joining her in the view of the canyon. The light caught her face in a way that shed years, giving clues to the beauty that had captivated London and Paris way back in those analog days.

"You found her," she said. Not as a question. "I knew you would. You had to. I understand that."

"You win," I said. And I meant it. I couldn't remember the last time I had felt so depressed, so uncertain about what would happen next in my life. But as those words left my mouth I wanted to take them back. I felt like I was leaving myself defenseless. Annabelle could climb the riggings of your emotions, a verbal knife between her teeth, before you even knew you'd been boarded.

But something happened. It was my mother who appeared. My real mother, not the one I had known for most of my life. "There is no winning. There's only living. And we all lose. It's just life." She was talking quietly without any of the drama that always came draped over whatever words she spoke. "I've just lost something precious myself."

"What?" Usually I wouldn't have asked, learning long ago when not to fan flames in our brittle little forest. But this seemed different.

"My anger." She actually smiled when she said it. "I've lost it. Albert showed up yesterday. He paid me back as much as he could. Almost everything. I realized later that it wasn't the money I wanted from him. It was his badness. That was what I wanted. So I could be angry. So I could have a reason why it hasn't turned out all that well for me. A reason that wasn't me."

She looked across the canyon to the wreckage of the house. "I know, I know. You don't have to tell me."

"Tell you what?"

"That I was a lousy mother."

"Oh, stop."

"I'm too wrapped up in myself. That's what you're thinking, right? You're wondering why I haven't asked you anything about fighting your war and all that. You're wondering how you got stuck with someone like me as your mother."

"I wasn't thinking that," I lied.

"Then you're dumber than I thought. You're stuck with a mother who never figured out how to be a mother. I was too busy figuring out how I could get someone to take care of me." She walked away and was standing looking out over the ocean, turning away from the wreckage, her long mass of curls blowing in the breeze. All the theatricality had spent itself. "Someone who would just back off and let me go on making all the same mistakes," she said quietly.

That was when I remembered what I'd read somewhere: *Be kind. Everyone you meet is fighting a terrible battle.* "Hey, Mom, it's going to be okay." It was as if she hadn't heard me. She walked farther out to the edge of the little canyon where the view of the ocean stretched to infinity.

"Yes, it will be."

I waited for what was to follow. Nothing followed. "I tried," I said. "Annie doesn't want anything to do with me."

"Of course she does."

"No."

"Yes," she said with that Annabelle certainty of hers. "She does."

"You know, do you?"

Which is when she told me that she *did* know. It came in a confession of sorts—at first I thought it was praising the mirror in the way she did. But it was more than that. Because Annie was her. Didn't I see it? Annie was all that Annabelle once was. "Surely, you must have seen me reliving all *those* days? Through her? The days when I mattered."

I tried to see it. But like images overlaid on one another, Annie and Annabelle just did not come into focus as a single soul. Not even close. So instead I told her that I had heard of her grand days of modeling in Paris, of almost owning the 8th Arrondissement with her beauty, and fending off Greek tycoons bearing yachts.

Just as Annie, with her beauty was now—the thought froze me as it sifted into my words.

"No, no, no," Annabelle said so quietly that I hardly heard the word over the whisper of traffic from the distant Pacific Coast Highway. "I invented my beauty after I had it," she said. "Back when I was physically beautiful I didn't even understand the word." Then she did something she hadn't ever done before. She reached out and took my hand, holding it as if it gave her strength.

"I spent three years living in ways that no mother can ever tell a son. I had been in love with a man, an American who worked in Paris, who loved me more than I deserved. And because he loved me, I hated him, or so I told myself. Couldn't he see that I didn't deserve him? No, he couldn't see that, the fool. So I was determined to *make* him see it. And I put him through hell. For three years. Because I thought I was saving him.

"That was how much I loved him."

A question wedged itself loose. The question that in different words, over all the years, had flickered and then extinguished itself in the darkness.

"My father?"

She nodded ever so slowly.

"Where is he now?"

"I have wondered that. Every day of my life."

"It's not the same with Annie."

"Oh but it is. Don't let her do what I did. Find her."

25

We were hours away from having to head for the airport.

But there was no sign of Danny at the Star-Brite motel except for the handwritten note tucked into the torn aluminum screen on the room we'd stayed in, saying, *Back in the belly of the beast. Plse join. 12 noon session.* I parked Eugene's Dodge down the street from Constance's apartment and waited. Sometime around noon, Danny came shambling out of the building, his shirt flapping behind him as he loped through the daze he was in.

"You okay?" I said from across the street.

He looked over as if he'd just been yanked out of some fragile thought. "Naw, not really. You?"

"Not really."

"What's with you?"

I told him of my night on the beach. And he told me of how Constance had peered silently into that black mirror for what seemed like the whole hour.

We ended up on the other side of the L.A. airport, in Manhattan Beach, with its expensive houses jammed together in miles of California wholesomeness. It was Venice Beach without the freakiness, the family-pak of beach living, the amalgam of money and the quest for the eternal summer. But the bars on the streets that descended steeply toward the sand were good enough for what we needed, which was pretty much just a place to sit on some patio watching the sun get lower until it was time to head to the airport.

By two margaritas into the afternoon I must have heard Ariana's name a dozen times or more. Danny had suddenly become talkative in the way he got sometimes when he stepped outside of himself, when he didn't want to cope with what he saw before him. The other eight people in the bar, including the waitress, were drawn into rollicking conversations about everything from the surf conditions to their new betting pool on the beach volleyball game going on below them. First names were thrown around—*Jack, this is Tom and I'm Danny and this is Hank and that's*—Even the karaoke machine was hooked up, but against all their best efforts it played only the old Bee Gees song "Stayin' Alive," which they all took turns at mangling.

I sat back and watched, saying nothing until, just as suddenly, Danny sank into some other world, one that Jack and Tom and Connie and the rest of the world could never begin to peer into. About how it was his fault, he could have saved her, he could have stopped Omar from doing what he did.

"Omar came back evil," he said twice. "And I didn't protect her from him. Even Constance figured that out." It was that same old wound that just got ripped opened again. And again.

It was the way he talked about Ariana—dark-haired with big eyes, wild and fearful all at once, with her impenetrable independence tethered to a contradictory millennium of ancient customs. It was almost as if she was there, sitting across from us, sculpted out of pain and longing.

But I didn't understand why he couldn't—or wouldn't—see the vast avalanche of destiny that had come crashing down on him. He was fighting what had been foreordained. What she had been bred into. He was trying to change the immutable.

But then, maybe, so was I.

"Constance tried to bring her in today."

"I get confused. One day you think Constance and all that stuff is bat-shit crazy. And the next day you're simpering all over her."

"She's all I've got." He was looking slightly desperate. "How else am I going to hear from Ariana?"

"Yeah . . . So, what did she say?"

"Constance couldn't bring her in. She said all she heard was a baby crying. Oh god."

"Oh god what?"

"A baby."

"What's a baby got to do with anything?"

"You don't understand."

TORONTO

26

Omar had been gone almost two years. Danny knew that Ariana and her mother received letters he wrote from the madrasa in Miram Shah and, every month or two, a brief phone call. But he never asked what had been said, never mentioned Omar's name, or even thought to enquire how he was doing. It was not anything Danny had thought through; it was just what evolved as Ariana became so much more relaxed without the presence of her brother. There were more smiles, tiny jokes, and secret touching than he had ever known.

And there was the piano, the one that Mrs. Cach proudly pointed to when he met her by chance while passing her Polish restaurant on Roncesvalles Avenue. "She come back. She play. Only for me. Beautiful." The stubby finger was guiding Danny's gaze through the reflections on the window to the old upright piano inside.

"Thank you." Danny said it several times, staring through the reflections and not knowing how to explain to Mrs. Cach why he was laughing.

• • •

Ariana went back to the school and waited for the music teacher to finish rehearsing the student orchestra. He looked startled to see her, instantly remembering the way she had played. It had haunted him, he told her. And, he added, it infuriated him that she had walked out on all that talent.

"I need to keep playing."

"Then play," he snapped, peering at her through those little wire glasses that seemed smaller on his round, blotched face. "No one's stopping you."

"Yes." She never looked away, not even when his expression tightened into the fierce gaze that had intimidated two generations of student musicians. "I am so sorry for wasting your time." She turned and walked away, her footsteps making a staccato echo in the empty hallway.

"Wait," he called out before she got to the heavy double doors. She stopped. "I phoned your parents. After you walked out on all your God-given talent. And no one ever returned my call. Why?"

"For the same reason I am here now—in secret." There was something in her voice, some pleading mixed with defiance, that made him reconsider.

"How can I help you?"

They talked until the music teacher ran out of questions. She answered whatever he had asked, and then when there was nothing else to say, he looked away as if he was in a fog of his own thoughts. Then he said, "I'll arrange something."

A week later he told her that rooms could sometimes be made available in the Royal Conservatory of Music. The old building was about to be closed down for renovations and by calling in favors, he said he could get access for her. He did not tell her that in order to keep the rooms open after hours he would be paying the janitors himself.

Danny went to the looming Conservatory building next to the museum. It was a century-old Romanesque, red-brick structure, compacted and somehow foreboding as if tortured genius had been nourished in its gloom. Darkness fell as the music teacher approached from the subway station and entered. Danny watched and waited until he went in. After several minutes, Danny followed through the big wooden door, and after signing in with the security guard as *family*, he climbed the creaking stairs as if on some invisible thread that was reeling him toward the piano music coming from the only lighted room at the end of the high-ceilinged corridor.

As he had done several times before, Danny watched from the hallway. The music teacher sat on the only chair in the middle of the big room as Ariana played the grand piano. The music teacher would sit with his eyes closed, his head swaying slightly. Occasionally he would say, "Ah-ah-ah," in a gently scolding manner, and she would replay the previous few bars. He would allow himself the slightest of smiles and then close his eyes again. He was in his own kind of euphoria.

On this night, when Ariana had finished playing and the music teacher gave her his ecstatic comments, she thanked him as she always did, but this time allowing herself a smile he had never seen cross her face. After he had departed, she hurried out onto Bloor Street, looking for Danny, who would have been sure to leave the building just before the hour was up.

They were seldom together on Saturday nights because the logistics of the various cover stories for her were just too complicated. But on this night, Danny's mother would be away for a weekend of Pentecostal devotion in Montreal and Ariana's most trusted girlfriends had been enlisted and sworn to secrecy, a tiny network of the young and the loyal.

Wearing a headscarf even more concealing than usual and borne aloft by the joy that overwhelmed her from her hour at the Conservatory, Ariana hurried toward Danny's car. She looked around quickly and then got in. "Hurry," she whispered, and waited until he had turned south into the maze of the university streets. At a stop sign, she leaned over. "Wait," she said. And then kissed him fiercely, leaning across the console between them, pressing herself against him.

It was the sharp honk from a car behind them that made her release herself, slowly pulling back, smiling. Her eyes remained locked on Danny's. The horn sounded again and the headlights from behind pulled out beside them. She raised her head covering, shielding her face, staying covered by the folds of the headscarf until he turned onto Spadina Avenue, driving through the lights of Chinatown. He asked if having to wear the headscarf ever bothered her. It was one those questions he had always let drift.

"Yes . . . no," she said.

"Do you actually want to wear it?"

"Not really."

"But then why do you?"

"It's what I have to do."

"I don't understand that."

"I know," she said, reaching over and taking his hand. "You can't."

They drove to the southern edge of Chinatown where the lights were less bright. He pulled over to the curb, reaching behind him and holding out something in his hands. "Well, do you think you'd want to wear this?" Ariana took the little leather box he handed her; she was almost breathless, frozen. Then she slowly opened it and cried and laughed at the same time.

He had spent days worrying that the diamond on the ring was too small, and now watching her shake her head over and over again, he had no idea how to interpret her reaction. It was her tears, seeping from the edges of her large dark eyes, that confused him the most. They were so at odds with her smile, and the way she shook her head slowly, endlessly.

"What's wrong?"

"Shh." She pressed herself closer against him. "I love you. You believe that, don't you?" When he was silent for a moment, she repeated: "You know that."

He wondered why she was so insistent.

Only later did she tell him her fears of leaving the Umma, the terror of being absolutely adrift from all that she was, all that had given the structure of her life. "So we'll have to go away, far away," she said. "Where everything will be new. Where we'll be starting as new people."

"As far away as you want. It's no problem. There's nothing here." Danny motioned around him, thinking of the stillness of his family home, small, gloom-ridden, and empty after his father had killed himself. Danny's mother would increasingly spend days, sometimes weeks, away with her Pentecostal church group. "We can forget about the past."

She looked out into the passing traffic. "No. We can't."

27

It didn't look like Omar.

A few weeks later, walking along Bloor Street, Danny turned, jarred by the collision with a memory. The tall, thin man with the wiry beard that flowed down across white robes was almost unrecognizable. Danny could see almost nothing remaining of the boy who had been forced into the rusting Buick by Zadran's bodyguards almost two years ago.

Danny had stopped on the street, struck by some vague sense of recognition. He turned to watch the figure who had just passed him. "Omar?" he called out.

The tall figure hesitated and then turned back to face him almost as a necessary courtesy. *"Assalamu alaikum."*

It was the look in his eyes that unsettled Danny the most. The irreverent, hell-raising gleam had been drained off, replaced by some pale light that came from a distant place.

A few minutes later over tea at the Starbucks in the nearby bookstore, Danny awkwardly faced the austere presence seated in front of him. It was a facade, it had to be; it just had to fall away. And the old, wired, and crazy Omar would suddenly burst through with all that chaotic energy—*Bonnie Frangilatta, man, I'm tellin' you she's—!*

But instead, Danny found himself facing the uncomfortable fire of utter certainty. The specter across from him was only Omar in fragments. Something, someone, had replaced the Omar he knew. Now a man with a serene, unyielding gaze unnerved him and spoke in a soft, cold voice. The old stammer was gone and phrases like *In the name of God, the Compassionate, the Merciful* were woven into talk of memorizing the suras, all one hundred and fourteen of them, at a madrasa in Miram Shah.

"We're playing hockey tomorrow night." Silence. "C'mon, we need a defenseman." Meant as a joke, an awkward way of diving into what they had shared.

"I am here only for a week. I serve only the Prophet, peace be upon him," replied Omar, his voice barely above a whisper.

"Serve the Prophet and play defense." Danny found himself in withering range of an unsettling stare. And the disdain of Omar's chilling serenity as he explained—as if he was talking to someone incapable of understanding. There was something called a caliphate that someone named Maududi had commanded people like Omar to fight for. A kind of Islamic rule that would wipe out kafirs— people like Danny.

"People like me?" Danny asked, waiting for the punch line.

"Yes," said Omar with that unbroken gaze.

Danny waited.

"Unless you submit," said Omar.

"To what?"

"La ilaha illa Allah."

"Oh well, that explains everything," Danny said, hoping to summon up the old Omar.

"There is no God but Allah."

Danny said nothing, choosing to focus on the prayer beads that were circling through Omar's hand, the only part of him that was not perfectly still. The stare that Omar held until he turned around in the chair and saw only two women and a man standing nearby at the magazine shelves. "This is the work of Satan. I cannot stay."

"Hey Omar, it's me, Danny, you're talking to. What's with this Satan business?"

"*Haram,*" he said, motioning to the readers. *Forbidden.*

"Reading *People* magazine? Or *National Geographic*?"

Silence. Omar reached into a satchel and pulled out a DVD case. Looking closer, Danny could make out the images on the box cover of the DVD.

"Is that what I think it is?"

"What do you think it is?" Omar asked with a slit of a smile.

"A photograph of dead people. And something that got blown up."

"Nairobi. We blew up the American embassy. And also their embassy in Tanzania. On the same day."

"We?"

"*Allahu Akbar.*"

"We?"

"'Then when the sacred months are drawn away, slay the idolaters,'" Omar said, his eyes drifting as he summoned up what he had memorized, "'wherever you find them and confine them and lie in wait for them at every place of ambush.'"

"What the hell is that supposed to mean?"

"Al-Taubah 9:5," said Omar, as if that settled any possible debate.

"That's it?" Danny took one of the DVDs and looked at the cover photograph more closely. Through the smoke and confusion, bodies of Africans were scattered through the rubble.

"Keep it. It's yours. A present."

Danny stared at the DVD, about to push it back across the table toward Omar. He changed his mind and kept his hand on it. "Will I like it?"

"Maybe. Maybe not." Then in a low, sharp voice: "I learned many things from the Zadranis. Some was from Pacha Khan Zadran. He is a military genius. I revere him for how he plays men like instruments. And other things I learned from a scholar, my teacher in Miram Shah. He told us that for centuries we have been fools—like wolves in the freezing mountains who are trapped by cunning men who leave a bloody knife for them to find. The wolf is driven crazy by the smell of the blood and pounces on it, licking the blood, which it loves. But it does not notice that the knife is slashing its own tongue and the blood, which now pours onto the knife, is its own. And the more blood it gets, the more it is dying, bleeding to death from its own stupidity and greediness." Omar pointed to the magazines. "This is just one of the bloody knives left for us by the cunning men of the West. But we are finished with all that now. We are the ones with the knives."

"We?"

"You will know soon, my Danny." Omar looked around. "It's late. And I have family business."

Danny would later wonder about the way Omar looked at him when he asked, "What business?"

"Business. Zadran and my father are making a trade." He turned and walked away and as he went, Danny was struck by the way his robes flowed and caught the light of the late afternoon sun.

Danny went home, unsure of what of he had just been told. He tried to contact Ariana using their new e-mail accounts, and after several hours of getting no response, tore his memory apart wondering what he had missed in the talk with Omar.

My Danny?

That night Danny was overrun by fears he could no longer smother. Ariana still had not e-mailed him. He waited, paced, and raged against himself for not asking her to marry him months ago. Before Omar. Before this video. Eighteen bloody minutes of executions, carnage, and bombings interspersed with brightly colored lens flares as an attempt at artistry. All of it accompanied by prayers and cries of angry joy in a language he could not understand.

Hours later, she still had not responded.

The waiting and the pacing goaded him to do something, *anything*. Whatever was happening, Omar just had to be somehow involved. He reactivated an old code, the one he and Omar had used years ago for meetings. Over and over again he let the phone ring once and then hung up. Then he waited for his own phone to ring once, anywhere from one to five minutes later—each minute representing the hours until the meeting with Omar. Finally, his phone rang once, less than a minute after his last call.

He waited in the deserted parking lot of the restaurant on the hill in High Park. The wind in the trees on the hill was howling in a way that first irritated, and then chilled. He thought of the howling winds in "The Legend of Sleepy Hollow" with its Headless Horseman thundering along the roads.

It was this specter of decapitation that sent waves of scalding images hurtling through instincts long atrophied by civilization. It was the head on the pole. At least, that's what it looked like on that website. The one in the video. *Allahu Akbar!*—the cry that came with the bloody human head swiveling at the will of whoever held the pole. Or was it even real?

He waited. Walking back and forth through a darkness intermittently fought off by a palsied streetlight, flickering out of place in the huge park. The wind tore through the trees at will.

Omar arrived. He appeared in the distance as a visage in white, almost floating through the darkness of a far-off hilltop, his long robes flying like a banner around him. "Ah, you waited, my Danny!"

My Danny. That there is no *my* anything remained unsaid. And Danny did not even attempt to match the same slit smile that Omar flashed across the darkness. "What is it you want?"

"Remember a couple of years ago? When one of us made the coded phone call? It wasn't because anyone wanted anything. It was just the signal for meeting."

"Things are different now."

"I didn't understand anything you told me today."

Omar smiled in that way he had. But to Danny, it was a smile that didn't reach his eyes. "Perhaps because when the truth is revealed, only an infidel would not understand."

"And you know the truth now?"

"*I took shahada. And I follow* in the footsteps of the Prophet, peace be upon him."

"Then what's with that DVD you gave me? And that website?"

"It is the way of the Salaf."

"Hey Omar, help out the infidel here—speak normal English. Instead of all the jargon."

"Ah, my Danny. How you have changed."

"*Me?* You go over there to spend two years memorizing some junk—"

Omar's hand flashed to Danny's arm in a pincer grip. "Do not blaspheme, I warn you." The smile was gone.

Danny shook loose. "You come back practically a fucking Nazi? Telling me to watch a video that shows some guy getting his head cut off?"

"Ah, I see. Danny, Danny. We had no choice. The man was against jihad, and providing information to our enemies in Kandahar, and—"

"Oh Jesus Christ. C'mon, Omar, tell me it was all staged or something—"

"You blaspheme even as an infidel."

"That scene where the guy's head was being cut off? And you're standing there in the background? It *was* you."

"Is there a point to all this?"

"Oh, probably not. Or maybe that somewhere in our old schoolbooks it said that heads getting cut off was something out of the Middle Ages, and wow, aren't we all civilized now."

"There was no choice. The man was in the pay of the enemies of Allah. We went across the mountains to where he was betraying us and would not repent."

"We?"

"My father is very powerful there. And now, thanks be to Allah, he and the Zadrans are as one. My father is helping to train Salafist warriors."

"Training them to do what? Wipe out ten centuries?"

Omar stepped up on a small concrete parking divider, rising past his full height, making him taller than Danny and more visibly powerful, with a strength made menacing at will. "Danny, Danny,

I hear this pain in you. The days we had together were what you would call 'fun.' And I won't lie to you, Danny—I loved this 'fun' we had, the way that fools love what poisons them. It is this 'fun' that all of you here in these countries need like a drug. It stops you from thinking of your emptiness. It is an emptiness that is like pollution, sewage, and you have tried to drown us in it."

"Hey Omar, no one's ordering you to go to Disneyland, watch MTV, or cheer for the Yankees."

"Ah, Danny, Danny."

"Joy and happiness are only an option, Omar. No one's forcing it on you guys."

"I pity you, Danny." Omar turned and walked across the grass leading to the treed hillcrest. He stopped. The smile held, but barely. "My father and I understand each other now."

"I'm happy for you."

"Why have you been wasting my time? You just want to know about her, don't you? That's the real reason you contacted me tonight, isn't it?"

Danny froze, fighting the breathlessness that surged through him. "Her?"

"Aha. I was right." Omar was walking toward the crest of the hill that overlooked Grenadier Pond. "The wedding," he called out.

It was an invisible tether that suddenly snapped. Danny spun around and confronted the renewed slit of a smile, gleaming in the night. "What wedding?"

Omar just smiled.

• • •

Now!!!! Where streetcars turn!

When her e-mail came hours later, he was staring into the screen, fighting off sleep by occasionally tapping the keyboard to keep his computer from going dark. He raced out into the rain, skidding through the remains of a yellow traffic light, his car fishtailing onto the wide road near the lake and racing toward where four streets converged at jagged angles and the streetcars from downtown turned north.

She had never been able to meet him anywhere near this late. It was almost midnight. *Now!!!!* Whatever was driving them both into the night appeared as jumbled fears beyond the rain-swept windshield—the emptiness of the streets and the figures in doorways that vanished when he looked a second time. At the junction of the four streets converging, just east of the big hospital, some synaptic alarm system was tripped in the rain-lashed streets that usually had life stumbling through them. Now there was only the silence of a night where usually the clanging trolleys, the horns, the drunks, and the Parkdale hookers were all heard in their own loud arias.

He turned onto Queen Street and idled without headlights, searching the shadows and the neon reflections shimmering across the slickness of the pavement. Then getting out of the car, his hand warding off the rain driving into his eyes, shapes and colors merged in watery convolutions that yielded nothing.

Until, in the distance, he saw her. Huddled under the edge of a roof at the old streetcar barn, at the far edges of the geometric collision of streets. For a moment he wasn't sure; he had never seen her on the streets without a headscarf. *Ariana!*—the wind sucked his voice out of the air. She was grasping onto what looked like a backpack and some clothes. He began running toward her, using parking meters to pivot onto the street, slipping and careening across it with headlights bearing down and then suddenly slowing as he stumbled once, pushing off against the sides of parked cars, yelling into the wind.

He could see her coming toward him. At first hurrying, but then suddenly stopping and motioning wildly with her arms. His shadow from the headlights behind him became sharper. It was etched as if some magnetic force of light would not release him until it vanished in that instant before a violently opening car door was slammed into his back, sending him crashing to the road.

Lights and the voices spun into jagged strands of consciousness. He was picked up and slammed back onto the street, barely able to form thoughts as boots appeared near his face, were cocked, and then fired into his ribs. Voices and more lights ripped through volleys of pain as he rolled away from the boots, lurching up and grasping a side mirror, catching the last glimpse of Ariana with hands clamped over her mouth as she was forced into the other vehicle, a van with no windows.

He screamed out her name, or part of it before the fist drove into the back of his neck and Omar smiled down at him, drenched and filthy on the road. "Ah, my Danny. You are so lucky. I should have killed you for what you have done to our family."

Danny struggled to get up until the boot came down again.

"You serve a purpose. Thank you. Alive, you are why she will be quiet when we take her."

"Take—"

"Take. She knows you can be killed. If she behaves badly."

The silence returned as the sounds and the lights raced away, the van's tires spinning in a rain-sizzled whir as it roared almost over him while he called out her name from where he lay in the street.

And when he was found, he was barely aware of the blue lights of the ambulance that were blasting across his eyes in a pain coming from somewhere far away.

• • •

St. Joseph's Hospital, about a mile away, had a series of rigid protocols for checking a patient out of its care. Danny observed none of them. When he awoke from the narcotic-induced sleep, he felt the bandages around his ribs and the plaster on the cast on his arm, making sure it had hardened. He groped for his clothes in the locker. Stumbling out some back entrance, fighting off orderlies, he kept going up to Sunnyside Avenue, circling back.

Always circling back. Groping toward Jameson Avenue, asking passersby what day it was, what time it was. Tuesday. *Tuesday?* Early evening.

But standing in front of the apartment, and feeling the pain arcing through his right arm, he had no idea what to do next. He walked into the wheezing elevator, pressed 8, and when it opened again, he went to the apartment they all lived in, knocking on the door.

A muffled voice sounded from inside. The door remained closed. He knocked several more times. Finally it opened, and Ariana's mother, looking more ancient than he remembered her, peered up at him.

"Ariana? Is she here?"

"No. No here."

"Omar? Is he here?"

"No. Omar no here."

"Where?"

"Where?" She did not understand the word.

Danny tried again, shrugging this time.

"They go. All go."

"Go where?"

"Miram Shah. Go Miram Shah." She made a fluttering airplane motion with her hand.

"When?"

"Today. Go today."

Danny felt the floor falling away beneath him.

"Marry. She marry."

• • •

Almost a week later, Danny wrote *family* next to his name in the after-hours registry of the Conservatory. Then he climbed the creaking stairs and went to the silent, lighted room at the end of the high-ceilinged corridor. The music teacher was seated in the single chair in the middle of the big room. Unlike the last time he was there, Danny entered the room. The music teacher, who had seen Danny before but never acknowledged him hovering in the shadows, peered through his little wire-rimmed glasses.

Danny was haggard and disheveled. He walked slowly up to the piano, touched it, and then stood there as if he was waiting for it to start playing on its own.

"Is something wrong?"

It took Danny a long time to answer. "They took her," was all he could think of as a response. "She'll be in Afghanistan by now. Maybe Pakistan."

The music teacher looked at the floor for a while. "I see." An infinite sadness had settled over him. Then he got up and slowly left the room. Danny remained, turning out the lights and sitting on the floor beside the piano, where he talked to Ariana as if she was there. After a while he absent-mindedly reached up and tapped one of the keys. The single note sounded several times.

He felt the key more closely. The top of it was loose. He was sure it was a sign. On his knees he examined it, wiggling the flat, ivory-colored surface until it loosened some more. Definitely a sign. He kept loosening the piano key until the top of it came away in his hands. The broken music. He apologized silently to the gods of music and held the smooth rectangle between his hands.

The next morning Danny woke up under the piano, still holding the top of the key. He left, walking through the corridors, hearing a different sound. It was harsher, urgent voices coming from a television set in one of the offices. A small cluster of people was huddled around it, some letting out groans or gasps.

The Twin Towers in New York were on fire. Danny stayed until the first one crumbled.

Then he got a phone book, looked up an address, and an hour later was at an armed forces recruiting center. When he was asked why he wanted join up, he said simply, "To find the woman I love."

The recruiter asked the question again, got the same answer, and then wrote *For patriotic reasons* on the application form.

And then asked Danny to sign the form.

THE MOUNTAINS

28

We got back to Afghanistan sixteen days after we left. Bagram was my first stop and then the smaller base in Khost, over against the mountains leading to Pakistan. Danny got to Kandahar at about the same time. It would be six more weeks before I got out of the base at Khost, linking up with him and the Princess Patricias, who were OpConned to our brigade on an operation in the mountains.

By then I was glad to get out of Khost; the mortar attacks from the Taliban were relentless. Entire nights were spent wondering when some overheated little ball of death would fall out of the darkness and reconstitute your earthly presence as a fine spray and a few chunks. You got to know how close you were to that fate by listening to a strange whistling sound turn into a sharp *fffft!* sound just before the mortar exploded. The sharper the whistling *fffft!*, the closer you were to becoming spray and chunks.

For an added treat, they used 107mm rockets that landed inside the base, beginning sometime around midnight. They were like alarm clocks from hell—just when you gave in to exhaustion and drifted off to sleep, *wheeeeee-BLAAAM!* and you'd be shot out of exhausted stupor, stumbling for cover, not knowing up from down. By the time the tenth one fell just before dawn, conscious thought had been shredded worse than the supply tent on the west side of the base.

The whole California interlude seemed like a hallucination to me, as if I'd dreamed it. Everything in my existence was in play now. I couldn't figure out what I was doing back there; in those sixteen days I'd lost the adrenaline-fueled rhythm of war that I'd left with. In its place were memories of Annie that could seep into the most tightly sealed vaults of my mind like a mist.

And the war had changed too. Maybe it took leaving it for me to notice what was really happening. What had been a wild, mostly improvised attack on the fourteenth century was more than ever becoming the Big Army war, rappelling the sheer face of a thousand-year-old culture with systems analysis, massive numbers, and Burger Kings. And all of it eternally dependent on the raw courage demanded of those few who went outside the wire.

The roaming of the mountains as Danny and I had done was more difficult now. The command structures in the field were hardening by the month. Vertical Integration was fusing paper trails from the Gods of Tampa down to the lowliest grunt. What we had done only a couple of months earlier was still barely possible, but only when official backs were turned. Or, when the very edges of a court-martial were tested. Which was what Danny was in the early stages of doing.

Looking out from the Chinook, descending onto the single-ship LZ about eighty kilometers west of Miram Shah, there were signs of what was to come. Strapped into a seat on the side of the big helicopter, I'd drifted into some altered state brought on by the roar of those two screaming engines over our heads. The quilted ceiling billowing slightly above us did nothing to keep out the noise. I was suddenly aware of hands motioning to me. Some of the other Rakkasans were trying to get my attention, pointing to the door gunner, a skinny kid manning a machine gun and waving me over toward him. I stumbled across the metal floor, and holding on to the webbing, I knelt beside him.

"Pilot wants to know if you're the guy who was with the Canadians," he screamed through the roar. I nodded to him and he said something into his intercom. "Hold on," he shouted to me a moment later and then the Chinook banked to the right. "Coming up at about four o'clock!" He was pointing to something below us, something standing up on the edge of the LZ. "Pilot wants to know what'n hell that is." I told him and he looked at me strangely.

Then he clicked on his intercom and yelled, "Sir? He says it's some guy named Liberace."

There was still something different about Danny. He loped out of nowhere, like some camouflaged dust devil arriving just in time to save Liberace from being blown into the next valley. Even from a distance I could see the piano key hanging from a chain around his neck. It swung out around him like the talisman it was.

"She's always here with me," he said, holding the piano key up with his crooked finger after the Chinook had landed and we were laughing just from seeing each other again.

"Liberace would understand that."

"Of course he would. I feel that piano key on my skin and then I know why I'm still fighting. He's the same. Just look at him." Liberace beamed in that same prancing leg kick he'd been doing for the whole war.

Danny took a laminated contour interval map out of his rucksack and spread it out on the ground. "Ratlines!" he said exuberantly in some way that made no sense. He was almost laughing. "Your Special Forces guys gave us a company-level briefing last night." He was pointing to a contour line. "We're here. And there's a ratline right here." His crooked finger had moved across the map, pointing to a town called Neka, and then tracing a route almost from where we were, through the mountains and into Pakistan.

Ratlines were what some of our guys had started calling the unmarked routes through the mountains between the two countries. They were sort of the Ninjas' highways, which meant that at best they were glorified goat trails through hellish terrain that no sane person would ever want to be on. But the Taliban used them all the time, moving in whatever direction suited them at the moment.

"Almost an entire tribe is on the move."

Suddenly I knew where this strange euphoria was coming from. "Zadran?"

Danny nodded. And then went back to studying the laminated map. Ariana, or some spectral incarnation of her, hung around him in a way that had never happened before we went to L.A. "I've been thinking. Constance said it'll be different when I meet her. I'm wondering exactly what will be so different—what I'm missing." He was unconsciously running his fingers across the piano key as if it was a chain of beads, the kind the warlords always carried loosely in their hands.

"You think Ariana's one of the people on this ratline?"

"Don't know. The intel we got said whole families were on the move."

"Omar?"

"Who knows?" He thought about it for a moment. "Probably," he said.

· · ·

It was called Operation Jukebox. It got the name because the battalion commanders had decided that, for a little money, Zadran would play any tune you wanted to hear. And the consensus was he was moving back from Miram Shah in Pakistan to his Afghan base near Khost, where someone from his tribe had told him the CIA operatives were debating whether or not to pay him any more money. To Zadran's way of thinking, he was automatically due a few million, give or take, merely for the honor of letting him play us off against the Ninjas. So Zadran was trekking back to this side of the mountains in order that Yankee dollars could rain down on him in a deluge.

Which, on the surface, was a perfectly viable strategy they'll teach at business school someday. Because at a time when the CIA was running around the mountains with trunks of cash, loyalty was definitely a marketable commodity. Even if, as in Zadran's case, it had a shorter shelf life than a carton of milk.

We were one of three recce teams, each taking a different elevation of the ratline. The whole idea was to do what the Predators overhead couldn't: try to figure out what Zadran was planning. Officially, Danny and I had been tasked with reconnaissance and surveillance. If things got hairy we would attack and then call in air support, waiting until reinforcements got to us. At least that was the plan.

It was a difficult trek we made. It became a grim, destined march through the freezing cold, climbing up into snow and then descending, following a camel path down into a dirt-road village. The headman of the village greeted us suspiciously and then invited us into his earth-brick compound. The compound was a kind of medieval fort on a smaller scale, with high walls that had little openings for shooting down at attackers, and a steel door big enough to drive a pickup truck through.

Everything was mud-colored beige except for the doors and window frames, which were almost turquoise. We entered, shoeless, into a large room with log beams protruding from the ceiling overhead. Sitting on the thick rugs scattered around the room, we had sugary tea brought to us by weathered men with white or gray beards with *pakol* hats and the baggy shalwar kameez outfit that was almost the uniform there. There were maybe a dozen of them, silent, turbaned men who muttered among themselves and examined us as if we might be some kind of prey.

They were surprised that Danny could speak enough Pashto to carry on a conversation, and soon the headman was leaning toward Danny and talking quickly.

"Basically, they hate us," he said, smiling for the benefit of our hosts. "They're all tied in with Zadran. But we are their guests, so they are honor-bound to extend hospitality to us. So they won't attack us now. And probably not even after we leave. They think we might be useful if they decide to go to war against another tribe."

We left and descended quickly through about a dozen contour lines into a spectacular valley, green and crudely terraced, with towering, snow-capped mountains off in the distance. The riverbank fell away into a deep, narrow chasm, traversed by a bridge of a dozen long logs laid side by side over the roaring water far below. Two men were whipping a white mule loaded with wood strapped to its sides. It was clumsily traversing the logs, braying in terror and slipping until it crossed the bridge and then bolted awkwardly into a field full of opium poppies.

The smoldering remains of a compound destroyed by the Hellfire missiles were at the base of a large hill. Through the blossoming smoke, a door could be seen clinging to shattered hinges as it swung, creaking in the low flames. We moved cautiously past the ruins. A mumbling sound came from somewhere in the smoke. An old man with a long beard, dyed bright henna-red, sat in the rubble. His toothless mouth was moving as if he was chewing air. At his bare feet were animal skins, some filled with a thick brown paste. Opium. Or maybe hash.

I motioned to Danny, who nodded and slowly edged closer. Both of us were doing 180s, waiting for the Law of Unpleasant Surprises to kick in. But the old man was alone, sitting there mumbling to himself. When Danny said something to him in Pashto he didn't even look up. He simply waved his hand dismissively as if he was tired of some long-running argument and kicked at the goatskins around his feet, spilling the brown paste out onto the ground.

"Gramps has been sampling a tad too much of his own product," said Danny, quietly looking around. The whole place had a *Night of the Living Dead* aura to it.

We got out of there, leaving the old man suddenly coming to life, yelling madly into the wind.

The sun plummeted.

The warm twilight glow of the distant peaks settled into a coolness that we fought off with the chemical packets in the MREs. For a while we hunkered down on our little plateau encampment, listening to the radio traffic coming in. Off in the distance we could hear the alternating whine and roar of an AC-130 gunship whose radio chatter was what passed for tonight's Top 40 countdown here on the murderous edges of the Clash of Civilizations. The AC-130 Spectre was an airborne platform of sheer hell, capable of firing rounds the size of toothpaste tubes down onto the heads of obstinate Ninjas.

It was flat-out eerie, lying there in the pristine night with the entire universe once again playing in wide screen in that Ultimate Drive-In of the night sky above our heads. And on the double bill tonight, vying for attention with Orion, the Milky Way, and Venus, was this AC-130, the flying boxcar from hell off in the distance, rattling through the darkness, providing special effects, lighting up a whole map quadrant.

But the really freaky part was the voice on the radio, a woman's voice from the AC-130—call sign Zinger. Now I know we're supposed to be past all that in these post-liberated times, but a few socially recessive genes in the middle of my brain were arcing at the thought of a woman—who really sounded more like a girl— piloting that plane, raining down death in the night.

Zinger had one of those naturally bouncy and somehow youthful voices. She requested confirmation on coordinates from the guys on the ground. One of them, the attack controller, sounded like they'd done business before, calling her Sugar.

"Sugar this," came the reply from Zinger. "Waiting for orders."

I was trying to think of whose little sister that voice reminded me of.

Tracer bullets hosed down the darkness, and Zinger's voice notched up a little when someone on the ground radioed, "We are taking heavy fire. I-6 is hit." A moment later another voice from the tactical command post miles away cleared Zinger to go in hot. Instantly the night was stitched with flame. Over that radio, Zinger again sounded to me like someone's kid sister working the taxi dispatch office. Then she annihilated whatever had been targeted in a series of minor fireballs.

I couldn't get the thought out of my head: Little Cindy or Tiffany or Ruthie. The thought of *sis* up there pouring 105mm cannon fire down into some Ninjas just plain stuck. Like Dorothy in *The Wizard of Oz* wiping out whoever was behind the curtain with machine gun fire.

Can't help it—that's the image.

"Ariana," said Danny out of nowhere. He had drifted into his own space right there in the middle of that light show going on out there. The attack controller was yelling into the radio, telling Zinger to be advised that her guns were hitting fifty meters from the tree line.

"What about Ariana?"

"We're listening to a woman piloting a plane in combat."

"And?"

"Forget it." Silence. "She's out there. Somewhere."

"You really think she's with Zadran?"

"Omar's somewhere here too." We watched the patterns of flame in the night, some linear, others irregular. From here it sounded like the sky was some huge piece of cloth being torn.

"I'm worried," he said.

"About what?"

"About virginity. And other stuff."

I watched for a moment to see if he was making some kind of weird joke. "We're watching a rerun of the Armageddon show and you want to talk about virginity?"

"Yeah." He was as serious as I'd ever seen him.

"Virginity's complicated."

"Yeah." Silence. "What if she gave birth?"

"Wanna run that by me again?"

"Zadran would go crazy when he found he wasn't getting a virgin. Crazy she could handle. Maybe. But what she couldn't handle is what he would do if he found out she was pregnant."

"Why are you thinking she was pregnant?"

"Constance. She said she heard a baby crying."

"It could be any baby."

"It's not," he said. With complete certainty. "I been thinking about it for all the months and years since I saw her. Wondering what our last night was all about. We always used to take all kinds of precautions. She even had a girlfriend who was giving Ariana her own birth control pills for a while. But that last night was different. Nothing."

"You think she wanted to get pregnant?"

"I don't know. She could be killed for it."

Zinger had gone off station and an Apache helicopter named Wild Monkey had come in, its chain gun cutting up the sky. Somehow it seemed all so far away.

I wished I had not known what I knew now.

Just the thought of a child, Danny's child—if he or she even existed—set the whole survival equation ablaze. And would demand recklessness from Danny. It sent scenarios and premonitions rocketing through our solitary corner of darkness.

• • •

At daybreak, we awoke and stepped into a postcard. The rising sun caught the snow on the distant mountain peaks, and the lushness of the valleys at the lower elevations had the feel of an oasis. Glassing the hills, there was little sign of the carnage of the night. Only a few black scars on the earth and a charred tree on the far side of the valley gave any hint of what had happened. It all invoked the Inverse Law of Horror and Beautiful Places: The more picturesque the scene, the more terrifying what happens there.

India team came up on the radio. They were the second of the three reconnaissance teams and were reporting in. Saying that Zadran's people were closing on us, descending on the path beside the river at about two contour lines an hour. "Be advised, they may have shadows," India added. "About a hundred meters above the main party. Cannot confirm." There was nothing to do but wait. Breakfast was a couple of cans of Chef Boyardee tossed into a C-4 fire and then cracked open with Ka-Bar knives. Speaking about inverse laws, there has to be one for food and where it's eaten. The fanciest restaurant in Beverly Hills cannot equal the culinary splendor of Chef Boyardee served charred to the ravenous at six thousand feet in a war zone.

Suddenly I dropped my can of Chef Boyardee and ran for my rifle.

On the western side of the highest hill, a cavalcade of humanity made a jostling appearance. Coming through the notch between the hills, hard against the rushing waterfall, were a group of men wearing baggy shalwar kameez outfits swaddled in bullet belts, and carrying AK-47s. Some of them wore suit coats and matching vests, which was a little like seeing your banker dressed for a shootout.

We made no attempt to conceal ourselves as more of them poured over the notch. They were fewer in numbers than I had thought, maybe a hundred and fifty men, women, and children. The bankers in bullet belts were in the lead, and behind them was a curious concoction of epochs. A few donkey-driven wooden carts with rubber-rimmed, spoked wheels carried supplies, jostling over the rutted path beside the river. On the last of those carts, seated on mounds of cushions, was Zadran like he was in some royal carriage.

"He probably can't even walk, not after what happened to him," said Danny, leaving out the details. He was busy setting up the spotting scopes. The scopes could pick out details from five kilometers. "A couple of guys on motocross bikes," he said, peering into one. "They must be his outriders. You know, like the Queen has all those guys on horseback looking like they're dressed in chrome and bouncing all over when she goes out in that gold carriage? Well, Zadran's got his two scraggly motocross guys covered in mud."

The whiny roar of those two bikes as they bounced across the rock-strewn path was like listening to a chainsaw having a breakdown. It pitched up and down until you wanted to put a round into the crankcase. But Danny wasn't even hearing it. He was completely focused on what had just come over the hill, following Zadran and his entourage.

It was like a parade of ghosts. It was the women—maybe thirty of them, covered from head to foot in burqas. They were a flock of shrouds of different colors, obliterating whatever individuality was under them. Of everything I saw there in that country, this image disturbed me the most, for some reason even more than the terrible violence. This was a different kind of violence. And whenever I saw a little girl laughing and playing, all I could think of was that hideous shroud awaiting her in a few years. *Always.* And now I thought of Zinger. And what these incarcerated souls under those burqas would make of her, up there in the air waging war.

Through the telephoto compression of the scopes, the women appeared jammed together, jostling along the descending path in hues of orange, black, brown, or blue. Some held plastic mesh bags filled with what looked like food. I knew Danny was doing what I was doing—focusing the scopes on the heavy latticework grids across the eyes of the women, seeing if any tiny detail, anything physical, revealed itself. An eye. A nose. Part of a mouth. Anything that hinted at Ariana.

The burqas were impenetrable.

"Goddamn. Goddamn." Danny was muttering. His voice was quavering. "Constance was right." *Will I recognize her?* We were both picking the same thoughts out of the air.

In all the situations I'd seen him in, this was the first time Danny lost that coolness. In all those combat situations, he'd barely showed a pulse, but now he was breathing like a sprinter after a marathon. "Oh God," he kept saying.

"You okay?"

"No." He shifted back and forth on his feet. "Lookit, lookit." He was pointing at the head of the cavalcade. "Kids." Ringed around Zadran's donkey cart were little children, maybe five of them, all somewhere around six or seven years old. There were at least two little girls, bouncing up and down. Totally unaware of why they were there. *Collaterals.* Again the thought shot through two minds. Zadran had placed those children around him so that from the air, any pilot—even our Zinger, *Sugar*—would have to radio tactical command and, in one way or another, pose the baby-killer proposition: *The old bastard's surrounded himself with kiddies. Hit him, hit them—maybe. It's fifty-fifty. Do we risk it? Huh?*

Danny and I were both playing Cyclops, stumbling around with our scopes to one eye, practically falling over each other.

"He's even got a little kid on the wagon with him!" Danny whispered. I flailed and focused. It was true. A little kid, maybe two, maybe three, sat on the big cushions. *Checkmate!* Zinger, in her most war-crazed, collateral-damage state—*How was I to know that there were kids?*—would drop teddy bears and rose petals at the sight of that cute little kid sitting beside Zadran. The little kid made that old tyrant Apache-proof. No one was going to vaporize him while *that* little kid was beaming all around.

"That little boy . . ." I whispered into the mountain air. *Danny?* Was I imagining something about the smile—the grin—on the face of that little boy?

"No, no, no, no." Danny was trembling like a leaf. I turned to look at him. I put my hand on his shoulder to steady him. It was almost like he was going to pitch face forward into the stream below.

"What?"

"Constance!"

"Constance?" At that instant, Danny and I were in different worlds.

"The white veil," he said.

Not far behind the bobbing horde of blue and orange and black and brown burqas, there was a solitary white burqa. Apart from the rest, it moved in front of several armed men in turbans.

Maybe it was my imagination, but the white burqa had a different rhythm to her stride. I know Danny felt that too.

We raced about fifty meters south to a place near where another of the log bridges precariously crossed the chasm above the rushing stream. The caravan descended and drew closer. We were neither hidden nor obvious, merely standing among the trees. We waited as it approached on the other side of the chasm.

"You sure about what you're doing?"

"No. There's only one thing I'm sure about." He was looking through the scope again.

On the path, the white burqa was a kind of beacon apart from all the other colors. It moved—were we imagining this too?—with a kind of grace. Watching it, for some reason at that moment, I was seeing *her*. And I knew Danny was too. He was standing there, no longer using the scope because Zadran's donkey cart and the caravan of ghosts was less than a hundred meters away from us. "The white burqa," he said again. "I know her walk."

"You sure?"

"I'll know it till the end of my days. It's Ariana."

The procession followed the path, turning along the other rim and heading toward us on the far side of the chasm. We stood stock-still, among trees and boulders, waiting for them to see us. We'd instinctively made a calculation—that Zadran was not going to do anything to derail the gravy train loaded down with the American money he knew he so richly deserved for a whole month's worth of loyalty. Maybe two. And so, to him, we'd just look like a couple of soldiers—Americans who happened to be there watching. In these times there was nothing that unusual about that.

At least that was the thinking. Our thinking.

It was one of the motocross guys who saw us first and raised his hand. After a fair amount of jabbering and nodding from Zadran, they kept going. From his cushioned perch, without even looking at us, Zadran raised a hand in a majestically disinterested greeting.

We attempted the same.

They were closing on us, separated by the rushing stream below. The noise of that small torrent grew to a roar within my mind.

The closer Zadran got to us, the more uncomfortable and angry he appeared, as if he was embarrassed at being seen riding in the cart. He snapped a sudden barrage of orders, making sure we knew he was the boss. They were directly in front of us now, only about fifty feet away, passing by in categories. The motocross went by first. Then some of the men, followed by the children, the little shields. A couple of them looked at us with eyes like dark pools. Then a few more men.

And finally, maybe thirty meters away, the ghosts—the burqas moving toward us—all of them looking straight ahead. Only the white burqa turned to look toward us.

Danny took a half step forward, almost like he was going to say something. The white burqa faltered for a moment but kept walking. "No," whispered Danny. "No, no, no." The white burqa was almost in front of us.

Will she recognize me?

"Oh shit, no, no." He dived into the rucksack, his hands shaking so badly that I had to help him unzip one of its compartments. *Just another foreign soldier, lean, toughened, with shaggy hair, sunglasses, and unshaven for days? Will she . . .* He pulled out the little speakers and his new iPod. I thought they were going to fly out of his trembling hands. He sank to his hands and knees, pressing buttons on the iPod, listening through the headset. "C'mon, c'mon, c'mon," he muttered. Then he took the headphones off and unplugged them from the iPod.

Through the little speakers came the sound of a piano. "Für Elise." Echoing off the walls of the chasm as Liberace filled the air with music.

On the other side, many of them shot a glance toward us, afraid, as if stopping to look would bring Zadran's wrath down upon them. But the white burqa almost swiveled, for an instant frozen, and then took two quick steps back toward us.

"Wait!"

It was Ariana's voice.

That one word shot through Danny as if he'd just grabbed lightning.

In a blur of motion that shot confusion through the whole procession, she ran through the burqas and the men. It was the shock of a perfect social order being shattered, an order where everyone had their place. She raced over to the cart where Zadran was angrily trying to turn his bulk around to quell whatever nuisance had broken out. The white burqa—Ariana—grabbed the child from the cart and ran back toward Danny, who tried to stay across from her on the other side of the chasm. You could feel it burning from within that white shroud—some force of defiance and joy and fear shining through. She held the little boy up for Danny to see. The boy chortled as if it was a game and pointed to Danny.

"Danny, Danny!" Ariana called out from inside that burqa.

"Deenee," laughed the little boy. In an instant you could see Danny all over that child's face. The wide green eyes, the mouth that crinkled up in response to the world's foolishness, even the hair, the reddish-blond thatch.

"Oh, dear God." Danny was crying and laughing all at once. He was making little baby waves to the boy, who gurgled a chuckle and then squealed, burying his face in the burqa.

Ariana brushed the hair away from the boy's eyes. He laughed and shook his head, sending the hair tumbling all over. "Your hand!" yelled Danny, louder, more urgently than anything he'd said to her.

She whipped her hand behind the burqa. I only caught a glimpse of it—twisted and mangled in ways no hand should be.

From the donkey cart, Zadran let out a snarling, guttural shout. He had shifted himself around enough so he could see Ariana. That giant mustache, like a dead black squirrel in rigor mortis across his top lip, curled and bounced in rage at this spontaneity from one of his own burqas.

He shouted to a huge turbaned man with deep lines on an angry face and bullet belts crisscrossing his chest. Holding a rifle in one hand, the man raced toward Ariana.

"No!" Danny said, almost to himself.

The man prodded Ariana with the butt of his rifle, moving her in the direction of Zadran.

"Don't touch her," Danny yelled, his voice getting stuck in his throat. I moved closer to him, ready for anything.

Ariana spun around the man, circling back and calling out, "Danny, don't do anything. I'll be okay." She was moving toward him when the squirrel came to life. I was watching Zadran, not the others. One of the deadliest species in all nature—the tough guy facing humiliation. Zadran bellowed again. The man nodded and drove his rifle butt into the side of Ariana's head. She collapsed. The little boy spilled out of her arms, wailing. On the ground she lurched on hands and knees, the white burqa soaking red with blood as she staggered to her feet, groping for her son and wiping the red smear away from the latticework across her face. The man was moving toward her . . .

. . . as Danny, in one unnaturally swift motion, fired a round that caught the man in the chest, sending him twisting, spinning, and then toppling backwards into the chasm, landing in the stream below, a fraction of a second before our world exploded.

•••

It was Zadran's bellowing that silenced the firing. For a moment his angry shouts were mixed in with other, weaker voices as if some kind of argument broke loose and then was smothered. Then there was only the clanging clatter of hooves, feet, and a motorcycle engine. All of it mixed with bursts of Zadran's yelling. The sounds receded down the path on the way to their hurried destiny of a rendezvous with Americans dispensing cash at lower altitudes. The *Pashtunwali* code of retribution would wait for proper financing.

What we did not understand until the chaos had subsided, until Zadran's caravan had scrambled and jostled its way further down into the valley, was that the real attack on us was coming from the hill high above.

In that instant after Danny fired, the top of his sleeve blossomed red. A bullet had not quite missed him, slashing through his shirt, leaving only a thin gash. But the bullet had not come from Zadran's caravan. In that second or two while his armed fighters and the men guarding the boxes of American money were still scrambling for cover, I lunged at Danny, sending us both tumbling down behind the boulders and trees. He struggled to get up, but fell back as the bark on the tree above our heads exploded.

Through it all I heard "Für Elise" in all its intimations of beauty and passion. Strangely, I had never appreciated music as much as at that moment while I lay there struggling to breathe, waiting for the end, and wondering what it would be like to die to Beethoven.

Beethoven as played by the incomparable Liberace. I mean it. Never has Liberace played with such meaning, such passion as he did when we were about to die. The beauty of it will soar for as long as there is memory.

Danny had struck the back of his head on something and now he stumbled twice as we tried to climb up from the gully to level ground. We got up there just in time to see the donkey cart rounding a bend in the rutted path. Ariana, in the white burqa, had been put on the cart next to Zadran, facing away from him and supporting herself with one hand on the cart. The other hand went to the top of the white burqa, which was splattered with blood.

Danny stumbled toward the rucksack that had the big McMillan sniper rifle. He grabbed the rucksack and was dragging it toward me when the iPod and the little speaker exploded in a wild kaleidoscope of flying metal and plastic. We both tumbled behind rocks.

"Ah, my Danny," said a voice from somewhere very close. "You know I always hated that music."

29

All you really need to know about military radios—or at least, the ones we were using—is that right when you desperately need one is when you're most liable to be holding a piece of junk in your hands. In the midst of all the modern miracles that could not have been imagined by Patton, Sun Tzu, Bismarck, Napoleon, and all those other warrior gods, there are times when two kids communicating through tin cans connected by a taut piece of string have more effective equipment than what we had.

I've had higher command refusing to give us the frequencies we needed to communicate with a different unit on the opposite side of a valley. And then there's those green, bricklike batteries we get for laptops and sat phones that curl up and die in the cold. Which leaves your radio pretty much like a small rock to be thrown at the enemy.

But other times there are those miracles of irony and communication, the kind you'd find on dead Ninjas, cheap little radios that Radio Shack wouldn't sell but were working just fine for the bad guys. And could yield a treasure trove of eavesdropping once our linguists were hustled in to eavesdrop on what the Ninjas are saying to one another over the airwaves.

Which is what happened us to us in reverse.

I had been using a handheld military radio officially designated an MBITR but known among the troops as an Em-Biter. All day the thing had regularly quit working every couple of minutes. I had just pitched it away when a dozen different taunting inflections of *my Danny* suddenly came curling over the Em-Biter lying at our feet.

The Taliban had gotten one of them from someone they had killed or captured. And Omar had been listening to us from somewhere up on that hillside that we couldn't see.

Danny picked up the source of the taunts and stared at it like he was trying to make it melt. He almost spit out the words. "What did you do to her hand?"

"Ah, my Danny," came the silky reply. "How nice to hear you. I knew you would show up."

Danny repeated the question. Yelling this time.

"Danny, my Danny. It was not me who destroyed her hand."

"Who was it?"

"Why, her husband, of course. She violated his will when she told him she would play *your* piano again. So he smashed her hand. It is his right. As the husband."

"I should have shot Zadran."

"Noo-noo-noo-no! Danny, my Danny! Zadran did not do this." Omar's words were not so much spoken as unfurled.

"He's her husband."

"He was. Until he found out that she was not a virgin. Do you know how that happened, Danny, my Danny? That my sister was not a virgin?" A silence louder than a barrage followed. "Did you see her face, Danny? No, of course not. She is not pretty anymore. Zadran is not a man you ever want to give a whore to as his bride. So he beat her and then divorced her and gave her to the worst man in his tribe."

Danny was staring into the radio. Like he was trying to make his mouth work.

"Even you wouldn't want her now that she's not pretty. Would you?" Omar laughed. "But she's available now—after what you did to her husband."

"What *I* did to her husband?"

"You just killed him."

. . .

I'll say this about Liberace: He was brave. A true hero. He definitely took one for the team.

After we'd sat through a few more of Omar's taunts, we had the problem of finding some way to crawl out from behind the little gully we were in. It all got worse when we figured out we had absolutely no idea where Omar was. Only that he was somewhere up on that hill. One wrong move and we'd be in his sights without knowing it.

Which is where Liberace in all his cardboard glory came in. Danny unpacked him from the drag bag. We unfolded him and put the support brace up so he could stand there in that gloriously outrageous pose, his leg kicking out, wearing those oh-so-tight little silk shorts and his hands fluttering out just beyond all that Fifties cowboy fringe hanging down from his arms.

And with that million-watt smile, he was ready for showtime.

I crawled to a place below the little ridgeline at the top of the gully. About thirty feet away, Danny was ready with his rifle and a laser-aiming device he almost never used. In his hand was the Em-Biter.

"Omar, *my* Omar," he said softly in a rasping voice. "I will keep playing music. Your sister will keep playing music."

"Oh my Danny, you are still so ignorant. Zadran will sell her to another tribe now. There will be no music. Trust me, my Danny."

"Oh, there will be music." And then Danny laughed. A curling laugh that was my cue to whip Liberace up above the ridgeline— *Ladies and gentlemen, the one, the only*—Liberace stood there prancing for his audience of one. The biggest performance of his career.

And still Danny kept laughing at Omar through the Em-Biter.

Within seconds Liberace took three direct hits. All that was left of him on that cardboard poster were those tight little silk shorts and those prancing legs. The rest of him had been obliterated. Liberace had died for the cause.

It was the muzzle flash that gave Omar away. From the shadows of the trees above us, Danny saw it repeatedly. Now utterly calm, in that altered state of his:

He gauged the wind and elevation.

Fine-tuned the scope.

Slowed his breathing.

Exhaled.

Stopped breathing entirely for the moment.

And gently, *gently*, pulled the trigger.

And at that instant, from somewhere high up on the hillside: *Ayyyyeeeeeeee!*—a scream that echoed into a pinwheel of shrieks as legs and a torso tumbled, flashing through rocks and trees, crashing against a boulder with a cracking sound that could be heard down in that gully. Still shrieking and writhing, Omar pulled himself up in plain view, holding his shattered leg. The bullet had obliterated most of where his knee had been.

From all that distance, Danny centered the laser device on Omar's chest. A red dot bounced across it.

"Ah my Danny, a laser dot," rasped the voice through the Em-Biter. It was a screeching, shakier voice than the one we had heard only moments before. "We're back to paintball, are we?"

Danny left the laser dot on Omar, jittering all over his chest. And then on his face. Omar tried to brush it away. Then he tried to move but his shredded leg would not respond.

Omar grabbed the radio again. "Are you going to k-kill me, Danny? Is that it, Danny?"

"No," said Danny.

"Kill me."

Omar was thrashing on the hillside, yelling at Danny, taunting him in a jumble of Pashto and English. And then lapsing into angry cries.

"Kill me!"

Danny smiled. "Goodbye, Omar." He shut the laser device off. The red dot vanished from Omar's face. Danny turned and walked away from the screams on the hillside high above him.

HOME

30

"Just go," she said.

That tiny room at the back of Eugene's office was the one favor he ever did for me. Or at least he claimed it was a favor. Like everything else he did.

He had let her stay there, living in a storage room with the faint rasping sounds of Sunset Boulevard as the white noise of a world beyond the darkness. It was to be for a few days, just to keep her from being out on the streets.

And it became her living space for the last four months that I was away from America.

"Make it like you just dropped in to see me," he'd said when he phoned me. "Don't let her think I told you she was here. Or that you showed up because of her."

"Why not?"

"You'll see."

And I did. When I opened the door the flaring of her eyes said it all in shame and fury. *Why was I there? Why was I intruding? Leave! This is my business. My fight. Goddamn you. Please. Oh God please.*

I waited it out. Watching her hands betray her, trembling as she fought to subdue them into enforced normalcy in whatever guise she could grasp. With the pill bottles on the floor beside her, silent informers. She held it together for as long as she could. Piecing together words coming in batches from whatever clothesline of thought she could reel in.

And then she fell silent, shaking her head as tears flowed down her cheeks. "Oh God," she said after a while. "Save yourself." I sat next to her and took her hand. She did not pull it away. And after a while she squeezed my hand harder than seemed possible.

"How can I help?"

"You can't. You never could. I tried to tell you that. But you wouldn't listen."

"No. I wouldn't."

"I have to do this myself."

"Do what?"

"For once in my life I have to do something on my own." We sat in silence for a while. "I'll be going soon."

"I'll go with you."

"You can't." More silence. "Don't you feel stupid?"

"About what?"

"Wanting to be with me."

"No."

"Please go."

"No. I'm here."

"You can't be." I waited a while and then looked at her. "Ridiculous," she said.

"What is?"

"No one should have to have a junkie loving them."

• • •

She vanished. The storage room was empty by sunset. Except for the pill bottles left behind, half-full and with a voice all their own. I went to all the obvious places looking for her. The Playboy Mansion. The clubs. Even the ferret's office. Everywhere but the one really obvious place that never occurred to me until the end of the second day.

The disintegrating little house on the Venice canal seemed held together by memories. Behind the ragged exterior only stillness prevailed. There were no more addled hippies crashing for days, weeks, or months now that her father was dead and her mother circled dementia in ever-tightening anxieties over the tea she made endlessly . . . *how do I know for sure that it's organic chamomile? . . . the government puts things in tea you know* . . . and then pouring it out for fear that *they* had put something in the tea. The little house roared with silence broken only by volleys of groans and cries from the bedroom she had once shared with her sister.

"The dreams," her mother murmured, making another pot of chamomile tea. "She has these dreams."

They were more than dreams. It was as if parts of her life were being pulled through blades. And then flayed and driven from the darkness where she had locked them away for her own protection. In the bedroom she lay writhing on a mattress, part of a strewn collage of clothes, her legs and arms thrashing wildly as she tried in vain to subdue them, curling into a shivering ball and staring blankly through raw eyes, red-rimmed stains on a hollow white face that had tightened into a mask.

"Please," she rasped. "Go. For my sake. *Go*."

I stayed.

In the front part of the house, watching her mother make tea, worry about the government, and then throw it out and start over, it was as if she were unaware that I was even there, shuffling around in tattered loops and muttering to herself. She didn't bother to look up when the angry face at the front door demanded to know what *he* was doing here.

Susie Boo had lost none of the spittle and hissing with which she embellished her proclamations. Almost kicking the door open, she barged forth, glinting in a wardrobe from another world. Screaming at her mother, who merely poured the tea through the strainer, checking it for foreign substances, Susie headed straight toward the bedroom. In her hand was a pill bottle.

Without an instant of thought, I slapped the pill bottle away from her. It skidded into the kitchen, where I got to it a moment before Susie Boo hurled herself on me in a clawing frenzy, her shrieks almost smothering the shaky voice from the hallway.

"Stop."

Annie's voice came so quietly that it was barely heard.

She was standing, shivering and blank-eyed, holding onto the door frame for support. "Stop," she said again softly. The maelstrom between her sister and me ended abruptly, leaving a moment of stillness before the pill bottle was plucked from my hand like talons snatching prey.

"Open it," Annie said. "Please."

Susie Boo was already holding out the pill bottle, like some kind of offering. In triumph, she snapped off the cap on the bottle. Annie shuffled toward it. "Give it to me."

I made not a single move.

Annie took the bottle in one hand, turned on the kitchen faucet with the other hand, and then looked at her sister for a long time. At first I didn't understand why she was looking at her sister in this strange and teetering silence. Then I saw that it was her eyes that were laboring, burning through some inner haze to focus into a stare as sharp as the one she now confronted, the same one she had confronted all her life.

As she turned the opened bottle upside down. Holding it above the drain, and watching the pills spill out and disappear.

31

The official papering-over that went on among the military bureaucrats listed Danny as *missing in action*. I was interviewed by a couple of concerned officers from two different armies and each time I gave the same story of seeing Danny, white shirt flapping in the wind, vanish into that hillside, going after the enemy, and never seeing him again.

Probably captured, I said to them. Actually, *definitely* captured. Had to be.

But I know better. I know that we clasped hands in full view of Omar crying out in pain and crawling up the distant hill, pulling the remnants of his leg behind him. And then with only part of his equipment, Danny took off.

The last image I have of him is of a distant figure running. As if he was trying to catch up to something.

• • •

Danny's letter when it arrives is mottled and stained with long-dried mud. I wait until far into the night to read it in the only place where I can will myself into its world—in the farthest reaches of my backyard where the newly laid sod stops abruptly at the barrenness of the California desert. My coordinates would show me out behind a house that looks like all the other houses, jammed up against nameless desert hills on newly made streets with names like Tally Ho Lane. Where coyotes and mountain lions prowl unseen, wreaking revenge on all who have so recently embroidered their arid kingdom with asphalt. Family pets will pay the price for decades to come.

Here, under the stars, the darkness is as close as I can come to those tar-black nights Danny and I peered into over there in the mountains, waiting to be attacked.

But soon the silence is shredded by the sounds of civilization at night: *The Late Show*, sitcom reruns, and the death throes of a marriage sound in the darkness as I sit staring into Danny's letter.

Old habits live on. In other words, please send peanut butter. (Crunchy not smooth.) And by the way if you still have your usual bedraggled collection of minor gods and B-list deities hanging around, call in markers for me. I need all the help I can get. But just know that we—WE are okay.

It is not just ink and paper in an age of Skype and texting and e-mail; it is a portal arriving in an envelope inside another larger envelope with British stamps on it. With the letter comes a note scrawled on BBC stationery from a cameraman who had survived an attack over there. He survived because someone, *something*, had swept down out of the mountains, cloak flapping like the wings of some great bird or fallen angel that could not take flight again.

He had saved them, the cameraman said, by descending like a wrathful ghost, moments before the tribe—the Zadrans—were about to overrun them. They had heard stories that none of them had believed before this, stories about a human ghost stalking the mountains, living and fighting in ways no one could understand.

And all because of a woman.

The only thing the ghost asked in return, the cameraman wrote, was that his letter be delivered to me. Along with the explanation that *she* was still beautiful no matter what they had done to her.

And that he still loved her. No amount of damage they did to her would ever change that.

And that he would care for her. Protect her.

And that . . .

Danny, Danny . . .

• • •

Behind me in the stucco security of 42 Tally Ho Lane, Emily, three, and Josh, two, are being watched over by Annie. As am I. We are among the lucky ones, the survivors, she and I. And to one another we owe some facade of baseline sanity that allows us to function in restless contentment.

And sitting in the darkness behind my house, miles and eons away from wherever Danny is, I *know*. I know in that way some people can grab one another's thoughts out of silence. I don't need the letter to tell me. Or even the rumors that began months ago. Ones like "The Legend of Sleepy Hollow" type of story of some flapping creature and his disfigured bride haunting the mountains. And with those stories come others about Zadran's money being stolen from him by a single gunman who got away with duffel bags of cash. No one claims to really believe them, of course.

But once in a while, one of the NGO types who bring in aid or medicine will send back stories about a soldier who deserted and a woman he bought from one of the tribes for millions of dollars in money stolen from some warlord. There are different versions of the story, but they all have more or less the same two main characters. Sometimes the man is tall with a thick thatch of hair. And other times, the woman has some problem with her face.

The legends change: They are said to be living with aid workers in a compound near Gardez. Or maybe in a cave in Paktia, protected by local people. And then there is the music—piano music that is sometimes heard echoing through the mountains. Several reconnaissance patrols have been unable to find its source. And no one knows for sure if it is real.

But I know. As if I was still there with Liberace.

I can see it now. Hear it. As my children murmur in their sleep.

And I listen to music that no one else can hear.